DESIRE AND DECEPTION

As he cuddled her against him, Galen murmured, "I love you Renah Dhobi. You're mine, all mine. Don't try to escape me, because I'll never release you. I'd chase you from one end of this galaxy to the other to recapture you. If you can love me as I love you, our future will be brighter than a supernova."

We have no future, Galen Saar. Your parents saw to that long ago with their treachery. Now I must help punish them. Renah knew it was wrong and rash to get emotionally involved with this man. Even so, Galen Saar had stolen her traitorous wits tonight and was threatening to confiscate her troubled heart! It would be a cruel joke on her to find love with her enemy.

If only you weren't a Saar . . . If only . . .

PUT SOME FANTASY IN YOUR LIFE—
FANTASTIC ROMANCES FROM PINNACLE

TIME STORM   (728, $4.99)
by Rosalyn Alsobrook

Modern-day Pennsylvanian physician JoAnn Griffin only believed what she could feel with her five senses. But when, during a freak storm, a blinding flash of lightning sent her back in time to 1889, JoAnn realized she had somehow crossed the threshold into another century and was now gazing into the smoldering eyes of a startlingly handsome stranger. JoAnn had stumbled through a rip in time . . . and into a love affair so intense, it carried her to a point of no return!

SEA TREASURE   (790, $4.50)
by Johanna Hailey

When Michael, a dashing sea captain, is rescued from drowning by a beautiful sea siren—he does not know yet that she's actually a mermaid. But her breathtaking beauty stirred irresistible yearnings in Michael. And soon fate would drive them across the treacherous Caribbean, tossing them on surging tides of passion that transcended two worlds!

ONCE UPON FOREVER   (883, $4.99)
by Becky Lee Weyrich

A moonstone necklace and a mysterious diary written over a century ago were Clair Summerland's only clues to her true identity. Two men loved her—one, a dashing civil war hero . . . the other, a daring jet pilot. Now Clair must risk her past and future for a passion that spans two worlds—and a love that is stronger than time itself.

SHADOWS IN TIME   (892, $4.50)
by Cherlyn Jac

Driving through the sultry New Orleans night, one moment Tori's car spins out of control; the next she is in a horse-drawn carriage with the handsomest man she has ever seen—who calls her wife—-but whose eyes blaze with fury. Sent back in time one hundred years, Tori is falling in love with the man she is apparently trying to kill. Now she must race against time to change the tragic past and claim her future with the man she will love through all eternity!

JANELLE TAYLOR

STARLIGHT AND SPLENDOR

PINNACLE BOOKS
WINDSOR PUBLISHING CORP.

PINNACLE BOOKS are published by

Windsor Publishing Corp.
850 Third Avenue
New York, NY 10022

First Pinnacle Printing: October, 1994

Printed in the United States of America

Dedicated to:

my good friends Dave and Rosalee McFadden
of Polk City, Florida.

Acknowledgments to:

Rick Griner of Wallisville, Texas
And,
Wally and Noralee Askew of Willis, Texas
who helped with researching my Texas settings;
thanks!

One

Jana and Varian Saar looked at Amaya in surprise as she revealed the reason she had come to see them this evening. The intergalactic voyage their best friends, the Sangers, were about to take had been planned for a long time; but their daughter had not mentioned joining them until tonight.

Amaya repeated the unexpected statement. "I want to visit Earth with Avi and her parents. I haven't had a stimulating mission in a *yig*, and working Security at Star Base offers no challenge or excitement. All the other times the Sangers invited me to join them, I was too young, ill, or on assignment. I want to see your world, Mother. I'll be free to go if Father will give me a leave of absence."

"If I give you one? I don't understand, Amaya. You're an adult and a Star Fleet officer so why are you seeking our permission?"

"Not your permission, Father, your assistance with changing my schedule and orders. I don't have enough time accrued since my last leave." Amaya Saar looked at Varian and urged, "Please, do this for me."

"You've never asked me to intercede or do special favors in the past."

"Because I haven't needed any until now. I'll take leave without pay; I'll work double shifts for months. I'll do anything necessary to get this time off. You're the Supreme Commander of the Alliance Force, Elite Squad, and Star Fleet; as my highest superior, the final decision is yours."

"I'm not your direct superior, Amaya. Have you asked him for leave?"

"Yes," Amaya sighed. Her eyes—a fusion of green, blue, and violet like her mother's—showed her annoyance.

"What was his reply?"

Amaya looked up at her father. "He said I don't have enough time accrued for the voyage. You both know I've never taken advantage of my family's status to get special favors, and I've always taken only scheduled leaves. I deserve this time off. I have no defiance or failures on my record but plenty of commendations. To be frank, Commander Mohr has personal reasons for refusing my request; he wants to keep me close to him as long as possible. He knows I could receive an Elite Squad assignment at any time and be gone."

"Are you saying Commander Mohr is romantically interested in you and is basing his decision on personal feelings?" Jana asked.

"Yes, Mother, and I've done all I can in polite ways to discourage him. He's one of the reasons I must get away for a time, why I've used all of my accrued leave. He refuses to believe he cannot win me if he's persistent. I have tried to remain calm and pleasant, but I cannot do so for much longer. If it weren't for Mohr's rank and family, I would not hesitate to be cold and harsh to him. This voyage is important to me, Father, for that and other reasons." Amaya began to pace restlessly, her long blond hair with *platinien* streaks bouncing against her shoulders with each step. "I feel as if I'm floating in space. I'm so bored. I need new challenges, experiences, and settings. I want to go; I need to go. You can overrule Mohr's refusal; please, do this for me."

"Let me think about your request; hasty decisions cause problems." Varian walked to the nearby *transascreen* and gazed outside as he considered the situation.

Amaya knew he was a fair, honest, and intelligent leader. He didn't like to overturn another officer's directive without good cause. He would not want it to appear as if he was showing favoritism for his child. She saw him run his fingers through sable hair and stroke a shaven jawline as he considered every angle of her plea. As he did so, she asked, "Why have you never returned to your world, Mother?"

"I don't have any family there and my best friend is here. Long ago, I made a complete break with Earth and embraced this galaxy as my own. My family, friends, and work are here. I'm a Maffeian citizen."

"But don't you want to know what's happened there since you left?"

"Andrea gives me a full and colorful report following her visits every three or four years. The only reason she and Nigel are returning more frequently now is because her parents are advanced in age and becoming infirm. She doesn't know how much longer they'll be alive."

"That's why I want to take this particular voyage with the Sangers. If her parents are in *Kahala* by next year, there will be no reason to go again. I want to see and study Earthlings, and I want to do it with friends. Avi could be wearing a bonding bracelet soon; Sebok is making no attempt to elude her chase. We've been best friends since birth, and this might be our last chance to share a special time before she mates. All of my closest friends are mated and most have children. I'm making new ones, but it's difficult when I'm not in the same place for long." Amaya frowned and added, "With this current assignment at Base, time moves slower than a *yema* crawls."

"You should be happy about a peaceful reprieve from violence and danger. I worry every time they send you on a perilous, secretive mission."

"I'm always careful, Mother, and I love daring adventures."

"So does your brother. You're too much alike that way."

"We're twins, so that's normal," Amaya said with a merry laugh.

"Perhaps you should think about finding a mate as your friends have."

"Thinking is easier than finding, Mother. I've met no one who stands above other males, who steals my heartbeat as Father does yours. I can't settle for just anyone so can I wear a bonding bracelet and produce heirs."

"I agree love is too important in a good union not to wait for your perfect match. But you'll never find him if you wear a blinding visor all the time. The same applies to your brother. However, Galen is getting a reputation for his countless conquests throughout the galaxy."

"Galen is only looking for the right mate. None of the females he's met is a perfect match for him."

"But if he keeps up his current course as a *reacher,* when the right woman comes along, she isn't going to trust him or give him a chance to win her. On Earth, we called *reachers* 'playboys,' and smart females avoided them like *scarfelli* and *keelers.* " Jana almost shuddered as she remembered encounters with the huge spiderlike and snakish creatures.

Amaya glanced at Varian. "I hear Father was quite the elusive male until you came along and put an end to his *reacher* days," she teased. "You're famous, Mother, the woman who changed the history of our galaxy. Even after so many years, people have not forgotten your name and deeds."

Jana smiled. "I'm happy the *charl* practice was abolished before you were born and had to witness it, perhaps even be assigned to help capture alien females. I wouldn't want you and Galen to be the children of a slave-mate, or you to be afflicted by the virus that made most Maffeian women sterile long ago. It was time for that procreation method to be terminated."

"Yet you accepted the man and civilization that abducted and enslaved you."

"That was long ago and conditions were different in Maffei. They were a people faced with extinction. By the time I was abducted, however, there were few instances where the mating didn't work out for those involved from either world. I simply helped the Maffeians realize they no longer needed alien females to keep their species alive. And once they were freed less than ten alien females chose to leave their Maffeian mates. Of course, I wanted to remain with your father because I love him."

Varian and Jana exchanged smiles as he murmured, "And I love you."

As Varian and Jana teased and chatted for a few moments, Amaya observed their great love and easy rapport. They were more than mates; they were best friends and passionate lovers: that was the same type of relationship she desired for herself and for her brother. She watched her mother gaze adoringly at her father as they talked and joked. Dr. Jana Greyson's life had changed drastically since her departure from Earth. She was the wife of Supreme Commander Varian Saar, one of the richest and most powerful men in this galaxy. He even owned a private planetoid, Altair. His deceased grandfather was the past *Kadim*, the highest authority of the thirteen-planet alliance, a ruler whose word was law. Amaya wished she had known her grandparents, but all four had died before her birth. As for her mother, Jana was known and revered by friends, acquaintances, and strangers across three galaxies for what she had done for the *charls,* Maffei, and research science. Her mother, with her father's help, was responsible for obtaining intergalactic peace with the Androasian Empire of eleven planets and the Pyropean Federation of nine planets.

When her parents' banter ceased, Amaya asked, "Well, Father, will you give me permission to go to Earth with the Sangers? I don't have an assignment in sight for the Squad and I can't sit still much longer at Base."

"You and Galen have always been wiggly as Zandian mudworms. Let me check the schedule and confer with Mohr tomorrow before I give you an answer."

"Time is short and I must let the Sangers know as soon as possible. They leave in three days." *I'm going even if I must resign my rank to do so.*

"Are you certain we should allow her go to, Varian? I have a terrible feeling this voyage is unwise and dangerous."

"She'll be safe with Nigel and Andrea; they're our best friends. They've made this trip many times over the years and had no trouble. Remember, moonbeam, Amaya didn't make the Elite Squad, earn her *Spacer* license, and get assigned to Star Base Security without being smart and cautious like her mother."

"I know, but . . ."

Varian caressed Jana's cheek. "Don't worry, moonbeam; she'll be fine. She and Avi won't get into any mischief; Andrea won't allow it and neither will Nigel. I think this adventure will be good for our daughter; she's been too restless lately. Perhaps when she returns, she'll be ready to look for a proper mate. Her choices are many; so are Galen's."

"So were yours, my love, but you were still mateless at thirty-one."

"I was waiting for perfection to enter my life, and it did . . . unexpectedly."

"The same is true about our twins; they're highly selective. But their marital status doesn't concern me; Amaya's safety does. She doesn't know about things and people on Earth and there isn't time to teach her."

"Andrea will be there to help her. I doubt she'll come into contact with very many Earthlings at the McKays' home."

"But the McKays live in Houston now; it's a much larger and busier city than West Columbia. She won't understand my people."

"But Amaya has the usual audio-translaters embedded in her ear canals; the devices will interpret any language she hears, unless it's an uncommon word or something that doesn't exist in both worlds."

"Or slang, and there's plenty of *that* on Earth. There are so many possible problems and dangers for her to confront there."

"Amaya is more than capable of taking care of herself. She's carried out some of the hardest, most dangerous cases we've had in the past. I also believe she was right about Mohr's feelings for her; he was quite disappointed I intervened."

"Was he angry?"

"Not visibly."

"Perhaps she should be transferred when she returns to avoid a bad situation for either or both of them."

"I agree. This timing is perfect in another area, moonbeam; with our current planetary positions, her voyage will be fast and easy. If she doesn't like Earth, she can help with the ship's data-gathering mission while the Sangers complete their visit. It will be an interesting education for Amaya to see how other people live."

"I just hope her discoveries aren't disappointing and depressing. From what Andrea's told me, Earth hasn't improved over the years; in fact, things seemed to have gotten worse since she and I left. I pray these aren't the dark days preceding the eve of destruction. If only Earthlings could learn to live in peace and to pour their energies into worthwhile things for the people and planet, they could prevent catastrophic times."

"Don't worry, moonbeam; we won't allow them to destroy themselves and their world. We saved them once before without their knowledge and, if necessary, we'll do so again. But we must not and cannot interfere in person until there's no hope of them saving themselves. Our cloaking device will prevent them from discovering our presence."

Jana nestled into her husband's arms. "You're a good man, Varian Saar; I'm lucky you were the commander of the *Wanderlust* that fateful day it came to Earth."

"I'm the one who's luckiest, moonbeam. If not for you, my world would still be using the outdated captive-mate practice, or we would be at intergalactic war with one of our past enemies. I wouldn't have experienced these last twenty-six years of happiness, and I wouldn't be the proud father of twins who do me great honor and give me great joy."

"We are perfectly matched, aren't we?" she murmured, then kissed him. As they embraced afterward, Jana added, "I pray our children can find this same kind of love."

"So do I, moonbeam, so do I."

When it was time for the Sangers and Amaya to transport to the starship, Varian and Nigel shook hands and shared a bearhug. "Take care of my daughter, old friend; she's irreplaceable."

Nigel's dimples showed and his brown eyes softened as he smiled. "I'll guard her with my life, Varian."

Jana and Andrea exchanged final words as Avi and Sebok stood apart from the others to say a private farewell.

"Watch her closely, Andrea," Jana whispered. "For some reason, this trip makes me nervous."

"I told you yesterday to stop fretting. I'll keep both girls under my eagle eyes. I'm so glad you're letting her come. My daughter's so in love that she wouldn't have gone if not for Amaya."

"We both know how love can take control of our thoughts and feelings."

"And our actions. We've done some wild things since we were twelve. We're lucky to have such wonderful husbands and children."

"And to still be together and as close as sisters."

Amaya chatted with her brother and his other best friend. "You two behave while I'm gone. Don't let anything exciting happen until I return."

"Get out of orbit, we can't make that promise," Thaine Sanger jested. "It's in our blood to stir up mischief wherever we go."

"How true," Amaya retorted, then laughed.

"It's time to leave, Avi, Amaya," Nigel called to the women.

Hugs and goodbyes and final cautions were shared before the group transported to the ship.

As she settled herself and the vessel's crew prepared to leave orbit around the capital planet of Rigel, Amaya grinned as Galen used their twin connection to send her a telepathic message:

Don't get attached to any humanoid pets you can't bring home.

Don't you *get attached to any female pets while I'm gone and can't check them out for you in Security*.

Not to worry, Sis. I'm too young and swift for female tractor beams.

One day, you'll run out of sectors to plunder with those charms.

When the right woman comes along, I'll know it, just as Father did.

But he had to travel all the way to Earth to outrun his reputation, you handsome reacher.

Is that what women think about me?

Every day, Brother. We're losing range. Goodbye, Galen. I love you. Keep the peace and stay out of trouble while I'm gone.

Goodbye, Amaya. I love you, too. Stay safe or I'll

*hold you captive for Mohr to lock a bonding band on
that lovely wrist of yours.*

You wouldn't dare.

Never, so I'd have to cut that beautiful hair
again.

Amaya almost laughed aloud as she recalled the
incident when they were six and Galen cut off her
locks for helping a girl chase him down to steal a
kiss. They possessed a mysterious mental link for
communication when they were within a certain
distance of each other. Yet, farther away, they still
could sense each other's needs and pains. That ability had helped her track and rescue him years ago
when a *nefariant* had overpowered and wounded
him.

"What's so funny?" Avi Sanger asked.

"Galen. He sent me a warning not to get involved with the aliens."

"It's weird how you two can communicate that
way. I wish Sebok and I had that power. I miss him
already."

"Love him that much?" Amaya teased in affection.

"Pralu, he steals my thoughts and breath when
I'm near him or when he kisses me. We're so compatible, Amaya. I want to become his mate, and
soon. I can hardly endure being parted from him."

"Even if you put on his bonding bracelet, he'll
be away on duty for long periods, unless he resigns
when his commission ends."

"He would never do that; Star Fleet runs in his
veins, just as it does with Galen. But if we were
locked together by choice and law, I wouldn't have

to worry about another woman stealing him. You know those ships have as many female crew members as males. There's no telling what could happen on one during a long and lonely voyage."

"Not with Sebok; he loves you too much to betray you. If he tried, Galen and Thaine would drop him on a deserted planet to suffer and die."

"You're right, Amaya; I'm being foolish."

"Perhaps Sebok is hesitant to commit for the same reason Galen is: marriage is for life in our world; there is no dissolving it unless a crime is committed and the Supreme Council grants freedom." Amaya smiled at the brunette. "But I'm sure he loves you, Avi, so don't worry. Remember, his two best friends are single and on the same ship. Perhaps a desire for a little more fun and adventure holds him back from docking."

"But he can have me *and* them."

"As soon as he realizes that's true, he'll be signing the document. Perhaps you should coax him along by letting him fear losing you. Men are such strange and stubborn creatures. Little snares them faster than something they think they can't have. Give him a scare."

"If you met someone you wanted and needed as much as I do Sebok, would you pursue him?"

"With all my skills and energy. And no games; I was teasing. Just give Sebok time and I know he'll commit to you."

"When you fall in love, you'll understand why I'm so edgy. But you'd never do anything crazy or impulsive; you're so smart and levelheaded. Any male you select will speed to your side and sign the document as soon as you motion for him to join you."

"Not if he's as reluctant and choosy as I am. Somewhere a perfect match for me exists; I only have to locate and capture him. But I have plenty of time; I'm only twenty-five and I have plenty to see and do before I'm a mate and mother."

"What if he lives in another galaxy such as Androas or Pyropea or even the Milky Way? What then, Amaya Saar?"

"I can't imagine falling in love with an alien and marrying one, and surely not moving with one to another world."

"Our mothers did. And you've found no one in Maffei to suit you."

"I haven't seen every available Maffeian male. There must be at least one somewhere as wonderful as our fathers and brothers, and your Sebok. Our mothers were lucky our fathers were so like them in appearance. I couldn't endure for some aliens I've met to touch me. Do all Earthlings look like our mothers or do they vary like the Tuleons?"

"All possess the same humanoid appearance; but their races vary in skin, hair, and eye colors and in facial features and body sizes. During my past visits, I've seen many males who are pleasing to the eye and senses. But we are far advanced over the Earthlings. To mate with one would be like mating with a child under three years. Or mating with a *greeb.*"

"*Kahala* save me from such a fate," Amaya murmured as she envisioned a primitive and usually barbaric creature.

The ship changed from sublight to starlight speed. The U-shaped vessel rushed across the vast expanse of space between Rigel and Earth and hurled Amaya toward a perilous unknown.

Galen Saar returned to his elite position on the *Galactic Wind*. His best friends—Thaine Sanger and Sebok Suran—were with him; he was glad they were serving together on the lead ship of the Alliance Star Fleet. He was also happy they had been in port to see off their loved ones. As he entered the off-limits area of Security Control, a lovely female rose from a seat, approached him, and introduced herself.

"Third Lieutenant Renah Dhobi reporting for duty, Chief Saar. My file is loaded into the computer and awaiting your scrutiny, sir."

Galen's multi-shaded gaze swept over the blonde who wore a saffron uniform with silver stripes on each wrist and a thirteen-pointed sunburst emblem above her left breast. The expression in her silver-gray eyes was unreadable.

"What are you doing in a secure area before confirmation of orders?" Galen demanded. "How did you gain entrance?" He glanced at the man at the monitors.

"Commander Vaux cleared her and told her to wait here for you, sir," he responded. "He wanted to be ready to leave orbit immediately following your arrival."

Security and Weapons Chief Galen Saar dismissed the man so he could question and judge his new female crew member. He saw that she didn't blush, flinch, or stare as most women did around him. She had to be aware that he—not their ship's commander—held the power to accept or refuse her assignment. Yet she didn't appear worried about his impending decision. "At ease, Lieutenant Dhobi, while I scan your record and qualifications."

"Yes, sir."

Galen sat down at the acquisition-input system and read her data. He was impressed by her record and amazed that a woman so beautiful and seemingly delicate could be a *Spacer* pilot, skilled in communications, knowledgeable in science, and an expert with hand and ship weapons. He noted her physical stats. She was twenty-four years, five feet eight inches tall, and weighed one hundred twenty pounds. There were no scars or marks listed. According to her file, she was one of the most intelligent officers assigned to him. She was certainly one of the most ravishing and composed he had ever met.

Galen glanced at Renah to find her standing with feet apart and hands crossed behind her, straight and tall and formal. "Why do you want to be a crew member on the *Galactic Wind*?"

"To serve on our fleet's lead ship and under Commander Vaux. Also, sir, they decommissioned my last vessel. I was told to list three choices of preference for a transfer and was fortunate enough to receive my first."

"Are you as smart and skilled as your record claims?"

"The report is accurate, sir."

Galen grinned and chuckled as he leaned back in the chair and eyed her. "That's a clever way to keep from boasting, Lieutenant Dhobi. Most women with a file like this would be stressing every entry to me."

"Vanity is dangerous, sir. It makes one impudent and reckless."

"But honesty and pride are safe attributes?"

"Yes, sir, if they do not endanger one's rank and mission."

"Have you ever made a perilous mistake, Lieutenant Dhobi?"

"Not to my knowledge, sir. I try to remain alert and cautious."

Renah didn't vacillate or fidget; nor did her expression change. Yet Galen was aware she focused on his forehead and avoided his gaze. "Excellent attitude. Excuse me while I finish this task."

As the Chief of Security and Weapons studied her alleged record, Renah scrutinized her new superior officer. His hair was ash blond with lighter steaks running through it. His eyes were like a rainbow prism of blue, green, and violet. His six-foot frame carried the perfect weight for his muscular physique. He was handsome, charming, and desirable, but, according to gossip and video observation, he used those predatory traits too well on women. Yet she was anything but helplessly attracted to him. Since birth, she had trained and prepared to help extract revenge from the Saars and Maffeians. All she had to do was get close enough to this self-indulgent sybarite to win his trust and she could use him to obtain victory and justice, as ordered. But, Renah warned herself, she must go slow and easy, as Galen was alleged to be an impossible catch. The best way to seize his interest, she reasoned, was to show none in him. He was captivating and virile, rich and famous, and had a tantalizing smile; but he was the enemy, son of enemies, citizen of the enemies of those she loved, those the Saars and Maffeians had—

"Tell me about yourself and your experiences on the *Space Rover.*"

Renah didn't worry about that question, as she was well versed on her assumed identity, one that could not be disproven. Yet she wondered why he wanted her to relate what he had just read on the screen. "My parents were scientists on that exploratory ship. I was born and raised during their final deep-space mission. We were gone for twenty years; it was supposed to be twenty-five, but problems arose with the vessel and equipment so we were forced to return five years early. That's where I was trained in science, weapons, *Spacers,* and communications. That last day, I was testing an emergency escape unit when something went wrong. My pod was automatically jettisoned. A boundary patrol saw the ship's explosion on their monitors and came to investigate. They rescued me and took me to Rigel for debriefing, but I couldn't tell them what happened. They couldn't explain it, either, because communications were out and no final message was sent. Nor was anything ever recovered in the debris to expose the cause. Star Fleet concluded something went wrong with our fuel and power system, something too fast for the others aboard to be alerted to the danger. Since I was in a pod, they think the control panel detected my presence and jettisoned me. That was fortunate because my unit wasn't stocked with survival supplies and had only one air tank. I finally gave up hoping others had escaped so someone could explain the tragedy. Afterwards, I was allowed to further my training and join Star Fleet."

Galen hated to press the painful topic, but he had to become familiar with anyone who was joining his team and who would be involved in ship and galactic security and protection. He had to make certain there were no flaws in her character or exaggerations of her skills. "What was the purpose of that deep-space mission?"

"The *Space Rover* was to gather data, do tests and experiments, and explore the outer reaches. We mostly found planets and aliens in the early stages of development. From what my parents said and I overheard, no mining or medical possibilities were discovered. None of the worlds we found warranted further study within the next hundred years." *At least that's what the ship's computer banks revealed when they were scanned before destruction so I could give an accurate report. I just wish its crew didn't have to be held captive until this matter is settled.*

Galen witnessed a reaction of sadness. "I'm sorry you lost your family and friends in such a tragedy."

"Thank you, sir, but they understood and accepted the risks."

He watched her formal demeanor and unreadable expression return. "And they taught you to think and feel that identical way?"

"Yes, sir. Isn't it the same with you and most Star Fleet members?"

Galen nodded. "You served on two other ships and rose fast in rank. That's quite an accomplishment for a woman so young."

"Determination to succeed, to do one's duty, and to do one's best should be all that matters to me or anyone, not my age or sex."

Galen heightened his alert. "Did I offend you with that statement?"

"Only if you meant it in a wrong light."

"I didn't, but I'll alter it. You've accomplished a great deal for *anyone* so young."

"The same applies to you." Her gaze moved to his first lieutenant stripes before she said, "To have those and Chief of Security and Weapons on our lead ship for a man so young. Your parents must be proud of you."

"They are. Have you met any members of my family?"

"No, sir, but everyone knows who and what they are."

"I earned every promotion without unfairly using the Saar's status."

"Did I offend you, sir?"

Galen replied with her words, "Only if you meant it in a wrong light."

"It was a compliment in return, sir, nothing more. I'm sure it will be interesting and an honor to serve with and under Chief Galen Saar."

Honesty or only a smooth extrication? "I hope so, Lieutenant Dhobi, and thank you. Do you have any other family?"

"None, sir."

"I'm surprised our paths have never crossed or I haven't heard of you."

"Star Fleet is large and we've served in different sectors." *But I've kept up with the Saars . . .* "And since I've done nothing outstanding to date, there is no reason my name should have entered your ears."

"Do you have a special relationship with anyone?"

"Sir?"

Galen knew she understood the question, so she was stalling for time to decide if his motivation was personal or professional. "Is there or was there a relationship with a male left behind that might affect your job performance?"

"No, sir."

"None?" he asked in a skeptical tone.

"No, sir. I've had neither the time nor the inclination for one. I've concentrated on my training and duty at Star Base and on my last two ships."

After satisfactory answers to other questions, Galen said, "Excellent responses and attitude, Lieutenant Dhobi." He faced a different screen and called up another file, then copied the information onto a disk and passed it to her for use in her quarters. "Your schedule and duties are listed there and in this monitor under your name. The officer you're replacing had a fatal accident. We're fortunate someone of your quality is available."

"Accident"? "Fortunate"? Neither is true, Galen Saar, but you'll wish they were before we finish with you and

your family. "Thank you, sir. I'll do my best to prove Star Fleet's faith in me is justified."

"I'm sure you will, Lieutenant Dhobi."

"Thank you, sir. Will that be all?"

"Check your schedule and duties listed on the screen to see if you have any questions, then get settled in and review the necessary tapes. If the introductory program in your quarter's computer doesn't fill your needs, I can assist you with a tour of the ship this afternoon or evening."

"Thank you, sir, but it's unnecessary. Am I accepted and dismissed?"

"Yes to both, Lieutenant Dhobi, unless your impending tests alter my preliminary decision. We'll begin them tomorrow." *I'll judge for myself if your talents match the claims on your file. If not . . .* "See you at the evening meal." He watched her check the monitor, nod understanding, then depart, without smiling or lowering her guard a single time.

Galen stared at the sealed door. *You're a strange and cool one, Renah Dhobi. Seems as if you haven't learned social skills since your return from deep space. I wonder what you'd be like if you learned to mellow.* For a moment, he wished his sister wasn't speeding out of their galaxy so Amaya could collect every detail there was to know about this stirring creature who had seized his interest in a flick.

As the three friends dined in the officers' mess hall, Galen couldn't keep his furtive gaze and wandering thoughts off of Renah, who sat at the far end of the oblong room. Thaine and Sebok noticed his interest in the lovely newcomer, and exchanged knowing looks.

"She's a loner, Galen," Sebok warned, "quiet and reserved and serious. When Commander Vaux guided her around this afternoon, she was as distant with me and others as Star Base is to this ship. She couldn't have been more formal than if the *Kadim* were present. If she continues to behave in that curious way, the crew isn't going to take to her at all."

"I noticed it, too," Thaine added, "when they visited engineering. Why didn't you give her the welcome-aboard tour since she's part of your staff?"

Galen winked at Thaine and murmured, "I tried earlier, but she gave me a shoulder of ice and rejected my offer. Now I know why; she had a better one—our unattached commander."

"Was she as cold to you as the Kudoran surface?"

"Maybe colder, Sebok. She could have been sending me a message to fly clear of her because she misunderstood my motive when I queried her personal life."

"I'm surprised you couldn't thaw that frozen layer of reluctance covering her."

"Get out of orbit, Sebok, if you doubt the high level of our friend's charms," Thaine joked. "Most women think he could melt a comet's icy trail if he touched it or smiled at it for more than a *preon*."

"Perhaps my colorful reputation is too familiar to that wary beauty."

"It is well known to others, but that didn't stop

them from chasing you across the galaxy or sliding into a *sleeper* with you."

"She's different, my friends, very different from the rest."

"She'll take more time and effort to conquer?" Thaine hinted with a playful grin, exposing the same deep dimples his father possessed.

"She strikes me as a woman who can't be conquered or fooled. She's intelligent and talented, according to her record and my assessment."

"Stars afire, you mean she's as special as my Avi?"

"Avi better be special to you," Thaine quipped.

"You know I love your sister. I wish she were here now."

"Kahala above, Sebok, you're missing her so soon?"

"You would too, Galen, if you met someone like Avi Sanger."

"Perhaps I have, Sebok; I'll know soon."

"Why don't you go over and ask her to join us, or ask if you can join her? It would be easier to work your charms at close proximity. Too late, Commander Vaux has stolen your chance. Get into orbit, she can smile!"

And what a smile, Galen mused. *She can radiate and soften like a sombian cloud.* His gaze drifted over the alluring object of his unexpected desire. Her short blond hair was thick and full; it framed her face to perfection and accentuated her stardust eyes. Her figure was exquisite and tantalizing in a black jumpsuit with one shoulder bared. Thin silver loops dangled from her ears and matched the wide band on her left wrist. Her pert nose was kissable. Her full lips were enticing. He wanted her to glance his way, but her attention was captured by their superior. Her cheeks glowed with pleasure and her laughter was soft and musical.

"Galen is getting a favorable reaction from her. Obviously high rank and power appeal to her."

"Respect and admiration, Sebok, that's all. And he deserves them."

"Galen *hopes,* that's all," Supreme Councilman Suran's son whispered to a laughing Thaine Sanger, who nodded agreement.

"Is her clever challenge working, old friend?"

"What do you mean, Thaine?"

"That pretense of disinterest, Galen. You know women's tricks, old friend; they have a cargo of them big enough to hold a nebula."

"Women should know by now deceptions don't work on me."

"But all females keep trying them and coming up with new ones. You said yourself she isn't like other women. Maybe she thinks she can outwit you."

"Not every female wants to capture me, Thaine."

"Since when did two moons fail to orbit Zamarra and when did her cities rise above sea level?" Nigel's son jested.

"If all women craved me, no man would have a lover or a mate. I'm only appealing to some because of who I am: Varian Saar's son, Jana Saar's son, a past *Kadim*'s great-grandson, a rich man, an officer, somebody with powerful friends and acquaintances. I'm just a good prospect for a mate."

Thaine knew Galen didn't take offense at their teasing, as the three had been best friends since childhood. Although Galen outranked them, they were too close for jealousy and rivalry to intrude on their camaraderie. Besides, Galen had earned every promotion and stripe with expertise and valor. "Your looks, personality, and prowess don't matter?" Thaine argued.

"To some. I don't mean to be cruel to women. I never lie to them before we begin a relationship, even for one night. I try to fill any needs with females who convince me they understand and accept me as I am. The problem is, they want more as soon as we've become lovers. You fly around doing as you please without gaining a reputation and hurting women, Thaine. Why can't I?"

"As you said, you're a Saar; you're a challenge; you're what many females want. I'm fun, a nice substitute, a considerate lover."

"You're also Nigel Sanger's heir. He's a high-ranking officer, my father's shadow, a wealthy man. You have as much going for you in looks, personality, and prowess as I do. So does Sebok; he's a Supreme Councilman's son. He has respect from women and he found the perfect choice for him."

"She has him thinking wild thoughts, doesn't she, Sebok?"

"Who?" Galen asked with a roguish scowl as he saw Vaux leave.

"That rare flower over there. She's alone now," Thaine hinted.

Flower . . . That's an excellent idea, Galen decided. "I have to leave before I'm overly tempted to invade her defensive space."

Thaine and Sebok remained at their table as Galen rose and exited.

From the corner of his eye, Thaine saw the new arrival glance at his departing friend, then focus her gaze on an untouched drink. Within a few minutes, Renah left the officers' eating room. Thaine stared beyond the large *transascreen* into the darkness of space. He watched distant stars appear to twinkle. He sent Sebok a roguish grin, and suppressed chuckles.

"What's that for?"

"Our friend had best watch out; she's definitely interested. I think this is going to be a stimulating voyage, Sebok, a historic one. This time, I believe Galen will be the hunter and a female the prey."

"Stars afire, I hope not."

"Why? She's beautiful and intelligent. And she's available."

"There's something about her I don't like."

"Galen's an elusive prize, so she's only trying to play the game to win."

"I don't think so. Her eyes are too cold and shadowed to suit me. Every time I was near her today, she gave me an odd feeling. She isn't the kind of woman Galen deserves, in my opinion."

"Maybe she's just nervous about being assigned to Commander Vaux, the *Galactic Wind,* and Chief Galen Saar; they're all legends in their areas, so she probably doesn't want to make mistakes. Maybe she's only shy, or been singed by a man, or has other veiled reasons to behave as she does. Let's not judge her before we know, especially since she's caught Galen's interest."

"Well, I'm going to keep a close eye and ear on our new crew member so she can't mislead our friend."

"Galen can take care of himself where a woman's involved, Sebok."

"I'm not so sure this time, Thaine. I've never seen him act like this, particularly over a stranger, and one who's giving him the icy treatment. I'm glad you're here to help protect him from her tricks."

Thaine realized he wasn't going to change Sebok's mind, so he changed the subject. "If we didn't have those new units in engineering, I'd be on my way to Earth with my family and Amaya. I'll miss seeing my grandparents this year. They don't have many years left. But nobody except me and the chief touches those replacements. So far, they're humming like happy children."

"Did I misread my orders, sir? Am I supposed to be on duty tonight?" Renah asked as she faced her target in the doorway to her quarters.

"No. I thought this might brighten your area. It's a welcome-aboard gift," Galen explained as he handed her the exotic plant. "It's a *Tarkitilae Moosi*—the Eyes of Kimon—my mother's favorite."

Kimon, mythical Goddess of Love and Beauty . . . A minor victory so soon or just arrogant flirtation? A delightful fragrance exuded from the flower. Renah gazed at the blue-and-green blossom with its vivid splotches of crimson and yellow. "Do you give all new crew members welcome presents?"

"No, because all of the others have been males." He chuckled.

"I don't think you should make an exception for me, sir."

"Do you prefer not to become friends with team-mates?"

"You're my superior, sir. Displaying favoritism causes ill feelings."

"A friendly overture isn't showing partiality, Lieutenant Dhobi."

"It could appear that way to others, sir, since I'm a single woman and new here. I don't want to cause problems."

"Is this a polite way of telling me to ignore your existence off-duty?"

"Not exactly, sir, but I don't need complications in my life."

Galen turned serious. "I'm not trying to be a *reacher*, Lieutenant; I'm only attempting to become friends with a new staff member."

"I didn't mean to imply you were misbehaving, sir."

Galen's gaze roamed her exquisite features as he perceived the tension in her. He wondered if, due to his ridiculous reputation, she was afraid of falling under his spell and being hurt. "For now, Renah Dhobi, getting to know you is all I'm seeking. Welcome aboard. Good night."

She halted his departure for a moment as she said, "Thank you for the flower, Chief Saar; it's rare and beautiful."

Like you. Galen saw her send him a tiny smile and nod before she pressed the button to close her door. He seemed to warm from head to foot. *You make me think of gathering splendor in starlight, my nervous beauty. We shall see how fast and hard you wish to run from me.*

Two

"Before we begin our tests and briefings, Lieutenant Dhobi, I want you to know I do this with everyone who comes under my command. This has nothing to do with you being a female. You're aware we're the lead ship of the Alliance fleet, so any crew member in Security and Weapons must be totally trustworthy and superior in skills. Your record says you're both, but this is standard procedure both for the *Galactic Wind* and me."

"I understand, sir, and agree with your precautions. This is a very important position; such information and power could be perilous to the ship and Alliance if placed in the wrong hands."

"First, I want to test you in a *Spacer.*"

Galen put another officer in charge of security until he returned to the ship. He and Renah entered a *trans-to,* which took them along the length of the starship's first level to one of six docking bays that were positioned at the rears on both sides of the U-shaped vessel and on all three levels. They walked by a large shuttle and a one-person *Spacer* that were secured in place in the center of the wide and tall bay. As they passed busy workers, crew men nodded in respect or spoke greetings to

Chief Saar and politely acknowledged the presence of the stranger in a saffron uniform at his side.

Emergency escape pods in cylindrical containers lined both walls. Galen watched Renah stare at one. He assumed that memories of her survival in a similar unit four years ago had seized her thoughts. He felt a wave of compassion for her suffering. It must have been difficult for a girl of twenty to face that terrible incident and its aftermath alone. He had to give her extra credit for her recovery and ensuing successes.

When they reached a two-passenger craft that had been readied for flight, they climbed inside, secured their safety straps, and closed the clear, heat-resistant domed roof.

Galen relaxed in his seat. "The controls are yours," he said.

"Use optical scanners and manual control or instrumentation only?" Renah asked.

"Manual first."

Galen observed a calm and confident Renah check the sensors and indicators then make needed adjustments. She gave instructions to the control room for the interior door to be sealed behind the craft and the exterior one to be opened for departure. She guided the craft to freedom and set a course for an asteroid belt as Galen had ordered. The swift *Spacer* covered the distance in a short time. Without error, she maneuvered them around and beyond obstacles of various sizes. Changing to instrumentation, she did a close flyby of a plasma cloud. Galen remained silent and alert during the two demonstrations. Afterward, they returned to the ship and she docked as the expert she had proven herself to be.

As Renah fluffed her short blond hair after removing her helmet, Galen asked, "Do you handle shuttles with the same perfection?"

"I'm as qualified with them as with *Spacers,* sir."

He noticed she didn't use a smile or words to express gratitude for his compliment. Again this morning, she was serious and formal, and focused solely on work. "I'm sure you are. Tell me, Renah, is piloting a *Spacer* only a necessary part of your position or do you enjoy the power and sense of freedom as much as I do?"

"Flying is one of my favorite tasks, for all the reasons you mentioned. It also makes one feel important and needed."

"I agree. I've found that people who love flying and don't fear it make the best natural pilots. Well, it's time to eat and relax a while. Meet me in the weapon's simulator after you finish. Dismissed." Galen approached a *telecom* panel to check in with security before he went to his quarters to order food from the *servo* unit there and to escape Renah's pull.

Later, he joined Renah in the simulator. Galen was amazed and impressed by her efficiency with the particle beam, photon, and chemical lazer weapons that were used to defend the vessel and attack enemies. They entered a *Spacer* facsimile where Galen pressed computer keys to simulate a mock battle with other starships and speedy crafts. He offered no clues or advice on the types of battles or numbers of vessels involved.

He looked at the female beside him. "Ready

when you are. Just let me shift backward out of your way and view."

Renah nodded, straightened, took a deep breath, and pushed the start button. The simulations varied from first appearance of an enemy or fleet or ally ship on sensors to visual sightings on the screens before and to each side of her. The sound effects used for the fake weapons and successes were loud in the confined area. Renah's head turned from side to side and moved up and down as she constantly checked the view and instrument panel for her next target. Some of them came several at a time and from different directions. She knew the enactment tested her aim, dexterity, acumen, daring, self-control, reflexes, instincts, and cunning. She was relieved when the computer told her to return to base and dock: that meant she had survived the "attack" and her skills weren't found lacking. She leaned back in the seat, closed her silvery-gray eyes, and took a deep breath. She waited for her superior's praise.

Galen decided not to tell her she was the only person to score as high as he himself had during that particular test, and said simply, "Excellent victory, Lieutenant Dhobi."

Renah decided it was time to soften a little. She hadn't dared do less than her best, as she needed the rank and trust her score would bring to her. Yet she must be careful of outshining and vexing her target too frequently. "Thank you, sir. It was scary there for a while."

Galen smiled. "You're a master, so don't worry about a real battle." He was warmed when she shifted in the seat to glance at him and smile in what he assumed was appreciation. "I suspect you need a breather and something to drink."

"Both would be nice, sir."

As she rested and sipped on a green liquid, Galen questioned her about Maffei's cloaking and anticloaking devises and their starship force shield. He told himself he shouldn't be astonished when she exposed complete knowledge of them, yet he was. Also, he soon discovered she was proficient in many areas, including engineering, life support, environmental control, and ship systems. "You know a lot about many things, Renah."

"I try to learn everything I can, sir; one never knows when one will get stranded and require a certain skill for survival."

As they discussed ship's weapons again, Galen remarked, "I suppose your background in science familiarized you with all the chemicals needed."

"Yes, sir. Our world is fortunate to have a superior supplier like Trilabs. I've never been there, so I'm looking forward to it."

Galen witnessed a brief display of excitement about their impending destination. That was natural, as Trilabs was a powerful and crucial three-faceted company that created and produced drugs, chemicals, and weapons. It was an indestructible and impregnable complex on the planetoid of Darkar that orbited Caguas, fifth planet in their solar system. Long ago, it had belonged to Ryker Triloni, his father's half brother and his mother's first mate. Jana Triloni had inherited it and presented it to the Maffei Alliance upon marriage to his father, as she felt it was too dangerous and vital for one person or family to own. Galen pushed aside those private thoughts. "I'm certain you'll be fascinated. *I* am, every visit. Trilabs also supplies our decontamination units, you know. You're aware you never bring a captive or visitor aboard without sending him through a unit?"

Renah noted how long it had taken for Galen Saar to respond and guessed he'd been thinking about a past she knew well. "Yes, sir. A rogue germ or virus could be detrimental to us. Maffeians learned that bitter lesson long ago when we almost faced extinction."

"You seemed to have caught up quickly on our history and politics since your return from deep space."

"I was fortunate my mother wasn't afflicted with that sterilizing virus or I wouldn't be here. I'm sure everyone is happy that conditions changed. As for catching up, I read and study during free time so I can learn everything about Maffei. So much happened while I was out of this galaxy. Our ship received reports, but they lacked sufficient details to become well informed."

"You have a quick and inquisitive mind, Renah Dhobi. I've never met anyone like you. I'm pleased you've joined our crew." Galen changed the subject in a hurry when his statement seemed to make her uneasy. "Your file said you had been through the *Rendelar* process, so we won't have to worry about an enemy using *Thorin* on you and learning our secrets."

"I was treated during my last assignment; truth

serum would have no effect on me. Doctor Triloni was a genius; I've read a great deal about him. It's a shame he was so evil-hearted and hated the Saars and Maffeians to such a self-destructive point." Renah lowered her head a moment before speaking. "I apologize, sir; I should not have mentioned anything so personal."

"I doubt there are many people who aren't acquainted with Triloni's actions, since they almost provoked intergalactic war with his grandfather's empire."

"Your mother is responsible for the truce we have with the Androsians. From what I've learned since my return from deep space, *Effecta* Triloni was under his grandson's spell. I'm relieved it never came to war."

Galen nodded his agreement. "Families do tend to believe and support their own members. Now, I think we've done enough for one shift. Meet me in the morning in the weapons room and we'll continue. Dismissed, Lieutenant Dhobi."

"I'll be there, sir."

Galen watched her exit after the pressurized door swished opened; as it closed behind her, the room exuded a strange emptiness and quiet. He sat there for a long time thinking about the unique and fascinating woman. She wasn't too good to be true, because she constantly proved her reality and talents. He couldn't put a finger on why he was so drawn to her so soon after their first meeting. It wasn't totally because she was beautiful and desirable; there was an aura about her that affected him in an uncommon and potent manner. She had matching skills, interests, and intelligence. She seemed to be the female closest to an equal he had ever met; she was the kind of woman he wanted and needed for a mate, as the time had come for him to think seriously along that trajectory.

Renah Dhobi was a dedicated officer who gave duty her all, but she seemed restricted when it came to personal emotions. Perhaps, he reasoned, she had been hurt by love in the past or had lost a lover on the tragic deep-space mission. Or maybe she just didn't trust him as a man. He wished again that Amaya was on Rigel so his twin sister could gather more information about the stunning creature, and he would ask her to do that favor after her return.

Galen went to his quarters. It seemed a good idea to avoid Renah for a while in a social situation so she wouldn't become too nervous about his difficult-to-mask interest in her.

"I'm sorry I'm late, sir; the *trans-to* stalled with me inside."

"Did you or someone else repair it?" Galen grinned.

"Someone else. I wasn't alone." *Your friend from Ship's Systems handled the problem and Sebok doesn't hide his dislike of me. I must deal with him soon or he'll become a problem.* "Shall we get busy?"

The man in a perse uniform took a seat and nodded toward the target area. "Show me your skills," he said.

Renah lifted the disintegrator. It was an oblong,

hand-size weapon that emitted a narrow ray of intense light and low hum when fired; the beam froze any target it struck, causing it to give off an iridescent glow before both dissipated. She pressed the button to create both stationary and moving goals of simulated friend and foe, images that came and went fast to test wits along with skills. That undertaking ended with a perfect score.

Renah chose a laser gun next and pressed the second button to call forth a similar test, which she passed without mistakes. She was surprised when Galen made no comments after each task, but she sensed he was paying close attention to her successful demonstrations. Renah pushed the third button to summon two androids to expose her deftness with a beam knife, a blade that used a laser for cutting. However, the mock weapon only made a colorful mark on contact with an opponent.

Galen witnessed the female's graceful and agile movements as she completed the two endeavors within minutes. She had disabled them for "capture" first; then she had slain them for "survival" or "secrecy." She glanced at the one bright orange mark on her left arm; if it were a real injury, a *latron* beam could seal it without leaving a scar or disability. She looked at Galen. "I'm glad he wasn't going for my throat."

Galen chuckled, then brought her a drink from the *servo* unit. "Are you just as adept in hand-to-hand fighting?"

Renah eyed him over the rim of her drink, lowered it, and replied, "Why don't you challenge me and obtain the answer for yourself?"

"So you won't have to appear to boast the truth?" he teased.

Renah pretended to suppress a smile of amusement and pleasure. She had practiced expressions and reactions countless times, so she knew her silvery gray eyes reflected an enhancing sparkle and her face an appealing glow. She was aware that Galen Saar noticed and responded to both.

"You're an amazing woman, Renah. We're lucky to have you here."

"Thank you, sir. I can't think of any place I'd rather be. Perhaps with my best efforts I can rise in rank under Commander Vaux's leadership. It's also an honor to . . ."

"Continue, Lieutenant Dhobi."

"To train and work with you, Chief Saar."

"Please don't hesitate to speak your mind, Lieutenant Dhobi, for fear of me misunderstanding your meaning or trying to take advantage of it. If you check the talk-round, you'll learn I don't fuse work and pleasure."

"I'm sorry, sir; I didn't mean to imply misconduct on your part. I simply didn't want it to sound like forwardness on mine, when that is not how I intended my statement."

"I assure you it did not sound like an enticement, and I thank you. Now, about your hand-to-hand skills . . . let's examine them."

"With you, sir, or an android?"

"With me, if you don't object."

"No, sir, I do not."

They walked to a matted area and began their struggles. Renah held her own during most of the exertions but Galen's strength, quickness, and cunning were superior to hers. When he had the female pinned to the mat and breathing hard, he noticed the sheen of moisture on her lovely face and how her short golden hair was mussed before he stared into her softened pewter gaze. Her lips were parted and he longed to cover them with his.

"Is something wrong?" she asked in an almost breathless tone.

Galen mentally shook off her effect on him. He rolled to his back to get control of himself. "I was just thinking that whoever disciplined you, Lieutenant Dhobi, did an excellent job."

Renah propped on one elbow and gazed down at him. "But I lost, sir."

"Only to the ship's champion. I believe you could have bested any other opponent aboard, because I've worked out with all of them. Actually, it's nice to have competition for a change; it helps hone skills and instincts."

"Thank you, sir. Practice keeps me sharp and ready, too."

"Any time you need a partner, feel free to ask me," Galen offered as he reached up and fluffed her tousled bangs into place.

"Thank you, sir."

He hoped she would add, *I will,* but she only retreated from his touch and eyed him with suspicion. Galen sat up and frowned. "Sorry, but I do that with my sister; she's always pushing her hair out of place."

"Amaya Saar, right?" He nodded. "I've heard

she's very beautiful and smart. I never had any sisters or brothers. Are you two close?"

"Yes, we're twins, but we're in different areas of Star Fleet."

"Perhaps I'll meet her one day. She must be fascinating."

"I'm certain you two would become friends; you have a lot in common, and you're close in age: she's twenty-five."

"Will we be in the same location any time soon?"

"No, she's on extended leave with friends. When she's in Maffei, she works at Star Base in Security. She's also a *Spacer* pilot and an expert with weapons and in hand-to-hand combat. Perhaps when she returns and we're on Rigel, I can introduce you two."

"That would be nice. I've been so busy since my arrival in Maffei that I haven't made any close friends. I suppose I'm not very adept at doing so because I was the only child born and present on the ship. Somehow games with the virtual reality device isn't the same as playing with real children."

Are you explaining your personality to me? "I was lucky to have Amaya when I was growing up; a man couldn't have a more perfect sister."

"It sounds as if you have a wonderful family."

"I do. Perhaps you can meet my parents, too, if they're on Rigel when we dock there. I'm sure my mother would delight in discussing the deep-space mission with you, since she's a scientist. Unless you prefer not to discuss that tragic period in your life, that is."

"I haven't done it often, so I'm unsure how it would affect me. During your questioning, I was too nervous to think about anything but the right answers."

Galen chuckled as he gazed at her. "It didn't show; you appeared as calm as a day without wind. Go shower, change, and eat, then come to the small conference room on the other side of the ship, top level, between communications and the botanical gardens. Dismissed."

After eating in his quarters again, Galen entered the secluded conference room to play *lauis,* an alien form of chess.

As he placed the board on the table and positioned the pieces, Renah asked, "What is this for, sir, when we're supposed to be on duty?"

"We are. Do you know how to play?"

"Yes, but . . ."

"What better way to test your strategy skills?"

"May I ask if you're the ship's champion in *lauis,* sir?"

"Yes, but only because my parents taught me well; both are masters."

"Do you have a lucky color?"

"No, do you?"

"No, but you take the red and I'll take the blue."

Soon, each had forfeited and captured the same number of pieces.

When it appeared that Renah was attempting to lure him into a clever trap by sacrificing a shuttle and endangering an android, he grasped her ploy and, within two moves, conquered one of her vital guards instead. "Your ruler is in jeopardy, Lieutenant. You might need that shuttle to carry her to safety."

"Only if she fails to defeat your ruler and win the heart of his empire." Renah made her bold moves and locked gazes with him. "Do you surrender to me, sir?"

Her last words and tone in which they were spoken sent flames burning over Galen's body. His wits cleared only after she lowered her gaze to the clear board with dark white lines and he did the same. He was astonished to see his ruler trapped by her remaining guard and two cyborgs. "That took cunning and courage, Lieutenant. I should have taken your shuttle. I thought in your vulnerable position, you'd use it for escape, not attack."

"Doing the unexpected and using nerve often provide a victory, sir."

"Or a defeat," he murmured as his cyborg captured her ruler.

"Or an exchange situation. We both have something the other wants; I have your ruler and you have mine."

Galen lifted his hand and curled his fingers around the female ruler. "You are my captive, Renah, and I rule your blue world; but I am only trapped in my red empire. In a real crisis, help could arrive and rescue me. Or I could pull a sneak escape."

Renah studied the predicament she had created for herself. She needed a move to take his ruler prisoner, but it was Galen's turn to have an extra one as reward for his victory, if it was required to win the game. She had failed to outwit and out-maneuver the enemy. "Do you want a final move?" she asked in a last attempt to trick him with an oversight.

"Yes." He used his shuttle to shift his ruler to safety, then announced the game was over.

She sighed her defeat, "Sometimes everything can fail one."

"Perhaps in a game, Renah, because only two players' emotions are involved. During a real con-flict, there are many forces and feelings at work. Your ploy probably would have succeeded when confronting real enemies. I defeated you because I've observed how you think and act; I was on alert for all the skills you would use. Besides, you chose the female ruler, so I would think you'd go for a win at any cost and make normal errors in judg-ment. From what I've ascertained, greed, reckless-ness, and vanity aren't qualities of a superior officer like yourself."

Renah smiled. "I think that's a compliment; thanks."

"No, just a statement of fact as I see it."

"Perhaps I should be more careful if you can decode me so well."

"We need to be well acquainted to protect each other and do our best during perilous times. In the face of danger, we should know how to func-tion and think as if one being. There may be situ-ations where talk is impossible, perhaps even hand signals. We might need to communicate with a look or simply intuit how the other will react."

"How do we accomplish that, sir?"

"Time spent together: experience during missions, exercises and observation in between. Our team must have rapport, trust, unity. In Security, you must be yourself for the rest of us to get to know you."

"I'll do my best."

"I'm sure you will. Now, let's go to the officers' rec room and see how much stamina you have. If you crashed and were stranded on a planetoid, do you think you could walk for hours without liquid to a rendezvous point or to safety?"

"Yes, sir. I'll change and meet you there."

It was nearing mealtime when Galen told Renah, "You can turn off the *walkometer.* That's enough; you were telling the truth, as usual." He tossed her a towel to mop perspiration from her face and body; and she thanked him. He brought her a refreshing drink and watched her drink it as she relaxed and cooled down.

"What's next, sir?" she asked.

"Tests are over, Lieutenant Dhobi. Tomorrow you begin training to take your place in Security. You'll need to learn our codes and procedures. You'll have to become familiar with every inch of this ship and with every crewman aboard. You'll be given your clearance for all areas. Our directives are to patrol and keep the peace, to check out anything and anyone suspicious, to be a show of force to intimidate potential enemies, and to investigate and solve interplanetary and intergalactic crimes. In the event of an attack, we're the lead ship. If you have no questions, dismissed."

"None, sir."

He nodded, and left for his quarters.

Galen responded to the signal at his door, to find Sebok and Thaine waiting there. "I wondered when you two would check on me. Drinks?" he offered his two friends as they took places in the small sitting area.

"*Zim* for me," Sebok replied, asking for a beverage similar to Earth's coffee.

"*Pate,*" Thaine requested a cola-type liquid.

Galen fetched the refreshments and took a seat. "What's the news?"

"News?" Thaine echoed with a grin.

"There must be some or you two wouldn't be here this late."

"Why are you avoiding the mess hall? The lovely lieutenant's had her eye out for you at every meal. She even peeked into the Stardust Room."

"How do you know that?"

"I followed her," Thaine admitted, and chuckled.

"Maybe she was only taking a look at it. As a member of the security team, she has to learn this ship from top to bottom and end to end."

"I don't think that was her motive. You've caught her interest."

"I hope so, because she's captured mine."

"So why avoid times and places you can see her off-duty?"

"I don't want to panic her by constantly being in her way."

"Do you want her to worry and wonder where you are and with whom? Are you trying to whet her appetite to make her eager to eat off your plate?"

"It's hard for her to miss me at night when she's with me all day."

"That's all work. Nothing's happened yet, right?"

"Right, but she opened up a little this afternoon. I'm trying to relax her and I can't do that if I come at her like a shooting star."

"Most women want you to overtake them at first encounter."

"This one's different, Thaine. She's smart, skilled, and cautious."

"Be wary of this one, Galen," Sebok warned. "She gives me a strange feeling."

"Such as?"

"I don't know; she just pricks my instincts in a bad way."

"I've always been one to give intuition its due, Sebok, but I haven't detected anything suspicious about her."

"You wouldn't, because she's blinded you with her allure."

"Have you had a problem with her?"

"No, but I believe she's out to beguile and snare you. I overheard her asking Commander Vaux questions about you and your family."

"The same kind you asked me about Avi and the Sangers?"

"Yes, but it was different. She has Vaux disarmed; he's never been talkative to strangers about his crew members and friends."

"Perhaps it's because he knows what a hard life she's had." Galen told his friends about Renah's past and revealed other things she had told him, then asked, "What's so peculiar about her desiring me, anyway?"

"It's her pretense of not wanting you or chasing you. If she's as smart as you claim, why not be open and honest? At least, not act disinterested."

"With my reputation as a heartbreaker, can you blame her for being leery? I really like her, my friend. Give her a chance, Sebok; that's all I'm asking." He watched the teal-eyed man nod with reluctance. "What about you, Thaine. Any reservations?"

"I've seen nothing wrong with her. She's warmed up to others since that first night. I guess she was a little shy in the beginning."

"With good cause considering her tragic history. Don't worry, Sebok; Thaine's wits are clear; he won't let me jump into a vortex."

"I hope not," the worried man replied.

The following morning, Galen gave Renah an instructional tour of the U-shaped vessel's three decks. He began on the lower right side where the crew members' quarters and their mess hall and rec rooms were located. Toward the curve, they visited the transporter sight, then the engineering and ship's systems sections along the front portion. He wished Thaine and Sebok had been present so

Renah could charm them as she was charming him.

Environmental Control and Life Support, the brig, data processing, and geological/meteorological areas were covered on the left side. They went up one deck to the astronomy/astrophysics labs, more crew quarters, storage for robotic and android units, the library, history and political science, weapons arsenal, various types of research and science labs, sick bay, and lower-ranking officers' quarters where Renah lived.

They took a *trans-to* to level one. Commander Vaux's quarters were on the top right end, followed by several conference rooms, higher-ranking officers' quarters where Galen lived, and officers' mess hall and rec rooms. They skipped Security Control, the bridge, navigations, and an observation bubble in the center front to check out communications, cozy suites for visiting dignitaries, activities rooms, and two special locations.

"As you already know, there are docking bays with *Spacers,* shuttles, and escape pods on each level at the rear," Galen informed Renah.

Standing in the passageway between the Stardust Room and botanical garden, she asked, "Is this where you got the flower you gave to me?"

He only nodded to minimize the romantic gesture. "You'll enjoy the Stardust Room if you like dancing and fine dining. The view from there is awesome. The same is true of the observation bubble above the apex of the bridge; few people aboard can go there without permission, so be glad a security badge gives you clearance to visit anywhere. The Stardust Room on any ship used to be for officers only; my father changed that requirement. Now, everyone aboard has an assigned night during the week they can use it. I think that was smart; it makes the crew feel more a unit if they can socialize when off-duty."

"Your father must have superior intelligence and talents to have risen so high in the Alliance. Despite being a Saar and grandson of the past *Kadim,* only exceptional traits would lift and keep him at the top. Otherwise the Supreme Council and *avatars* would replace him." She spoke of the three-man ruling body of the Maffei Galaxy and the thirteen planetary leaders. "Do you think your father will become *Kadim* in the future?"

"I don't think he wants the responsibility of an entire galaxy on his shoulders. A *Kadim's* word is law. Even the other two councilmen cannot challenge his edicts. That's tremendous power for one man to possess. I believe our *Kadim* is doing a fine job; so does my father."

"Are they close friends?"

"Yes, since youth. But Commander Nigel Sanger is my father's best friend and second in control of Star Fleet and the Alliance Force."

And second after Varian in charge of the secret Elite Squad, of which your twin sister is a member. "He's Thaine Sanger's father, correct?"

"That's right."

"And Sebok Suran is Supreme Councilman Suran's son, correct?"

"That's right, too. Have you been studying the personnel files?"

"No, sir; I haven't been given access to them yet. Commander Vaux told me who they were the other night in the mess hall."

"They're my best friends."

"That appeared obvious to me. It must be wonderful to have . . ."

Galen resisted stroking her cheek or hair. "A best friend?"

"Yes."

It was a struggle, but Galen managed to keep a sexy huskiness out of his tone when he offered, "We can be friends, Renah, if you don't object."

"As long as it doesn't interfere with our duties, I do not object at all. You're a fascinating and intelligent man, Chief Saar. I can learn a great deal from you. I appreciate you making this transition easy for me. I like the *Galactic Wind* and her crew; I'm going to enjoy my tour on her."

"I hope she will become the last ship you serve on, Renah."

"So do I, sir. If I don't make any mistakes, she will be." *That's true.*

"From what I've seen, I can't imagine you ever making an error. But if you do, don't take it too hard because everybody makes them sometime."

"Even you and your father?"

"Even the Saars, Renah. We aren't perfect; we're just men."

"Men who do extraordinary things. You're fortunate to have a family that has earned such honor and respect. Everyone in the Tri-Galaxy knows the Saar name and their glorious deeds. I would like to meet your father in the future; your mother and sister, too." Renah halted and looked at him. "I hope that didn't sound too forward."

"It didn't, and I promise you'll get to meet them. But now it's time for you to meet the bridge officers and crew."

Galen and Renah—now attired in the perse Security uniform—headed for the heart of the ship's power. Following instructions, she was shown the ship's multispectral scanners and sensors to acquaint her with the vessel's systems and capabilities. They discussed navigations and weapons and procedures for peacetime and defense-attack.

During a break in the instructions while Galen was speaking with Commander Vaux, Renah walked to the large window spanning the front wall of the starship. She gazed through the *transascreen* at the vast expanse of space. The panorama was wondrous. Vivid and harmonious shades of green and yellow cloudlike formations were scattered across a seemingly endless backdrop of pale blue. They almost glittered as the sun to the ship's rear danced on their surfaces. It was as if she were standing on the edge of forever, an invisible door to the future.

But what, she mused, would her future hold after this enormous game of retribution was played and won? She had been trained since birth to help punish her loved ones' enemies. What would she do after victory was obtained? How would she feel about herself? Was it right, she fretted, to endanger innocents to punish the guilty? Not every Maffeian was to blame for what happened to her family, even though they followed the rule of leaders who were responsible. She wished her family hadn't made recent distressing changes in their strategy, tactics with which she didn't agree. Yet she was duty-bound to do as they ordered, and she was too entrapped in the darkening plot to ever turn away from it. Wasn't she?

Perhaps she was allowing herself to become too close and friendly to her targets. Perhaps Galen Saar was disarming her. She had expected to hate him, to use him without guilt or remorse; and she had in the beginning. But in four days, he was warming and softening her as no male had ever done before, and that worried her. She must remember who and what he was. Besides being son of the enemy, he was a pleasure-seeker, a self-indulgent *reacher* who drifted along in freedom and irresponsibility; he captivated, used, and jettisoned females. He would do the same to her if she did not keep a clear head.

Renah realized it was going to be hard to get close to him without losing herself in that task. Soon, to accomplish her secret mission, she must become his lover and confidante; then she must use that role and facts gathered to betray and destroy him and many others. Could she follow through?

"Ready to go?" Galen asked a second time of the distracted female.

Renah focused her silver-gray gaze on him and smiled. To explain her lapse of attention, she murmured, "No matter how many times I stand on the bridge of a starship, the view always amazes me."

"I understand. We both worked hard to get to this point and place."

"Yes, we did. If fate is generous, all of our goals will be grasped."

In the *trans-to,* Galen asked, "What are your goals, Renah?"

"To do my job on this ship to the best of my abilities."

"What about personal ones?"

"To date, I haven't had time to make any."

"Once you complete your preparations and things slow down, perhaps you can create dreams of your own."

"Perhaps, Chief Saar." *After I'm free to do so.*

"Eat and relax, then join me in Security Control." He left the *trans-to* to head to his quarters while Renah continued to hers on the next level.

In the Security section, Galen gave Renah the clearance codes to call up personnel files. "It's vital for us to know the people aboard. Anything they do of consequence on and off this ship is put into our files. Sometimes the tiniest fleck of information enlightens us to a future problem or helps us solve one that's developed. Unless someone has worked in Security in the past, a crewman doesn't realize we know everything about him; that way, he won't get nervous or irritated around us. Except for the Commander and other Security personnel, everybody's files are accessible to you with that code; never reveal it to anyone or use it without a valid reason. It's your responsibility to learn this crew and ship as well as you know your own name and history. This electrocard," he began as he handed one to her, "will get you into unrestricted sections of the ship even if they're ordered sealed; never misplace it or loan it to anyone or misuse it yourself. That voice-activated signal we inserted moments ago will allow you to enter any location that's off-limits to other crew members; we use voice-activation for absolute security in those areas because an electrocard could be stolen. We're the only ones who are permitted to wear weapons aboard the ship, and we do so at all times. One never knows where and from whom trouble will strike. For safety purposes, only stun guns are carried. Any questions so far?"

"None, sir."

"As to communications in the event of an emergency, Security has certain ciphertext, ciphony, and frequencies that can't be understood or detected by the *Galactic Wind*'s or any other ship's retrometer systems. I'll go through the codes and procedures with you."

"Is this precaution so other ships can't pick up and decipher our messages during trouble?"

"Yes, particularly if the trouble is within the ship, such as a traitor sabotaging or monitoring regular communications. Whatever dispatch leaves this special unit remains unknown to our ship and others. Whoever sends the missive is the only one who knows of its existence. As a fail-safe, only Security-cleared voice activators can make the unit function."

"Who has voice-activated clearance?" Renah asked.

"Security, the Commander, and the First Officer."

Later, when Galen felt certain Lieutenant Renah Dhobi was capable of handling the Security section for a while on her own, he left the control room to head for sick bay to get his routine injection of *liex*, a male birth-control shot that lasted for three months.

Renah sat in the quiet room filled with high-tech equipment deliberating if it was wise to send a cryptographic message to her family that the first two steps of her mission were accomplished: her acceptance in Security and by Galen Saar. She needed to file a report to let them know she was safe and had succeeded, but if she were caught . . .

Three

Renah entered the Stardust Room and paused to take in the view. It was a striking setting that gave one the feeling of being outside in starlight and moonglow. There were artistic murals of outdoor scenes on three walls, while the remaining one was of a transparent material that gave the illusion no barrier was there. It seemed as if one could walk across the green floor and stroll into the indigo sky. The ceiling was a retractable panel that was moved aside to expose more of the space surrounding the vessel. Small silvery-white lights were mounted to blend unnoticeably with sparkling stars. Furniture, fixtures, and decorations were a harmonious and elegant mix of amber, sky blue, and forest green. Soft music seemed to come from every direction, as if it were part of the very air. Muffled laughter and conversations drifted between the dreamy and melodic strains. The room was imbued with a gay and tranquil aura.

Security Chief Galen Saar approached her and asked, "Would you care to join me for dinner and conversation, Lieutenant Dhobi?"

Renah smiled. "It's so beautiful and peaceful here. Darkness and starlight seem to transform this location into a magical place. It's as if we're no longer on a moving vessel, more like standing on a terrace in the sky—high in the sky. I'm utterly amazed and impressed. The evening rooms on my past two ships were not this enchanting."

"The *Galactic Wind* is the lead ship and we often transport important leaders and intergalactic guests, so ours is the best. Will you join me at my table?"

"Will I be intruding when your two friends arrive?"

"They aren't joining me tonight, so I can use the company. They prefer the officers' mess hall to the Stardust Room. I like it here."

"I thought I would check it out for myself, since it fit into my schedule tonight. I was hoping that someone I know would be present."

"I'm delighted I can accommodate you," he said as he guided her to his table and seated her. "What would you like to drink?"

"Since I'm off-duty, Eirean wine. It's the only evening beverage I'm familiar with, as I rarely have strong drinks."

"An excellent choice; it's what I'm having." He pressed the appropriate button to place the order on a small and decorative unit in the center of the table. "I suppose I have a fondness for Eire's wine because it comes from my great-grandfather's planet."

"Yes, *Kadim* Trygue, a famous ruler in our history. Your family is very special, Galen. You must have had a fascinating and happy childhood."

"I did. We spent many wonderful days on Eire. Amaya and I called him Grandfather. He died when we were twenty. That he lived to one hundred and two years was fortunate for us. He was a unique and wise man. He and my father were close, especially after my grandparents' . . . deaths. Amaya and I are named after them, in case you didn't notice that in your studies."

"I did. *Kadim* Procyon seems to have made a good replacement during the last five years. I was fortunate enough to meet him briefly on Rigel. He struck me as being the perfect mixture of gentleness and strength. I can't imagine being a *Kadim,* or *avatar,* or *zartiff.* Do you have aspirations to be galactic ruler? Or a planetary or a regional leader?"

Galen responded honestly to her question. "No, I'm happy and satisfied being in Star Fleet and ship security."

"You aren't interested in becoming a starship commander?"

"Not for at least ten years. I enjoy being in the heart of action, not being the one to order others into it. What about you?"

Renah glanced around and lowered her voice as if she were revealing a secret. "I wouldn't mind becoming a starship commander in ten years or so. There aren't many female commanders because most women become mates and mothers before they can climb that high in rank. But for now, like you, I enjoy the adventures and challenges of my position."

"From spending the last four days with you, I had a feeling we're much alike in many ways. It's good to have a friend who's so compatible."

"It does make spending time together nicer."

An android delivered Renah's wine and Galen proposed a toast, "To becoming best friends and a perfect team."

Renah smiled, tapped her glass to his, and sipped the mauve liquid. As she set down her glass, she asked, "Sebok Suran doesn't like me, does he?"

"What makes you say that?"

"When we were in ship's systems, he watched me as if I were a *scarfelli* sneaking around to attack and cocoon him in my web to devour later. It was almost as if he were giving off a chill as cold as Kudoran winds. Since we haven't socialized or worked together, I don't know what I could have done or said to offend him."

"Neither can I, Renah. Perhaps his mind was elsewhere or he wasn't feeling well because he isn't normally rude or cruel."

"Perhaps I was mistaken. If not, please help me settle the matter with haste, as it could create trouble for either or both of us."

"I'll speak with him later."

"On second thought, it would be best not to mention it to him at this point when I'm trying to make friends and learning how to fit in here. If I'm wrong, confronting him could incite hard feelings where none existed. I'm not good at socializing. I seem to make people uneasy because I appear so serious and distant, or *unfriendly*, as many have said. I don't mean to be or to appear aloof and cool to others; it's just that I spent too many of my early years around serious adults."

Renah gave a wry laugh before she admitted, "I

suppose I was always a tiny adult myself. When I was a child, instead of playing, I was always studying and learning. In my teenage years, I wasn't around girls and boys my age; I didn't go to parties or dances or sports. After my rescue, I was alone and grieving; I had no family, home, or friends; I felt I had to prove myself to be accepted and had to stay busy to distract my mind from that tragedy. It seems as if I've trained and studied all of my life to be right here. I have a duty to perform, and I don't want anything or anyone to damage or destroy it. If I lost my place in Star Fleet, I'd have nowhere to go and no friends where I landed." *And I'd be in deep trouble.* "I need to remain here. Teach me how to be accepted and help me do a good job."

"You miss your family greatly, don't you?"

"Yes. Everything has changed so much since I came here alone that it's difficult at times to know the right things to do."

"One day, you'll create another family for yourself."

"I'm unsure I want to take that risk, sir; losing all you have and love is devastating." *According to my parents, and they should know. I wonder if they truly have been forgotten by the Saars and the Maffeians. Soon, son of Varian and Jana, I fear everyone will recall and curse their names.*

Galen wanted to remove her sad expression. "You don't have to worry, Renah; I'm certain you'll do your duty."

"I've sworn to try my best to accomplish everything I came to do."

"Which would you like to do first tonight: eat or dance?"

"Dance?" She queried the sudden change of subject.

"Move around on the floor in time to the music," he teased.

"Would that be proper for us?"

"Here, we're off-duty. Here, everyone has fun and relaxes. I don't devour my teammates, Renah; you don't have to be afraid of me."

"I'm not," she replied, but knew that wasn't true. Galen Saar was not the kind of man she had expected. He was wriggling his way under her defense shield and, if allowed to complete his tunneling, could become a threat to her mission and survival. She must get closer to this blazing star, but without getting burned.

Galen studied the array of conflicting emotions that came and went in Renah's gaze. "Then, what makes you nervous and distrustful of me? Sometimes I sense a wariness and retreat."

Renah realized she had made a slip, so she took advantage of an opening to mislead him, to guide him in a fake romantic direction. "I'd rather not answer, sir; this isn't the appropriate time."

Galen smiled in pleasure and didn't press the stimulating issue. "But it *is* time to have fun. Let's dance. I'll behave; I promise."

"I'm convinced by now, sir, that you always behave yourself."

As they danced with a proper distance between their bodies, they chatted about security procedures, the starship, and past adventures.

"Do you know all the Council members personally?" Renah asked.

"Yes. They're close friends of my father's and were good friends of my great-grandfather's. I suppose you know that my father was assigned to Breccia Sard's position when Brec became a Council member."

Renah nodded, familiar with that enemy's name and history.

"Suran, Sebok's father, was *avatar* of Zamarra before he became one."

Suran, another foe to be defeated. "Didn't I read that his family were the creators and builders of Zamarra's undersea domes?"

"That's right, fifty years before the last three continents sank."

"Is that why he's so rich and powerful?"

"In the beginning, but he's also a wise investor and excellent leader."

"Kadim Draco Procyon is a close and longtime friend of your father's and your mother's, correct?" *Their staunch ally in past treacheries . . .*

"Does that mean you know he was the one who purchased my mother when she first arrived in Maffei?"

"Yes, I read it in the history files on Rigel. The *charl* practice and laws were fascinating data, but I'm glad they were abolished, thanks in part to your mother's arrival and influence. I can't imagine living as a slave and not selecting my own mate. Those must have been frightening experiences for those alien captives, and I'm sure most Maffeian women envied and resented their fertility. It's good those problems and feelings were conquered."

"I agree. I suppose your parents told you it was necessary to raid the Milky Way Galaxy because Maffeians dared not breed with Androasians and Pyropeans. They couldn't provoke more trouble with either galaxy by stealing mates from them or even by accepting seemingly willing ones. Long ago before our births, neither race could be trusted."

"Those intergalactic conflicts no longer exist with the Trilonis and Tabrizes gone. We have truces." *For a while longer* . . .

"Thank the stars they're all dead and peace rules; they were evil and greedy. Intergalactic war is a horror too great to imagine."

"I'm sure you're proud of the roles your parents played in obtaining those treaties. They're fortunate they found each other. But why didn't your mother and the *Kadim* stay together? Or is that private?"

"Private, yes, but I'll answer. Draco realized my parents were in love, so he agreed to sell Mother to Father. Before they mated, she won her freedom by saving my great-grandfather's—*Kadim* Trygue's—life during an assassin's attack. She bonded to Father by choice." Galen waited to see if she mentioned the fact that Jana had bonded to Ryker Triloni first.

"Why didn't your father just keep her after her capture from Earth?"

"It was against regulations for a commander or crewman to take charge of their female cargo, or every starship commander and crewman would insist on seeking out their choices. And he didn't realize he had fallen in love with her from the first moment he cast eyes on her. He enjoyed his freedom and adventures, like we do, and believed he wasn't ready to settle down. He also believed it was his duty to marry a Maffeian because of who he was, but there were few fertile Maffeian females, and none who suited him. He also had many enemies who would have endangered Mother's life if he had claimed her before those *villites* were defeated."

"It's a good thing he destroyed all threats to them and realized his mistake while there was time to correct it. Love triumphed because of friendship. It's advantageous the Council consists of such good friends since they have to work together to rule our galaxy. What would happen if the Council members disagreed on crucial issues and became enemies?"

"With three members, a *Kadim* has the deadlock-breaking vote."

"What would happen to the man who disagreed with the other two? Could he cause trouble, perhaps provoke rebellion?"

"Theoretically, I suppose so. Fortunately, that has never occurred in our history. Men chosen have always put the welfare and safety of our people and world above their own desires and goals."

"*Theoretically,*" Renah began, and grinned, "if a member was on the brink of causing severe trouble, what would the others do?"

"I don't know, because I can't imagine one of our three leaders becoming twisted and going to such an extreme."

"Neither can I." Renah laughed, and said, "Surely no Supreme Council member would battle the others; nor would any of them sink to betrayal. Their unity explains why we have truces and peace with Pyropea and Androas. If our leaders didn't have such a strong bond, another galactic ruler might be tempted to ally with a troublemaker and break the treaty."

"With our technologies, multi-galactic war would be catastrophic for both sides and for the innocents trapped between them. All rulers know and respect that powerful truth, so any disputes are handled with words instead of with weapons."

"Do we ever have missions to seek out and destroy such threats? Do we ever cross galaxy borders and intrude on the leadership of other rulers to prevent such a horror?"

"If you mean, do other leaders or their families try to incite war, the answer is no, not since those past threats were removed."

"From Androas and Pyropea: the Trilonis and Tabrizes?"

"Correct again. You've done your studying, Renah."

"My parents and I missed a lot of history in progress while away from Maffei. Shortly before our births, Galen, a great deal took place in a short time. Wouldn't it have been fascinating and exciting to have been a part of those times? We could have risen to high rank within months. Think of the adventures and challenges we could have shared."

During those perfidious days when the Saars, Trygue, and their friends were stealing control of the government, I wonder if you know all they did to get rid of their rivals. Perhaps Draco was promised the Kadimship *in exchange for giving Jana Greyson to your father. She got what she wanted in exchange for Trilabs: freedom for her and her captive friends, marriage to Varian, and abolishment of the* charl *practice. It's doubtful that your uncle's death on Caguas was an accident, and I might find a way to prove it. The murder of Prince Ryker Triloni and theft of Trilabs by the Saars would displease and provoke the Androasians. Evidence that Prince Taemin Tabriz had been accused falsely and wrongfully exiled would turn the Pyropeans against the Saars and their friends. Both galaxies would surely seek revenge. The Maffeians think their leaders are honest and honorable; what will they do when they learn the truth? What will you do, Galen, if you don't know the truth already?*

"I hope those are colorful daydreams you're having," Galen teased.

"Being a part of glorious history would have been nice, but I'm realistic, so I'll become a part of future history," she finished with a laugh.

"You have all the qualities to do just that, Renah Dhobi, and I hope we're teamed up when it happens."

"We will, because this is the last starship I'll serve on." To dupe him, she made a comical scowl. "Unless I make an error and get jettisoned."

He smiled and vowed, "I'll make certain you don't do either one. I like and respect you, woman, so we'll get along beautifully."

On the way to their table, Galen halted to speak with an officer.

Renah's mind was racing. *Trying to charm me, my*

handsome rogue? Can none of you Saar men be trusted? Must you snare, use, and discard countless females to sate your lust? Soon all male Saars will suffer agony and destruction. When trouble soon comes to every planet of this star system, Maffeians will curse the days they allowed greedy men to take control and darken their futures. When Star Fleet and the Council cannot help or protect their worlds, they will rebel and the Alliance will be broken. After your past crimes are revealed, expect attacks from Androas and Pyropea. Who knows, perhaps my side will conquer and rule this galaxy . . .

Sebok Suran observed the couple and worried over the icy glance Renah gave Galen when his friend's back was turned. It was obvious she did not see him watching her. Somehow, he worried, he must find a way to convince Galen that Renah was trouble.

As Renah sipped wine and Galen ordered their meal, the plot for retribution sliced like a laser through her troubled mind and torn emotions. Yet, she must not weaken or fail. She was the only person who could carry out this area of the mission. Besides, what she was doing was right, she told herself, though her part was becoming more difficult as unwanted emotions threatened to confuse her. Perhaps that was because the plot had grown in scope and severity since she began her active part four years ago. She hadn't learned of the distressing changes until the day she boarded this ship. Could she, Renah worried, do *everything* ordered of her? Could she let *everything* that was now planned come to pass? She must!

"Would you like another glass of wine?"

"No, thank you." She leaned in his direction to whisper, "I wouldn't want to embarrass either of us by exceeding a safe limit."

His gaze drifted over her sunny hair, fair skin, and stardust eyes. "Then I suppose I should keep my head clear and my conduct proper."

Renah gave his hand a brief touch. "Please, have another if you wish."

"I don't need it." *Your beauty and company are plenty potent, and your contact is intoxicating.* "Ah, swift service. Excellent, I'm hungry." *And I need a distraction from you badly. Kahala above, you're enchanting!*

"Me, too. I need to leave right after the meal; I'm a little tired."

"I'm sure you are; it was a long and busy day."

As they dined, they chatted little; when they did, it was about the ship's personnel and their impending assignment at Darkar. Yet, Galen perceived that something was bothering Renah. She exuded an aura so intense he could almost touch it. Perhaps, he reasoned, she was being drawn to him, and that— because of his unfair reputation—frightened her. He'd never intentionally hurt any female and had tried to be honest and kind to every companion he'd had. Why did so many people think that because he didn't have a long relationship with a woman and enjoyed a variety of them that he was a *reacher*? His father had endured that same unjustified affliction. Varian Saar had been only discriminating, never cruel or greedy. Now a woman had come along who he wanted and, as with his parents and paternal grandparents, perhaps he was in for a long and painful fight.

"Galen?" Renah spoke his name for the second time. "I've finished my meal and now I'm leaving. Good night. I'll see you in the morning."

"I'm finished, too, so I'll escort you to your quarters."

"I don't think it would look proper, but thank you."

"Goodnight, then, Renah. Sleep well."

"You, too, sir."

Galen watched her exit the softly lit room and took a deep breath. Sebok joined him. "I thought you were eating in the officers' mess hall."

"I did. I just came by to visit with friends."

"Do you want a drink?"

Sebok shook his head. "Did you enjoy dinner with the lieutenant?"

"More than you can imagine, old friend."

"Aren't you traveling this new course too quickly?"

Galen leaned forward and propped his forearms on the table. "Did I ask you that question when you lost your head over Avi?"

In a serious tone, Sebok replied, "As a matter of fact, you did."

With hopes of lightening the sudden heaviness in the air, Galen chuckled and asked, "And what was your response?"

"I had to be fast to win her before another did."

"Well, old friend, that truth applies to me, too."

"She isn't like Avi Sanger, Galen."

"If she were and that's what I wanted in a female, I would have gone after Avi."

Sebok frowned as if insulted. "What's wrong with Avi?"

"Nothing, but she's like my second sister. I should be asking, what's wrong with you? We've been best friends too long for my choice in a woman to come between us. This relationship—if it can develop into one—is my decision. You know nothing bad about Renah Dhobi, my friend. She has an outstanding record and she's done you no harm, so you're being unfair to her and to me. Give me one fact to go on, Sebok, not just a personality clash. I think Renah and I are perfectly matched. If you can't give her a chance, at least stay out of the matter." Galen stood, looked at his somber friend, then departed.

The following evening, Renah went to hopefully end the problem. "May I enter and speak with you, please?" she requested.

Sebok's teal eyes frosted. "Of course, Lieutenant Dhobi, but what brings you to my private quarters?"

"I would prefer for you to call me Renah, if you don't object," she told him.

"Why should I?"

"May I ask why you take such strong offense to me?"

"Why do you think I dislike you?"

"Your reason is unknown but your behavior exposes its existence. Every time we come into contact with each other—you stare at me with a coldness and revulsion I do not understand, since we're strangers. When we're in the same area for any length of time, I find you studying me with the intensity of an enemy. Your dislike is so strong that it's unnecessary for you to verbalize it for me to perceive it. I lived in deep space with only adults until a few years ago, so my social skills with peers have suffered. I've worked hard to get over that tragedy and to become a qualified officer. I want my life on the *Galactic Wind* to be happy. I want to make friends here. If you don't tell me what I'm doing wrong and why I repulse you, I can't correct that flaw and fit in with the others. Help me, Sebok, to adjust to this new life and position. What have I done? Please, be honest."

The man ignored the twinkle of near tears in her eyes and the tone of sincerity in her voice. "What is your interest in Galen Saar?"

She stared at him in feigned confusion. "What?"

"You heard me, Renah, so I won't repeat the question."

"Yes, but I don't grasp your meaning. How is that a flaw? Why would 'interest' in him offend you to such a degree?"

"I'll be clear and succinct. Reason: love and defense of a best friend. Meaning: the peculiar way you look at him."

"Why does Chief Saar need defending against me, and how do I look at him that so disturbs you?"

"Do you deny you want him?"

Renah coaxed her body to bring a flush to her cheeks and a look of astonishment to her face. She lowered her gaze for a moment, swallowed, and took a deep breath. "I . . . I like and respect him. I . . . enjoy his company. I'm sure most females find him attractive and pleasurable. We're working well together. We're becoming friends. But we aren't . . . close that way."

"Not yet."

"As fellow officers, we will never get that close."

"Is propriety going to stop either of you from doing so?"

"Why worry about such a vague matter? Besides, why are you getting involved in something private?"

"Galen's one of my best friends."

"It's an honor and privilege to work with him; he can teach me a great deal, professionally and personally. Don't begrudge me this opportunity and friendship by sabotaging them because I'm different. Besides, he would never do anything he didn't want to do. We're only becoming friends, Sebok. Is that so wrong, so unacceptable?"

"But you want him, don't you?" he persisted.

"I admit he's the most unique and captivating man I've met, but he can have his choice of countless females. What would he want with me? I have no family, no wealth, no elite status, no important friends; in fact, no close friends at all. I'm a stranger to Galen's type of life, and I won't become any man's temporary conquest or plaything."

"Is that why you stare at him so coldly when he isn't looking? You hate him because of his ridiculous reputation? You want to teach him a lesson? Or do you believe a faked disinterest will challenge him to pursue you?"

Renah lowered her head. When she lifted it, tears sparkled again in her eyes. "None of those things, Sebok; I'm cursing the fate that made me a nobody who can never seize the serious interest of a special man. If the *Space Rover* hadn't exploded, my family would have returned to great honor and public attention. I would have been placed in the elite circle and been deemed worthy of a man like Galen. As it is, even if I desired him, I could chase him from now until Maffei no longer exists and it would make no difference because he will select a mate who is his equal in all ways. We both know I am not, through no fault of my own.

"Yes, Sebok, he's everything a woman could desire in a man and I've fantasized about a romance with him. But as his friend, you should know I stand as much of a chance of winning Galen Saar as a meteor does of staying aflame after striking Kudora's icy surface. Whether or not you allow me to try to earn your respect and acceptance, it will not affect my chances with Galen. Dislike and reject me if you must, but do so for a reason more important than my ill-fated desire for him. I can no more halt my feelings for him than you can control yours for the woman you love. I'm no dark and deadly threat to him; I would never hurt him even if I possessed the power and skills to do so. Nor do I want to be hurt by rejection or to suffer a great personal loss again."

As she turned to press the button to open the

door in order to make a hasty exit, Sebok urged, "Wait, Renah, we haven't finished our talk."

She whirled. "I have confessed, apologized, humbled myself, and explained; what more is there to say or do? I don't want people to dislike and avoid me. I want to enjoy the same rapport and warmth I witness between almost everyone aboard. Listen to what you're saying; analyze your thoughts and emotions. You know Galen Saar too well to underestimate him in this matter. Do you really think I or any female could fool him? I've been around him for only five days, but I know him better than that."

Renah did not give the man an opportunity to interrupt. "For *Kahala's* sake, Sebok, you're talking about *the* Galen Saar, son of *the* Supreme Commander, great-grandson of a past *Kadim.* Galen and I deserve credit for knowing we're worlds apart in countless ways. Even if he found me appealing, he would never view or accept me as more than a brief affair. Perhaps I should be flattered that you would even consider me enough of a threat to worry about. Well, I want to make one request: we're going to be aboard this ship for a long time; so I think it would be wise for us to be polite and professional so others won't get drawn into this problem you have with me. If you can cooperate that much with me, then I promise to stay out of your path as much as possible. That's the best compromise I have to offer, Sebok, so I pray you will accept it for everyone's sake. Under the circumstances, that's the only solution I can think of to prevent problems and embarrassment for us, the crew, and especially for Chief Saar. We don't want to trap him in an uncomfortable position between a team member and a best friend."

"Renah—"

"Please allow me to finish before you respond. If you wonder why I am as I am, I'll tell you what happened before I was assigned here. When I first returned to Maffei and was accepted by Star Fleet, most of my classes and training were with instructors or computers or simulators because I was advanced beyond the point of the classes in progress; I can see now, in a way, that was a terrible disadvantage because I didn't get to mix with peers and become familiar with what it was like to be twenty. It was as if I'd been an adult all of my life. Aboard my first two ships, most of the crew thought I was too reticent, too serious and dull. Some believed I was arrogant and self-seeking because I concentrated on work, tried to learn and do the best job possible and not make mistakes that could endanger others or stain my record.

He's actually listening, Renah, and being touched! "During one of my first assignments, I outperformed two other *Spacer* pilots—males—so they and their loyal friends were annoyed with me and shunned me. Despite our advanced society and the abolishment of *charl* laws, women still do not possess the same freedoms as men; no female has held the highest rank in Star Fleet, or been an *avatar* or *Kadim* or Council member; their primary role in life is to reproduce. Eventually, most women become mates and mothers, no matter what work and deeds they have performed before that period. Those who reveal little or no interest in those areas are judged as being different, as I was. I want to make a fresh beginning on the *Galactic Wind*. To succeed as an officer and to become a real person to others, I must make the right start and avoid the mistakes in my past. I'm trying to do that, and Galen is helping me. If you can't like me and accept me, Sebok, that's your right. I'll even understand your choice because no one knows better than I do that I truly am different."

"I'm sorry I hurt you, Renah. Now that you've enlightened me about yourself, it's obvious I misjudged you. I compared you to the women of Maffei, when you were not born and reared here. Now I understand why Galen is so impressed by you. He's told me and Thaine about your record and skills and how hard you've worked to get to this point in your career. I misread your actions and expressions because I didn't understand your history and personality. It isn't like me to be unkind or unforgiving, or to intrude on Galen's business. But it isn't like *him* to take to a stranger this fast, so warning beacons flashed in my head."

"Galen and I are compatible because we have the same or similar likes, abilities, and positions. We're *Spacer* pilots, skilled with weapons, both love adventures and challenges and want to be career officers."

"You two have learned a lot about each other in a short time."

"Galen said it's important for security team members to know each other inside and out, to become synchronized, so a unit can react as one person in a crisis. I believe he's right, so that's what we've been doing: getting acquainted and bonding as a team, and hopefully as friends."

Sebok noticed how her eyes glowed and her voice softened each time she mentioned Galen's name. If she wasn't already in love with Galen, she was running fast in that direction, whether she wanted to or not. "I was suspicious of you at first because you were pretending not to be interested in Galen when it was clear you were."

Renah summoned a guileful flush to her cheeks. "I'm trying not to allow an interest in him to be born, but if it happens I know I must prevent its growth because that surely would be foolish and futile."

"You're right, Renah, it *is* none of my business, so I'll stay out of it. It's between you and Galen."

Renah put on an expression of astonishment. "You're serious about that?"

"Yes, and I think we might even become friends with a little work."

She brought tears to her silvery-gray eyes and a quiver to her voice. "Thank you, Sebok, I appreciate your candor and generosity."

"Why don't you refresh yourself in your quarters, then we will meet for dinner in the officers' mess hall? Perhaps Galen and Thaine will join us?"

Renah smiled and thanked him again before departing. As she headed to change garments, she stunned herself with the realization that she liked and respected Sebok Suran for his reaction. She even experienced a few twinges of guilt for deluding him. But not everything had been a lie. She'd truly never had friends her age and hadn't learned how to make them. It felt good to be accepted and liked now.

When Galen and Thaine entered the mess hall, they were surprised to see Renah and Sebok laughing together and chatting. They were asked to join the table.

"I've been telling Renah about some of our past adventures and introducing her to other crew members," Sebok said.

"He's also been telling me about the ship's systems and his romance with Avi Sanger. It sounds as if you have a wonderful sister, Thaine."

"I do; so does Galen."

"Is there a romance between you?" she asked the grinning male.

"No, we're just good friends. She's like my sister, too."

"You're fortunate to have a family you love and respect so deeply."

"I agree. It's belated, but please accept my condolences for the loss of yours. I'm sure it was a painful period for you."

"Thank you; that's kind of you to say. Anything happen in Security after I went off-duty, Chief Saar?"

"Nothing; all's quiet aboard the ship."

"With luck and hard work, it will remain that way."

"I hope so, Renah; it means a lot to me."

Every person at the table caught Galen's double

entendres but pretended his statements had only a single meaning.

"If anyone can help you keep matters under control, it's Renah."

She smiled at Sebok. "I hope you're right. I'll try my best."

"We'll reach Darkar tomorrow, Renah; that should be a treat for you."

"I've never been there before, so it will be. Tell me about it."

"Why don't I let you make that discovery for yourself? Your first impressions, particularly of her security, will be of interest to me."

"Another test, Chief Saar?" she teased.

"No, but perhaps you can spot something we haven't. Since Darkar and Trilabs are unfamiliar to you, you can look at them objectively. I want you to pay close attention to their defense capabilities and systems."

"The planetoid and laboratory complex are impregnable," Renah responded. "The surface has an impenetrable force shield. It has the most superior attack and defense weapons in existence. The complex itself is constructed of laser-resistent material, and the labs have an ability to automatically lower themselves underground if the shield and structures don't hold against attack. If the lowering procedure is carried out, only the *Kadim* knows the code to raise it again. The complex is accessible only to certain personnel, and with a secret code that cannot be deciphered or imitated or even extracted from the minds of those who know it. If entrance is gained to the complex, each section automatically seals itself off to invasion. With those weapons and safeguards, what more could it need?"

"Where did you learn so much about Darkar and Trilabs?"

"From our security data files; I wanted to know all I could about them before we reach there tomorrow. You ordered me to study everything. Was I in error, sir?"

"No, but your efficiency took me by surprise. I intended to go over the facts and plans with you later this evening; that's no longer necessary."

"Here comes our food," Thaine remarked.

"Excellent, I'm hungry. What about you, Renah?"

"Hungry, too, Chief Saar." She sent forth a blush to charm them and it seemed to work when all three males grinned and Galen chuckled.

The security team traveled from the orbiting starship to Darkar's shuttle port to collect needed supplies. Chief Galen Saar journeyed in the craft piloted by Third Lieutenant Dhobi. Following the pleasant dinner with Renah and his friends and delighting in Sebok's change of heart, the son of Varian and Jana Saar was in a cheerful and relaxed mood.

Renah was on full alert. She was eager to impress Galen with any flaws or suggestions about Darkar's security, something of vital interest for another reason: her secret mission. She had learned the shield lowering code when he sent it to the surface from the ship. Soon, perhaps she would discover the entrance code to the complex, if she stuck to Galen like the hairs on his skin. After her return to the *Galactic Wind*, she must find a private moment to send those codes to—

"You're quiet today, Renah," Galen observed. "Are you tired? Did we keep you up late?"

"No, sir, just concentrating on following your order to study the defenses here. This area of the planetoid is beautiful."

Galen peered at the view beyond and below them. "It's where things are grown to use in drugs and chemicals."

"Do you ever wish you could have met Ryker Triloni before he died?"

"Yes and no."

"I don't understand."

"I'll explain another time."

"Galen, if I'm ever too nosy, please don't hesitate to tell me. I can't help being intrigued about a man who could build a place like this and create so many powerful drugs, chemicals, and weapons. Anyone would have to admit he was a genius. Imagine what he could have done if he'd poured his energy and thoughts into more helpful discoveries instead of hatred for your father. Because of him and Trilabs, Maffei is the most powerful galaxy in known existence."

"There are some things I wish you hadn't learned about our world."

Renah checked the instrument and sensor panels. "Such as?"

"Such as anything that makes me and my family look bad in your eyes."

She glanced at him to respond, "Nothing I've learned has done that, Galen; in fact, just the opposite." *To my dismay!*

"Are you certain, or just being kind and polite?"

"Why are you concerned about that?"

"Because I like you, perhaps too much for my own good."

"How is it possible to like someone too much and why is that wrong?"

He reasoned it was too soon to answer that question. "Forget it for now. There's the landing grid. Time to go to work."

Yes, it is, and without getting caught.

Four

As Galen spoke with the men who greeted his shuttle, Renah eyed their surroundings. The domicile where Jana Greyson had lived with Prince Ryker Triloni sat in the distance. The tan dwelling was comprised of a large rondure center with four smaller semispheres attached by short corridors. Reflective *transascreens,* flush with the walls, mirrored the view of lush landscape with interconnecting walks. The living chambers sat on a thick base that lowered them into a subterranean bastion if defenses failed. Galen had told Renah it was occupied now only by a three-man security team. She noticed many other edifices: storage pods, green-domes for raising plants, an enclosure to house pleasure-riding creatures, an aqua-shell for swimming, and a compound of many laboratories.

In every direction, plants, trees, and flowers grew to create a colorful and striking setting. She knew from Galen that more gardens and animal shelters were located elsewhere. There were no birds or insects flying free, and plant pollination was effected by mechanical means with a technology Ryker had invented. Renah wondered if the scientific mind of Jana Greyson had been stimulated by this impressive location; and if Jana had been mesmerized by the genius, exceptional good looks, and elite status of her first mate.

Renah knew it was no secret that Varian and his half brother had been bitter rivals and lethal foes until shortly before Ryker's alleged "accident." Supposedly Jana Triloni had made the Prince a better man, a different man. Different? Yes, if it wasn't Ryker with her during those final days when the Trilonis helped obtain two intergalactic treaties. If things had been different, she mused, Galen could have been Ryker's child and been heir to Trilabs, Darkar, and the Androasian Empire; as the Triloni heir, he would have commanded great wealth, power, and prestige. If so, she would not be here seeking revenge. Considering the timing involved, it was possible for that speculation to be true. Galen favored Varian Saar, but so had Ryker, as both men resembled their deceased father. Since Jana loved Varian, it was fortunate for them that Ryker was "killed in an accident." What better wedding gifts could an alien ex-slave give her illustrious husband than Trilabs, peace, and twins? And what better things could an enemy take away in vengeance?

Galen led her to the portal of the complex's heart, where he entered the digital and verbal codes to open it. Once inside the threshold, remaining doors responded by floor pressure or voice-activated commands. After giving his instructions to the technician who met them, Galen took Renah on a tour while they waited for the order to be readied and loaded.

They left the entry nucleus to visit an aggregation of domes constructed in a half-moon pattern. Assorted laboratories and edifices were located at the ends of long corridors that were reached by mechanical conveyors that operated automatically. Some parts were involved in creative research and development, some in production, and some in testing their output. Most of the labor was performed by androids, but some of the tasks were handled by an intricate computer network. Both systems were alleged to be inaccessible to an enemy.

The complex was composed of an almost impenetrable substratum, and it lacked *transascreens* that would provide breachable points to an attacker. The interior environment was controlled by an automated life-support system; it and lighting controls were situated beneath the entry core to prevent destruction and invasion. Also included in that secure area was a large food and water supply.

During a break in a comfort room following excursions to the shuttle base and storage structures, Galen asked his companion for her impressions.

"What protection do loaded shuttles have if defenses are breached?" Renah asked. "Some of their cargoes would be lethal to this area."

"Shuttles are loaded only when a starship on full alert is in orbit to protect them, especially during their return flights."

"What if several enemy crafts arrived and our vessel was kept busy while the shuttles were destroyed or stolen by tractable beams?"

"They couldn't approach without detection, so

we'd have time to enclose the shuttles and reenergize the force field."

"What if they had a cloaking device?"

"It wouldn't work against our anticloaking unit."

"Suppose an enemy galaxy created their own sophisticated units?"

"So far, none have. When they do, we'll deal with the problem."

"What about the weapons in the storage area? There's little to safeguard them if an enemy-landing occurred."

"Little is needed because those kind of weapons are useless without the chemicals that make them function, and the chems can't be reached."

"Suppose someone did get his hands on the necessary chemicals?"

"It wouldn't matter. Any attempt to analyze them for reproduction would result in a self-alteration sequence. Ryker put tags on one of the substances included in each of his formulas so no one could discover their contents. Also, they have a limited life span; that's why we have to restock. Lucky for us, we have all his formulas in the main computer. Only androids are permitted to mix them, and they're programmed to terminate if questioned without the right code."

"Has the complex lowering procedure been tested?"

"Never, to my knowledge."

"Then how do you know it will work? If it doesn't, an explosion and dispersion of the chemicals would destroy this sector of space and put it off-limits for thousands of years. In addition, imagine what would happen if any of those germs or viruses escaped. And worse, in a blast like that, there's no guessing what mutations could evolve."

"Those are horrifying contemplations, but what if the labs failed to rise again under the *Kadim's* command?"

"Isn't that a necessary risk, considering the consequences of a malfunction during a natural disaster or an assault? As you told me, destruction of the storage pods would contaminate only Darkar's surface and atmosphere. What is in this complex would be blasted and spread to Caguas and into open space. Also, the landing grids are too close to the storage area. If a shuttle crashed and exploded, it would be endangered."

Galen was impressed with her excellent observation. "I'll report that oversight," he said.

"Also, the codes for lowering the force shield and gaining access to Trilabs' heart should be changed at intervals in case someone became a traitor," Renah added.

"Another excellent suggestion, one I've made previously. But the *Kadim* and Council believe it's perilous to transmit code changes to those entrusted with it, even via our secret frequency and cipher."

"Who is entrusted with such crucial knowledge?"

"The *Kadim,* Council members, my father as head of the Alliance Force and Star Fleet, and certain Security chiefs on lead vessels. In the event of an attack, we need access to weapons and supplies, and codes couldn't be transmitted with enemies in Darkar's sector."

"Why can't a guard on this surface open the complex for you?"

"That isn't necessary, since Darkar Security controls the force shield. If a man isn't allowed past it, the entrance code is useless to him."

But with the force shield code . . . "That's the perfect precaution."

"Anything else?"

"Someone besides *Kadim* Procyon should know the lifting code—your father or the Councilmen. Procyon could be slain by an enemy, killed in an accident, or just die of natural causes. It is unwise for only one man to possess a fact of such grave importance to Maffei's defense and survival."

Renah witnessed Galen's broad smile and the glow in his eyes. "Why are you staring at me like that? Do my words amuse you?"

"On the contrary, your intelligence astounds and pleases me. What a rare and special woman you are, Renah Dhobi. Lucky the man who . . ."

"Why did you halt? What were you about to say?"

"Are you sure you want to know? It's personal, maybe inappropriate."

She pretended to observe him for a moment before saying, "Yes."

"Lucky the man who wins you, Renah Dhobi."

"I have little to offer the kind of man I'd want, Chief Saar."

"You require nothing more than what you are and have."

"Is that a personal or professional assessment?"

"Both."

Renah gazed at him, her thoughts scattering and her heart beating fast for a moment. "I don't know how to respond, sir."

"There's no need to do so, unless my words offended you."

"They do not, but they alarm me."

Galen moved closer to her on the long *seata*. "Why?"

Renah felt his magnetism pulling at her and she tried to repel it. "Because I might read more into them than you intended."

"You could never read too much into them, or enough."

She stood to put distance between them. She stared at him as she spoke. "But we're near strangers; we're fellow officers, teammates. How could you feel such a way so soon?"

"Only *Kahala* knows, but I do. The first time you smiled at me and touched me, it was as if my emotions had been sleepwalking and suddenly were jerked awake. I find myself thinking about you, just wanting to be with you, to gaze at you, to hear your voice. If you feel the same way, we should explore the attraction between us, test how good we can be together. If not, tell me to keep my place, and I will. If I have spoken too soon, it's because I feared another would catch your eye before you learned of my feelings toward you."

Renah paced the floor as her mind spun with wild thoughts and her body burned with fiery feelings. Was he being honest? Surely not. Should she pretend to believe him, accept his overtures, and get on with securing a bond to him? She had the Trilabs codes, but she needed more . . .

Galen joined her. His hands cupped her chin and lifted her head to fuse her gaze with his. "Have I frightened or angered you?"

"No and yes."

"Explain, please, so I'll know how to behave with you. I'll never speak of this again if that's what you want. Rest assured, Renah, it will not present a problem for you."

"I—"

Galen's transmittor sent out an emergency signal then, which he answered with haste. He and Renah listened to the surprising report. Their private conversation was delayed as they rushed to the shuttle base to return to the *Galactic Wind*. Following recover of their supply crafts, the enormous vessel headed for Caguas, a planet of numerous mines that provided a vast wealth of ores and gems, the planet Darkar orbited.

En route, the security team made plans for capturing the smugglers sighted there. Elite Squad members spying on them had been ordered not to interfere or expose themselves to the criminals unless the starship failed to arrive in time to use their cloaking device to shadow the *spacekis* to their base and in that way discover everyone involved.

As Galen and Renah awaited approach in Security Control, where they received occasional updates on the smugglers' actions, he asked her, "Will you answer my earlier question?"

Their positions at the monitors were so close that she felt his breath on her face. His flaxen hair fell forward as he leaned over to gaze into her eyes. The rainbow of colors in his were vivid. His features were perfect. His husky voice wafted over her as a solar wind. She tore her eyes away from his. "A relationship between us wouldn't work," she said simply.

Galen stroked her cheek with the tips of his fingers. "Why not?"

"Because you're *the* Galen Saar."

"And you're *the* Renah Dhobi. Am I not good enough for you?"

She locked gazes with him again. "Of course you are, but people will think I'm not good enough for the son of Varian and Jana Saar and a past *Kadim's* great-grandson; I do not travel close to that eminent level."

Galen turned in his chair, then pulled hers around until they were knee-to-knee. "Even if that were true, what difference would it make to us?"

"Why me, Galen, when our worlds and histories are so distant?"

He covered her clasped hands with his. "Only *Kahala* knows. Surely generous fate has thrown us together for this reason."

"But you can have your choice of females, women like yourself."

"My choice is you, Renah."

Her gaze searched his to analyze his verity, and she was aroused and frightened by the strong emotion exposed there. He was much too disarming and irresistible to suit her. He was the enemy, son of enemies, her target. He was offering her a path to him; thus, to victory. But should she take it? "Are you sure this is wise?"

"I've never been more convinced of anything in my life."

"But we hardly know each other."

"From the moment we met, it's been as if I've known you and waited for you all my life. I'm not an impulsive or reckless person, and my intention is not for conquest and brief pleasure. At least give me a chance to prove myself and earn your affection."

Gehenna, she wished he didn't appear so honest! And his words, why did they have such an overwhelming effect on her? She must not get emotionally ensnared by this man, or *any* Maffeian! He was only trying to seduce her, to add her heart to the string in his possession. She had been warned about the Saarian males' sensual prowess, but she hadn't expected it to be so potent.

"I promise I will not misuse and hurt you, Renah. Please, trust me."

How can I when Saar and Trygue bloods run within you? "What if a romantic relationship between us doesn't work? What if you change your mind tomorrow or next week? How could I remain aboard afterward? I have worked hard and long to reach this point. You ask me to risk much. When you change your mind, I will suffer great humiliation."

"Become my present and future. I will never change your mind."

Yes, you will one day, for reasons you can't even imagine. You will hate me and curse me, if you live. "What if we aren't as alike as you think?"

"We'll never know if we don't give it a chance."

"I'm too inexperienced for you."

"What do you mean?"

"You've . . . had many women; I've had no man. After the feminine skills you've enjoyed, you would find me disappointing."

"How could I when you'd have no man with whom to compare me and find me lacking? If you're worried because of my reputation, I promise you, it's exaggerated. Because I've had no serious or lengthy relationship with a female, people assume I must be a *reacher.* I'm not. I simply haven't found the right woman for myself, until now. Do you want me? Just answer that one question, then I'll be patient," he urged.

"I do not want you . . ." She saw a crushed look come to his face before she could finish with, "to keep your distance." She saw him smile and exhale in relief and joy. "But do not ask or expect more from me this soon. Give me time to think about possible repercussions."

"There would be none, but I will not press you further. I—"

"We're in position, Chief Saar," the communications officer injected.

"I'm on my way to the bridge," Galen responded. He stood and looked at Renah. "Ready for our first action together?"

"Yes, sir."

He extended his hand and murmured, "Let's go face their challenge."

Renah grasped his hand and was assisted from her seat. For a moment, she thought—and found herself hoping—he was going to kiss her. Instead, his eyes roamed her face, he smiled, then guided her away from the provocative privacy. As they walked down the short corridor, she warned herself, *Never again forget who you are and who he is. Become his lover when the time is right, but only because of your duty and mission.*

They reached the bridge and went to a monitor that displayed Caguas' surface. The mining area was mountainous, and desolate. Tall and barren rock formations jutted from the ground. The atmosphere was tinged with yellowish smoke and brown dust coming from ventilation shafts. No creatures or birds were in view, and scant vegetation was visible. Everyone aboard knew that to escape the harsh climate and arduous terrain, dwellings had been gouged from the sides of cliffs and constructed atop flattened peaks or dirt mounds. Most had one wall that was a clear *transascreen* with an awesome panorama. Large cavelike areas were used for governing purposes, social functions, and businesses. An interior-exterior tunnel system connected the chambers and domiciles, in which trams transported inhabitants.

Galen leaned forward and instructed the crewman, "Scan to the right, fifty *migs,* to those blue rocks. I thought I caught movement." As he obeyed, Galen frowned when he saw four men concealed there. Nearby was a tube-shaped rover with a clear bubble top, a vehicle used to skim the surface. The largest mines were protected by force shields; at others, androids were used as guards. Yet no automatons were sighted; no doubt they had been disabled. "Blast it, a Caguas patrol unit preparing to attack," Galen observed. "They can endanger this mission and themselves. I wonder if they know they're outnumbered and outgunned." He glanced at the communication's officer. "See if you can contact them and warn them to not interfere. Tell them to leave the area without taking action or risking exposure."

"No response, sir," the crewman reported. "Trans-mittors are off."

"I guessed as much. That's standard procedure to prevent *nefariants* from picking up a signal. Our squad knows we've arrived, so they've gone to silence; and they're too far away in the other direction to see that patrol."

"What if the *spacekis'* craft has sighted them?" Renah ventured. "What if the patrol unit called for help before going silent? That area could get crowded and dangerous very soon. If we do nothing, those men are going to be slain. But if we act, we'll expose our presence and destroy our chance of shadowing them to their base. Which is more important, sir?"

Before Galen could do so, Commander Vaux asked, "Which would you choose to save first, Lieutenant Dhobi?"

"The men's lives. Then I'd capture and question the *spacekis* and hope they reveal the location of their base and their group's names. Even if they take flight, there's no way they can escape or defeat a starship."

"Our new security officer is intelligent and cunning, Galen."

"Thank you, Commander Vaux," Renah said.

"What is your suggestion, Galen? Time is short."

"I recommend a laser blast near the attackers to alert the patrol to their peril and to warn the *spacekis* that unit has help. Move the ship fast so the enemy craft can't trace the beam to us. I'd hover them; since the cloaking device picks up the images above us and displays them underneath us, no distortions will appear to let them know we're there."

"Any other quick suggestions from your team?"

"If we send out a *simboyd*," Renah said, "it would attach itself to their ship, drill a hole, and shoot in *gracene*; the gas will disable them so the craft can be boarded through the *jerri* hatch for capture. No lives would be lost, the stolen cargo saved, and clues to others could be extracted."

Galen concurred.

"All right," Commander Vaux agreed. "Ready laser and—"

"Sir, a patrol shuttle is onscreen!" came the warning. "Arrival in two minutes."

"The unit did get out a message. Can you hail the shuttle?"

"No, Commander, they've gone silent, too."

"Sir, the *spacekis* are firing on the patrol craft!"

"Fire weapons at—"

"Sir, the shuttle is hit! She's going down."

"Fire at the surface attackers and let them know we're here. Planetary Defense should have sent a *Spacer* to battle them, not a shuttle. Prepare a *simboyd* and launch it the minute we're in position over them. Ready a boarding team to capture our targets. Summon help for that shuttle crew."

The men got busy obeying their commander's orders. A loud buzz registered as a brilliant beam of light shot to the planet's surface; dirt and rocks flew in all directions. The blast alerted the ground unit to approaching enemies and to help nearby, and it sent those foes hurrying back to their friends. Within minutes, the *spacekis* had transported to their waiting craft. Before they could energize their force shield and mount a defense, the *simboyd* spewed gas into their vessel.

Vaux ordered the boarding team to carry out their task. Galen, Renah, and five security men used the connection to the craft and the *jerri* hatch to enter the smugglers' vessel, as it was too hazardous to transport into it without proper coordinates. With the environmentally controlled attachment, it was unnecessary to don pressurized suits and helmets; only *breathers* were needed, which made the job go faster and easier.

After the unconscious men and the security team were transported to the *Galactic Wind,* the smaller vessel with its stolen cargo was turned over to the Caguas patrol unit which had arrived during the procedure. The local authorities took control of the ground rescue so the starship could depart with its prisoners. During the commotion, the Elite Squad members left the area to avoid exposing themselves.

"You take charge in the Control Room while we place these men in the brig, revive them, then question them," Galen told Renah.

When she was alone in that off-limits area, Renah

wondered if she should use her mission cipher and frequency to send out the Trilabs codes. If she did so, a vital and powerful Maffei weakening secret would be in the hands of their enemies. Until now, she had obeyed orders. But her role was becoming dangerous, confusing, and treacherous as she helped to imperil an entire galaxy of lives, and used and betrayed Galen and others befriending her. Was she birthing a conscience, she worried, when she had been reared not to possess one? Was it because she knew of the many horrible episodes in store for the Maffeians, and in progress now?

She didn't have to concern herself about being exposed by the men captured. When they were questioned, even with Maffei's most powerful drugs, it was impossible for them to reveal their leader or what their real motive was. The memory blocks used on the alleged *spacekis* were too strong to be penetrated; not even Ryker Triloni with all of his genius could have done so, nor could he or they thwart the plot assailing this galaxy. She also knew Galen and the others were in for an enormous shock within the hour when the captives were exposed as Earthlings.

Five

Three days later and far away on the planet Earth, Amaya Saar and the Sangers beamed to an uninhabited area of the Houston airport. With terrestrial baggage in their hands, the four walked to the entrance to hail a taxi to take them to the McKays' dwelling. After they made contact with Andrea's parents, remaining possessions would be sent to them.

Amaya sat in the snug confines of the backseat with Avi and Andrea while Nigel took the front with the driver. A mixture of clatter and sights bombarded her senses. Horns honked and vehicles of many sizes and colors whizzed past them; some put out offensive smoke and odors and grating sounds. Noisy people scurried about with items clutched in their grasp, sometimes an infant or the hand of a child. Dirt and debris danced in gusts of brisk winds. She heard airplanes take off and land, and observed several with great interest. Bright sunlight caused her eyes to squint and water. A variety of unknown smells filled her nostrils and some caused them to tickle as if she were about to sneeze. Even the taste on her tongue was unfamiliar when she inhaled alien air through her mouth. It was almost like witnessing chaos, she concluded.

Andrea's words matched those impressions as she murmured, "I forget between trips how much racket we have here. Commotion," she explained to the confused girls. "Racket refers to excessive noise."

Amaya was glad she had aural canal implants to translate alien words—except for slang—into her language. Andrea McKay Sanger, an Earthling until twenty-six years ago, could explain those peculiar words to her. To help her speak English, a doctor had inserted a microchip in the speech center of her brain that would tell her how to respond. With the English she used translated back to her upon hearing it, she knew if what she had said was accurate. During the intergalactic voyage, she had practiced with the Sangers. Also, as children, she and Galen had played word games with their mother. But Amaya could not read or write English, and had no device to assist her in those two areas. Each of them had American money that had been duplicated with accuracy, and Avi had made a game of teaching her the amounts of the numbers on the bills and coins.

As the taxi weaved in and out of traffic, Amaya was amused by the terrestrials' behavior as they shouted or mouthed insults, blared their horns, made crude finger signals, and rushed along the highway with expressions of agitation. She stared at huge signs with pictures or symbols on them: "billboards," Andrea clarified for her. As the ride continued, the former Earthling explained about fences, mailboxes, telephone and power lines, and the road construction that slowed their progress. Amaya noticed diseased and dying trees and plants and wondered if the Earthlings lacked the knowledge to prevent or correct such conditions.

"What are those?" she asked as she turned to gaze out the back window at some strange creatures.

"An armadillo, an animal," Andrea explained; "probably killed by a fast vehicle during the night. The birds are buzzards; they eat dead flesh and clean up the road."

The taxi driver glanced at the tawny-haired beauty behind him and assumed she was from a foreign country or was a country hick.

Amaya noticed the man's reaction, but pretended she hadn't. She decided her query—along with others—had made her seem dense. It didn't matter, she reasoned, as they'd never meet again. She was experiencing too many wonderful sensations and emotions to allow a stranger to inhibit her. She was filled with curiosity and exhilaration about visiting her mother and maternal ancestors' world; she wanted to see and absorb all she could while here. She admitted she was a little apprehensive about making mistakes in language and conduct, as she didn't want to appear foolish, or endanger them. Yet, she chided herself, nothing terrible or *that* humiliating could happen in only two weeks of Earth time. After all, her world's technology and knowledge far excelled this one's. She was an adult. She had wits and discipline and Elite Squad training.

At a stop sign, the driver conversed with another in the next car. She tapped her ears several times with her forefingers, and Avi inquired if there was a problem. Amaya divulged in a low tone that her aural devices were malfunctioning, as they weren't translating the men's words.

Avi laughed and whispered, "It's Spanish; they're from Mexico, another language and country; that language wasn't placed in our units. Mother knows it from living in Texas, but Father and I do not; it isn't necessary, so relax."

Amaya was relieved that broken tranlators weren't to blame, as that would spoil her trip until they could be replaced or repaired. Avi smiled and nudged her as they reached the condominium complex where the McKays lived after having moved from West Columbia where the two females' mothers had been born, reared . . . and abducted by aliens.

Amaya observed the setting after they entered a tall gate with a sentry on duty. A high and decorative iron fence also guarded the location to protect its inhabitants. She noticed living quarters of various shapes, heights, and colors—all pleasing to the eye. The landscaping of trees, bushes, flowers, and grass was lovely and verdant. The streets were clean and smooth. The sidewalks were wide and often lined with flowers or shrubs. Benches for resting and visiting with friends had been placed here and there, usually beneath shade trees. The area was quiet and serene and large, and mostly older Earthlings dwelled there, she had been told, who no longer worked. The McKays' site—"property" Andrea called it—was situated on a large lake and possessed a huge yard with garden areas to its rear. As the vehicle drove into their driveway, she noticed a covered structure extended over the water with leisure furniture for enjoying the scenery and outdoors, Andrea had also explained.

The elderly couple came to greet them, smiling and chatting in excitement. Nigel paid the impatient driver and the man left in a rush to return to the airport for another fare. Hugs and kisses were exchanged between the relatives, then Amaya was introduced.

As taught, Amaya shook hands with the older man and returned an embrace from his wife.

"Come inside where we can talk and you can rest. Mercy, it's good to see my child and granddaughter again. Right on schedule as you promised last year. Glad you're a man of your word, Nigel."

"It's a good thing, too, or Martin would be camped on the lawn day and night watching for you. My, but you look lovely, Avi; all grown up now."

"Thank you, Grandmother. You look well, too."

"Martin and I are doing fine. We love it here. Life is much easier."

"What Grace loves is having less housework and cooking."

"No more than you enjoy less yardwork, you old cowpoke."

Once inside and with the bags deposited by the door, they took seats on a cushiony sofa and comfortable chairs. The whole room was decorated beautifully and comfortably, and the McKays were nice people, Amaya decided in pleasure.

"Andrea, you and Nigel can use our guest room and the girls can stay in the Phillips' condo next door. We're house-sitting for them; they'll be gone for months. I'm sure the girls will enjoy a little privacy. How about some refreshments before you unpack?"

"That sounds wonderful, Mother; I'll help."

After Andrea and Grace left the room, Martin asked, "Do your parents work with the same people who employ Nigel and Andrea?"

"Yes, sir, they're with the Secret Service."

"I've learned over the years not to ask questions they can't answer, but it surely is hard not knowing where or how to reach them. Don't get to see them enough, either."

"We're sorry, Martin, but that can't be helped."

"I know, and Grace and I have accepted it. But we still don't have to like it."

"We don't, either, Grandfather, but maybe things will change later."

"Maybe you can move here when you marry, Avi. We'd be more than happy to help you tend our great-grandchildren. That's the problem of having an only child, Amaya. Once she leaves, there's nobody to fill in for her. Are you an only child, too?"

The man was courteous to include her in on the conversation, Amaya observed. She liked the warmth in his hazel eyes and neat style of his gray hair. "No, sir; I have a twin brother; he's also with the Service."

"Well, I'm glad you could come along and visit with us."

"Thank you, sir, so am I."

Martin focused on his granddaughter. "Tell me,

Avi, what have you been doing since last year? Got you a sweetheart yet?"

"Yes, Grandfather, and he's wonderful."

"Watch out, Nigel, from that glow, this girl will be lassoed soon."

"He's a fine young man, Martin, so we approve of the match."

"Bet he's in that Secret Service, too."

Nigel and Avi laughed and both nodded.

"Figured as much," the elderly Texan jested.

Andrea and her mother returned with trays loaded with cookies and lemonade.

Mrs. McKay smiled at the group. "I made these this morning especially for you all."

Amaya accepted the glass and plate passed to her. Watching the Sangers and McKays for clues on how to do things, she placed the glass on a coaster on the nearby table and balanced the small plate on her lap. After chewing one bite, she smiled and offered her comment. "Delicious."

"Toll-house were always Andrea's favorites."

"Mine, too, Grandmother."

Amaya savored the textures and flavors of the alien treats. She had worried about not liking Earthling food and drinks and craving those of her world. But as with Avi, she took two more from the platter.

"I'll have to make you girls a batch to take home with you."

Amaya didn't know the word "batch," but she replied before Avi could speak. "That will be kind."

Avi laughed. "That's her way of saying she loves them," she said.

"Then I'll be certain to make plenty. You can freeze them for later."

Amaya grasped those words and knew of the ancient hardening process.

The group chatted for a while about local, national, and world news; and about people the McKays knew. Andrea finally suggested they get settled in before dinner.

"Martin, you take the girls and their things next door," Mrs. McKay instructed. "I'm sure they'd like to rest, bathe, and change."

"Be right back. Come along, little ladies."

Amaya watched him insert a metal object in a hole to unlock the door. He handed the "key" to Avi for their use, then set their bags in the "foyer," smiled, and left after hugging Avi again.

"They're delightful, Avi," Amaya commented. "And those refreshments were tongue rapture. Imagine, a whole dwelling chamber to ourselves. Too bad you can't beam in Sebok. I'm sure he's missing you as much as you're missing him."

"I hope so. I'll call the ship with the coordinates for our things."

After the transportation of their possessions, Avi suggested, "You use that room and I'll use this one; the space plan is like my grandparents' condo." Avi watched Amaya for a moment and asked, "What are you doing?"

"The door will not open," she explained as she stamped on the floor.

Avi burst into mirthful laughter. "It doesn't operate like ours. You grasp this knob, twist it, and push. *Pralu*, it opens," she teased.

Amaya playfully scolded, "How in eons would I have known that?"

"Let me familiarize you with everything here. First, the sleeping and bathing chambers are called bedroom and bathroom, or lavatory. The tub does not fill automatically; you have to employ these controls." She instructed her friend on how to use them, and the ones governing the sink and the toilet. "Alien homes do not have environmental control systems. If you get hot or cold, tell me to adjust the temperature unit. The lights work this way," she said and demonstrated them.

Amaya observed carefully before commenting, "It is primitive here when compared to our world. Our mothers had much to learn when they moved to Maffei. Can you imagine going from this planet years ago to our advanced one? We know other galaxies have life and we travel to them, but the Earthlings do not. Do you think they were terrified?"

"Unless they were too much in love with our fathers to notice or care," Avi jested. "I wouldn't mind if Sebok swept me away to his home. If you met a handsome and irresistible alien here, would you be tempted to stay?"

"*Kahala,* no, never; there are too many problems: pollution of air and water, crime, diseases, ozone depletion, a shortage of land and food for a growing population, wars, racial battles and hatred—and more."

"But think what challenges and adventures you could have."

"Not the kind I want and need."

"Are you not the same person who complained of sitting in Security at Star Base with no stimulating assignments in view? Think of how many missions you would get as an Elite Squad member of this planet."

"They have no Elite Squad, and you know that's a secret rank. Our galaxy is ruled by our *Kadim* and Council; planets are governed by *avatars* with *zartiffs* as their territorial helpers. We have one military power: Star Fleet and the Alliance Force, and they are commanded by one man. We have peace and prosperity. On Earth, there are countless countries and leaders who battle at the drop of a helmet. They spend more time, money, and energy on fighting than on the good of all as a whole. They are destroying their planet, their people, and their futures. Can you imagine driving one of those crude vehicles wherever you wish to go? No beaming or rovers. No *Spacers* or starships or shuttles. Trapped on the surface. And so much work for things done automatically in our world. You witnessed how these people are; most race in madness and anger toward their doom."

"You are right. That is why I wish my grandparents could come to Maffei with us."

"Why is that impossible?"

"Mother says they are too old to accept such an unknown. They have their home, friends, and life here; a change of such magnitude would be too traumatic for them. She says they will be happier to live and die here."

"Her reasoning is wise and her sacrifice is generous. I can't imagine never seeing my family, friends, and world again."

"Your mother was fortunate she left no family behind and her best friend was taken to Maffei. And she has her work there. It's strange how love can sometimes affect us."

"I wouldn't know, not yet."

"You will, because so many men pursue you."

"But none I care for as more than friends."

"What about *Kadim* Procyon's son? His eyes have trekked you."

"He does nothing for me, more than being a good time."

"You'll have to find a proper mate within the next five years. Few women remain unmatched past thirty."

Amaya placed her hands on her lower abdomen. "No child will come from this womb until it's conceived by the man I love."

"Then you must find a love, or he must find you. Surely there is at least one male who matches you in our galaxy."

"If there is, Avi, I have not seen or met him."

"Don't worry; after we return home, you will."

"The way things are going and looking, that brother of mine will be mated before me."

Avi sent forth merry laughter again. "Never in an eon."

Amaya jumped suddenly. "What is that?" she asked.

"The telephone. When it rings, you do this:

Hello," Avi demonstrated after lifting the receiver. She talked a moment, then replaced it. "It was Mother calling. She says to come over when we're dressed."

"This is how they communicate from place to place?"

"Yes. I'll give you lessons later. Now, tell me, do you like this garment?"

Amaya studied it as Avi turned around twice. "The color is pretty and the fit is nice. Earthling clothes are hard to don and remove."

"Be glad they're made in our materials and we have a renewal unit with us, or we'd have to wash and iron them as Grandmother does with theirs. This bra is the worst," Avi complained as she tugged at it through her top. "Why can't Earthlings create garments with support in them as we do."

"Perhaps they need your mother's skills and knowledge. She is the best designer in our galaxy. You're fortunate to get her beautiful styles free and any time you desire something new."

"Do not forget you cannot mention that to anyone on Earth or they'll wonder where they can buy them. Nor can you reveal your mother is from Texas, since Jana Greyson vanished years ago and left behind a large inheritance. Mother said it went to research and support for ill children."

"It did—the oil business, cattle ranch, and Stacy Aerospace Firm. Isn't it strange that her family was involved in the designing and building of shuttles, missiles, and satellites, not to mention labs and equipment for them? It's almost as if she had a fated connection to space before Father claimed her. Being a scientist, she had a perfect way to fit into our world. It's almost as if they were matched by *Kahala*. I wish I could visit her old home and firm. I would like to see what her environment was like. But without a logical reason and permission, I cannot, and there are neither. Perhaps your parents could arrange for us to visit the space center; it would be fascinating to see at which stage the Earthlings are."

"They told me they have plans to show us many things and places."

"Wonderful. We'd better hurry before a search patrol comes."

"Where are Father and Grandfather?" Avi asked.

"They went to the store to buy fresh milk."

"Growing girls need milk for beautiful skin, teeth, and hair."

Andrea laughed, as she'd heard her mother say that many times in the past. She glanced at Amaya, whose expression revealed her confusion. She caught the girl's eye, smiled, and implied she would explain later.

The doorbell rang; Grace asked Andrea to answer it. When the woman returned, she was laughing and guiding a tall and muscular man into the kitchen. "Look who's here, Mother, Avi. I do believe my cousin gets more handsome and taller every time I see him."

"Jason!" Avi almost squealed in delight and went to hug him.

Jason chuckled and held his second cousin at arm's length to study her. "Heavens, you're a grown woman now. I missed your last four visits and you've changed, little cousin. Aunt Grace kept me up on details of all of you."

"I'm happy to see you; it's been a long time. You've changed, too."

"The Navy and my job toughened me up. You're also looking lovely, Andrea. I'm glad I'm in town this week."

"He drops by all the time to check on us. Jason is a fine boy; his father would have been proud of him, God rest my brother's soul. We have company, Jason; Avi brought a friend with her: Amaya Saar."

Jason turned in Amaya's direction. His sapphire gaze widened a moment as it took in the beauty with ash-blond hair streaked with platinum. She had a California tan and the most unusual eyes he had ever seen, a coalescence of green, blue, and violet. At five feet ten inches, a six-foot-two-inch man didn't have to lower his head much to view her as she approached and halted near him. Saar, an unusual name, too, he decided. And she smelled scrumptious. He smiled and extended his hand. "Nice to meet you, Amaya Saar."

"It's a pleasure to meet you, Jason McKay."

"It's Jason Carlisle, Amaya," Grace corrected, "my brother's son."

"Jason Carlisle," she repeated, and committed the name to memory.

"When did you all arrive?"

"This afternoon. You will stay and have dinner with us, won't you?"

"If it won't be an intrusion on your reunion, Andrea."

"Don't be silly, of course not. I'm sure Avi and Amaya will enjoy chatting with someone their age."

"I reached thirty this year, Cousin, but thanks for the compliment."

"Mother told me about the death of your wife and child three years ago; I'm sorry, Jason, I know that was hard for you. I can empathize after losing a son two years ago."

"I was sorry to hear about Losch; Aunt Grace told me. How's Thaine?"

"Busy, happy, and making progress in his work," Andrea answered. "He couldn't come this year, but he will next time. He said to tell you hello if I saw you."

"There's the postman's horn," Grace said. "Will you fetch the mail, Andrea?"

"Yes, Mother."

"Avi, why don't you and Amaya set the table and chop the salad?" Grace requested. "We'll be ready to eat when Nigel and Martin return."

"What can I do to help, Aunt Grace?" Jason asked.

"You can select and open the wine and let it breathe."

Avi fused gazes with Amaya as she wondered how she could get her friend a message about how to do the chores. "Amaya, why don't you cut up these vegetables in this bowl while I place eating dishes on the table? Here's a knife. Just like *corvie*," she hinted.

"What or who's *corvie?*" Jason asked as he took a corkscrew from a drawer and a bottle of wine from the refrigerator.

Avi thought fast. "A friend who likes to chop the salads."

"Your sweetheart?" he asked with a grin.

"No, *corvie's* a female." Avi went into the dining room where her grandmother had placed the dishes, utensils, and napkins on the table.

So, not Amaya's boyfriend, either. Jason worked at the counter near the sink where the stranger was standing and staring at the vegetables in an odd and reluctant manner. Again, he was struck by her provocative fragrance. She was a ravishing female, so she probably had more dates than she could handle.

Amaya lifted the knife and began to slice the large green ball into wedges. She soon learned it didn't remain that way, but separated into pieces. The firm red ones cooperated better. When she began to do the same with long green items, Jason halted her with a whisper.

"If you aren't going to skin those cucumbers, best wash them first."

Her unit interpreted "skin" and sent a message along the relay system in her brain. "Should I have removed those skins, too?" she asked.

"Aunt Grace usually doesn't skin her tomatoes and she'd already washed them because they were wet."

Jason chatted with Andrea and Grace as Amaya peeled and cut the cucumbers into oddly shaped, large chunks. He observed her from the corner of his eye and concluded she didn't spend much, if any, time in the kitchen. He was amused when she leaned close to him to ask in a whisper if she should peel the carrots. "Just skin and grate them," he instructed.

"Grate?" she echoed as her auditory/cerebral communications microchips sought and found the best translation for the task involved. She wished English words didn't have so many different meanings, as that made comprehension difficult when the aural unit sent several possible interpretations to her cerebral intelligence center and she had to decide which one was correct. She was silent and still as she reasoned on how she was supposed "to reduce to small particles by rubbing against a rough surface."

"Why don't I lend you a hand?" Jason offered. "You do the radishes."

Amaya assumed the only vegetable left were "radishes," but wondered how he could remove an appendage and let her borrow it. Jason took a tool from a drawer and began to pass it over the "carrot's" surface, removing the outside layer. He used another tool to pass them over at a swift pace that cut them into small and thin slices. "Do I peel these?" she asked.

"Just rinse them under the tap," he said, as he touched the faucet.

Amaya figured out his instruction and obeyed. When she began the next part of her task, Jason suggested in a low voice that she cut off the radishes' stems and slice them thinner, which she did. She was glad he did not appear amused or suspicious. She was relieved he was there to advise her, and in such a polite and genial manner. But his voice had a strange and potent effect on her. *Only his voice*, Amaya's mind teased. *What about the remainder of this Earthling?*

Avi's cousin, she admitted, was more attractive than any male she had met, and she had encountered plenty in her galaxy. His hair trekked to broad shoulders in a mixture of curls and waves; it was as dark as a moonless night, and thick and shiny. Only one section, near his right temple, journeyed onto his appealing face. The sides were swept backward and the lower parts of his ears were visible. His strong jawline met almost in a point at his chin. His cheekbones were prominent; his nose, not too large or wide; and his mouth, full and enticing. Dark brows grew downward at their ends and were close to impressive deep blue eyes. From pictures Avi had shown her, she knew his garments and footwear were called western: shirt, jeans, and cowboy boots. The red material of the shirt created a striking contrast to dark hair and skin. The snug pants and fitted shirt revealed a superb physique. She sneeked a look at his large, strong hands as they labored.

After he finished with the carrots, he gathered the cucumbers and cut them smaller.

"Perfect," he murmured afterward, and couldn't help smiling.

"Thank you for your assistance, Jason Carlisle."

Their gazes locked a moment as he replied, "You're welcome, Amaya Saar." *Wake up, idiot, you're acting like she's the first girl you've met.*

She wanted to ask why and how wine "breathed," puzzled by Jason's earlier comment, but she didn't want to show ignorance. Nor did she want her voice to quaver when she spoke, which it might if she didn't get control of herself and these crazy feelings from being near him. She looked at her best friend who had finished the task of placing dishes and utensils on the table. Avi had a broad grin on her face and a merry twinkle in her brown eyes, as if she guessed how her cousin was affecting Amaya. She watched Jason join the brunette to chat. She wanted to offer further help to Mrs. McKay, but feared the older woman would request a task unfamiliar to her. Fortunately, Andrea McKay Sanger entered the kitchen before a long silence ensued.

"You were gone a long time, dear," Grace remarked.

"Daddy and Nigel returned and we started chatting. What's next?"

"Everything's done. Why don't you call them to the table? Jason, will you pour the wine? Avi, you bring the bread. Amaya, the salad, dear."

The seven people sat down at the table in the dining room. One side was snug, with Jason placed between Avi and Amaya. The food was blessed, and Grace told them to help themselves.

Amaya studied the setting arrangement in case she was asked to do that task in the future. She eyed the unknown foods and hoped they would have pleasurable textures and tastes. As to the man nearby, she tried to keep excessive attention off of him. That was difficult when their arms and legs touched ever so often, his tantalizing smell assailed her every sense, and his voice poured over her like sweet wine.

Although Jason was talking with Nigel and the others, his true attention was on Amaya. She was watching the others closely as if trying to learn what to do from them. Perhaps she simply didn't want to make an error in etiquette. Or maybe he was too vigilant or his brain too inquiring because of his work.

"So, how's the P.I. business, Cousin?" Andrea asked him.

Jason grinned when she asked about the last thought on his mind as if she'd read it. "Couldn't get any busier. Keeps me hopping."

"Is it any safer and easier than being a Navy Seal?"

"Not really, Andrea, but it's certainly different and engrossing."

"You enjoy facing challenges and dangers and catching criminals; don't you?"

Amaya glanced at the terrestrial male. She was eager to speak with Avi alone to ask questions about him. Avi had previously mentioned her relatives on Earth, but her best friend hadn't told all about this particular and fascinating one!

Jason chuckled and said, "Somebody's gotta do it."

"You must like it and do well at it or you wouldn't be so successful."

"I earn a nice pocketful of money and I never get bored."

As they ate, Martin and Nigel began talking together, as Grace did with Andrea and Avi.

Jason looked at the guest. "Aren't you going to eat?" he asked.

Amaya had watched the others long enough to learn what to do during the meal. She smiled and said, "Yes, thank you," after which, Jason passed her several bowls and platters and condiments.

Amaya was pleased and relieved to find the unfamiliar foods delicious. She ate and listened to the others as they talked about many subjects. Warned by Avi, she sipped the wine with caution.

"Jason, perhaps you can take the girls sightseeing while they're here, if you have time," Mr. McKay suggested.

"I'd be glad to, Uncle Martin," Jason replied. "We'll make plans later."

"That sounds exciting and fun," Avi remarked between bites.

"Does that suit you, Amaya?"

"Suit" me? The best definition was far down the list, so she pretended to chew her food until the word made sense and she could respond. "It pleases me, Jason. Thank you."

After the meal and dessert, Nigel and Martin retired to the living room while Jason helped the women carry the dishes and leftovers into the kitchen. Again, he noticed how Amaya watched the dishwasher loading and clean-up process with a baffled expression.

Amaya mused on the whole process and preparation of the terrestrial dinner. She thought about the way dishes were cleaned and stored. She was accustomed to *servo* units and androids doing those chores. When she was hungry or thirsty, she simply pushed buttons and food or drink appeared. When she finished with her meal, either an android cleared away the mess or she put everything into an apparatus that handled dishes and debris. She watched Grace and Andrea wipe the table and counters, and vacuum up crumbs. Jason took the trash to a container outside while she and Avi washed and dried "pots and pans" and fragile wineglasses. These alien females, Amaya concluded, had to work harder and longer with their meals and clean-up than those of her world did. At least Avi and Andrea were familiar with the procedures and could guide her through them.

Jason hugged his aunt "I have to take off now to do some shadowing tonight. Dinner was delicious, as always. Sure is good to see you all again," he told the Sangers. "If it's all right with you, Avi and Amaya, I'll come by tomorrow at six to take you for a drive by Lake Houston and to a movie."

"Amaya, how does that appeal to you?" Avi asked her friend.

"It sounds like fun, Avi. Thank you, Jason."

"Avi, you stay close to Amaya while you're looking around," Nigel remarked. "I promised her parents we'd keep her safe."

"I will, Father; I won't let her out of my sight. And we'll have Jason to guard us."

"I won't let them get into any trouble, Nigel. See

you at six, Avi. It was a pleasure to meet you, Amaya."

"It was a pleasure to meet you," she echoed.

As they had done many times over the years, Amaya and Avi sat on the bed and talked for hours after leaving the McKays. Grace had told them to sleep as late as they pleased after their journey, then come over for breakfast or lunch, whichever the hour.

"You kept a big secret from me, Avi Sanger," Amaya accused in a playful tone after listening to countless words about Sebok Suran.

"What secret?"

"Jason Carlisle."

"I've mentioned him to you."

"Mentioned, yes; related everything, no."

"You liked him that much?"

"I found him interesting and enjoyable."

"What was going on in the kitchen while I set the table?"

Amaya related the salad-making episode. "He must think I'm dense."

"From the way he was stealing glances at you and helping you, that couldn't have been his thought. You're a big surprise to him; I'm sure he never expected to meet someone like you at Grandmother's."

"How long have you known him? Tell me everything."

"We met as children during one of our visits, and I've been with him many times since that day.

Jason is fun; he's nice, polite, and smart. He's taught me many things about Earth and terrestrials, without knowing it. Like my grandparents, he thinks we're with their Secret Service and can't tell where we live or what we do. If he asks any questions you can't or must not answer, tell him it's classified information. After school—called college here—ended, he was a Navy Seal; that's similar to a mixture of our Alliance Force *Bejors* and Elite Squad. He's a private investigator now and owns his own business in Houston. He doesn't live far from my grandparents."

"What exactly *is* a private investigator?"

"He seeks out criminals or facts that people need; they pay him to do such jobs for them. A document—a license—gives him the government's permission to do secret work, but he doesn't have to tell them what he learns. If necessary, he can shoot criminals or capture them for the law to punish. In a way, his work is similar to yours, just not his rank and duty."

"Does he have a mate?"

"A *wife*, remember? He married a female who was close to him for many years; they had a son during his last year at college. After he became a Seal, he went to Dallas to work; Dallas is another city in Texas, a large one. They were killed in a vehicle crash three years ago. He moved here to begin a new life. He has not yet chosen another wife."

"Did you know his wife and son?"

"I met her several times, but only saw the boy's

picture. He was dark-haired and handsome. The woman was pretty and nice, but quiet."

"Those are terrible losses."

"Before they married, I never sensed great love and passion between them. I was surprised to learn from Grandmother they had become a unit."

"If they did not share great love and passion, why would they marry?"

"I do not know, but . . ."

"But what, Avi?"

"I never saw him gaze at Kathy as he did at you tonight, and I've never seen you do the same to another male. Something is happening here."

"You're imagining things; we're strangers, totally different. We'll never see each other again after this visit."

"I don't know," Avi murmured. "Strange things happen at times."

"I could never unite with an alien."

"Our mothers and fathers did."

"That was different."

"I suppose so," Avi replied in an unconvinced tone, then laughed.

"Are you still watching those silly programs on that Sci/Fi channel?" Avi asked Amaya later. "I only turned on the television to show you how theirs functions. As I told you, they have no *telecoms* or voice-activated units; use that remote control to change it to something else if you want to learn real things about them."

"Why do Earthlings think life-forms from other

worlds are ugly and mean? Most of the time, aliens
are depicted as monsters and invaders. The terrestrials always defeat and destroy those superior
forces."

"Those are only movies, Amaya, make-believe,
entertainment. Most Earthlings don't believe other
worlds and aliens exist."

"The news program I watched earlier was not
make-believe; many Earthlings are hostile and cruel
to each other, especially to other races. I do not
think I would want to live in such a misguided and
backward world; now I understand how Mother
could leave and never return. Imagine what the
Earthlings would do to us if they discovered who
and what we are."

"Don't even hint at such a horror. Now, let's go
and join the others."

"Do you like to camp or sail?" Jason asked Amaya
the next day as they viewed Lake Houston during
a stroll. "I know from experience Avi doesn't."

As a result of previous remarks between Jason
and Avi about people in tents and motorhomes
and the crafts on the water, Amaya grasped his
meanings. "I have never done those things. Are
they fun and safe?"

"A lot of people think so, including me. You
probably know Avi hates water that deep, but I'll
be happy to take you sailing while you're here.
Perhaps Sunday? Nigel said you all have plans to
look around on Saturday."

Having learning about the days of the week,

Amaya replied, "It would be an interesting experience. If Avi's parents agree, I can do it."

"I'll ask their permission when I take you two home tonight."

"If you promise to defend her with your life, Jason, they will say yes," Avi interjected.

"They can trust me with her. Now, we'd better leave if we're going to eat a hamburger or hotdog before the movie."

"You eat dogs?" Amaya said in revulsion, having seen many pet ones.

Jason looked at her but didn't chuckle because she seemed so serious. "You've never had a hotdog?"

"Never, and I do not want one. Why would you—"

"They're called dogs, Amaya, but they aren't," Avi interjected. "It's slang. They're delicious; I've had them many times during visits to America."

"I understand. I'll try a hotdog."

"Where are you from, Amaya? Where do you live?"

"Sorry, Cousin," Avi said quickly, "but that's classified information. She works where my father and brother do."

"You're with the Secret Service?" he asked in amazement.

"One of the best agents according to our parents and her superiors."

Jason stared at the beautiful female. "I would have never guessed that fact in a hundred years."

"Amaya's intelligence, courage, and skills would astonish you."

"I'm certain they would. I wish you could tell me more.

"You know we can't. Sorry," Avi murmured.

Later, as they traveled toward the city, a train streaked past them. With he and Avi occupying the front seats and Amaya in the back, Jason stole glimpses of the woman in the rearview mirror. She appeared to be observing the train as if she'd never— No, he told himself, that was ridiculous; everyone knew what a train was.

Inside the theater, Jason watched her eat popcorn. She smiled and claimed to like it, just as she had with the chilidog. She behaved as if both foods were unknowns that she—almost like a scientist— was analyzing. She'd been the same way last night at dinner. Where, he wondered, could Amaya live and work without knowing such things? His keen mind jested that it was more like she was from another world than from another country. But if she were a top agent, he mused, how could she carry out assignments without knowledge of such common items and situations?

While they waited for Avi to return from the ladies' room before the return drive, Jason asked, "Would you and Avi like to attend a concert Friday night if I can get tickets?"

"A concert?"

"You know: music, singing, entertainment?"

"I don't know the songs."

"It doesn't matter, but you will if you're familiar with Joe Tarp's hits."

"Hits? Who does Joe Tarp strike? Why?"

"Hits are someone's best songs, and they're performed at a concert."

"I understand. American slang is always difficult for me. I would enjoy attending a concert. I'm sure Avi will, too; she loves music and singing."

"I'll check tomorrow to see if tickets are still available."

"Tickets for what?" Avi inquired upon rejoining them.

Jason explained, and Avi accepted the invitation enthusiastically. When they reached the car, Avi insisted on sitting in the backseat so Amaya could take the front and view the sights during the ride.

En route, Avi watched her cousin and best friend as Jason related facts about Houston, Texas itself, and other general topics. It was obvious to her they were attracted to each other. Perhaps, Avi's romantic heart plotted, she should "become ill" so they could attend the concert alone. Amaya was learning fast, so she shouldn't have any problems at the performance. Besides, what harm could a short and innocent romantic interlude cause? She closed her eyes as she tried to envision what was taking place in her world with her lover.

At the same time, Amaya was thinking, *Oh, Galen, if you could see me now, you'd never believe this predicament. How is it possible to find an alien so irresistible, for one to turn my emotions inside out? Surely you would tell me that to experience and yield to such feelings for a near stranger is rash.*

* * *

But Galen Saar didn't have time at that moment to think of his sister far way, not after the shocking emergency message he had received.

Six

Galen sat in Security Council following a *telecom* conference from Star Base with Commander Vaux, First Officer Zade, Chief Medical Officer Mirren, his security team, and his father. He took a deep breath and focused his troubled gaze on Renah. "I don't understand what's happening. Neither does my father, the *Kadim*, or the Council. First, we have that weird *spaceki* incident; now, this. Those smugglers refused to answer questions. When Mirren tried *Thorin* on them, some kind of chemical reaction occurred and put them in comas. The med staff and scientists at Star Base are still in the dark; they can't rouse those men, and tests have confirmed they're Earthlings. Pure Earthlings, Renah, never been bred with Maffeians. How did they get here? Were they smuggled in by other *spacekis* to do their illegal work and take their risks? Who could have created such a powerful mind block? Why?"

"What about the Earthling colony that was on Anais long ago? I read about it in our security files. Could they or their heirs be responsible?"

"Father is having Anais searched, all terrestrials not returned to Earth years ago will be found and questioned. But that theory is doubtful."

"He'll send us a report as soon as the investigation's finished; then, if you're right, we can eliminate that possibility."

"Two of the men captured on Zandia also proved to be Earthlings. Why would they attack Zandia without any means of escape? When *Avatar* Kael refused to pay the *katoogas* they demanded, they actually sprayed four rain forests with defoliant. Containers found by Zandian patrols say they're from Trilabs. How is that possible? They've threatened to spray the remaining forests as well. Without plant life and breathable air, Zandia would be uninhabitable for years. I don't know where we could transplant a whole civilization and its creatures, or how long that task would require even if we found a suitable location. An entire planet will suffer chaos and we don't know why or by whom."

Entire planet . . . "We may get answers tomorrow when we reach orbit. We should be on alert for a cloaked ship; they must have an escape means. Surely not even a band of *nefariants* would entrap themselves on a surface they intend to slay if their demands aren't met."

"Zandia patrols reported there's no vessel registering on their sensors. *Avatar* Kael said the attackers demanded a small cargo ship with a cloaking device and plenty of supplies in addition to the fifty million *katoogas*. Kael doesn't know how the group landed there without detection, but they *did* have an escape plan, even if it was a wild and reckless one."

"How can they believe such a scheme will work?"

"I don't think they do. It sounds like a suicide mission to me."

Renah was shocked by that speculation. Galen couldn't be right. The plan related to her was to be a scare tactic which would injure a small section of two jungles; *and* nothing was said about all of those involved dying. "You mean their leader intended to sacrifice them before they landed here? Why?"

"To protect his identity after they destroy Zandia for him," Galen explained. "Without *nefariants* to question, there is no risk of clues pointing to him."

"But we can interrogate them if we can capture them."

"Like we did those we took at Caguas?" Galen reminded.

"We know now to be careful and to not use *Thorin*. Even if we don't capture more, they're holding two prisoners for us; and Zandia patrols can't use truth serum, only Star Fleet Security has that authority. Those still free must realize Star Fleet forces are en route and time is short. Once they realize their leader has abandoned them, they'll halt and surrender."

"I don't think so, Renah; that mind-control process is too strong for them to resist. I hope the realization we're en route doesn't panic them into more spraying or suicide."

"We need to learn their motive."

"I doubt we'll learn anything our *villite* doesn't want us to know. I can't imagine killing innocents for greed, vengeance, or deception."

"Deception?"

"Yes. If it becomes necessary, rescuing and relocating Zandia's population would require numerous starships, cargo vessels, manpower, and time; with us distracted in this sector, another target could be struck."

"What other target could be his real objective?"

"I don't know, but this could be a decoy plot."

"Perhaps you should warn your father to have our forces on alert in all other sectors and for them to report anything unusual immediately. What if a threat is coming from outside our galaxy and an attack is imminent? We can't summon our forces here to help and leave ourselves vulnerable."

"Let's see what we learn at Zandia before I relay my suspicions."

"Commander Vaux, *Avatar* Kael reports there are four groups of hostiles in four different locations," First Officer Zade said. "Zandian patrols are keeping a watch on them. He wants to know how we plan to help."

"Do the enemy camps still have communication between them?"

"Yes, sir, in a frequency and cipher we haven't broken. The *fiendals* said if any camp is attacked, the others will release their chemicals into the air. They have laser weapons capable of destroying a shuttle that comes within range. Even if patrol *Spacers* fire on them simultaneously, the blasts will rupture those containers and spread the defoliant."

"Mirren, give me a possible injury, death, and

damage report if we decide to use our *Spacers*,"
Vaux ordered.

"All life—human, flora, and fauna—within fifty
migs will die either from the blast or soon after
from the chemical. Beyond that range, injuries and
illnesses will begin within hours to days, according
to distance. Some, my medical staff can treat; others will eventually die. If all four or at least three
of the explosions occur, Zandia is doomed for ages.
This chemical was never intended for use on an
inhabited planet. Its sole purpose is to destroy diseased or dangerous plant life on surfaces that
would either grow new life or be replanted with
ours for future colonization. This much should
never have been in existence during a time it isn't
needed."

"Galen, make a note of that for our investigation."

"Yes, sir, Commander Vaux."

The superior officer continued. "Zade, keep
working on deciphering their code. Vaiden, keep
your eyes and ears on those communications monitors. Mirren, get me every fact our data and med
banks have on this lethal chemical. And Jarre,
when will we reach orbit?"

"Within an hour, sir," the navigations' chief replied.

"Keep me posted on anything that wiggles on
your screen."

"Yes, sir."

"Commander?" the communications chief called
out.

"Yes, Vaiden?"

"*Avatar* Kael is hailing us. On the *telecom* now, sir."

The planetary ruler revealed the criminals' threat to terminate the stand-off in two hours if the money and escape demands weren't met.

Vaux asked Galen, the weapons chief, if he had any suggestions.

"Why don't we try that new *x-nythene* bomb Tri-labs created?" he responded. "We picked up six to carry to Star Base. We can on-load them to four *Spacers* and have pilots drop them at the same moment on those camps; they wouldn't have time to move the containers or themselves out of range. They won't even suspect our plan since no one knows of the new weapon's existence. *X-nythene* is designed to instantly disintegrate matter beneath its cone on impact; the sudden creation of a deep hole sucks in everything above and around it; dirt and rocks cover and seal the cavity. It was made for this type of danger. If the tests are accurate, Commander Vaux, the episode should occur too quickly for the chemical to escape into the air, at least not much of it. Later, *Avatar* Kael, Environmental Control can remove and destroy any contaminated soil and debris. There will be local surface damage, but the closest cities are too far way to be endangered. Aftershocks will be felt for *migs*, but—if we order all patrols out of the target area—the only loss of lives should be the *nefariants'* and any wildlife nearby. It's a risk using a new weapon, but I can't think of anything else. We certainly can't pay them and give them an escape route with that hazardous cargo; even if they kept their word and left Zandia unharmed, which I wouldn't trust them to do for a blink, they'd probably use it elsewhere, and maybe without warning."

"What do you think, *Avatar* Kael? Do you want to make the decision or shall we consult with the *Kadim*, Council, and Star Base headquarters? Our time is limited to prepare and execute Chief Saar's suggestion."

"Will the *Spacer* pilots be in jeopardy, Commander Vaux?"

"Chief Saar, can you answer that question?"

Galen looked at his superior officer. "Not if we select the four best pilots aboard, sir, to carry out the mission," he said. "If the bombs are fired in unison and the *Spacers* use starburst speed, they should be out of range before the explosion begins. The *nefariants* should think we're only doing a surveillance flyby with only one craft visible on their screens in each area."

"What if they fire on the *Spacers* as they did on that shuttle?"

"If we time it right, *Avatar* Kael, we should be in and out too fast to take a strike, even if they possess such weapons capability. The shuttle was vulnerable because it flew lower and slower than we will. There is minor risk to a pilot if his craft or sensors malfunction, but that's our duty, sir. It's better to endanger or lose a few men than imperil an entire planet. We have to decide now, sir, to give us time to get ready."

"You're as intelligent as your father, Chief Saar," the Avatar complimented. "Proceed."

"Commander Vaux?" Galen hinted for confirmation of Kael's words.

"You're in charge, Chief Saar. Select your pilots and brief them."

Familiar with the skills of everyone aboard, Galen called out the names of the pilots he wanted to use. "Vaiden, alert them to a meeting in docking bay one. I'll be there as soon as I change."

Galen and Renah left the bridge. In the *trans-to*, he said, "Change fast and meet us there. And be careful during this mission."

"You be careful, too."

"If you weren't one of the best, I wouldn't send you. Stay alert and come back safe or I'll demote you, woman."

"Don't worry; I'll be fine."

Galen moved before her and gazed into her eyes. "I will worry."

"You mustn't be distracted or I'll be safe and you won't."

He leaned forward tentatively. When she didn't prevent his lips from covering hers, he gently held her face between his hands as the kiss deepened. Warmth and elation spread over him; heat, delight, and apprehension washed over her as she savored his desire. After the computer control announced his stop, Galen pulled away, smiled, and left her inside to continue on to the corridor to her quarters on the next deck.

Renah leaned against the hard surface behind her. She ordered herself to ignore her warring emotions and to concentrate on her dual roles and conflicting duties. She knew she couldn't sneak to

Security Control to send out a warning about the attack. She also knew she mustn't fail on her part of this Star Fleet assignment; she was too skilled in a *Spacer* and with weapons to do so without casting suspicion on herself. Yet, foiling Zandia's threat would be an unexpected blow for her side. She didn't know the Earthlings on Zandia's surface, but she hated to destroy them. She wondered if there was a credible way for her craft or weapon to malfunction. If so, she wouldn't have to kill innocent aliens. Also, if she allowed one group to carry out its orders, this part of the plot wouldn't be a total failure. *But,* her mind argued, *aren't the Zandians just as innocent as the enthralled pawns of our side? Perhaps,* she concluded, *but every failure will weaken our plot. I must use my skills and knowledge to assist my side's triumph, even if they are going to horrible extremes not mentioned to me. Perhaps I shouldn't tell them about my true involvement in the Caguas and Zandia episodes; they might think I've disobeyed my orders and am being swayed toward the enemy's side.*

Commander Vaux was enthusiastic in his praise. "Congratulations, Chief Saar; your team destroyed Zandia's threat. *Avatar* Kael is most appreciative and relieved; he insists each of you receive our highest commendation; I've already informed Star Base of our success. We're en route there, so your team will be honored upon arrival."

"Thank you, Commander Vaux; luck was on our side with *x-nythene*. I doubt they had time to realize their dark fates. I only wish we could have captured more than two. Mirren is examining them now. As soon as I change out of this flight suit, I'll see what he has to report."

In the *trans-to,* Galen told Renah to change, too, and meet him in sick bay. "Let's see if we can figure out a way to get at the facts," he suggested. "Use your keen mind to come up with some tricks to help me break them without any injuries."

"I'll try, sir."

"Sir?" he jested, and grinned.

"We're on duty, remember?"

"What about when we get off duty later? Can we share a meal in private?"

"In your quarters?" Renah watched Galen nod and broaden his sexy grin. "Would that be proper? What if someone sees me enter?"

"It's a risk we'll have to take to get to know each other better."

His playful tone and expression caused Renah to smile. She told herself that in order to extract what she needed to learn from him, she had to get closer, and he was offering the perfect opportunity. Yet she mustn't appear too eager or too easy to conquer, or a *reacher* like him would lose interest too fast. A challenge and chase were needed. "We'll just eat and talk, correct?"

"For tonight. I promise to be patient and I will."

"On those terms, I accept. I'll meet you later."

Galen took Renah with him to confer with their superior. "Mirren ran tests on the captives to see if interrogation with *Thorin* was possible because nothing we've said or done so far has provided answers. The tissue and blood samples were attacked when treated with our truth serum, so we dare not use it on those captives. Mirren said he'd never seen anything like it, and all attempts to analyze it failed. If we put these prisoners into comas, we'll never solve this mystery. If we can't extract the truth from them, perhaps the med or research staffs at Star Base can find a way to prevent or bypass that chemical reaction. I'd surely like to know by whom and how something was created that renders our *Thorin* helpless. I didn't realize anybody possessed the same skills in chemistry as Ryker Triloni."

"But someone does," Vaux said. "I requested a check on the defoliant and laser weapons they were using. We still haven't deciphered that code or traced the frequency they were using. I wonder if they had special plans for the money they were demanding from *Avatar* Kael and the Zandians."

"I assume you mean for more than personal greed?" Vaux nodded. "Frankly, sir, I don't think they were after money or believed they would escape Zandia," Galen ventured. "I think destroying the planet's surface was their real intention; the denial of payment was a cover excuse."

"Why would anyone want to destroy Zandia? Especially Earthlings?"

"I don't have a clue, sir, but for the simple reason Earthlings were used as disposable weapons, I suspect an insidious plot. When we add up stolen chemicals and weapons and that unknown drug, it appears a certainty to me. I think we were allowed to capture two of them so we'd discover they're Earthlings, just like those *spacekis*. Whoever is behind this wants to confuse us."

"Have you reported your suspicions to Star Base? To your father?"

"Not yet, sir. I planned to wait until we get our report from them about Trilabs, and I want to keep trying to break those captives' silence."

Galen agreed to keep the commander informed of his plans and progress.

Renah sat on a stool at the eating bar in Galen's quarters. She watched him make selections from the *servo*, a wall unit that transported food and drink from the galley on the lower deck to the apparatus from which it was ordered. The service was quick and simple, and meals arrived with cold items chilled and hot items warmed to perfect temperatures. She glanced at the dishes he placed before her and grinned at his beverage choice: wine.

"What's that sly smile for, woman?"

"Are you trying to weaken my defenses, Chief Saar?"

"Naturally."

"You promised to go slowly, remember?"

"And I'll honor my word. But your rule didn't forbid a pursuit altogether, did it?"

"No."

"Care to qualify that response, Lieutenant?"

"Not tonight; not this soon."

"Fair enough. Did I tell you how beautiful you look this evening?"

"Only twice since my arrival."

Galen took the seat next to hers and began to eat to distract himself from her potent allure. She was wearing a fitted jumpsuit in a silvery gray shade that matched her striking eyes; its shoulders were cut out to bare silky flesh that he wanted to graze with fingers and lips. He observed the way she cut her meat and slipped the piece into her mouth; he watched a small chunk of fruit follow that same enticing path. When she sipped wine, he almost squirmed at the way her lips caressed the glass's rim. Her fingers were long and slender; her hands were soft, and he imagined them stroking his body. He yearned to make love to her, but he would be satisfied to just be with her for now.

"Delicious, Galen." *And I bet you are, too. I can feel you taking possession of me with your eyes. I know I shouldn't experience a reaction like this to you, but I can't seem to halt it. You're being so gentle and patient, as if you truly care about me. I mustn't fall captive to your charms, even after I allow you to seduce me. If only you weren't so handsome and virile, such good company, this part of my duty and assignment would be easier. The way you look at me, the tone of your voice when you speak to me, the manner in which you treat me—they're like wit-stealing drugs I can't resist. I find myself wanting to be with you all the time, day and night. I find myself wondering what a future would be like with you and in your world. That's foolish because it could never be. I must keep reminding myself you're a* reacher *and I'm nothing more than your current prey.*

If only I weren't becoming so confused about so many matters! I must obey orders or all is lost.

The following afternoon in Security Control, Galen received another shock; this time, from his father. "How could anyone breach security at Trilabs and what in *Kahala's* name made them think it was you?" he asked.

"Somebody who got possession of the defense shield and complex entry codes, an impersonator who could pass for my identical twin in looks and actions: the portal monitor proved their claims after they *telecomed* the evidence to me," Varian replied. "Whomever he is, he was good enough to dupe them. They reported I picked up a secret cargo soon after your ship left orbit. Supposedly, I strolled in with my own team, collected what I wanted, and departed. No one there has the rank to question or halt me from doing as I please, so the bold impostor succeeded. A rapid inventory revealed what they believed I took: chemicals, drugs, weapons—enough for a small war. Not that I need it, but I have an indisputable alibi. I ordered the codes changed and they'll come through your unit at the termination of our communication. It's top priority for us to find that duplicate of me and recover the cargo; not all of those men and chemicals were destroyed on Zandia. I'm glad you were aboard the *Galactic Wind* and used *x-nythene*. I'm proud of you."

"Thank you, Father. It was risky, so I'm relieved

it worked. I'm puzzled as to how those *nefariants* could reach Zandia so fast and undetected?"

"Only with starlight speed and a cloaking device," Varian replied.

"Who else has those capabilities besides the Tri-Galaxy?"

"We don't know. But we are certain Earth doesn't. How terrestrials got involved is baffling. Whoever is behind this, Galen, is clever and dangerous. This mind-control drug worries me; so do these supposedly random crimes. Now, a replica of me appears. If I wasn't convinced Ryker is dead, I'd say this is his insidious work. He could easily pass for my double, just as I did for his long ago. It's almost as if my evil half brother left records that somebody is using, one with additional and powerful secrets we don't possess."

"Did Ryker have any children or other family?"

"Not to our knowledge, and none were mentioned in the private files we searched after his death. The Triloni bloodline ceased with *Effecta* Maal's death shortly after Ryker's."

"Could there be another half brother? Could Ryker have a twin that was kept hidden all these years, perhaps in another galaxy?"

"I'm certain that isn't the case, Galen; and Ryker himself wouldn't have been born if his mother hadn't drugged my father into unwanted submission long ago."

"In a strange way, sir, his existence profited us."

"That's true and, in all honesty, Ryker wasn't totally to blame for the way he was; his wicked mother gets the credit. But let's get back to our current trouble: I'm also convinced the Caguas, Zandia, and Darkar episodes are connected. Another angle has arisen: Alliances Forces have investigated an eruption of crimes across the galaxy: murder, rape, robbery, kidnappings for ransom, arson, explosions, and the assassinations of two *zartiffs* and one *avatar*. Every miscreant captured has been an Earthling, the worst of their species. All of them self-destructed before interrogation like programmed androids."

"We have no clues to the leader and motive?"

"None, Galen. I've assigned Elite Squad teams to seek answers, but without a course to follow, it doesn't look promising for now."

"Who could want to create chaos in Maffei? Why?"

"The bigger question is: who has the power to seek revenge or to attack for conquest on such a scale? We have treaties with Androas and Pyropea; as far as we know, they're the only two galaxies that possess technological and military advancements anywhere near our own. No suspicious ships have crossed their boundaries into ours. Needless to say, your mother is upset about the involvement of people from her old world. She's afraid that if this violent rash continues Maffeians will recall she and others are from Earth and will become prejudiced against them. She's also concerned about that Trilabs facsimile of me making more appearances and damaging my credibility."

"That would never happen, Father."

"If people are given persuasive evidence, Galen, I've learned from experience that anything is possible. At least Trilabs is safe; only certain people have the new codes and security has been tightened. However those codes were stolen last time, it won't happen again without somebody falling under suspicion. Without Trilabs, Maffei would be plunged into chaos."

"Our secrets were never in jeopardy, Father. Those files can't be accessed or copied and no virus can be inserted, thanks to our failsafes and a smart computer. Only you, the *Kadim,* and Council can get into that system; there's no way your duplicate can steal that particular code. The Trilabs androids would self-destruct if anyone tampered with them. With the codes changed, our impostor can't reenter the complex to sabotage it. Why don't you feed me the details on those other crimes so I can see if I can build something from them?"

"I'll transmit everything I have on file. We'll talk after you reach Star Base with those prisoners from Zandia. Keep them alive and well, Son, and perhaps we can find a way to get past that block."

"If the other *nefariants* are connected to these, somebody wanted us to capture them alive or they would have terminated themselves, too. For an unknown reason, the lead *villite* wanted us to learn they're Earthlings."

"Perhaps to confuse us because he knows we have Earthlings here."

"He must be aware we'd realize it's a trick."

"I'm sure he does, Son, but what's his point?"

"Hopefully we'll locate clues soon."

"Yes. Now, come to see me as soon as you arrive. Your mother's on Rigel, too; she's working with the scientists here to find something to counteract that mind block before you bring in your prisoners. The others are still in comas, and their bodies and minds are deteriorating fast."

Galen tried to soothe Varian's mind with what he hoped would be good news. "If there's time and opportunity, Father, there's someone I want you and Mother to meet."

Varian's sapphire gaze studied his son for a minute on the *telecom* screen. "That sounds intriguing, Galen. Is this the kind of surprise that will please your mother?"

Galen chuckled. "I hope so, Father, because she surely pleases me."

"Who is she?"

"Third Lieutenant Renah Dhobi, my newest Security and Weapons team member. She is as brilliant and rare as a *sombian* cloud."

"It's serious?"

"Yes, sir."

"You haven't mentioned her before. How long have you known her?"

"Since my return to the ship after Amaya's departure for Earth."

"Isn't that a swift flight?"

"It couldn't be slowed, Father."

"Dhobi? Why does that name sound familiar?" After Galen related more details about Renah, Varian nodded. "I remember that incident. In fact, her file was put into my system for consideration on the Elite Squad," he said.

Galen stopped smiling and his father questioned

his reaction. "I want to keep her on the *Galactic Wind* with me, sir; I need her here."

"Is that a personal or professional request?"

"Both, sir. Truthfully, she's the best team member I have; Star Fleet needs her here, especially now, with trouble threatening us. And *I* need her here; I've almost won her, but I must have more time to complete my task."

"I take that to mean she's giving *you* a chase for a change?"

"Not exactly, but I do have to earn her trust. I know you have to do what's best for the Alliance, but wait as long as you can."

"I'll let you know my decision after I meet this special woman."

In his quarters that night, after relating most of the talk with his father to Renah, Galen concluded that it didn't look good. "But there are many people working to solve this mystery and terminate this threat," he added. "We'll do our best to help them. I'm happy to have you at my side during this situation; I mean that personally and professionally."

"You said you told your parents about me, about us?"

Galen stroked her soft blond hair. "Yes, and they're looking forward to meeting you after we reach Star Base."

"Have you ever taken a woman home with you before?"

"Not like this, only for an evening on a social

occasion. Don't worry; they'll like you and accept you. I hope you'll feel the same way about them. I want you to be a vital part of my life, Renah Dhobi, and I'll prove it to you."

"What if your parents *don't* like and accept me, Galen?"

He trailed his fingers over her cheek. "They will."

"But what if they don't?"

"The choice of a woman is mine alone to make; I choose you."

Renah stared at him. She asked herself if she comprehended his real meaning: mate. "You . . . choose me?"

Galen cupped her face between his hands and locked their gazes. "I promised I wouldn't press you and I won't, but I think you grasp my feelings and what I'm saying."

Should I ask you to clarify? "Will Amaya be there so we can meet each other?" *Will I be able to dupe all of the Saars or am I only duping myself?*

"No, she's away on leave with friends, but she'll love you, too." For a moment, he wished his sister was there to befriend Renah. He prayed, with rogue terrestrials involved, that Amaya had avoided contact with the *nefariants* on Earth and with the *villite* bringing them to their galaxy to create havoc. Yet, he didn't know where his twin was safest, far away or here.

Seven

Amaya was delighted with the concert that featured singing, dancing, dazzling lights in multiple colors and patterns, billowing mists, and assorted sound effects. The music had a beat that caused her body to want to move, and it often seemed to vibrate off her chest with its loud volume. She took special notice of the instruments and their sounds, and the wildly dressed men playing them. She was amused by the way many fans of the rock star behaved: both sexes stood and yelled compliments or made special requests, many sang along, and many waved their arms in the air and shook their bodies in time to the music. Some females threw flowers on the stage, others screamed and swooned or shouted romantic overtures, and a few tossed lacy panties or keys to the lead singer. Amaya watched Joe Tarp laugh as he collected some of the items. A selected few received kisses, appreciative words, or a simple handshake. For certain, Joe savored his work, talent, and the audience's adulation.

"Are you enjoying yourself?" Jason asked.

Amaya looked at him. She smiled and leaned closer so he could hear her response. "Yes, it's wonderful. I really like Joe Tarp's hits. He gives a good performance."

"You've never been to a rock concert before?"

"No. Thank you for giving me this unusual experience."

"You're welcome." *Unusual,* Jason's mind echoed. *That describes you, Amaya Saar: unique, radiant, more than beautiful and charming. You seem so natural, so fresh. Yet there's such a contradiction about you: innocence versus seductiveness, openness versus mystery and reserve, intelligence versus simplicity. There doesn't appear to be anything artificial or superficial about you. You have warmth, glow, and smile that can light up a room. And those eyes. Mercy, I've never seen such a blend of vital colors, prettier than a Texas sunset; they make me want to gaze into them forever. Kathy didn't affect me in this crazy way even in the beginning of our relationship.*

There was an enchanting magic about the alluring and enigmatic female, and Jason realized she was rapidly weaving a spell over him. He wasn't against love and marriage; he just hadn't met anyone who tempted him to try them again; until now, he admitted. He wanted to have a wife and family again, and assumed someday in the future he would. He still loved and missed his son and no one could replace Scott, but a wife and child could fill the empty holes in his heart and life that his son's loss had created. Since the fatal accident three years ago, he had tried to ignore his loneliness by filling his days and nights with work. Then the flaxen-haired beauty beside him swept onto the scene and into his life. Perhaps this unexpected and swift attraction to a stranger should alarm him, but it didn't; the only thing that almost panicked him was not having enough time to test his feelings or do anything about them. He leaned toward Amaya. "Nigel and Andrea asked me to go sightseeing with them tomorrow. Is that all right with you?"

Amaya gazed into his sapphire eyes. She liked how he always looked as if he were about to smile. His air of confidence was appealing and she enjoyed just being around him. He was masculine and self-assured without being cocky; he enticed without pressing. Why, she mused, couldn't she find an irresistible and potent man like this in Maffei? Why weren't there males in her world with his stirring personality and character; and yes, his superior looks and breeding?

"Is that all right with you?" Jason repeated. He liked the way she was looking at him. Nothing she said or did came off as casual flirtation. She gave him the impression she liked and enjoyed him, but definitely wasn't the type to jump into bed at the first available opportunity. If only she weren't leaving soon . . .

"You know many things about Texas and America you can share with us and teach me. I like you and enjoy your company, Jason Carlisle."

"I like you and enjoy *your* company, Amaya Saar, a great deal. I'm usually too busy or too tired to go out much and have fun; or—to be frank—not many women seem as if they'd be as much fun as you and Avi and Andrea. I'm glad you all came to visit. I'd be happy to show you other interesting places: the Houston area has plenty of them."

"You are kind and well-mannered, Jason."

"Is that a yes or a no or a maybe I can be your tour guide?"

Amaya laughed. She was warmed and tickled by the way he teased her. *You do strange things to me, my forbidden terrestrial. But what harm could come from a few diversions with Andrea Sanger's kin?* "That is a yes if Avi and her parents approve."

"Thanks, because I haven't enjoyed myself so much in years." *If ever.*

"We shall become friends, Jason, if that pleases you."

"It more than pleases me, Amaya," he whispered during a soft love song that quietened the audience for a while. *Mercy, woman, don't you realize what you do to a man? I wonder if there's a lucky guy waiting for you back home. I sure hope not. Maybe you aren't as perfect as you seem, but, who is? I wonder if there's any way I could do some nosing around about you without tipping off your boss. Maybe I should call in some favors to get the lowdown on you . . .*

"I wish your visit wasn't so short so we'd have more time to get better acquainted."

"Perhaps I can return with the Sangers next year."

"A year is a long time. Couldn't you and Avi stay longer or visit over the holidays?"

"Holidays?" *Which ones do Earthlings have and when?*

"July Fourth, or Labor Day, or Thanksgiving, or Christmas, or all of them. Aunt Grace and Uncle

Martin miss their family. They're getting up in years and their health's been failing for some time. Maybe you could hint around for the Sangers to stay longer or visit sooner."

"I'll try," Amaya promised with a radiant smile and glowing eyes.

Avi caught bits of the words her second cousin and her best friend exchanged. She perceived the mutual attraction and rapport between them. Perhaps a little romance would be excellent for both. Of course, they would need her help escaping her parents' watchful eyes. Amaya and Jason, what a nice match, she mused, at least for a short time . . .

"I'll work on Andrea during our sightseeing trip tomorrow," Jason continued. "Don't forget we're going sailing Sunday. Uncle Martin is taking Nigel to play golf, and Aunt Grace and Andrea are going shopping. Avi said she'd come with us and wait at my place. We'll have a picnic lunch. Next week, we can catch another movie and have dinner; I can't let you leave Texas without trying our famous chili and authentic Mexican dishes. I know of several five-star restaurants that will put that hotdog joint to shame."

Amaya nodded as her brain echoed. *Five-star? Joint? What are those? Keep quiet and let Avi or Andrea explain their meanings later.*

"Ever been to a vintage air show?"

Amaya reasoned he wasn't referring to old atmosphere, so she hoped he would explain after she replied, "No."

"They'll have lots of old airplanes doing stunts and demonstrations. They'll also have hot-air balloon rides if that interests you. You and Avi might want to taste some of Houston's nightlife, too. Just choose what you want to see and do and I'll be there as chauffeur, escort, and guard."

"We'll ask the Sangers for permission."

As she pretended to listen to several songs, Amaya reflected on things she had discovered about Earth. As her mother and Andrea had told her, there were many problems on this planet. During every spare minute, she watched their television system to learn all she could and to help prevent errors in speech and conduct. News programs revealed that there were numerous areas of turmoil and fighting; horrible natural disasters and manmade ones; that there was a terrible disease called AIDS that had just become the leading killer of men ages twenty-five to forty-four and the fourth leading killer of women in the same age group. She heard about vicious crimes and attacks on men, women, and even children. She learned of countless ways Earthlings were destroying themselves and their world. She wished that weren't true for her mother's and the McKays' world . . . and Jason's.

Jason Carlisle. Her mind whispered his name in rising desire. She longed to kiss him, to touch him, to be in his embrace, to mate with him. Those were reckless and foolish thoughts. She mustn't get physically or emotionally involved with him or any terrestrial male. It wasn't because he was inferior or uncivilized, because he wasn't. It wasn't because they weren't biologically compatible; her mother, Andrea, and other *charls* had proven they were. In fact, she was half Earthling herself. It was because nothing could come of their relationship; she was leaving in nine Earth days. She couldn't abduct Jason and take him home with her as her father had done with her mother, though that was a tempting fantasy. Nor could she expose who and what she was: an intergalactic alien.

"Tarp will come back and sing one more song for an encore." Jason broke into Amaya's thoughts. "If we want to miss the traffic and crowd, we can leave now," he suggested, and both women agreed it was a good idea.

They headed along the Eastex Parkway toward the Lake Houston area where the McKays and Jason both lived. Amaya eyed the city's skyline with its buildings of various heights and shapes. Most of the tall ones were clustered together like *Kahala*-seeking rock formations; many displayed reflective glass, often in green, that mirrored their surroundings. She watched them rush past giant high voltage towers with numerous power lines stretching between them. She noticed traffic signals and quickly learned Jason stopped when they were red and drove when they were green. She observed how he remained within certain lines painted on the roadways. Streetlights prevented darkness from engulfing the land. Signs, which she could not read, were hung over highways and on bridges. Many of the congested spots Jason called cloverleafs, underpasses, and overpasses; they seemed to twist, turn, circle, and loop in a confusing maze. They passed the North Loop and continued onward. Soon, they were within sight of the airport. In a short time, they reached the McKays' home.

Amaya was fascinated by Space Center Houston, "Home of NASA." She watched films on a screen that was said to be five stories high. She listened to plans for impending missions and realized they had a great deal to learn about controlling gravity and living and working in space. She tried on primitive space helmets and a jet pack and studied the astronauts' suits in glass displays. She toured the shuttle mock-up and admitted the Earthlings were making excellent progress in their infant program. She heard how their shuttle flew upside down and backward, that a "roll-over" was necessary to get into correct landing position, after which a series of *S* maneuvers slowed the craft following reentry. As a *Spacer* pilot, she found the differences in technological levels enormous.

Jason was amazed and baffled by how riveting the beauty found this place, and more so by how many intelligent questions she asked Nigel or the center assistants. It almost sounded as if she knew a great deal on the subject; yet she was like a student making discoveries and observations. She wanted to see everything and almost appeared to memorize certain things. At times, it was as if she forgot others' presence, as if she were lost in a world of wonder and stimulation.

While the Sangers were distracted, Jason couldn't resist jesting, "I think you possess an inner longing, a secret desire, to be an astronaut."

"There are female space travelers on this planet, correct?"

"That's right. Does that mean you'd like to become one of them?"

"Does it not excite you to think of challenging space and visiting other worlds? To fly across the galaxy at starlight speed? To view the wonders of the Universe? To meet other lifeforms? To observe and learn from them?"

"I'm content keeping my boots glued to the ground or a boat deck. The closest I want to come to visiting another world is deep-sea diving. My work gives me as many challenges and adventures as I can handle. I certainly don't need to poke my nose into aliens' affairs, and probably lose it to some laser beam or cannibalistic mutant. What makes you sure there are other civilizations in the great blue yonder?"

"The Microcosm is larger than you can imagine. Why would Earth be the only planet with life? There are countless worlds and species beyond this atmosphere, and surely more civilized ones than this."

"Considering the condition of our planet, that wouldn't require much. If scientists and governments don't get it in gear and make some changes, we won't have a planet to worry about in a few hundred years."

"People should never destroy what gives them life."

"But they do. It's one of our human weaknesses. Some people take what they want without regard for others or consequences."

Amaya smiled at Avi, who joined them. "That's dangerous and selfish."

"More of our human flaws. I guess we all have our share of them."

"What are *your* flaws, Jason Carlisle?"

He stared at her after that unexpected query. He watched Avi whisper into Amaya's ear and noted the female's concerned reaction.

"I withdraw that question; Avi said it is not a polite one to ask. I apologize for being rude." *Pray those are the correct remarks, Amaya.*

"You weren't rude, just direct and honest," Jason replied. "I don't see that often, so it caught me off guard. Truth is, I probably have too many flaws to list to a lady."

Amaya smiled in gratitude and in amusement. "Thank you."

"You're welcome. Now, shall we continue our tour?"

Amaya touched a moon rock that had been brought to Earth, and she thought of the many kinds of geological wonders she had seen in Maffei and other galaxies. Her wide gaze examined the Mercury, Gemini, and Apollo spacecrafts and their launch rockets. She strolled through Skylab, which she knew her scientist mother would find intriguing. She couldn't help but wonder if her mother's past company—Stacy Aerospace Firm—had built parts for any of the sights she was viewing today.

Amaya particularly enjoyed the simulator that allowed her to "land" an alien shuttle. She used the control throttle with skill and triumph. Nigel, Andrea, and Avi congratulated her; and she beamed with pleasure.

"You're a natural pilot, Amaya," Jason remarked. "You didn't have a moment's trouble. You would make an excellent astronaut. Maybe you should go and enlist today." *That would keep you around a long time.*

"Thank you. Try this," she coaxed as she urged him into the seat and pressed the mock apparatus into his grasp.

Jason's attempt ended in a runway crash. A disheveled astronaut with hair sticking in all directions appeared on the monitor screen to give a disaster report. "Whoops, that would have been a billion-dollar catastrophe. I would have set the space program back ten years because taxpayers would have screamed about funding a replacement."

"They would be foolish to hinder advancement. Where do they think they will live when Earth is no longer habitable?"

"Perhaps by then we'll have underwater cities. That would suit me."

"That technology is too far in your future to profit humans."

"Your"? what about "our"? He was getting the impression Amaya was far more intelligent than he had realized, and he'd already placed her in a high level. Perhaps, he reasoned, she was a scientist or engineer or worked in a technological field; that would explain her knowledge and interest. She certainly knew a lot about a great many things.

The stop at the Manned Manuevering Unit was

amusing to Avi and Amaya when Jason was selected from the crowd to demonstrate tasks in the "frictionless environment of space." Those awkward and difficult chores, she knew, could be almost simple if the Earthlings knew what the Maffeians did. As she observed him, Amaya knew he would be astounded by the things he could see and do in her world. Her appreciative gaze roved him, from his black hair down the full length of his virile physique.

"*Pralu,* are you memorizing every *hapax* of him?" Avi whispered.

"Yes," she admitted. "I just might be doing so. Your cousin is a superb specimen, my friend."

"I think so, too. If not for our kinship and Sebok, I'd seize him."

"He is unique. I like him. I wish— Here he comes."

"Let's take the tram to Mission Control," Andrea suggested.

Inside that separate structure, Amaya viewed the nerve center for space flights from a glassed-in observation deck: there, Jason told her it was fortunate no mission was in progress or that area would be off-limits. That wouldn't have mattered much to her, as she learned little from seeing row after row of monitors and large screens on the distant wall. Yet she didn't allow her disappointment to show to others.

Jason noticed how elated Amaya was with everything she saw. She was like a child at Christmas with so many wonderful toys that she didn't know which one to play with first. Her vitality and pleasure were contagious, and he found himself laughing and smiling all day. In one area, he asked Amaya and Avi to have a picture taken with him in a "realistic space scene"; then, he had three copies made so each of them had a souvenir. He hoped it wasn't obvious that a photo of him and Amaya—actually just of her—was what he wanted.

"We need to head to our next site as soon as we have lunch," Andrea suggested. "The Silver Moon Cafe has a nice buffet with many choices of foods, drinks, and desserts, according to the brochure. Is anybody hungry beside me?" she asked with a laugh, and everyone nodded.

Again, Jason noticed how Amaya watched others in a subtle way to see which items to select and how to eat them. It was as if every food and drink she saw and tasted was unfamiliar to her.

Later, Andrea told Amaya, "If you want to purchase mementoes of this day, there is a shop available. I'll guide you there and help after I finish eating."

"Yes, I do, if it won't delay our departure."

"I'll be happy to escort her there while you all finish," Jason offered. "Really, it's no bother," he added when Andrea looked hesitant to allow his request.

"I have money, so I'll be fine," Amaya said to end the odd silence.

Jason assisted her with her chair, grasped her elbow, and led her from the quiet group. He wondered if the Sangers were afraid to let Amaya out of their sight, then decided that couldn't be so because they had allowed her and Avi to go out with him Tuesday night. On the other hand, they hadn't been alone then. Surely, he reasoned, his first cousin didn't think he would take advantage of Amaya! Besides, how could he in a public place? Amaya could surely shop by herself. Yet, she didn't strike him as being . . . *What, old boy?* He couldn't guess if she was American or not; her accent didn't give away her heritage, but there seemed to be many common things she didn't recognize. *Amaya, what a mystery you are, and a sheer delight.*

In the SpaceTrader, she chose five items: replicas of the shuttle, Lunar Rover, Command Module, and an astronaut in suit and helmet. Last, she lifted a small globe of Earth and studied it.

Jason's finger pointed at Texas as he murmured, "I hope you won't forget where Houston is and you'll come back to visit often."

"I'll try," she said, as their hands touched on the globe and their gazes met for a stimulating moment. "We should hurry."

When she started to withdraw money from a pocket, Jason insisted paying the clerk.

"That was unnecessary," Amaya protested, "but thank you anyway." She was glad Andrea had invited her cousin along today and she was sorry Andrea's parents had been too weary to join them.

As they were returning to the Sangers, he asked, "Are the gifts for a little brother or do you have a special friend with a small child?"

Amaya hoped she grasped his underlying meaning. "I have one brother, a twin, named Galen. But these are all for me," she told him as she wiggled the bag. "I plan to display them in my quarters."

Jason halted and gazed at her. "Your quarters?"

"Where I live," she corrected. "That is all I can say about my location and work," she added to prevent further questions.

"I know," he muttered, then chuckled. "It's a secret, classified. Sorry. I just find you utterly fascinating, Amaya Saar, so I want to know all about you. I'll try not to be too nosy. If I am, just tell me to shut up."

"You are an understanding and polite person; thank you."

Amaya learned many things about Earth and terrestrials at the Museum of Natural Science and Baker Planeterium: their next stops. Her gaze took in the dinosaurs and other prehistoric remains and mockups of either free-standing or glass-enclosed specimens. Murals vividly recreated ancient settings, creatures, and vegetation. She realized she couldn't ask questions about the extinct animals.

When a giant armadillo seized her attention, Jason asked, "They've really gotten smaller since those prehistoric days, haven't they?"

While distracted, she said, "I saw one dead on the highway near the airport; he was small. Birds, buzzards, were about to eat his body."

"It's more likely they were investigating a roadkill; I've never seen a buzzard or crow dine on one of them, but maybe they do. Busy highways are their biggest threats because those little knights in tough armor are hard to defeat. When attacked, they curl up in balls to protect their underbellies."

"That's an excellent defense system. Are they savage?"

"Nope; in fact, very gentle."

Amaya was glad animals and birds from around their globe were depicted in their natural habitats. She was delighted by the gem and mineral displays, especially the amethyst, which was her favorite color. She strolled past wall units with countless seashells and she thought how lovely and interesting it would be to take a framed case of them home.

"They're . . . exquisite. Can I buy some?"

"Not here, but you can collect all you want of certain kinds at the beach not far away. I have a vacation house on Galveston Island. It's quiet and beautiful there and the beach is loaded with shells. I'll be happy to take all of you down next weekend for a few days if your schedule permits."

"Sorry, Cousin," Andrea declined, "but there won't be enough time during this visit."

"The invite stands open any time you want to accept it."

Amaya sensed Jason's disappointment when Andrea refused his offer. She, too, was disheartened.

They continued onward to the IMAX Theatre that used a six-story screen, a device which made one feel almost a participant. They observed a laser show with a musical background where various sizes and shapes seemed to dance in time to the merry strains.

Then they headed for the zoo with its tropical

walkways, rushing waterfalls, authentic rock formations, lush foliage, and numerous specimens of wildlife. Amaya watched sea lions frolic in the water and leap out to perform tricks for fish; their antics often caused her to laugh aloud. She watched many species snuggle and interact with their mates and offspring. The creatures' patterns and colors were magnificent; she particularly liked the big cats, zebras, giraffes, and some of the snakes. The Touch Tank and petting areas where she could make contact with the unknown creatures of land and sea and air intrigued her. She didn't mind that mostly children were involved in that activity, as it was also fun and educational for her.

Jason became more confused as he watched Amaya studying the specimens. She giggled like a teenager when she handled a live sea urchin and a starfish, played enthusiastically with miniature goats and lambs and stroked a pony happily. She seemed to stare at most animals as if she'd never seen them before. She seemed astonished to see birds drinking blood from a small bowl; so he explained bats to her.

Amaya envisioned the large parasitic annelids that once lived in the jungles of Zandia in her galaxy. "Are there other animals or birds that suck blood from humans?" she asked.

"Just mosquitoes. And perhaps vampires," he added with a chuckle.

Amaya knew about the flying pest that forced them to spray on a repellent when going outside to walk. "Vampires are fiction, correct?"

"I was only pulling your leg; of course, they

are." Jason saw her glanced down at her long and sleek limb as if she didn't grasp his meaning.

Andrea injected by way of explanation, "Jason has a habit of teasing people, Amaya, so keep a close watch on him."

Amaya smiled. "A sense of humor is a good possession."

In the gift shop, she had difficulty selecting which "animals" to purchase. She finally decided on a leopard, a panda, a zebra, and a seal.

As Jason carried the package to his car for Amaya, Andrea asked if she was enjoying herself.

"I'm so glad I came. Mother's world is fascinating and unusual. It's not what I imagined. We're more advanced in many areas, but I like Earth, its people and its creatures. Do you suppose she ever misses it?"

"At times I think she might miss certain things about it. But Jana's too happy where she is for those feelings to linger very long. You appear to be adjusting fast."

"Parts of their language are difficult and many terrible things occur on this planet, but Earth is a nice place to visit. I would not want to live here; I do not think I could become a good terrestrial." She laughed. "These females have too much work to do: cooking, cleaning, washing, shop—" She hushed as she saw Jason approaching them with a wide grin, and she knew this would be an unforgettable day for her.

Jason came to the same conclusion as he tried not to stare at Amaya. He wished he hadn't agreed last week to go on a double date this evening, as he'd prefer to linger at the McKays as long as possible. He couldn't call his friend and cancel this late, but he should have thought to do so earlier after meeting Amaya. He didn't want to go out with the sister of his racketball partner's girlfriend. He had agreed only to silence the man's constant pleas. At least he would have Amaya almost to himself tomorrow, but her remaining eight days were vanishing too fast.

"Are you certain you don't want to come with us?" Amaya asked her best friend as Jason prepared his sailboat for departure.

"I'll be fine. I know how to use everything, remember? I'll relax and watch television and daydream about Sebok. Deep water and boats frighten me. I lack your courage and eagerness for adventures."

"Jason said we will be gone only a few hours, but I hate to leave you."

"Stop worrying. I had to come to conceal our plans from Mother and Father. They would be nervous for you to go out alone, even with Jason. As long as you're with me, they'll give permission. I've been to Earth and with my cousin many times so they give me freedom to come and go."

"I don't like misleading them, but we had no choice. Correct?"

"Correct, so don't think about it again. There are certain things we cannot tell parents because they worry too much about us even as adults. Go and have fun, and be careful. Do everything Jason says so you'll be safe."

"Everything?" Amaya echoed, and laughed.

"You know what I mean."

"Yes, I do. His home is lovely and comfortable," Amaya remarked as she gazed around the large living area with plush sofas and pillows in beige, smoky glass-and-brass tables, a fireplace, decorative items, and lots of greenery. The carpet was thick and soft; it was in a deeper shade of tan than the furniture and walls. A tall pillar supported and separated dual archways into an overflow sitting and an eating area with wicker furniture and many verdant trees in buckets and greenery in hanging baskets. The wall beyond was spanned with glass doors and windows which revealed a view of the marina where Jason's apartment was situated. A large porch was suspended above water. A docking slip was beneath it like a garage for a boat. Amaya liked being up high where she could enjoy the splendid setting. The waterside "villa" had an open and airy yet cozy feel to it. Jason had given them a tour of the kitchen, bath, half-bath, and two bedrooms. His dwelling was clean and neat and possessed a happy aura, just as its owner did. During her stroll around the adjoining rooms, she noticed several pictures of a little boy that Avi told her was Scott Carlisle—his deceased son, an image of him.

Amaya was aware there were no pictures visible of his dead wife. She wondered what kind of woman Kathy had been. It must have hurt him deeply to lose his two loves, and perhaps he never wanted to replace them or to risk being tormented by anguish again. She didn't know why he hadn't stayed to visit last night following their glorious day of sightseeing; he had excused himself after saying he had a "chore" to tend to. She wanted to ask him countless questions about himself and his past, but that was unfair and rash when she couldn't respond to any queries he might ask about her. She heard Jason coming up the steps from the bottom floor so she quickly seated herself near Avi to prevent appearing too nosy about what his dwelling revealed of his life.

"Ahoy, mate, ready to skim the water?" he asked Amaya, whose gaze locked with his as he approached the sitting area.

Amaya's translator told her "mate" was a companion or a crew member on a ship. She assumed his first word was a nautical greeting, as not every word in English was in her embedded chip. She was glad their scientist had included contractions that were so popular in this world, as it made their speech less different. "Ready to go, Captain."

"Ah, a woman who understands and respects rank; I like that," he jested with a broad grin. "Sure you don't want to come with us, Avi?"

"No, thank you. I'll be fine here. Just protect her with your life or my parents will kill me for letting her go alone—and don't tell them I did."

"I'll guard her as if she were Fort Knox or the President, or the best treasure in the world. Feel free to look for anything you want or need. There's food in the fridge and snacks in the pantry. Now, let's shove off, mate."

At the bottom of the stairs, Jason motioned to a

closed door. "That's my work room; I keep it locked because of weapons and private files. I'll give you a peek when we return, if you're interested."

"I will enjoy learning about your weapons and work."

"Too bad you can't tell me about yours; I'm sure it's fascinating."

"It is, and I'm sorry I can't talk about it to anyone."

"I understand because my job has plenty of secrets, too."

They exited the villa and he locked the door. He grasped Amaya's hand and led her along the wooden deck to his boat. He hated to release it to help her into the craft, but had no excuse to prolong the stirring contact. He untied two ropes from their cleats, tossed the ends into the boat, and leapt over the rail with agility.

"Sit there while I get us under way," he instructed, then guided them from mooring with skill after she was seated.

When they were a sufficient distance from land, Amaya watched Jason raise and secure the sail in place. The craft caught the wind and their adventure began. She loved how the breeze wafted through her long hair and over her skin and how the boat danced and sped along. She listened to the sound of the water slapping against the hull and the popping of the material overhead. She noticed the sky was a clear blue and the sun was brilliant. Many others were enjoying the lovely spring day, just as she and her companion were.

"Well, how do you like sailing so far?" he asked.

"It's exciting and fun. Do you sail often?"

"I do it a lot in the summer, but usually alone. Getting out here by myself helps me think and relax. It stirs the blood to challenge the wind. What tricks do you use for relaxing and thinking?"

"I swim. I walk. I exercise. I read. I visit family and friends."

"You said you have a twin brother. Are your parents still alive?"

"Yes, they do work similar to mine. Do you have parents?"

"I lost them a few years back to food poisoning."

"It is sad and tragic to lose loved ones."

"Especially to foolish accidents. I sued the restaurant that killed my mother and father; that's where I got the money to go into business for myself. No amount of money replaces family, but I wanted them to suffer for their carelessness."

She wondered if he turned away to prevent her from viewing his expression. "I am sorry you have suffered so much."

"I suppose Andrea told you I lost my wife and son in a car accident?"

"Yes, but you do not have to speak of them if it hurts you."

"I don't want to spoil our day with black talk; I promise to tell you another time. I still miss them, but I've finally accepted what happened."

"When something cannot be changed, it is best to adjust or the pain continues and one can be destroyed."

"You've got a smart head on those lovely shoulders."

"Thank you."

For a while, they were silent as they observed the sights and savored each other's company. A noise caught their attention and both looked upward to where a small plane was pulling a banner behind it.

"That seems like fun. Want to try it sometime this week?"

"Try what?"

"That," he said, and pointed to the banner.

Amaya stared at the symbols, then asked, "Would it be interesting?"

"You could see and learn a lot during a helicopter tour of Houston."

She was relieved he explained the unknown words and his offer. "I don't know if the Sangers would think it was safe for me to do."

"I'll ask them if that's okay with you." She nodded. "I bet you've never flown in one before."

"No."

"I'm almost positive you'd love it. I doubt Avi would." He chuckled.

"Avi is not daring like I am. She prefers to . . . have her boots planted on the ground," she said, using his past analogy. "Tell me more about Houston, sailing, and other things." She listened and observed as Jason complied. He even lowered the sail and anchored the craft so he wouldn't be distracted while he explained about his private investigative work and gave details of some of his most stimulating cases.

After several hours on the water, Jason asked if she was getting chilled.

"The air *is* becoming cooler."

"Here, put this on," he suggested, and helped her into a windbreaker.

She snuggled into his garment gratefully and gazed into his sapphire eyes.

Jason couldn't help but stare back into her captivating ones. "You're beautiful and special, Amaya Saar. You're the most interesting woman I've met in ages, maybe ever. I wish we had more time together."

She noticed the huskiness to his tone and the desire in his gaze. "You are also special, Jason Carlisle, and I shall miss you."

Jason's fingers stroked her cheek and toyed with a long wave of soft blond hair. "I hate to think of you leaving. I wish you could stay longer or return sooner."

"I feel the same way, but it cannot be changed."

Jason leaned forward very slowly to see if she was receptive to a kiss. When she didn't attempt to halt his obvious intention, he pulled her into his embrace as his mouth explored hers. He was thrilled when her arms slipped around his body and she responded with eagerness. His kissed her several times, then trailed his lips over her face and neck. He wanted her like crazy but knew this wasn't the time or place to see how she would respond. He craved to see and touch every inch of her. He wanted to spend days and nights with her, share a future with her. Yet he couldn't tell her such an important thing so soon after meeting or she might not take him seriously. Kissing him was one thing but making love to him was different, something he couldn't rush. Even if this was their last private moment, he had seven more days to convince her to stay with him.

Jason leaned back and smiled. "I suppose we should head in; we don't want to leave Avi by herself much longer. No, I should be truthful, Amaya; I find you too desirable to stay here any longer and behave myself."

"Sometimes it is hard to . . . behave," she replied with a smile.

"You've gotten to me, woman, and I didn't expect that to happen."

"I did not expect to meet a special man like you during my visit."

"I'm glad the attraction is mutual. Let's see where it goes, okay?"

"We shall see where it travels before I leave."

"Maybe far enough so you won't leave."

Amaya's smile vanished. "I must return home on schedule, Jason."

"We'll see," he jested, "because I'm going to try every trick in the book to keep you with me. I'm skilled at being sneaky and persistent."

"That will be an interesting game to watch."

"And a pleasant one to play. Let's pull anchor, mate."

After Jason showed Amaya and Avi his office and weapons' displays, they chatted for a while and had some refreshments he had prepared. "Why don't we play cards if you two have time?" he suggested. "Perhaps gin?"

Amaya almost panicked because she knew she wouldn't be able to read the cards and didn't know how to play Earth games. Avi spared her by telling Jason they should get home and spend time with her grandparents. Amaya wanted to hug her in gratitude.

"If we're gone too long today, they might not let us sneak out again and we have many plans for this week."

"You're right, Cousin; I'm being selfish, but you two are fun. I'll drive you back and see you tomorrow night."

"You are not staying for dinner?"

"I should give the Sangers and McKays some privacy, Amaya; I've been over there every night but one since your arrival. They might get tired of seeing my face. Plus, I have a few things I need to check on." *Like my case in progress, and you. I can't fight unknown competition.*

At dusk, Nigel caught Amaya sneaking up on an armadillo that was browsing in the bushes near the water's edge. As she extended her hand to touch it, Nigel yelled, "No!" He heard her shriek and saw her jerk around to face him. As he hurried to the scene, the spooked creature scurried into hiding. "Don't ever touch alien animals and plants without permission;" he ordered firmly. "One could bite or prick and give you lethal germs."

Amaya smiled in appreciation of his concern

and caution, but she was an adult and she had confronted countless perils in the past. Obviously, he was forgetting she was an Elite Squad member and a Star Fleet officer. Even so, she relented to politeness, as she was in his charge. "I'm sorry, sir; I didn't realize there was any danger. He looked so gentle and slow-witted that I didn't think I was taking any risk. We had countless inoculations and decontamination so there's no danger to me, is there?"

"You mustn't take unnecessary risks; the med team might not have covered everything we could encounter. We don't possess the same germs and viruses and immunities these Earthlings have. A risk could be fatal. Even if not, medical treatment could expose your identity."

"If an injury or illness occurred, I wouldn't seek medical treatment from the terrestrials. If I couldn't resolve it myself, I would return to the ship."

"What if you were out alone like now or only with Jason and you were rendered unconscious? He or someone else would carry you to one of their medical facilities. Tests would expose and endanger us all."

"I'm sorry, sir, but I would never endanger myself or any of you. When Avi and I aren't with you and her mother, she's there to protect me and I'm there if anything happened to her. I promise we'll be careful and alert. We wear our survival-emergency units at all times as ordered," she told him as she placed her right hand over the device on her left wrist. They were made especially for trips to

Earth and other alien worlds. The apparatus that appeared to others to be a watch-data bank combination held miniaturized versions of a medical analyzer, surgical laser, stun and disintegrator beams, and a personal force shield. The desired function was activated by lifting the cover and making digital contact with one of five buttons which were marked with Maffeian symbols; as a safeguard against accidents and exposure following theft or loss, the survival-emergency device worked only after scanning and identifying its owner's fingerprint. "I have med and self-defense training. I can sterilize and seal any cuts and disable any threat or encase myself from peril with my wrist unit. In my work, sir, I never know when I'll be forced to treat or protect myself during a mission gone wrong."

"I know from your record you can take care of yourself in our world," Nigel affirmed. "But it's different here on Earth, Amaya, where danger can lurk in seemingly simple things. I don't want to spoil your fun, but please be cautious and alert. Your parents would never forgive me if I allowed anything to happen to you."

"I will be extra careful from now on, sir," she promised Varian Saar's second in command.

After Avi went to bed, Amaya lay in hers and thought about her parents, brother, friends, and galaxy so far away from this planet. Soon she would be back at home and work, back facing her persistent superior.

Forget Commander Mohr or you'll ruin your mood

and trip. If he were anything like Jason Carlisle, I would chase him down and capture him in a preon. Who, Amaya, are you going to find to match Andrea's cousin? Star fire, how he can kiss! And smile. And laugh. Imagine what it would be like to mate with him . . . No, you'd better not or you might find that temptation too hard to resist.

To distract herself, she watched the "cult classic" movie *I Married A Monster From Outer Space*. It was silly and tragic but romantic. She couldn't understand why most Earthlings who believed in aliens considered them to be horrible and vicious creatures. She wished her people could make themselves known to these terrestrials so they would halt their foolish and inaccurate ideas. One day in the far future, when and if Earthlings became more advanced and civilized, they would reveal themselves. But that would be too late for a relationship between her and Jason.

Eight

"Mother, Father, I want to introduce you to Lieutenant Renah Dhobi. She's the newest and probably the best security team member I've ever had. She's also a close and special friend of mine." Galen glanced at his love and smiled. "You should see her in action; she has superior skills and intelligence, and we're lucky to have her aboard the *Galactic Wind*. Renah was the person who came up with the idea of how to defeat and capture those *spacekis* on Caguas with a *simboyd* and *gracene*, and she was one of the four pilots who attacked those *nefariants* with *x-nythene* during that Zandia incident. I have to admit she continues to amaze and please me every day. I've never enjoyed myself more than I have with her during these last few weeks. I doubt any two people could be more compatible than we are. Renah, these are my parents."

As he spoke, Jana witnessed Galen's proud and possessive tone of voice and the tender expression in his eyes, particularly when he looked at and touched Renah. She had never seen that kind of blissful smile or that adoring glow in his eyes before. Her son was definitely enchanted and in love. "It's so nice to meet you. Varian said our son was

bringing a dear friend with him tonight. Welcome
to our temporary home."

Renah was astonished by the way Galen introduced her to his family. It sounded to her as if he
were speaking about his prospective mate! "Thank
you, Doctor Saar; it's an honor and pleasure to
meet you and Supreme Commander Saar. I hope
I'm not intruding on a family gathering, but Galen
insisted I come."

Jana clasped Renah's hand and smiled. "Certainly not. We're delighted to have you join us.
We've looked forward to this evening ever since
Galen mentioned you to Varian. We're glad to
meet someone who's so special to him."

"Jana speaks the truth, Renah," Varian affirmed.
"We're happy Galen brought you to visit with us,
even if time is limited and current matters are
grave."

You're as handsome and beguiling as your offspring.
"Thank you, sir. As a Star Fleet officer, I've wanted
to meet our commander for a long time. After my
return from deep space, I came across your name
often in my studies. We're fortunate to have an illustrious leader like you."

Varian smiled. "That's kind of you to say,
Renah."

"You must be very proud of your son's accom-
plishments. He's the best superior officer I've had
during my four-year career. I hope I stay assigned
to the *Galactic Wind* for a long time because I'm
learning so much from Chief Saar, and it is an
honor to serve on the lead ship of our fleet. I
appreciate this warm welcome, Doctor Saar. I con-

fess I've been nervous about meeting two people of such high rank and esteem."

"There's no reason to be uneasy around us, Renah," Jana replied.

Varian and Jana had sensed apprehension in Galen's companion before she mentioned it. They assumed she was anxious about this occasion because she was afraid they wouldn't like or accept her in their son's life. Both concluded Galen was serious about his feelings and intentions toward the lovely officer. They hoped Renah felt the same way so Galen would not be hurt by his first endeavor into love. Surely, they reasoned, Renah wouldn't have agreed to come if she weren't just as serious about their son.

"We have a few things to discuss, Father, either now or later."

Renah noticed the resemblance between the two men. It was a genetic trait of Maffeian fathers and sons to look nearly identical. The resemblance here would be even stronger if Varian Saar hadn't mated with an alien. Varian and Ryker had been almost duplicated images of their father. It wasn't known why daughters didn't have that same genetic tendency; and, in her case, that was fortunate . . . For a moment, she remembered the laser surgery she had submitted to long ago to enhance her facial beauty and to remove any clue to her real identity.

"Renah, you and I will go into the other chamber to talk while Varian speaks with Galen," Jana said, smiling. "Then, we can enjoy our meal and relax after business is completed."

"Is that all right with you?" Galen asked Renah.

"Yes, I would enjoy conversing with Doctor Saar. With our mutual interests in scientific research, I'm sure we can have an informative talk."

Galen released Renah's hand so she could leave the entry area with his mother. He followed his father into a room that Varian was using as an office during his lengthy stay on the capital planet, as the Saars' permanent home was on a private planetoid called Altair that orbited Rigel. He watched the older man take a seat behind a desk that was translucent except for pedestals at each end that contained drawers. He sat down in the chair before it. "How bad are things, Father?"

"Getting worse by the day, Galen. Maffei hasn't experienced this much trouble since Ryker and Taemin were defeated and we won treaties with *Effecta* Maal and Supreme Ruler Jurad. The Androasian Empire and Pyropean Federation have good leaders now in *Effecta* Agular and Supreme Ruler Leumi, so this shadowy threat isn't coming from either of them. None of the other nearest galaxies—especially the Milky Way—have the technology and daring to carry out something of this enormous scale."

"Does that mean you think it's coming from within our boundaries?"

After Varian ruffled his sable hair, he leaned forward and propped his arms on the desk. His handsome features were creased with worry. He focused a trouble blue gaze on his son. "I can't imagine that being true. I'm totally baffled, and that doesn't happen often. First, we had those incidents on Caguas and Zandia and Darkar, and now one on Mailiorca. Every time, Earthlings behaving like programmed automatons and supplies stolen from Trilabs by my imposter are involved. Those are the only clues and evidence we have, and they provoke questions instead of giving answers."

"What's happened on Mailiorca? We didn't receive orders to stop there on our way to Rigel. We came here at starlight speed."

"I received the bad news just before your arrival: more Earthlings were caught after poisoning half of their *majee* spinners. If I hadn't ordered all thirteen planets to full alert and *Avatar Kwan* didn't have patrols out, they would have achieved their goal of exterminating the entire species."

"That stratagem could have crippled Mailiorca's economy. Without those annelids to make *majee*, we'd lose the strongest and finest thread for fabrics. You know that *majee's* the only natural fiber we use in clothing; it wears and survives our cleaning process better than the highest grade of synthetics. And Mailiorca is the only planet where those particular annelids can survive. That clever *villite* knew exactly where and how to strike. Any other news?"

"The Elite Squad members I assigned to the Caguas incident made new discoveries today; those *spacekis* weren't just stealing and smuggling ore and gems to get rich or to finance their scheme; they were tunneling to other areas to plant explosives. If they hadn't been stopped and if those *tremolite* caves had been set afire, over a third of

Caguas's surface would be burning by now and polluting their air for eons. Ingression was almost completed to the largest mines Ryker once owned. Those *fiendals'* disintegrating laser was powerful and undetectable to surface sensors. It's nothing like we have or we've seen before, Galen. It didn't even leave dust or debris behind, and those hollow-outs were as smooth as a baby's flesh. They knew they couldn't get past force-shield domes and android guards protecting the mines, so they burrowed toward their targets."

"That laser apparatus the Squad confiscated offered no clues?"

"The minute after tests began, it self-destructed. Sound familiar?"

"And contradictory," Galen added, with a slight nod. "Sometimes our *villite* makes certain we obtain no clues; other times, he makes sure we do. There must be a reason behind which facts he allows us to discover."

"Or he's simply taunting us, because we haven't learned anything he doesn't want us to know at this point. Taking prisoners doesn't even give us help or an advantage; if we attempt to interrogate or treat them, we annihilate them. It's apparent to me and the Council that somebody is trying to destroy our planets or their lead product one by one. When we add the outbreak of violence by assorted *nefariants*, it's even clearer there's an insidious plot to induce havoc, misery, and death throughout Maffei. Whoever our *villite* is, he is a genius like my half brother was."

Galen had never met his half uncle. No matter

how much he read, heard, or was told about Prince Ryker Triloni, he was disappointed that chance was gone forever, as it was undeniable the mixed Androasian/Maffeian had been a matchless genius. He remained quiet and thoughtful as he waited for Varian to continue.

"We haven't detected a pattern to their attacks, so intercepting them before their next strike is impossible. To move around as ghosts, they must have a sophisticated cloaking system even our anticloaking device can't penetrate. And how they created a convincing double of me and got those Trilabs codes is an alarming mystery."

"I surely would love to get my hands on their leader and learn why he's doing this to us."

"I'm meeting with the Supreme Council again tomorrow. Draco, Brec, and Suran want swift action taken; and I'm doing my best to comply. The Alliance Assembly of *Avatars* will meet with the four of us the following day. We need answers and suspects, and neither appears forthcoming. No drug, threat, or bribe has extracted information from our prisoners; at least, those we haven't put into comas by accident or those who killed themselves to prevent exposure. The *Galactic Wind* will be in charge of collecting captives and getting them safely to Star Base, and she'll provide any force needed during conflicts."

"I'll keep my team ready to respond immediately, sir."

Varian leaned back in his chair and took a deep breath. "Jana wants Amaya home and out of any danger on Earth from whoever is abducting and enthralling those terrestrials. She's worried Amaya might get snared."

"How could our *villite* discover she's there?"

"Perhaps the same way he got hold of those codes and posed as me. He's cunning and dangerous, and persuasive. Think what would happen if Amaya became his prisoner, especially if he used his vile drugs on her."

"She's been through the *Rendelar* process, Father, so he can't force secrets from her; *Thorin* would have no effect."

"If he doesn't know she's an Elite Squad member and has been made immune to truth serum, he could use his vile chemicals on her."

"Have they tested the effect of our *villite's* formula in that area?"

"There's no point because we can't analyze and reproduce it; it self-destructs."

"Just as Ryker's formulas react to testing. Very strange, Father."

Varian's brow furrowed and his blue gaze chilled as he recalled past horrors with his half brother, including the day of their final confrontation. "He's dead, Son, believe me, because I'm the one who killed him. The only place his secrets exist is in that computer in Trilabs, and nobody can access that except me and the Council. Not even my imitation knows that code or can get his filthy hands on it."

"Do you trust the *Kadim,* Sebok's father, and Breccia Sard implicitly? Do you know for certain none of them are involved in this?"

Varian was stunned by the query. "Yes, as close

friends and as Supreme Council members. Why do you ask such a question, my son?"

"I have no reason to doubt our galactic ruler and Councilmen, but you've known those men better and longer than I have. If this threat comes from within our galaxy, a man of great power and wealth and acumen must be responsible. Do not forget each of them has possession of the Darkar and Trilabs codes which were used recently during those thefts. They know each planet's vulnerable point and its defense systems and methods. They also know about the duplicate of you that was used long ago when you assumed Ryker's identity to trick Maal Triloni and Jurad Tabriz into peace."

"That impersonating unit was facially altered and its memory erased."

"But at that time he was a perfect replica."

"Only because I programmed him myself."

"Who else but someone who knows you well could do the same?"

"For the part my new double played on Darkar, anyone who's studied and spied on me could have programmed him. No one there questioned a man who appeared to be me and who had the correct access codes."

"The fact remains no area can be left unchecked, Father, no matter how incredible it seems. The fate of our world is in peril. Do any of them doubt your innocence? Try to blame you?" Galen watched his father shake his head to both questions. "What if this fake is perfect or close to it and he's used as a weapon to get to them?"

"They won't be fooled if he tries to approach

them. He can't get past our new safeguard. We have a secret word to prove who I am when we meet or talk by secured *telecom:* your mother's middle name."

At the mention of Jana and to get off the dismaying topic, Galen asked, "Have you calmed Mother's worries any about Amaya?"

"She'll return soon, but not fast enough for Jana. I haven't told her I'll have to assign your sister to one of the investigations in progress. I have no choice; our daughter is an Elite Squad member and Star Fleet officer. Of course, Commander Mohr isn't going to like losing her at base."

"So, Amaya told you about his determined pursuit?"

"Before she left for Earth. I hope no problems result from it."

"If Mohr will forget she exists, there won't be. But now that a woman's caught my eye like Amaya caught his, I doubt he can forget or ignore her."

"Are you saying you're in love with Renah Dhobi?"

"Yes, sir. I feel like I've been struck by a meteor and sent spinning."

"How do you know it's not just infatuation or a challenge?"

"I'm positive it's not, Father. I've never met a woman who's my perfect match. Most women either try to prove they're better than me to grab my attention, or try to appear not as good so they won't annoy or embarrass me. Renah is herself. She uses her exceptional skills professionally and as naturally as breathing, but she's not a show-off. She's impressed by my family and heritage, but who and what I am doesn't matter to her like it does to other women. She's refreshing and invigorating. Everything within me says, 'This is her, the one you've been waiting for.' "

"Are you going to ask her to become your mate?"

"Yes, but after I give her more time to get to know me. I don't want to panic her. She has little to no experience with men and romantic relationships. With my reputation as a *reacher*, she has to make certain I'm serious and honest. That's the only area she's a little insecure about, how *the* Galen Saar could fall in love with and choose her over all the others. It must have been the same way with you and Mother when she first came to our world and met you. Nobody would understand our situation and other feelings better than you two. Any suggestions, Father, on how I can make certain I don't do anything to lose her?"

"Be yourself, Galen, and never lie to her about your feelings. A woman can't see what's inside your head and heart, so you have to tell her. If you love her and want her, don't lose her by being too cautious and distant."

"I'll follow your advice, sir, and thank you."

"There will be a commendation ceremony tomorrow for you and your team's victories on Caguas and Zandia. Public acknowledgment of those defeats and of the skilled forces in our fleet should allay any citizen's worry and fear, and prevent perilous rumors from spreading. Why don't we let it be a surprise for Renah? Receiving two citations should boost her confidence and self-esteem. It will also prove to everyone she's a perfect match for you, and our presence at her side will reveal she's been accepted by and is special to the Saars and to Star Fleet. In fact, perhaps she's earned an elevation in rank and pay."

"Don't take both actions on the same day, Father, or others might become jealous and resentful if it appears we're showing favoritism to her."

"You're right, Son, we'll promote her later."

As the men discussed other matters, Jana and Renah were talking on similar topics. As a Star Fleet officer and security team member involved in them, Jana knew she wasn't revealing any secrets she should withhold.

"This *villite* astounds me with his intelligence and alarms me with his evil. He knows *majee* can survive only in the combination of Mailiorca's soil, air, and water, just as he knows Caguas needs its mines and Zandia its jungles. That tunneling laser is beyond even our technology. Their cloaking device ranks with ours. And that mind-control power amazes me. Whatever drugs and processes he's using, they remove any fear of dying and insert total loyalty to him in those captive Earthlings; that makes his thralls dangerous, unpredictable, daring, and determined to please and obey him at any cost—even at the price of their lives or lives of innocents. I've been working with the med staff and scientists at Star Base, but we haven't made a breakthrough yet. I have my research staff at home working on the same project."

"In the laboratories on your private planetoid?"

"Yes. Altair is quite large, so it doesn't interfere with our privacy. Varian and I plan to stay here while he handles the investigation and I assist with the medical angle. I hope it doesn't take much longer because I miss being home. You must come to visit after our return; Altair is lovely and peaceful, but I'm needed here." Jana paused, her lovely face troubled. "I wish it weren't my old people involved. Those Earthlings are like mindless thralls to that *villite*. So many have died and more lives are in jeopardy, but I doubt he cares as long as he needs them as slaves to do his bidding. With the technology, chemicals, targets, and workers in use, there's more to this attack than crimes for greed. I hate to imagine what he's plotting at this moment for helpless victims. I pray he'll make an error soon so we can expose and defeat him. To think he could create a convincing replica of my husband is frightening."

"I'm sure his identity and motive will be made known soon," Renah said soothingly. "Since he doesn't appear to be after wealth, he cannot complete or enjoy his plot if he doesn't eventually reveal it to whomever or whatever it's aimed at. Perhaps these assaults have been to seize our attention, to terrorize and arouse our people, to show us he can and will attack at any place and time, to prove to Star Fleet and our people we're unable to prevent his actions. After he decides we're intimidated and powerless to battle him, then he'll make his real demands on us, whatever they are. For certain, if these acts continue or worsen, Maffeians will doubt our ability to protect them.

He could even use that mind block on our citizens to enslave large numbers of them, turn them against our forces and leaders. Perhaps conquest of this star system is his long-range goal."

Jana was horrified by those speculations. "In your travels on the *Space Rover,* did you ever come across any planet or star system with such capabilities as we're confronting?"

"No, the *Space Rover* only found uninhabited or savage worlds. In a way, it was good I was born and reared out of Maffei because I learned so much. I only hope I can use my skills and knowledge to the best of my ability during this crisis."

"I'm sure they will serve you and us well." Jana left the dismaying subject for a while. "Did you like living and working in deep space?"

"Yes, but it denied me many crucial things."

Between sips of warm and dark *zim,* Jana remarked, "Your knowledge, skills, and rank prove you've studied and trained to your best since your return to our world. I know losing your parents in that tragedy was hard, but they prepared you well for your present existence."

"Thank you, Doctor Saar. Deep-space exploration is interesting, challenging, and educational, but it's lonely when there aren't others your age in the group. My childhood was so unlike those of my shipmates that many tend to have trouble understanding me. Galen has been kind and generous in helping me adjust to my new assignment and life on the ship. Sometimes it's frightening and painful when you seem to be a *hapax* mark trying to fit into a *mig*-size hole." Since most of what she was saying was true, Renah realized it was easy to sound honest. For a wild and crazy moment, she wished she *were* being truthful about everything.

Jana's aquamarine gaze softened. "Coming from another world myself, Renah, I know how difficult and intimidating change and adjustments and acceptance can be. I was terrified when I first arrived in Maffei, but things were vastly different then. Don't get discouraged; you'll do fine; you *are* doing fine. Just be yourself and don't worry about the few people who might dislike and reject you: they aren't worth knowing if they deny you a fair chance. You're a charming young woman, and very lovely. I can see why you're the one who captured my son's eye and heart."

Renah displayed genuine surprise. "He told you that?"

Jana laughed. "Not in so many words. Even so, I would have guessed the truth; I know my son. It's as clear as a *transascreen* that he loves you. May I be so forward as to ask if you if you have deep and special feelings for him?"

Stars around me, how should I respond? "I . . ."

Jana lay a comforting hand atop Renah's. "If you prefer not to answer, please feel free to do so. I won't be annoyed. I just don't want to see Galen suffer. I know he doesn't need his mother to protect him at his age, but it's a habit that's hard to break. A parent just doesn't want her child to experience rejection."

Renah dared to venture, "Would you be upset if we fell in love?"

Jana laughed softly before she replied, "Of course not. I can't imagine a better choice for Galen than you."

"But you don't know me well. I'm not a match for your level of prestige."

"That doesn't matter to us, Renah; only Galen's happiness does."

"What if I can't make him happy?"

"If love is real and strong, Renah, it can conquer any obstacle."

"Any and every obstacle?"

"I'm living proof that's true. So is Varian. Do you know our history?"

"I've read and heard things about what occurred before I came to Maffei. It's said you two have one of the greatest love matches of all time."

"I'm biased, but I agree with that," Jana said, and laughed. "It can be the same for you and Galen if you both surrender to your feelings for each other and don't let anything or anyone come between you."

Renah glanced toward the closed portal to the sitting chamber before meeting Jana's gentle gaze. "Love and commitment frighten me because I've never experienced them before. I can't discuss my feelings with my parents because they aren't here. Nor with a friend because I have none that close. Galen has become my best friend and favorite companion. Yes, I love him."

Jana almost sighed aloud in relief and joy. "Then tell him, Renah, if you haven't done so already."

"I have not, but I'm sure my feelings are obvious to him."

"Sometimes men can be blind and foolish when it comes to emotions. Trust your heart, Renah. Your heart never lies to you and true love never betrays."

Was it possible, Renah's troubled mind questioned, that Galen Saar—one of her targets—was truly in love with her, his unknown enemy? Was it possible this woman—another target—was coaxing her to become her son's mate? What would both do if they knew the dark and bitter truth? Within the Saars' hands was the power to destroy her if she were exposed, and, to save themselves and their world, they would surely do so if that awesome moment arrived. "I don't know how to respond, Doctor Saar."

"There's no need to say or do anything impulsively, Renah, just think about what I've said." As Renah considered her advice, Jana was aware that the girl had not asked questions about her first "mate"—Ryker Triloni. No doubt Renah was too polite to mention him, though it was no secret that Maffei had obtained ownership and control of Trilabs through her. It was also no secret that Ryker was Varian's half brother and bitter rival. Since Maffeian unions were for life except in certain grave circumstances, only Ryker's "accidental" death had allowed her to join with Varian.

Jana looked pleased and unknowingly misled. "I promise you I will do what I believe to be fair and right," Renah responded. "Galen and I are so compatible that it's tempting to move swiftly but we need to take time to adjust to our feelings, to strengthen our bond and to give his family and friends time to get to know and accept me as he has."

"Those are important and smart goals, Renah," Jana said approvingly. "Friendship is the best first step toward real love and the best advantage to have for achieving a lasting and strong relationship. If one doesn't truly love and respect a person above all others, a long and happy bond isn't possible."

"I agree. I—" The doors opened then and the men entered the chamber and silenced her.

Jana stood, walked to her son, and embraced him again.

As the two chatted, Renah realized she had prepared herself to hate Jana Greyson Saar and Varian Saar on sight and to be willing—if not eager—to make them suffer extreme agony. Yet she found herself respecting, liking, and warming to both people. The couple she had met were nothing like the monsters she had been told about since birth . . . Had they changed so greatly in twenty-six years, she mused, or were they both just adept at guile?

Jana whispered to her son as Varian joined the young woman. "Your Renah and I have been having a wonderful talk; she's utterly delightful, Galen. I hope you bring her to see us many times. I'm sure she would enjoy a visit on Altair when everyone's schedule allows."

"I'm glad you approve, Mother, and I concur with all my heart. I was sure you would find Renah just as irresistible as I do." He sent Renah a satisfied smile which she returned in kind as she spoke with Varian.

As her son headed to sit by Renah, Jana suggested, "Let's order Eirean wine to celebrate your visit. Then, we'll share a meal."

"Well, didn't I tell you this evening would be fun and easy?"

"You were correct, as usual, Chief Saar," Renah quipped with a smile. "Do you want to stay and talk? It isn't very late." *Perhaps if I get you cozy, you'll drop clues about the private meeting with your father.*

Galen glanced around the comfortable setting. "Are you sure you'll be safe with a hungry male prowling your chamber?" he teased.

"How can you be hungry when we ate not long ago?"

"I'm starving for you, Renah Dhobi, not food. My family adores you, as I do. After Amaya returns from her visit to Earth, you'll meet her, too."

"Your sister went to another galaxy during her leave?"

"She went with the Sangers. Nigel's mate has family there. Amaya and their daughter, Avi, are best friends. They asked my sister to go with them. She needed a rest and diversion so she accepted their invitation."

To prevent suspicion now and later, Renah didn't ask any more. She knew Amaya's location was a crucial—perhaps useful—fact she must report to her side as soon as possible. "Avi Sanger, Sebok Suran's love. Will they mate one day?"

"I expect her to be wearing his bonding bracelet soon." *Just as I hope you'll be wearing mine when this threat is over.*

Renah recalled the exquisite jewel-encrusted one Jana wore to signify she was mated to Varian Saar. She wished the woman had talked about her bond to Ryker long ago; perhaps after they got closer, Jana would trust her enough to speak freely. "Now that Sebok and I have resolved our problem, I like him. Thaine, too. You have chosen good best friends."

Galen stroked her short hair. He enjoyed its fullness and softness, and the way it framed her oval face. "You're at the top of my list now."

"You're at the top of my list of friends, too, though mine is a short one."

Galen captured her hand and kissed her fingertips. "You'll make plenty of friends soon. How could anyone not like you? Is that what you and Mother discussed, us being close friends?"

"We had female-only talk, so I can't tell you," she said, and laughed as she sat down on a plush *seata*. She motioned for him to join her.

"Secrets already in progress?" he murmured.

"I wouldn't be interesting to you if I weren't a little mysterious."

Galen rested his arm atop the seatback and toyed again with her hair, then her earlobe. "Since I met you, I feel as if my emotions are trapped in a vortex. Until I'm certain you're mine, I can't pull free and relax."

Renah's gaze captured his. "What can I do to help you?"

"Become mine tonight, Renah. I'll never make you sorry you trusted me. I love you, woman: I need you. I don't mean to be impatient, and I won't be angry if you say not yet. You're worth waiting for, Renah, for as long as it takes to win you. We're perfect for each other. If you're not ready to commit to me tonight, at least tell me I stand a chance of winning your heart. And please tell me if I do anything wrong during my pursuit. A great many people believe everything comes fast and easy for me because of who I am. But I swear to you, I have worked hard for all I have and am. I'm never giving up on you, woman; I'll fight for you if necessary. You're unlike any woman I've ever met; you're unique and special, like my mother. I've never wanted to make a female totally mine before; there hasn't been one I couldn't live without. As soon as the time and occasion are right, I want you to become my mate."

Renah could hardly believe her ears. "Are you certain? It's so early in our relationship."

"I've never been more convinced of anything in my life. There's a magic between us, Renah, a potent connection, as if we were destined to meet and mate. I hope you also sense it."

"I just don't want our love to blaze like a comet across the sky so fast and hot it burns me up in the process."

"It won't. If you want me to prove my words, I'll announce I'm going to ask you to become my mate. I just didn't want to do it this soon and have people think we're being impulsive. Or worse, think we shouldn't be working together because we're too close."

"I think that's a wise decision; so, yes, I will become your lover."

"You will?"

"If you do not expect too much of my innocent state. I fear it will disappoint and discourage a man accustomed to experienced females."

"Love is more than having sex, Renah; it's giving and sharing. It's how we feel and what we do off a *sleeper* as well as on one. Give me your heart and I'll cherish that prize and guard it with my life and honor."

Do your duty as ordered, Renah: deceive and ensnare and use him, but don't love or trust him. She suppressed twinges of guilt as she replied, "As I will do the same with yours, Galen, as your lover and friend."

"What about becoming my mate when this current trouble ends?"

I cannot allow you to pressure and confuse me with seductive words and offers. "We must take one trek at a time to see how compatible we really are. We should first explore and test our emotions and affinity so we won't make a grave error. There is no hurry; we're young and we have much to do. We must not rush into a more serious relationship until we discover if our feelings remain the same or grow even stronger. If that proves true, then we'll discuss a permanent commitment."

Galen's mind urged, *Teach her she can have a bright and happy future with you if she dares to accept*

*it. Prove to her you and love are risks worth taking.
Show her she has nothing to fear from you, that she's
your equal and your consummate match.* "I realize it
may seem as if I'm moving too fast, but there's no
logical reason to deny or resist what I know I want
and need. I swear this isn't about conquest and
amusement. I truly love you, Renah Dhobi. I swear
I will never hurt you."

"I will trust you, Galen, until you give me a reason not to do so."

"On my word of honor, my love, that will never
happen."

*I cannot make the same promise, even as a necessary
lie.* "I must prepare myself. I will summon you
when I'm ready."

"My *liex* injection is current, so don't worry
about that."

"I was certain you practiced safe birth control.
Wait for me to change."

Galen watched her rise and leave the chamber
for her sleeping quarters. He walked to the large
transascreen and gazed outside. He saw shuttle
lights and forms as they transported people to chosen locations. His gaze roamed tall structures of
various shapes and sizes. He knew he couldn't be
seen through the window's reflective material, even
with lights on inside. He didn't want to think of
the assignment facing them; he only wanted to
think of the woman nearby who would soon be
his. This was a big step for him, and also for her.
He wished they were far away from perils and duties so they could savor this glorious splendor beneath lovely starlight. He heard the swish of the

door as it opened when Renah put pressure on the floor beyond it. He turned and filled his senses with her beauty.

Renah waited while his glowing eyes roamed her from head to feet. She felt a blush warm her cheeks, as the filmy blue garment was sheer. She had been trained for this moment, but she fretted, could she please this man who had been with many females? She trembled as he approached. Her gaze met with his. "I am yours for the taking, Galen Saar, if you will have me."

"Never have I wanted or needed any woman more, or ever will." He pulled her into his embrace so he could feel the full length of her against him. His lips closed over hers and he knew he wanted her forever, not just tonight and not just in this physical way. His tongue sought her mouth with tenderness and leisure, tasting her sweetness. Her skin was warm and silky beneath his wandering hands. His lips drifted over her earlobe, down her long neck, and back to her mouth. A fierce hunger gnawed at him but he was determined to move slow and easy. When Renah laced her arms around his neck and responded in shy eagerness, he sighed with satisfaction.

Renah allowed his hands to roam at will; they trekked over her back, waist, and hips, then moved upward to her breasts. When he cupped and massaged them and fingered their peaks to tautness, she was amazed by how wonderful and exciting those sensations were. He was skilled and irresistible, patient and gentle. Her breathing quickened and her heart beat fast in panic and rising passion.

A strange hunger coiled within her womanhood. She felt as if she were melting into molten lava. Soon her fears subsided beneath his fiery siege. She ignored who she was and the original motive for being there. For now, only sating her rampant passion was important.

Galen swept her into his arms and carried her to the *sleeper.* He lay her on its surface and gazed at her as he removed his boots and garment. Panels overhead gave off a glow of light that flattered her complexion and added a seductive mood to the chamber, as did soft music and a heady scent coming from concealed devices for guests' pleasure. He joined her and drew her into his arms once more. His gaze roamed her face as he murmured, "It's as if you left *Kahala* or the best dream I could ever have and stepped into my life and heart. Sometimes I fear if I close my eyes, I'll open them to find you gone forever. Never leave me, love."

Renah hugged him as her troubled mind whirled. *Soon you will believe I came from Gehenna and I'm the worst nightmare you could have.*

Galen's questing lips founds hers and his hands explored her inviting territory. He groaned in increasing need but commanded himself not to rush this treasured moment. She was real. She was here. She was his.

Renah's hands traced his sleek shoulders, muscular back, and taut buttocks. Every area she touched or fondled was firm and smooth. She became intrigued by his body, his desire, his actions. She wanted to discover every *hapax* of him. There were no scars or blemishes to mar his splendid physique. He was strong, proud, and self-assured. He was the epitome of passion, the height of sensuality and sexual prowess. She felt herself quiver with longing and pleasure. His voice was tender and soothing; his movements, purposeful and deft. Her fingers played in his ash-blond hair. She felt his embrace tighten and heard him groan in rising desire that matched her own. She savored the force of their shared passion, as did he from his reaction.

Galen's pulse raced. The contact with her was more potent than any drink he had consumed. As their kisses waxed deeper and more urgent, his mouth trailed over her cheek before traveling down her neck then returning by a different route. He nuzzled his jawline against her fragrant locks and relished their texture against his skin. His hands roamed up her arms and drifted into her sunny mane where full strands surrounded his fingers.

Renah grasped his head and guided his mouth back to hers. She took and gave countless kisses until they were both breathless and trembling. Her fingers sought the pulse point in his neck so she could feel his heart pounding in desire *for her.* She felt it gaining speed with each minute he held her close and pleasured them. His hunger was enormous but he was clearly controlling it out of consideration for her. Her hands returned to a perusal of his torso. She was so aroused and receptive that she wondered if her throbbing heart could trick her into betraying her duty if she but relaxed her guard over it for a *preon.* From the moment they met, hadn't she known and feared deep inside that, under other circumstances, he was the perfect man for her? If only he wasn't out of reach . . . Soon, they would be endangering their lives when he challenged the awesome powers of her side. Eventually, the catastrophic truth would be exposed, as would she, and their relationship would be destroyed forever. He would hate and curse her instead of vowing love and showering praises; he would crave to slay her with his bare hands instead of caressing her with them. But before those events became realities, she would feast on every morsel of affection and pleasure he gave to her, and she would reprimand herself daily for being so weak and susceptible.

"Just relax and enjoy tonight," Galen murmured. His head lowered as his lips journeyed down her throat. He brushed them over the straining peaks of her firm breasts and lavished sweet nectar upon their pinnacles.

Renah felt his hands shift to venture over her naked body, stroking every part he could reach. Afterward, they traveled over her hips to the very center of her passion. With skill and gentleness, he stroked her moist and silky region. She moaned and squirmed in delight, her body sensitive and pliant to everything he did. She also wanted to touch, pleasure, and tantalize him. Her hand closed around his maleness. She heard him suck in air and stiffen a moment when she did so. She smiled at his response and continued to practice the actions she had observed on the monitor during her lessons. Her fingers worked on his hard, smooth length; and she found the deed as stimulating as he did. Her body soon was engulfed in a blaze of splendor that she—for one wild and senseless moment—wished could mold them into one.

Galen moved out of her grasp and guided himself gently into her welcoming heat. He halted a moment to regain self-control over it and to allow Renah to adjust to these new sensations. He didn't seem to have hurt her, only given brief discomfort, which was a relief and joy. He hugged and kissed her as he relished this magnificent union. Surely, he decided in dreamy bliss, it would bind them for all time. Each time he thrust within her and she matched his rhythm, it was sheer ecstasy. They moved with urgency, aching for release from sweet torment. Both were torn between wanting to claim their reward within seconds and wanting their rapturous quest to continue all night.

Soon, there was no choice for them to make. Their desires raced at starlight speed. Unable to wait another minute to begin the final leg of their voyage, they soared upward as ripple after ripple of wondrous pleasure washed over them, leaving them sated and content. They cuddled quietly for a while to savor the euphoric and triumphant experience of two people becoming one.

As he locked her against him, Galen murmured, "I love you, Renah Dhobi. I've never known a happiness such as I'm feeling at this moment. You're mine, all mine. Don't try to escape me, woman, because I'll never release you. If you try, I'll chase you from one end of this galaxy to the other to recapture you. If you can love me as I love you, our future is brighter than a supernova."

We have no future, Galen Saar; your parents and their friends saw to that long ago with their treacheries, and with what I have done and must do to help punish them. Yet Renah realized her feelings had changed since she began this mission four years ago; actually—her mind corrected—when she was born. She knew it was wrong and rash to get emotionally involved with this man, and especially with his parents. Even so, somehow Galen Saar had stolen her traitorous wits tonight and was threatening to confiscate her troubled heart! That would be a cruel joke on her if she found love with an enemy—only to lose it to uncontrollable ties to his past. *If only you weren't a Saar. If only I weren't a—*

"Do you want me to return to my chambers or snuggle up with you for the night?" Galen asked as his right arm encircled her waist to keep their bodies in contact. He didn't know what to think about her heavy silence. From her actions, their joining had been more than satisfactory, so he wondered what her odd mood meant.

Renah feared she was too aware of Galen's nearness and contact, his hand stroking her side, and his stirring breath near her ear. When he nestled her face against his chest and caressed her back, she didn't know what she should do and say. Duty demanded she keep him near; self-defense ordered her to retreat for a while until she mastered her emotions.

"Are you asleep?" he jested, and kissed her forehead.

"No. I was thinking about us. When I accepted my assignment, I never expected you to be as you are. I never expected to . . ."

"Fall in love with me? I hope that is what you left off," he teased.

He's trapped you with his words. If you disagree, all progress is lost. Say and do what yo must. "It is. But it is hard for me to say, to believe, to accept. This bond between us happened so suddenly, without warning."

"I know, and it surprises me, too. It's strange, but I'm not afraid of how I'm feeling. I love you and I know this is meant to be. The only thing that scares me is losing you. Father said matters are worse," he began, then brushed over their earlier conversation, omitting only private family matters and other secrets. "Somewhere, we have a dangerous and cunning *villite*. We don't know who he is, why he's doing this, or how he's accomplishing his evil goals. Destruction of Maffei appears to be his aim. While we're investigating and challenging him and his *nefariants,* I want you to stay close to me so I can protect you from any harm. That doesn't mean I doubt your skills and intelligence, Renah, because you've proven them to be superior to most officers' I know; I just can't bear for anything to take you away from me."

She embraced him without meeting his gaze, as hers might expose the ravenous torment chewing at her. "You can't imagine how it affects me to hear you say such tender words and to have such strong feelings for me. I want you to stay longer with me tonight, but I don't think it's wise for you to sleep here. It's best if we keep our relationship just between ourselves for now. As you said, Star Fleet could separate us if they think it will damage our duties."

"You will consider becoming my mate after this threat is destroyed?"

"I will think of it many times as I help seek victory for our side."

Galen grasped her chin, lifted her head, and gazed into her eyes before sealing their lips. Soon, desire commanded another union.

Renah was astonished the following morning when a small package and bouquet were delivered to her chambers from Jana and Varian Saar. The tropical flowers were colorful and rare, their fragrance soft and subtle. She opened the oblong box to find a *platinien* wrist band inside. Her smoky gaze widened and her fingers trembled as she removed the bracelet and rested it across her palm. It was made like delicate webbing, a darker shade of gold than the false shade of her hair. She lay the present on the table to listen to their message on an audio-visual correspondence device:

"Varian and I want you to know how much we enjoyed meeting you last night and look forward to spending many more such evenings with you. We extend an invitation for you to visit us any time you wish, with or without our son's escort. We know it must be difficult and lonely without a family, so we hope you will become a special part of ours. If there is anything you want or need while you're on Rigel or after your departure, please contact us or ask Galen to pass along your request. Stay safe during the dangerous days ahead, and follow your heart as we did long ago.''

Renah studied the expression on Jana's face and the tone of the woman's voice as she replayed the Earthling's words. Jana Greyson Saar looked and sounded sincere, kind, and thoughtful. It was as if the alien was welcoming her into their inner circle as their son's choice of a mate. This unforeseen predicament, she fretted, was unsettling and hazardous. She didn't need a bittersweet complication to confuse her!

Renah tossed the unit onto the table with the expensive wrist band and flowers and paced the chamber. *Don't be nice when you're my enemies and I must hurt you. Do you and your friends believe you'll never have to pay for what you did to my loved ones? Do you think you can destroy anybody who gets in the path of your desires and not be punished?* She snatched up the device and erased the message so she wouldn't be tempted to listen to it again. *I must not fall in love with your son or become friends with you two. I must do my duty; I have no choice, not now, not after all we've done so far.*

Renah knew once she returned to the ship she would have to find a private moment to contact her parents and report establishing a close relationship with Galen, meeting Varian and Jana, and learning of Amaya's whereabouts. She should warn them of the precaution taken to prevent Varian's duplicate from reaching the Councilmen to dupe them. There was no need to tell them the

Darkar/Trilabs codes had changed, as that action was expected. By now, they knew the good and bad results of the Caguas, Zandia, and Mailiorca incidents, but she wouldn't expose the extent of her actions with them, not yet. After a hasty report, to avoid taking risks of discovery, she would tell them this message would be her last for a while.

She wished she hadn't received unexpected news from her parents this morning, black news that had her distressed and afraid, news to which an instant reply was impossible. Even if she could have responded via their android, it was too late to stop their next steps or to warn Galen if she dared. Renah wished she hadn't told her family she would be on Rigel so they could send that horrifying information.

Renah's heart pounded in disillusionment and trepidation. If her parents hadn't already unleashed the lethal virus on each of the thirteen planets, would she attempt to halt its invasion? Would she go against her family to save the lives of their enemies? Regardless of what her mother and father said, was it right for innocents to suffer and die to punish the guilty? None of this violence had been part of the original assault plan. What, she fretted, happened to stealing ore and gems for finance and fuel, spraying a forest, and killing a few *majee*? No one said Caguas would be set afire, or the ecology of Zandia destroyed, or the economy of Mailiorca devastated. Yet it was her report about Trilabs which had enabled them to carry out those actions! No one had said a fatal virus and countless deaths would occur! If she had been enlightened earlier—

It's too late to take another course, even if I dared to commit treachery and betrayal and to risk my and my parents' lives. Soon, the Maffeians will feel the agonizing bite of the monster that's been loosed on them. They have no immunity and there is no cure even in our hands. My parents have made certain there's no turning back or even a slim chance of winning Galen. I'm as trapped as the Maffeians are.

Nine

Friday night, Amaya lay in bed and reflected on the past few days and evenings with Jason Carlisle. She had never responded to a man in such a way. Everything he said and did affected her—his smile, his touch, his voice, his character. He was all she needed and wanted. He was an ideal mate. How, she fretted, could she ever forget or replace him? Yet she was leaving soon and might never see him again. She wished she could tell him the truth about herself and ask him to return home with her; but she couldn't because the shock could destroy their relationship. He had made it clear to her that he found her desirable, but they were worlds—galaxies—apart.

Monday afternoon, he had taken her and Avi to AstroWorld, where they enjoyed numerous rides that included a log flume, a freefall, Thunder River, the Batman "escape," and several roller coasters, including the thrilling Texas Cyclone. Those adventures had been stimulating, often stealing her breath and allowing her to snuggle or be thrown into contact with Jason many times. They had watched entertaining shows, seen all kinds of sights. Jason had purchased her a souvenir: a miniature replica of the largest roller coaster.

That evening, Andrea and Nigel had joined them for dinner in a fine restaurant and then the ballet. The performance of *Swan Lake* had included lovely costumes and music, talented dancers . . . and a moment of panic when Jason asked Amaya to check the program to see who had the lead parts. Fortunately Andrea had overheard his request and the Earth-born woman handled the matter.

The following day, Jason had taken everyone to a vintage plane show to observe stunts by old planes and "daredevils." Amaya especially savored the hot air balloon ride alone with Jason. When he had asked her to go on the ride, she had been so enthusiastic that Nigel had agreed. They had floated for an hour above the planet's surface in a heavenly setting. The sky was clear and blue and there was little wind. The balloon was an array of vivid colors, and the basket was cozy and romantic. They had stood close together as he pointed out sights. Amaya cuddled against his tall and hard body; Jason's arm was around her waist. If only a pilot hadn't been present, they could have stolen kisses and embraces and shared private words!

Afterward, the exhausted McKays were taken home to rest, and the Sangers stayed behind to keep them company while Jason took her and Avi to a Mexican restaurant. She managed to conceal her inability to read by asking him to order something unusual for her to try, which he did with delight. She even tried a margarita, which she discovered was tasty to her palate and potent to her head, and her reaction to the drink was amusing to her two companions. Jason had chuckled and said she could only have one or she might get "smashed." That was one time she didn't require explanation for a slang word.

Wednesday with Jason had been a great thrill for Amaya. When the excursion began, she almost panicked after he asked if she wanted to drive his car. She quickly refused by claiming the traffic was too congested and scary to suit her. Jason asked Avi the same question, and her best friend also refused in a hurry, saying she didn't "like alien traffic, either."

Jason laughed and said, "We do have lots of foreign tourists, but most know how to drive in American traffic or they take taxis. Are you sure you don't want to tag along with us?" he asked Avi. "Amaya's in for a treat. I'm going to let her test her hunger for flying. If she likes what I have scheduled for her today, maybe she'll stay here and go into training to be an astronaut."

Knowing of his plans and wanting to give them time alone, Avi said, "I'd be too terrified to watch, so it's best for me to stay away. I'll wait for you two at your home. You take good care of her, Jason, or my parents will kill all of us."

"Don't worry, she'll be perfectly safe. I wouldn't let her take chances of getting hurt. I think Amaya loves adventure and challenges as much as I do, so this is one experience she'll never forget."

At the Air Ace company, she was "briefed" on the T-34 plane and its weapons, on maneuvers, strategies, tactics, and safety. She donned a flight suit and helmet, was strapped into the front seat of a cockpit, and prepared for takeoff with the help of a pilot in the rear seat. The propeller was noisy and the small craft vibrated during and after leaving the ground. Amaya's head and stomach had danced with unfamiliar sensations and suspense. She had flown the plane as taught— climbing, diving, attacking, evading, and firing infra-red laser "bullets" on enemies in a simulated "dogfight." After she landed the craft, there was a "debriefing" where the two watched a video of her "mission," which became a treasured keepsake, one she was eager to show Galen upon her return home.

No flying experience was necessary for the ride, but Amaya grasped the instructions fast and carried them out with ease and skill. Jason and the instructor said she was a natural pilot and fighting "ace."

"Just as I thought," Jason added. "Astronaut material to the bone. Are you sure you don't want to enlist at Space Center Houston? Who knows, maybe you'd get to visit the moon one day?"

"You forget I have a job, one I love."

"You could give it up for a good reason, couldn't you?"

"Not any time soon. I have duties and responsibilities there. Could you give up your work to move to another place and another . . . career?"

"I never thought about it. Like you, I love what I do and I do it well."

He had said those last words without arrogance,

just pride and satisfaction. They returned to his villa and showed Avi the tape.

Afterward, they ate dinner at the McKays', chatted, and watched television for a while.

Thursday, Jason took them to the Astrodome for a baseball game. The sports arena was enormous and had countless brilliant lights and windows. It was packed with people who created a great deal of "racket." There was loud music to stir the viewers' blood and support for their chosen team. She had listened closely as Jason explained the game to her en route, and she had found the sport interesting and pleasant. She also found the Coke, popcorn, and peanuts appealing. As a souvenir, Jason purchased her a pennant, as he'd learned by now she enjoyed mementos.

Afterward, they stopped by a grocery store to purchase food and drinks for a "cookout" on Jason's porch overlooking the marina. Once more she had panicked when he asked her to "pop the potatoes in the microwave" and she didn't know how to use the device. Fortunately, Andrea and Avi did. While the three men and Grace chatted on the porch and Jason cooked steaks, Avi's mother had a chance to explain the meaning of "rug rats" and "hits the spot" and other sayings she had heard during the day. That event was delightful, but she had found herself wishing she was alone with the virile Earthling who aroused her passions to great heights.

She and Avi had spent the next day with Avi's grandparents and parents, relaxing and chatting. Tonight, Jason had taken everyone to a performance of *Cats* at the Theater Under The Stars. Amaya found that "Broadway-style production" to her liking and even talked about wanting to see it again one day.

Now she was having trouble getting to sleep because she was too aware of the reality that she had only one and a half days left on Earth and with Jason. The visit had passed too swiftly to suit her. There was so much more she wanted to see and do, all with the irresistible alien. She was glad Avi had promised to help her steal some time alone with him tomorrow.

"Jason is certainly spending a lot of time and money on the girls," Andrea remarked to Nigel, in the guest room next door. "I've never seen him so happy. But I'm not sure we should let them go off tomorrow. We'll be departing Sunday evening, so Saturday is our last full day here."

"They're young and full of energy, my love, so let them have fun one last day. At least Jason's diversions have kept Avi from worrying about Sebok and wanting to go home every day. Amaya seems rested and relaxed; she's been enjoying herself. As for Jason, he needed to be revived. We know what it's like to lose a son; and he lost a wife, too. I think our visit has been good for him; so does your mother."

"Perhaps too good. I'm a little concerned, Nigel; he and Amaya seem to be enjoying themselves and liking each other too much."

"What do you mean?"

"I think they're attracted to each other. Jason said it was possible for him to take off so much time because he works for himself, has only one case in progress, and has an employee doing most of the investigating and tailing for him. I believe he's doing it to spend time with Amaya."

Nigel's dimples showed as he grinned. "What's wrong with that?"

"We've leaving soon, so a relationship between them is impossible. After what he's been through, I don't want to see Jason get hurt again."

Nigel's smile vanished. "You think Amaya is being unfair to him?"

"No, I think Amaya likes Jason too much. She could get hurt, too, if they've fallen in love and neither realizes it. Or even if they do. Amaya knows they're from different worlds, but Jason doesn't."

"They're both good people, my love, so they'll be kind to each other. Amaya knows we're leaving, so she won't make it hard for him."

"You're right; Amaya is as gentle and intelligent as her mother. She would never injure another for brief pleasure. Now, let's go to bed. I'm sleepy."

"I'm not," Nigel murmured as he drew Andrea into his arms.

After lunch the following day, Avi strolled into her grandparents' backyard and sat down with the group to chat.

Andrea looked at her daughter's playful expression. "I thought you and Amaya were going for a ride with Jason," she said. "Didn't he arrive a while ago? I thought I heard a car leave just now."

"I decided I didn't want to go."

"They went together? Alone?"

"I didn't see anyone else in the vehicle," the brunette jested. In a serious tone, she added, "Amaya will be fine, so don't worry. She's a grown woman, Mother. They like each other and have fun together."

"She'll be fine, dear; Jason will take care of her," Grace told Andrea, who seemed unduly worried.

"I'm sure she will be, Mother. It's just that Nigel and I are responsible for her safety while she's in our care. Amaya isn't like other women Jason knows; she's lived in a very different environment. I would never forgive myself if anything happened to her; nor would her parents."

As Jason pressed the buttons on his car radio, he asked, "What kind of music do you like best, Amaya?"

She called a television commercial to mind. "Easy listening."

Jason grinned. "Me, too. I like most kinds, but that's my favorite for background when I'm talking with someone as fascinating as you."

"You are also fascinating. I've enjoyed my visit and your company. You have been an excellent . . . tour guide and . . . chauffeur."

Jason parked the car at Lake Houston and released his seatbelt. "I can't remember ever having more fun than I have with you," he told Amaya. "I hate for you to leave. I'm going to miss you, woman. I wish we had more time together. I hope this will remind you of me and the hours we spent together," he said as he took a box from the dashboard and gave it to her.

Amaya had viewed enough television to know how to open the jewelry box. She gazed at the gold watch inside and smiled in joy.

"I'll help you put it on," he offered so he could touch her.

Amaya released her safety belt as taught and turned toward him to extend her right wrist. When he asked if she wanted to remove the other "watch," she shook her head. "It stores information for me," she told him.

"It's unusual. What kind is it? What brand?"

"I don't know; it has no company name on it; it was a gift from my parents. The data inside is listed in secret symbols, in private code. Most of it has to do with my work, so I can't show you its functions."

"That's all right because they'd be Greek to me anyway."

Her heart speeded up for a minute as he edged closer to put the gold watch on her wrist. "It's perfect, but I have nothing for you."

Jason placed his arm along the top of the seat and made contact with her shoulder, and his knees nudged hers. His fingers toyed with a flaxen curl. "These past two weeks are all I need as a souvenir. But what I want most in the future is to spend the majority of the hours on that watch with you."

Amaya met his gaze. "I wish that was possible," she replied. "For now, it is not. I must return home and to work."

"Work was the biggest part of my life until I met you. Now, other things seem more important to me, like you and a future together. I know this is forward of me, Amaya, but our time is running out. Crazy as it might sound, I love you, woman, and I want to marry you."

Amaya leaned against the door behind her and stared at him. She needed the distance to clear her wits and regain her composure. She didn't know what to say and do. She couldn't stay here and marry him without telling him the truth; she couldn't imagine his reaction to such shocking news. Yet she couldn't stay even without telling him; if she had a baby that would expose her not only to Jason but also to Earthling doctors, their scientists, their rulers. She didn't want to speculate on what those people would do to her, him, and their child. They would have no privacy or freedom. They could become specimens, prisoners, monsters. She must not endanger herself, Jason, the Sanders, the McKays, and any unborn child. Yet . . .

"Maybe I've misread your feelings for me, but I hope not. If we don't explore this bond between us, we'll never know what could have been. I learned from Scott and Kathy's deaths that life can be short and cruel. Give us a chance to see if we can make it together. I believe we can be happy."

Amaya did, too. "I did not expect to hear such words today."

"And I didn't expect to say them, but they're true. Is there any way you can remain here longer or return soon? Could you fall in love with me?"

Even if they couldn't marry and have children, they could enjoy their love and passion for a while. Perhaps once they were as one, he would love her enough to go to her world to live. They needed time alone, time together, just the two of them. Could she sacrifice true love without searching for a way to make a life together possible? Both things were too rare to lose if the obstacles between them could be removed. A relationship on Earth could not work for security reasons but perhaps one could in her world if he got to know her well enough to go. "I cannot remain, but I will try to come back as soon as possible. I will speak with my parents and superior the moment I return to my world."

Jason ignored her last words as hope filled him. "What about my last question? Could you love me if given time to get to know me better?"

"I do not need to get to know you better to love you and want you. But what of your first mate? Is she out of your heart and mind?"

Jason realized that Amaya had a strange way of putting things sometimes but that only endeared her to him. "Kathy is in my past. She was a good wife and we had a comfortable marriage. She was a kind person and wonderful mother. I loved her, but I wasn't *in love* with her. We were high school sweethearts and we stayed together during college. We always planned to marry after graduation; our friends and family believed the same thing. During my senior year, I realized I had to break it off with her because I didn't love her as I should; I just hated to hurt her because we'd been together for so long. We were like a pair of old boots that had been comfortable for years but had finally worn out."

Jason lowered his arm and rested it across his lap. "Before I could find the kindest way to end our relationship, Kathy told me she was pregnant. I couldn't let her get an abortion or have the baby alone; it was my child, too. We got married during our last year in college. Scott, our son, was born the summer afterward. I had already signed up to become a Navy Seal, so I left for training. Later, Kathy and Scott joined me at the base. I'm not complaining; we had a nice life. After I finished my tour of duty, we moved to Dallas and I went to work as a P.I. It wasn't long before Kathy and Scott were killed. I was angry and depressed; God, I loved my son. I sold our home and moved in with my parents for a while to comfort them and to escape tormenting memories. After their deaths from food poisoning, I sold everything and took the money I collected from suing the negligent restaurant owners and moved to Houston for a fresh start, opened my own business to give me more challenges and distractions."

To be certain she understood his past, Jason clarified, "We didn't have a perfect marriage, Amaya, but it was a peaceful one; we gave Scott a good home, and I made the best of the situation. I didn't want to divorce Kathy because I wanted Scott to have a stable environment and *I* wanted to help raise my son. After my parents' deaths, the man I worked for—a close friend of mine—told me I had to accept all those tragedies and get on with my life. He said the best medicine was a new love and marriage, but I hadn't met anybody who tempted me to believe him until you came along. I don't want to lose you, too, Amaya. I need you. I love you. Give me a chance to prove myself to you."

"You don't need to prove yourself to me."

"Is there somebody special you left behind at home?"

"No, you're the first man I've loved, but this has all happened too quickly. We need time together to see if our bond is strong and true enough to share a future together. I have duties to honor. There will be many changes to make. There is more involved than resigning a job. We must make certain of our feelings before either of us gives up so much. I was born and raised and I live and work in an environment very different from yours. This is my first trip to . . . America; I did not know I was coming until three days prior to departure so I was not well prepared for this land and its people. There are many things I do not know about and countless things I have never seen or done before. I cannot tell you about my work, but it is what you would call, behind the scenes, undercover, in carefully controlled circumstances. I cannot tell you much about myself and my parents because our existences are a secret."

Jason knew those last statements were accurate because he had been unable to get *any* information about her from *any* source he had tried. It was almost as if Amaya Saar—and the Sangers—didn't exist! "If you stay longer or hurry back, I can show you all kinds of things and teach you everything you don't know. I could take off from work so we could visit deserts, mountains, beaches, and other wonders of America. We could go camping in Yellowstone, the Grand Canyon, the Black Hills, New England, and other places you haven't seen. Let's take a walk and talk about it."

"I would like that," Amaya said.

"So where does the name Saar come from?" Jason asked as they strolled.

"My parents. Isn't it the same here with children?"

"Yes, but what I meant is, what kind of name is it?"

"My family's name."

He chuckled. "What country is it from. It doesn't sound American."

"It isn't American, but I'm sorry I cannot reveal its origin. I realize you have told me many things about you and your life, but I cannot do the same. I know that sounds unfair, but I have been sworn to secrecy. How could you trust me to keep my word to you if I broke it to others?"

"I can accept you at face value, Amaya. When the time comes that you feel you can tell me everything about you, you will. Until that moment arrives, what I know about you for now is sufficient."

She halted and gazed at him to ask in a playful

manner, "How do you know I'm not a criminal or a terrible person? I could be a spy or an alien."

"If that were true, you wouldn't be here with the Sangers, my cousins. Are you a criminal or terrible person?" he jested.

"I am neither; that I swear to you. But I *am* different."

Jason lifted his hand and caressed her tawny cheek. He loved her sexy, almost sleepy-eyed expression. He adored her soft and silky honey blond hair. He yearned to kiss those full lips. He liked the pants suit that hugged her small waist and shapely hips and firm breasts as he craved to do. He noticed the way its fusion of colors matched her eyes. He felt himself being aroused by her beauty and sensuality, her nearness and mutual attraction to him. He knew his voice was husky when he finally said, "I know, that's why I find you so appealing and lovable."

Amaya leaned against the tall tree behind her and allowed her gaze to wander over his handsome features. "You are unlike all men I've met and known; you stand far above them."

Jason propped one palm against the bark over her head and leaned toward her. "That's how we should be, special and unique to each other." His other fingers drifted into her hair as he meshed their mouths. He felt Amaya's arms band his body and her lips respond in eagerness.

Any space between them vanished as they clung together in a passionate embrace. As they explored each other with eager kisses and caresses, Amaya yearned to surrender to these enticing desires. Her fingers moved along his strong back and shoulders as he stroked her jawline and the smooth column of her neck. They pulled her away from the pine far enough so his arms could encircle her and hold her tighter.

As his mouth trekked down her throat, he groaned in hunger and pleasure. "I love you, Amaya Saar, and I need you. Stay," he urged.

Her lips sampled his neck and her hands roved his torso. "I'll try, but I can't make promises today. I'll—"

"Ain't that a purty sight?" a cold voice sneered from a short distance away.

Jason and Amaya jerked apart and glanced toward the intruder. They noticed a weapon in the disheveled man's hand, pointing at them.

Jason pushed his love behind him. "What are you doing here, Speaks? I thought you were in jail."

"I'm free on bond."

"Your brain's fried on drugs or you wouldn't be acting so stupid."

Amaya wondered at the contradiction of "free" and "bond." How could someone's brain be "fried" if he were still alive? She watched and listened.

Larry Speaks eyed the beauty peeking from behind his target. "You stuck your nose in where it wasn't needed or wanted. You cost me plenty. My old lady's hiding and I can't find her. She took everything with her. Some of that shit's mine and I aim to git it back. Her, too, the bitch."

"If you hadn't beaten your wife, you wouldn't

have gotten into trouble. I was hired to get evidence for a restraining order and divorce. You had no call to beat her senseless."

"She won't press no charges against me; she knows she deserves every licking I gave her. That bitch ain't sending me to prison."

"She doesn't have to; there are other witnesses against you—your buddies who saw you beat her—when you weren't doing it in private."

"My friends'll keep their flaps shut if you stop egging 'em on and scaring 'em. Now, hey, you there, woman, sally your pretty hinny to me."

"Leave her out of this; I'm warning you, Speaks."

Larry ignored Jason's icy tone and look. "Do it, woman, or he's dead."

"I don't understand your order," Amaya said as she accessed their surly attacker and the perilous situation.

"She's foreign, Speaks, so she doesn't know all of our language."

"How about, git yourself over here or I'll kill your man?"

When Amaya started to obey the command, Jason grabbed her elbow. "No, he's crazy and dangerous," he said. "Let me deal with him."

"Don't worry," she whispered. "I can take care of myself and him."

"Let her go, Carlisle, or I'll shoot both of you. I'm mad and I'm antsy. You took my woman, so I'm taking yours. After I'm done with her, I might give her back, ain't no telling. Git your paws off her and send her over or she's a gonner."

To stall for time, Jason released Amaya's arm.

When he tried to inch closer as she walked forward, Larry shook the .357 magnum and ordered him to be still or he'd take her out faster than a jackrabbit could run.

Amaya pretended to be frightened, and obeyed him. As she approached him, his gaze flickered over her from head to feet. She waited until he partially imprisoned her before him with an arm spanning her torso between her neck and breasts. After he focused his attention on Jason, she reacted with skill and speed that astonished both men. Her hands seized his wrist and, as she whirled around, they twisted his arm and she tossed him to the ground on his back. She jammed her knee into his vulnerable abdomen, the action stealing his breath. She used her forearm to knock the heavy weapon from his loosened grasp. He wriggled and grappled to get free and to attack.

Jason reached them and yelled, "I'll take him! Run!"

As her love pulled her away by the arm, Larry rolled free and grabbed the large pistol. Amaya shoved Jason aside and gave Larry's hand an agile and powerful kick that sent the weapon flying away again. She saw Jason leap on the man and watched the two scuffle for a few minutes. It didn't take long for Jason to disable his winded opponent.

With Larry's arm pinned behind his back, Jason told the female, "Get me my handcuffs out of the glove compartment." He noted how Amaya hesitated and looked confused for a moment or two.

As soon as her microchip translated his words,

Amaya rushed to the vehicle and obeyed his request. She returned and passed them to him.

"Thanks. I'll cuff him to this tree and call the police."

"Why?"

"He's a criminal. He broke the law, tried to kill us. He'll be arrested again. This time, he won't get out on bond."

They left the man secured to a pine and walked to Jason's car.

There, Amaya asked, "Will the . . . police ask us questions and take us to their complex?"

"Yes, they'll have to make a report and take him in. We'll have to give statements and sign them. Why?" he queried her apparent worry.

Amaya knew she could not read a "statement and sign" it. "I should not get involved in problems here. I must return to the McKays before the authorities arrive. It will look suspicious if I do not tell them who I am and answer their questions, and I cannot; I must not. If I get into trouble or my superiors learn of my peril, I won't be allowed to return to America and the Sangers won't allow me to be alone with you again before departure time."

"You're right. I don't want to anger or worry the others or get you into trouble." On the other hand, he reasoned, a witness would have to hang around to testify against Speaks . . . No, that was selfish. "Take my car and go home. I'll join you there as soon as I finish with the police."

"I can't drive," she admitted.

Jason stared at her. "You *what*?"

"I cannot drive a vehicle like this. It isn't far and

I know the way. I watched our course en route. I'll walk to their dwelling. This is our secret."

"It's two miles away and going alone could be dangerous."

"It is a short and easy walk, and I can defend myself."

"I guess you proved that minutes ago. But I—"

Jason's cellular phone rang. "Hello . . . I understand . . . Of course you have to take care of her . . . Don't worry, I'll cover for you tonight. I'll be there as soon as I turn Larry Speaks over to the cops. They let the bas— snake out on bail and he just attacked me. I was about to give them a call to come fetch him."

Amaya listened to the brief conversation and knew a conflict had arisen. After he hung up, Jason explained that his employee had a family emergency and he had to relieve him on a surveillance job.

"This couldn't be worse timing; tomorrow is our only day left. It can't be helped, Amaya; this case is in its final days and our target is making careless slips. I have to go watch him. I'm sorry."

"I understand; you must do your duty; it would be the same with me. We'll see each other tomorrow."

"I'll take care of this matter and not involve you." *I hope.* "Maybe Speaks will go for a trade: an assault on me instead of two attempted murder charges if he doesn't mention you were present. If he refuses, you'll be gone by Monday morning and can't be brought in for questioning. If necessary to keep you out of it, I'll drop the charges against Speaks; he's the kind to get himself into trouble again. Besides, he was carrying a weapon. Don't worry; it'll be fine. You watch yourself on the way home. Be alert and careful."

"I will, and thank you."

"You're back early. Where's Jason?" Avi asked as she let her friend inside her grandparents' home, peeked out front, and closed the door.

"He had work to do. I'll tell you about it later. Where are the others?"

"Outside. I came in to get something to drink. Do you want anything?"

"Yes, I'm thirsty." Amaya sipped the cola drink Avi handed to her.

"Pralu, tell me what happened between you two. I"m as nervous as an *espree* in a chamber filled with *scarfelli."*

Amaya glanced toward the patio doors and whispered, "Later, when we're alone. Everything is fine with us."

"From that glow in your eyes, I have no doubt it is," Avi quipped.

"Your cousin is wonderful, splendid, a man bigger than the stars."

"Pralu, you're in love with him! Does he love you?"

"Yes, but so much stands between us. You must help me get away for a while tomorrow to say goodbye in private."

"Don't worry, we'll think of something. Let's go

visit with the others now so they won't have an excuse to refuse our request in the morning."

* * *

In the borrowed condo the following day at noon, Jason came to visit before heading into Houston for a surveillance chore. "I'll be tied up for most of the afternoon, but I'll be back to see you. What time is your flight?"

Amaya realized she couldn't tell him the truth about their schedule or they would be exposed. "We depart at midnight," she was forced to lie, when six o'clock was their last hour on Earth. By the time he discovered she had deceived him, they would be gone and he'd have no way to locate her. She would get Avi to teach her how to use the telephone so she could leave an explanatory message on his answering machine; she would tell him goodbye was too hard to say in person and she'd return as soon as possible.

"Good, that gives me time to finish this job or be replaced. I'll be here at eight o'clock or see you at the airport, even if I have to put this case on hold. That'll give us four hours together, if you don't change your mind."

"I do not want to leave you, Jason, but I must. It will be good for us to have time and distance to test our feelings."

Jason pulled her into his arms and held her tight for a moment. "I'm just afraid I'll lose you forever if you leave. How can we test our feelings and get closer if we're separated? We can't even call or write."

"I know, but I must see my family. I must take care of my job. I'll have to get a long leave so I can return. Besides, the Sangers wouldn't allow me to stay behind."

"You're a grown woman, Amaya; how could Nigel stop you?"

"I'm in their charge; I vowed to my parents to obey them. I don't want to cause trouble between them; they're best friends."

"Your parents and boss will understand if you stay for love."

"I can't explain why today, but it's not that simple, Jason."

"Nothing worthwhile is ever simple, Amaya. Stay, please."

"I promise you I will think about it all day," she had to reply.

"That's a start. I'll see you tonight."

"I also promise to return as soon as possible if I can't remain here."

"That's better than a final goodbye. I love you, remember that today."

"I will, and I love you."

They shared a bittersweet kiss and parted.

"I'd better leave before somebody comes to check on us or my suspect skips out on me. Think about us before you make your final decision."

"I will," she vowed, but knew she couldn't stay this time.

"They've been over there alone for a long time,

Nigel," Andrea said to her husband. "I'm worried about them."

"You heard Avi; let them have a last visit together. We're leaving soon, so we should join your parents outside and do our own final visiting."

"I just don't want either of them getting any wild ideas."

Nigel stroked his wife's auburn hair. "Like what, my love?"

"Like Jason talking Amaya into staying behind or her revealing things about herself to him. Love and desire can make one act impulsive at times."

"They're adults, Andrea, and they're both intelligent. They wouldn't behave rashly. They've only known each other for two weeks."

Andrea's worries were not assuaged by his words because she knew how powerful and persuasive love could be. "Have you checked in with the *Aerostar* yet about our departure? Has there been any news from them or Varian since you contacted the ship two days ago?"

"No. I'll do it from upstairs, then join you outside."

"Come in, sir; I wanted to have a few words with you," Amaya said as she let Nigel into the apartment she and Avi were using.

"I saw Jason leave, so I thought we should speak alone. You two have been spending a great deal of time together; now, this private visit. Is there something Andrea and I should know, if you want to discuss it?"

"Is it possible for us to remain here another week or so?"

Nigel shook his head of dark brown curls and his chocolate gaze sent her a sympathetic expression. "I'm afraid not, Amaya. The planets are moving out of alignment and it would make our return voyage too long."

Before he could continue his explanation, she reasoned, "If we use starlight speed, it won't add too much time to our schedule."

"The misalignments of a delayed departure will lengthen our voyage too much, Amaya. Even at starlight speed, we couldn't make up lost time. The ship is on standby now. All preparations have been made, and the staff's data-gathering mission is completed. We can't ask them to orbit up there with nothing to do so we can extend our visit. Even more important, staying cloaked much longer will be a reckless drain on our power system. We can't risk losing our shield and being detected by their radar. Even if they didn't know we're an alien vessel, each country would suspect another of an imminent attack or of spying with some new weapon or satellite system. We must not provoke trouble or fear."

"But we'll have to lower our shield for us to transport aboard."

"Correct, and there's only one window to use any time soon: it's at six o'clock as I told you last night. A short intrusion on Earth's magnetosphere by a quasar will mask our presence. We must take advantage of it."

"That's our only safe opening in the near future?"

"Yes, so we must go. Your father has an assignment waiting for you, and we've both used up our leave time. We're Star Fleet officers and we have our duties to perform at home. Personal desires can't intrude; I'm sorry."

"You spoke to my father? How? When? What did he say?"

"I received his coded message earlier; it's an important mission, and you've been eager to receive one. I'm needed there, too, so I can't prolong our stay. I'm sorry because it's obvious you and Jason have gotten close." *I can't reveal the problems at home and alarm you three women when we're too far away to help. I don't want Andrea to worry about Thaine's safety or Avi to fret about Sebok's or you to panic over your family's, especially your father's with that replica on the loose. Varian needs me there for help and advice; our world is being attacked by a powerful and cunning force. If I had known about this trouble, we'd be under way right now.* "This request does have to do with Jason Carlisle, right?"

"Yes. I want to stay to get to know him better. I've never met anyone like him. We're very compatible, but we need more time."

"I can't leave you here, Amaya, so please don't make that request. It's impossible and dangerous to let you stay. If trouble arose, you'd have no protection or means of escape. It's also too early to risk exposing the truth to Jason, even if you two are in love. Being from another country is one thing, but from another galaxy and civilization is quite another. I know from experience with Andrea, Jana, and others taken to our world—it's difficult to accept and adjust. To push that kind of revelation too fast could destroy any relationship you have in progress. I believe it's easier for a female to change and adjust than for a male. Jason Carlisle is a good and strong man, but this is too soon to tell him you're an alien. You do need time with him to test and strengthen your bond before any commitment decision is made, but that's not possible at this date. Maybe you can return after your impending mission is finished."

Amaya knew she couldn't argue against his logic and intelligence. "I hope so because this relationship is important to me and to him."

"I can see it is," Nigel said. "But give it time, Amaya, that's what your parents would advise. You hardly know Jason; and a life here with him would be difficult, if not impossible. It would certainly be hazardous for you, him, and your children. You need time, distance, and a clear head to assess the obstacles facing such a union. Wait and see how you feel after you're separated. See how *he* feels when you return. I'll speak with Varian and Jana and help you plan another visit."

"Thank you, sir; that's very kind of you. I'll prepare my things for departure and join you soon. I'd like to be alone for a while."

"I understand. Is Jason coming by later to say goodbye again?"

"We will be gone when he returns at eight. I gave him the wrong time, so we wouldn't be exposed here or at the airport."

"That was smart of you. Take the time you need, then join us."

* * *

At five o'clock, Nigel stared at his distraught daughter who had summoned him outside to talk in private. "What do you mean Amaya's gone?" he asked. "The taxi is en route and we have to depart."

"I"m sorry, Father, but she isn't there. She left a message for us and one for her parents in the correspondence device. You told me to leave her alone following your talk with her, so I obeyed. She's gone."

"That's strange. We were sitting outside for most of the afternoon, Avi, and I didn't hear a vehicle approach or depart. Why would she go off with Jason to say goodbye when she knows what our schedule is? She should have returned by now. What if something happened to her?"

Avi had no choice except to disclose the truth. "It didn't, Father, not how you mean. She's decided to stay here with Jason and—"

"She *what*?" Nigel interrupted in astonishment and dismay.

"Listen to her message to us; it explains everything."

Nigel took the audio-visual unit and played Amaya Saar's news. "I can't believe she would do this. It's too dangerous. We have to locate her and change her mind. Did you know she was planning this defiance?"

"No, sir, and I would have spoken against such

wild plans. She isn't prepared for staying here, not even with my grandparents or my cousin. What are we going to do, Father? Time is so short."

"Give me the key to that place and send your mother over to join me. Don't worry your grandparents. Tell them we're handling private business by telephone. We'll try to find Jason and convince him to return her."

After Andrea joined her husband in the other condo and heard the grim account, she paled and said, "Varian and Jana will be furious. We can't leave her behind, Nigel; we must find her."

"Call Jason's place and see if they're there."

Andrea tried, but no one responded, not even the answering machine. "What are we going to do?"

"If Jason and Amaya want to hide from us, they can and will. Even if we missed our only departure window, we might not locate them."

"You aren't saying we'll leave without her, are you?"

"We have no choice. Varian wouldn't want us to miss the window and remain here. Amaya said she'd rendezvous with us at your parents' home next year. We must leave on time."

"How will I ever explain this to Jana and earn her forgiveness?"

"Jana will understand we had no choice. We have to hope and believe Amaya will be safe with your cousin . . . There's the taxi's horn. I'm sorry, my love, we have to go without her."

"What about her career? Her rank? Her assignment?"

"Obviously they don't mean as much to her as Jason does." *If I had revealed the truth to her, Amaya would be anxious to get home!* "The best I can do is let Varian decide about sending a search team back for her."

"Do you really think she'll be all right here?"

"I hope so, Andrea." *Especially with some villite raiding Earth for slaves.*

Grace answered the bell to find Jason standing at the door. "How nice to see you, dear. I'm sorry you missed the young people's departure. Can you join us for supper? We're eating late this evening."

"They're gone? When? I thought their flight was at midnight."

"No, at six; they left about five-thirty. It was a rush after Amaya decided to stay behind."

"Amaya didn't leave with them? Where is she? Still next door?"

"No, we assumed she was with you," Grace said with a smile. "I must say, Nigel and Andrea were miffed with you two for doing things this way. You should have spoken with them first, dear, so they wouldn't worry."

"I don't know what you mean, Aunt Grace. I didn't know she was staying. I came to tell her goodbye and see her off at the airport."

"Oh, my," the older woman murmured and tapped her lips with her fingers. "From what Andrea said, she thinks Amaya is with you. She asked me to look out for her if she returned here. Where do you suppose she is?"

Excitement filled Jason. "Perhaps at my place waiting for me. I hope so," he said to eliminate the woman's worries, because he knew Amaya was not at his waterside villa, or hadn't been when he left there. "I love her, Aunt Grace, and I plan to marry her if she'll have me. That sly woman snatched me right out of my saddle before I could think twice. Since she stayed behind as I pleaded, that must mean she loves me, too."

Delighted by that news and Jason's mood, Grace hugged him and kissed his cheek. "I'm so happy for you; she's seems like such a nice girl. A pretty one, too. But she shouldn't have worried everyone this way."

"I'm sure she took off because she was afraid Nigel wouldn't let her stay without permission from her parents and superior. If they call, tell them not to worry; I promise I'll take very good care of Miss Amaya Saar."

Ten

In a hotel room in Houston, Jason closed the door behind him and locked it. He gazed at Amaya and grinned. "This is a wonderful surprise, woman. I was going to track you down tomorrow when that taxi driver who picked you up returned to work; he's off-duty today and couldn't be reached. For a nice tip, he would have told me where he brought you; then I could've wormed your room number from the clerk. I'm surprised Nigel and Andrea didn't search for you and force you to leave with them."

"They didn't have time; they had a schedule to keep, and I took precautions. I am here under your name."

Jason chuckled, then warmed at that thought. "Nigel is smart enough to ask for Amaya Saar or Amaya Carlisle, so he would have found you with a little investigative work and given you a hard time. I'm glad he didn't."

"He would not think of me taking a taxi or coming to a hotel alone."

"How did you do this? I mean, how did you get away from them?"

"I spoke with Nigel and he said it was impossible for me to stay behind. He was right, but I felt compelled to defy his orders, and I will handle any repercussions later." From things she had learned from television, Amaya related her cunning plot. "I used the telephone to call the operator; I told her I was blind and couldn't see the dial, so she connected me with the taxi. I sneaked out and met the driver at the gate. I asked him to bring me to a nice hotel. I wrapped my hand in a bandage and told the man I could not sign the paper because of my injury. I told him I was here to see a doctor at the Texas Medical Center. He did everything for me. The man who guided me to these chambers showed me how to obtain food using the telephone. I have been resting and watching television while I waited for you to contact me. I tried to leave you a message yesterday but your unit was malfunctioning. I tried again today and it was repaired."

"I was on cloud nine after I heard that message. For some stupid reason, I forgot to reset my machine after I collected my previous messages. I got here as fast as I could without getting six speeding tickets."

"So, they did leave without me; I presumed they would."

"Yes, they're gone."

"My father might come or send someone after me. I gave him my word to obey; I have never broken it before now."

"I'm sorry it was necessary and I hope he'll understand after you explain things. I told Aunt Grace to tell everyone not to worry, that I'd take good care of you. I'm sure Andrea will phone home to check on you."

"Once they depart, communication is not possible, but a search team could arrive soon."

"Why don't we go to my beach house on Galveston Island. It isn't listed under my real name so we couldn't be tracked there. That's the only way I can have privacy and keep men like Larry Speaks away. We'll let Aunt Grace know you're safe, in case Andrea does find a way to call her mother."

"Can you take so much time off from your work?"

"Why not? You did it for me. And I just hired another detective."

"For how long?"

"We'll take it one day at a time. Does that suit you?"

Amaya's eyes glowed with pleasure. "That suits me very much."

Jasond caressed her cheek, "Why did you change your mind?" he asked. He needed to hear those words from her.

Amaya glued her gaze to his. "You asked me to take a chance with you, and I have never been a coward. I've always enjoyed challenges and adventures. Love and commitment are surely the biggest ones of all. Besides, I will have you to guide, teach, and protect me, so what harm could come to me?" *In one short year? By then, I hope you will know and love me enough to accept the truth and will leave your world for mine. If not, we must part forever because I cannot stay and risk endangering us.*

"I would never let any harm come to you, Amaya.

I love you. I'll make certain you're never sorry you stayed and gave us this chance."

Sunlight filtering through mesh curtains cast a soft glow in the secluded and cozy room, creating a romantic and seductive mood that teased at their senses and aroused their desires.

"You're an amazing woman, Amaya Saar."

She smiled at him. "You're also amazing, Jason Carlisle."

His fingers stroked her cheek. "We'll be happy together; I promise."

Amaya nuzzled her face against his hand. "Yes, we will be."

"I'm not scared often, woman, but when you said you had to leave, my gut knotted with it. I'm glad you changed your mind."

She toyed with the collar of his shirt. "So am I."

Jason's tender gaze roamed her arresting features as he wondered if this was the time and place to make love to her for the first time. He needed her badly but didn't want to frighten her with premature overtures. All he could do was hold her and kiss her and see how she responded.

Amaya was thinking along the same line and came to a matching decision. Now that she had him alone, she could begin to prove to him they were perfect for each other. Perfect, she fretted, except for one major problem. She must reveal how wonderful life could be for them as lovers and mates, so fulfilling that he would make the sacrifice necessary for them to remain together. Until then, she must deceive him about her origins.

"I'm lucky I was in town during your visit because some cases take me all over the place. I'm convinced destiny threw us together that day."

"You believe strongly in fate?"

"Yep. Good or bad, everybody has one."

"Ours is good."

"You're right about that. Do you really understand how much I love you and need you? Do you realize how bad it would be to lose you?"

"If you feel as I do, yes. I love you and need you, too."

"Do you want me and need me in every way?"

Amaya smiled and nodded.

"Do you want to make love with me here and now?"

"Yes, here, now. But I have no birth control. Do you take injections?"

He hadn't heard of shots for men but they must be available where she lived. "No, but I have a condom in my wallet. I bought a pack last week hoping we could get this close."

Amaya had been told about the Earthlings' various methods to prevent unwanted pregnancies and knew they were efficient, though primitive compared to the use of *Liex* injections. "That is good because this is not the time to mate to produce a child." *For reasons you can't imagine.*

Jason grinned, again amused by her unusual way of speaking. He took her hand and guided her toward the bed. "One day, it will be if I can persuade you to marry me; and I'm going to do that every chance I get. I'm not looking to replace

Now, for the first time...

You can find Janelle Taylor, Shannon Drake, Rosanne Bittner, Sylvie Sommerfield, Penelope Neri, Phoebe Conn, Bobbi Smith, and the rest of today's most popular, bestselling authors

...All in one brand-new club!

Introducing KENSINGTON CHOICE,
the new Zebra/Pinnacle service that delivers the best
new historical romances direct to your home,
at a significant discount off the publisher's prices.

As your introduction, we invite you to accept 4 FREE BOOKS worth up to $23.96

details inside...

We've got your authors!

If you seek out the latest historical romances by today's bestselling authors, our new reader's service, KENSINGTON CHOICE, is the club for you.

KENSINGTON CHOICE is the only club where you can find authors like Janelle Taylor, Shannon Drake, Rosanne Bittner, Sylvie Sommerfield, Penelope Neri and Phoebe Conn all in one place...

...and the only service that will deliver their romances direct to your home as soon as they are published—even before they reach the bookstores.

KENSINGTON CHOICE is also the only service that will give you a substantial guaranteed discount off the publisher's prices on every one of those romances.

That's right: Every month, the Editors at Zebra and Pinnacle select four of the newest novels by our bestselling authors and rush them straight to you, usually *before they reach the bookstores*. The publisher's prices for these romances range from $4.99 to $5.99—but they are always yours for the guaranteed low price of just *$3.95!*

That means you'll always save over $1.00...often as much as *$2.00*...off the publisher's prices on every new novel you get from KENSINGTON CHOICE!

All books are sent on a 10-day free examination basis, and there is no minimum number of books to buy. (A postage and handling charge of $1.50 is added to each shipment.)

As your introduction to the convenience and value of this new service, we invite you to accept

4 BOOKS FREE

The 4 books, worth up to $23.96, are our welcoming gift. You pay only $1 to help cover postage and handling.

To start your subscription to KENSINGTON CHOICE and receive your introductory package of 4 FREE romances, detach and mail the postpaid card at right *today*.

We have 4 FREE BOOKS for you
as your introduction to
KENSINGTON CHOICE
To get your FREE BOOKS, worth
up to $23.96, mail the card below.

FREE BOOK CERTIFICATE

As my introduction to your new KENSINGTON CHOICE reader's service, please send me 4 FREE historical romances (worth up to $23.96), billing me just $1 to help cover postage and handling. As a KENSINGTON CHOICE subscriber, I will then receive 4 brand-new romances to preview each month for 10 days FREE. I can return any books I decide not to keep and owe nothing. The publisher's prices for the KENSINGTON CHOICE romances range from $4.99 to $5.99, but as a subscriber I will be entitled to get them for just $3.95 per book or $15.80 for all four titles. There is no minimum number of books to buy, and I can cancel my subscription at any time. A $1.50 postage and handling charge is added to each shipment.

Name _____

Address _____ Apt. _____

City _____ State _____ Zip _____

Telephone ( ) _____

Signature _____

(If under 18, parent or guardian must sign)

Subscription subject to acceptance. Terms and prices subject to change.

KC1094

Scott, but I do want another child, children, when the time is right for both of us."

"Before that day arrives, we need to explore each other and ourselves. No child should enter a union where no strong and special bond exists. We must have our relationship in good control before we expand it."

"You're a smart woman, Amaya; we're going to be a perfect match."

"Yes, we are. That is why I stayed."

Jason pulled her into his eager arms and sealed their mouths. He savored her sweet taste and response. He kissed almost every inch of her face and neck until he could wait no longer to see the rest of her. When he grasped the hem of her tunic top, a joyful Amaya lifted her arms for him to pull it over her head. She watched him place it on a nearby chair. He knelt, removed her shoes, and set them aside. He grasped the waistband of her leggings and eased them over her hips, down sleek limbs, and off her feet. For now, he left on her lacy bra and panties to avoid making her nervous. After standing, he plunged his fingers into the long strands of her flaxen mane and spread them around her bare shoulders where they caressed her tawny flesh.

He stared into her multicolored eyes and smiled, "Your hair is the shade of ripened wheat but as soft as cotton," he said as he scooped her into his arms, swung her around once as he laughed in elation, and sat her on the bed. "We'll take this slow and easy; we have all the time we want."

Before he could rise and undress, Amaya clasped

his head between her hands and kissed him deeply. As her tongue played with his, she relaxed backward and they sank to the bed with him half atop her. They kissed many times as their hands trekked in several directions to caress each other. Wonderful sensations flooded their bodies and enflamed them.

Jason's fingers unfastened her bra and discarded the obstacle. His lips roved down her neck and kissed both breasts. She closed her eyes and moaned in delight as his tongue and teeth gently tantalized them. He shifted to her side and worked her panties off with her assistance. As his mouth continued to titillate her firm breasts, one hand wandered over her abdomen, hips, and thighs with light and sensuous strokes. When he lifted his head to kiss her, he gazed into her lovely face for a moment. Her large and expressive eyes seemed to engulf him. Though she was naked, she didn't appear to be embarrassed by her exposed body; she seemed to trust him totally. His lips claimed hers again as his hand ventured toward her womanly region, where he used his skills and knowledge to the fullest.

Amaya's heart raced with excitement and her body flamed with desire. Her entire being was enchanted by this man. She realized he was something she wanted and needed more than returning home to family, friends, duty, and safety. For now, this is where she belonged and yearned to be; this was the man who must share her destiny and future. Surely, after they heard her explanation and met Jason, her family would concur. All she had to do was make certain she stayed alive and well and unexposed so they couldn't find fault with her shocking decision.

Jason stroked Amaya's cheek tenderly. He hadn't even consummated their love and already this was the best experience he had ever enjoyed with a woman. Never had he wanted any woman—including Kathy—as he did Amaya Saar. She had a way of making him feel on top of the world. He was happy, truly happy. He could envision a bright and successful future with her, a rich and full existence. His life would no longer be consumed by work and simple diversions and unrequited longings; he wanted to do and see many things with Amaya; he wanted to make discoveries with her and through her eyes. She had so much to offer him.

Amaya peeled off his pullover shirt. The muscles on his torso were like rolling hills that enticed her to caress them. His biceps and forearms bulged with strength and firmness. It was obvious he took excellent care of his body. He smelled clean and fresh and manly. Her fingers journeyed over a broad chest that displayed dark and curly hair. Her hands drifted down the shallow depression from his throat to his flat, tight abdomen. She played in the hollows between his neck and collarbones. He was magnificent, totally masculine. When he looked at her, starlight seemed to glitter in his blue gaze. When he touched her, splendor filled her. When he kissed her, her senses spun swift and wild like a *Spacer* out of control. He was sheer magic and bewitchment.

Amaya lifted adventurous hands to his handsome face and traced his chiseled features, pausing a moment on high and prominent cheekbones. Several times her forefinger rode a tiny canyon between his mouth and pleasing nose. Others wandered over his full lips. Her admiring gaze locked with his evocative one. "You're a splendid specimen, Jason Carlisle."

"You're the most beautiful and desirable woman I've ever known. I'm the luckiest man on Earth to have you." As he spoke in a voice made husky by great emotion, his hands covered her breasts and rubbed them with his palms. He leaned forward so his tongue make circles around the tingling peaks. He kissed and teethed the tips, causing her to quiver with delight. Her breathing quickened and a flush crept over her face and chest. He shifted his hands so the sides of his thumbs could stroke her nipples and cause them to tauten even more. His actions made her next few words come out in a near breathless murmur, after air caught briefly in her throat.

"I am the luckiest woman in the Universe to have you."

Jason's mouth took a tasty path up her neck and to her lips. He put all of the love and desire he felt for her into the kisses and caresses that ensued. His love was so overwhelming and his hunger so large, he didn't know if he could control himself very long after he entered her. But if he didn't arouse her to a lofty pinnacle first, she would miss soaring the heavens with him.

Amaya let him do what he willed. It was as if

he wanted to possess her fully, stake a claim on her, enthrall her to him. "Love me, love me," she urged as she writhed in need of him.

"I will, I do," he murmured in her ear.

Amaya savored every intoxicating kiss, titillating touch, every familiar and new sensation. Each countless pleasure was potent and stirring, passionate. For now, he was the only thought in her mind, the only reality in the world—his and hers. He was the man she loved and wanted, wanted tonight and forever, wanted in and out of bed. She yearned to share every facet of life and every emotion with him. Her hands roved his virile body and took delight in that journey. But she craved full contact with him, with nothing between them. Her fingers struggled with his belt buckle, a large western one. When she couldn't unfasten it, he did so. She worked at the button and zipper on his pants and succeeded with determination. She gripped the garment on both sides at his waist and shoved downward.

Jason caught her hint and parted them only for as long as it required to finish undressing. When he pulled her back into his arms, their mouths fused in an urgent kiss. Their hands reached unclad regions and conquered them in fervent splendor and expertise. For as long as they could endure blissful torment, they gave and took.

"I need you now."

"Me, too," he murmured against her lips. He slipped his manhood within her and she wrapped her legs around his hips as if to imprison him there. He knew how much she wanted him and this union as she matched his pace and movements. He watched her expressions as he took her and was lost in the wonder and beauty of their loving.

Both gave moans of delight as their bodies moved as one. Entwined together, they continued their search for ecstasy until they reached it together. They rested as they snuggled in each other's arms, sated as never before.

Amaya felt wonderful, relaxed and happy. She cuddled with Jason beneath a sheet to ward off the air conditioner's chill. She was soothed by his caresses and the kisses he pressed to her hair and skin. She was so calm and limp that she could drift off to sleep in these safe and romantic surroundings. If he ever made love to her better than he had tonight, the pleasure surely would be maddening. His kisses and caresses gave wings to fantasies about their future, to imagines of countless unions like this one. It was arousing just to envision them! *You've bewitched me, my alien lover. Whatever shall I do if I can't win you?* She jerked upward and listened, her instincts coming to full alert.

Jason also sat up, noted her reaction. "What's wrong?" he asked.

Amaya realized what had intruded on the cozy scene—voices and noises outside the room. "I heard others," she said.

"Just hotel guests and employees. No one's found us and nobody's going to take you away from me for as long as you want to stay." Amaya's head turned toward him and she smiled. He noticed a glow in her eyes and on her rosy cheeks, a glow of love and desire. Her responses to him caused joy to flood his heart, plans to fill his head, and hope to run in his veins. "Why don't we get showered and dressed, pack your things, collect mine at home, and get out of town fast?"

Amaya witnessed his roguish grin and possessive gaze. "Yes, let's escape to your secret place. There, you can teach me everything about you and your world." *During this next short and wondrous year. I pray it is only the beginning of our life together.*

As they prepared to leave the hotel, neither could imagine the fears and dangers looming ahead.

Far away on the capital planet of Rigel in the Maffei Galaxy, a much different episode was taking place. Supreme Commander Varian Saar greeted his wife as she entered their rented chambers in the ultra-modern tower, "You're working too hard, moonbeam. You look so tired and worried today," he observed. "Still no breakthrough with that mind block?"

"None, my love, but that isn't all that troubles me today." Despite the numerous burdens on his powerful shoulders, Jana had no choice except to add another heavy one. "There is a new medical problem, an unknown and lethal virus. We've had blood and tissue samples and deathly ill patients and corpses brought to Med Complex. We are alarmed and baffled. This evil virus attacks and destroys the body's defense and repair systems and makes its victim susceptible to many types of infection. Once it enters the bloodstream, it locks on to almost anything present in the plasma and forces its transporters to carry it everywhere and wreak havoc. Before this evil struck, we had immunities or treatments for every known germ and disease in our world. Now, it's as if those infected have protection against nothing, even simple things like cuts or breaks."

Varian focused a startled blue gaze on the distressed woman. "Are you saying we have a new disease in Maffei and no cure or treatment for it?"

"Yes, and it's proving even swifter and more lethal than the one years ago that evoked the *charl* laws and practice which brought me to your world and your side. Women like me eliminated that trouble for your people but this one is more ruthless; it strikes at both sexes and all ages." To help him understand the gravity of the matter, she tried to explain it in simple terms. "Normally, if a germ, bacteria, or virus enters the body, specialized blood cells gather to attack, defeat, and dispose of them; that isn't happening in these new cases. Normally, when that primary defense system fails, a backup one goes into action to deactivate and neutralize; that isn't happening, either. Simple things which should not harm a healthy person are injuring and killing those infected by this new virus. We have patients with chronic infections, carcinomas, lymphomas, cutaneous disorders, and pneumonia. They're suffering from fevers, weight loss, digestion problems, nodules, acute fatigue, and respiratory failure. They aren't responding to antibiotics, or any other treatment or therapy. Most have too many tumors or in places we can't treat with chemicals or lasers. Every new medication we try has side effects as destructive as the condition. Most of the corpses we autopsied were emaciated and covered with dark-blue plaques. It's horrible."

"But what is it, moonbeam? Where did it come from?"

"We haven't identified it or its origin yet. For now, we're calling it DISD: Destructive Immune System Disorder. So far, we have over a hundred diagnosed and confirmed cases, with all planets involved. We don't know how these patients contracted the virus, and we've made no connection between them. If it weren't for the blood and tissue sample tests, we wouldn't know there *was* a connection. Since we rarely have serious and unresponsive illnesses and strange deaths on Maffei, these cases stood out to the doctors and they alerted us. We've sent special med teams to test water, food, soil, air; and also examine family members of those infected."

Jana summerized for her husband. "All we know at this point is that it's newly arrived, it's alien to us, it's fast and lethal, it kills the cells that defend the body against illness and infection, and . . ." She took a deep breath before finishing with, "It appears to be mutating at a steady pace into a new strain. Without creating a panic, we're requesting information on any unusual deaths and illnesses. We must find a way to inhibit the virus's assault soon or we'll lose all of our current patients, and more may become infected. Unfortunately we researchers are hindered by a lack of knowledge and the swift pace of the virus. What panics me most is its ability to integrate and take control of the DNA. It alters and strengthens itself every hour; perhaps that's one reason we can't identify it and make progress against it. By the time we complete our tests and try a chemical or action on it, it has changed itself and defeats all of our attempts. We don't know what it is or how to stop it."

Varian clasped her hands in his to comfort her. "You and your team are the best scientists in the galaxy, moonbeam, so you'll succeed."

"We haven't succeeded so far with that mind block. It's still as much of a mystery as this rogue virus is." Jana paled and stared at her husband. "You don't think our *villite* could be responsible for this new horror?"

Varian grimaced. "Is it possible to *create* such a wicked thing?"

"A germ, bacterium, or virus can be *altered* by a skilled scientist. He would have to take one in existence somewhere, restructure it, and inject it here. To accomplish that evil feat, he would have to smuggle it through decontamination points for all cargoes and guests, which is nearly impossible with our safeguards. Or he would have to make it in our world, but it is also nearly impossible for a secret laboratory to exist here and needed supplies to be obtained. He would then have to find a clever way to get it into his victims without their awareness. It would have to work fast, be introduced in many places, and in a cunning manner that wouldn't be noticed until the virus was functioning perfectly and out of control."

"Doesn't that sound like what you've been describing to me?"

Dr. Jana Greyson Saar had come to that same conclusion as she spoke, so she nodded. "I think we should move with haste on those inquiries and tests before this virus spreads and threatens us with an epidemic. I'll alert Star Base Med Center and you alert the *Kadim* and Council. I also think you should assign Elite Squad members to our investigative teams in case a deeper or secret probe is required to obtain needed facts. I'll get you a list of the names and locations of the patients and deceased victims. See if the same vessel visited those planets within the last two months. If so, check out their cargoes, origination points, and crews. I don't have to tell you to order your team to secrecy; we don't want to risk alerting the source of this threat to our knowledge; nor do we want to create a panic. Let's learn who and what we're dealing with before we inform the citizens, and clues are lost in a resulting chaos. Unless it continues to spread before we can gather everyone infected; then, we can't be silent and wait. Oh, Varian, what else can go wrong?" she fretted.

Varian cuddled her against him on the *seata* and stroked her shiny hair that was as golden as one of Zamarra's two moons. "At least my duplicate hasn't made another appearance anywhere. I dread to learn what he's going to do next."

Jana nodded agreement. "I worry about Galen and Renah always being sent into every target sector, especially with this deadly virus running wild. I don't want anything to happen to either of them.

And I want Amaya home. I hate to think of her being on Earth and falling into that *villite's* clutches during one of his frequent raids."

Varian felt deceitful for not telling Jana about their daughter's shocking defiance, news he had received from Nigel after their departure yesterday. He had concurred with his best friend's decision to leave rather than waste precious time searching for Amaya who apparently didn't want to be found. He needed Nigel Sanger here with him, as things seemed to worsen every week. Perhaps, he hoped, their daughter was safer on Earth; it was a large planet and no one knew she was there to reveal her presence to their enemy. Soon, he must tell Jana the truth, but first he wanted her rested and calm, as she'd been working almost day and night since the many crises struck.

Varian snuggled her closer. "I want you to be extra careful working with these ill patients, contaminated bodies, and hazardous samples so you won't get infected," he urged. "I couldn't bear to lose you, moonbeam."

"We're taking every known precaution, my love, so don't worry. Our preliminary theory is that it has to enter the bloodstream before attacking. So far, it doesn't seem to be airborne or to be ingested with food or water; but we're studying those methods anyway."

"Then how does it enter the victims?"

"Probably through injection into a vein, lovemaking, birth from an infected mother, and mingling of blood in an open wound."

"Spreading is by accident then?"

"That's what we believe at this point. If we can locate and gather all victims who've had physical contact with our patients, we can prevent any further infection and we can do our best to cure or treat those who are ill. I knew it would be hard for patients to leave families behind, so we plan to bring them along. We have large and pleasant facilities to accommodate them. So far, everyone involved has agreed to this precaution. By doing it this way, we can avoid panic of exposure and prevent further infections by accident. It also aids our research to be able to observe them daily and test them frequently. We must stay on top of this rogue virus since it's mutating steadily."

"Did any of the patients mention having a recent injection?"

"No, and that has us baffled about its original entry points."

"The victims who died, could they have been the initial carriers?"

"Some infectors were, but most patients had no connection to them."

"What if all patients were injected then given memory blocks?"

"We thought of that, but psychological testing didn't confirm it."

"But it is possible they could have been injected without knowing it?"

"Yes, there are units that inject without notice. But with our strict drug laws, someone carrying such a device would be seized and questioned at check points. Unless . . ."

Varian released her and faced her. "Unless what?"

Jana locked her gaze with his. "Unless that person could get past them without inspection. Who fits into that category?" She noted how reluctant he was to ponder that question and respond, but he finally did.

"The *Kadim,* Council, *Avatars,* me, Nigel, Elite Squad members, and Security chiefs, *Kahala!* Please don't tell me my double was used to smuggle in a deadly virus! Or that he stole germs from Trilabs and altered them! How can I order an Elite Squad to question my presence at the infection sites during the last few months without appearing crazy?" he muttered. If only Amaya was home, his daughter could use innocent ways to ask those sources if they had seen her father recently. If only she were en route, he could delay the investigation and wait for her to handle it. But since she wasn't, he had to select another trustworthy person to carry out that assignment; perhaps Galen, with Renah's help. They both knew about the replica and Trilab's encroachment. He had to know if *he* was to blame, and he had to make certain *he* didn't continue to visit their thirteen planets to spread certain misery and death.

Jana waited until she had his attention again before she replied, "Almost as difficult as investigating yourself, how can you check out those other men without provoking trouble and suspicion and tormenting yourself?"

"I can't bring them in and use *Thorin* to get answers because they're all immune to truth serum. And even I don't possess that power; only the *Kadim* does. Draco would think I've gone mad if I even suggested it to him, friend or not."

"You have access to all files, including voyages and passenger lists. That's a safe start and will eliminate most of them, if not all."

Varian leveled a troubled gaze on his astute wife. "Is that what it's come to, moonbeam, suspecting and spying on friends and leaders?"

Jana caressed his face as she told him what he already knew, "If necessary, my love, because we're doomed if you do not unmask our foe."

Two days later on the *Galactic Wind*, Renah stood in Galen's loving embrace in his quarters before the impenetrable *transascreen*. She gazed into dark space beyond the starship as she listened to him relate the talk with his father. She could hardly believe she was involved in something so horrible, and with a man who should be her hated enemy. Surely her soul and fate were as dark as the setting outside, her trap deep and secure. Even if she dared to expose herself and her family, Varian Saar and his son would not rest until they were hunted down and slain. Yet how much longer could she continue to perform her duty when so many innocents were getting harmed and killed? If only she could flee, she mused, return home and cease her terrible roles, but, despite her wits and courage, she could not think of a safe escape plan. Even if she could get off this ship and elude her lover, there was no way she could get off that planet and out of Maffei, not until she was retrieved. That wouldn't happen until she completed her mission, and she couldn't ask her side to rescue her without a logical reason. If she did return home, they would only ask her to become involved in another aspect of their plot. If she refused and they realized her motive, they would probably order Galen's death for tempting her to defiance.

"You're very quiet tonight, my love." Galen exhibited his concern as he nuzzled the side of her head with his cheek. She was clasped against his body and was a perfect fit within that circle.

Renah lightly squeezed his fingers. She closed her silvery-gray eyes and took a deep breath. "I was thinking of all you just told me. A disease without a cure or treatment is too frightening to imagine and more so to be a reality. It's particularly horrible for children, babies, to be affected. Why can't it strike only adults who resist it better? I hate for little ones to suffer and die." *I never agreed to participate in such an insidious attack. I never agreed to help destroy planets and their inhabitants. Why did they have to alter things after the plan was in motion and I was trapped in it?*

"If there's any way possible, my mother and her team will solve that mystery. Our job is to help learn how the virus got here and who brought it to our world. I strongly hope it wasn't Father's impersonator; that would be hard for him to accept and could possibly create doubts about him in others who don't know him to be a man of honor. These attacks weigh heavy on him because he feels he's responsible for the safety of our people and leaders, and he can't seem to provide adequate protection. This rogue virus can't be battled with prowess, so he feels helpless. If the strategy goes as planned, those infected can be quarantined to prevent further spread. But what has Mother worried is how it mutates and integrates. And there's been no progress on dealing with that mind block. As soon as we finish our work on Balfae, we'll have to do that secret favor for my father."

Renah thought how ironic it was that she—the enemy—was being asked to search for *their* enemy, which told her how much she was trusted. It would be a waste of their time and energy because the replica wasn't to blame. That should ease Varian Saar's conscience, also Jana and Galen's. She wondered if she should report Varian's probe of their leaders knowing that would infuriate those powerful and rich men. She decided to ignore that fact to her side.

"This Balfae incident could be dangerous, but we'll resolve it."

No, my blinded lover, you will not; but I wish—

"There are so many obstacles hindering us from defeating this unknown enemy. If only he would reveal his identity and motive, we could find ways to work against him."

Those are facts you will learn after Maffei is crippled. Even if you knew such things today, you could not defeat them, not with the potent secrets and weapons they possess. "Perhaps those medical and Elite Squad teams will make valuable discoveries. We'll know as soon as they complete their tasks and your father sends us a report," which she knew Galen would share with her. "But if our enemy's vessel has cloaking ability, visits to the planets involved would remain hidden to them and to us. I hope it doesn't become necessary to reveal the virus's existence; a panic would surely result. Infected people would hide in fear of being held captive or eradicated to prevent an epidemic and we could never isolate all carriers of the rogue virus. I hope your mother is careful in her work so she won't fall prey to it. We must also be careful to avoid catching the illness."

Since Renah knew how the disease was being spread, she knew she and Galen were safe; so were his parents, unless Jana was careless and let contaminated blood mingle with hers during a laboratory accident. She decided she would not report the Maffeian's knowledge and actions to her family, or her loved ones might find paths around those barriers. She despised using a lethal disease even against enemies and was angry her family had resorted to such a black deed for revenge. If only she could give them clues on how to fight that threat, without exposing herself. What if . . .

"Galen, your mother said the virus is contracted through blood or blood products, and she mentioned lovemaking. What if that is how it was smuggled in, in the bodies of carriers? What if infected males or females passed it to others during sex and they, in turn, passed it to others?"

Galen released her and turned her to face him. "That's an interesting speculation! I'll tell Father to check out all sexual contacts of those who are sick and have died. Perhaps our *villite* has a way to keep his carriers from taking ill or dying; he's proven he's a genius with chemicals. Look what he's done with that mind block. It's a cunning idea."

"Don't tell your parents and friends I thought of it. I just received two commendations and, if my speculation becomes fact, they could award me another one. I don't want to create jealousy and resentment in others who might think I'm receiving too much attention and praise; so please tell your family and others it's *your* idea." She paused a moment before continuing softly. "Better still, cunningly imply it to your father and let *him* suggest it to your mother and her staff. That way, he will get the credit he needs badly in his eyes and in the eyes of others."

"That's generous of you, Renah, but it's a great honor to be the person who discovered the clue to end this madness."

"I know; that's why I want my love and future mate or his family to receive the credit. If your parents learn I thought of it, they would be compelled to be honest. I don't want more attention focused on me; it will steal our privacy for people to be looking at me—at us—all the time." *I'm sure my family is wondering why I didn't tell them the truth about those previous episodes. I wouldn't have been exposed to them if not for those public commendations! I hope they think it's only part of my ruse to get closer to these people or that I was acting to prevent my exposure.* She realized she had to keep herself less noticeable to both sides. "It also may alert the enemy to us. If he thinks we're too smart, he could endanger our lives or hinder our progress. Please, make this our secret. I'll reward you," she hinted as her hands caressed his virile body in a sensuous and seductive manner.

"If that's what you want," he conceded, mainly to protect her from harm by not becoming a target.

"*You* are what I want and need this moment," she said to cease the disturbing talk and to distract her nibblings of traitorous guilt.

"I need you, too, my love, at my side always."

Galen's lips sought hers and he kissed her with hunger. He had to protect her. If necessary, he would sacrifice his life to save hers. His fingers wandered into her short, thick hair to press her mouth more snugly against his and savored her taste. His heart thudded with joy to know she was his. He was inflamed by her response. His hands covered her concealed breasts and kneaded them into firm mounds with taut peaks.

Between caresses and kisses, they removed their boots and garments, then sank to the *sleeper.* The raw intensity of imminent danger gave their union a bittersweet urgency.

Galen's talented hands roamed her supple terrain, as did hers over his sleek and taut frame. Passion held them captive in its strong and demanding embrace. Thoughts of troubles left them so they could concentrate only on each other and this fiery bond. Their overtures became bolder as their tongues danced and a fierce yearning consumed them. Her soft hand fondled his manhood as his caressed her pulsing core. Their anticipation and suspense mounted.

Exquisite delight coursed through Renah's mind and body as she enticed him with words, movements, and noises to continue his actions. She writhed upon the *sleeper* and thought of nothing except him and what was taking place this moment. When she could endure no more wonderful foreplay, she coaxed him to enter her.

Galen did so with fervor. As they moved together, they quivered as they tried to retain self-control of themselves and make their lovemaking last as long as possible. He rolled to his back and guided her atop him while keeping their bodies joined. He moaned in pleasure as she rode him with eagerness. From time to time, she leaned forward to take and give a brief and fiery kiss. His hands stroked her breasts as he moved within her. After a while, he altered their positions again, lying atop her and driving wildly into her receptive body. He knew when her climactic trek began and he did all in his power to make it the best she had experienced.

With her legs locked around him, Renah held Galen tightly and matched his pace and pattern to give him the greatest thrill possible. She felt the pounding of his heart through his chest. Until cruel fate intervened and parted them, she would cherish every moment with her love, as memories would be all she could take with her after these bittersweet days.

When their blissful journey ended, they remained entwined as their bodies sought to return to normal. They nestled together as contentment wafted over them like a calm breeze. They didn't want to part but both knew she had to leave soon.

Finally Galen hugged her. "I love you, woman," he said, "and one day we won't have to sleep in separate quarters. I can hardly wait to keep you in my arms all night. You're the best thing that could happen to me."

"You're the best thing that could happen to me," she echoed. *And I wish I could keep you forever, Kahala, help me, for I do love and need you. My parents never imagined this would happen when they sent me here, and they would hate and punish me if they discovered my secret. There is no way I can have you, my love, without betraying them and causing their deaths.*

Galen wasn't a part of those wicked treacheries, she reasoned, so why must he pay with his life for his parents' and ancestors' crimes? How could she allow him to die? She couldn't and she wouldn't! Her betrayal would be enough suffering and punishment for the Saarian blood he carried. *So little time left together, several months at the most. I hate to imagine the look in your eyes when you learn who I am and what I've done. If things on Balfae don't go as my side planned or if an error is made elsewhere, I will be unvisored soon and you will hate me and curse me.*

The following afternoon, Galen, Renah, and his chosen security team began to make their way toward the enemy's campsite on one of Balfae's many islands. The entire planet consisted of various sizes and shapes of land surrounded by one enormous body of emerald water. Combined with the lush and verdant landscapes, the smallest planet of their star system resembled a green ball from high above it. Even the sand on the beaches and the lowest level of atmosphere had a pale-green cast. The ocean teamed with countless edible fish and, as with the isles, no large and ravenous predators dwelled there. Birds with colorful plumage and playful creatures with agile limbs lived in the trees, and several species of animals roamed and foraged on the ground. Nuts, berries, and fruits grew in abundance, as did assorted vegetables. It was a setting that was too tranquil and beautiful to be imperiled or misused.

Each island had a regional leader who governed for and reported to Balfae's *avatar,* who in turn did the same to the Supreme Council. *Avatar* Salazar's locale was far away on the largest and loveliest island where enough jungle had been cleared for a large city with gleaming towers and perfect climate. Pictures transmitted from a weather satellite had revealed an encampment of strangers on the only part ordinarily uninhabited by people, a place where exotic and rare species were kept for reproduction and preservation. Further study had shown that the intruders were constructing a permanent position, and weapons were in view. Salazar had suspected it could be the *nefariants'* base and had ordered his patrols to avoid that area. The planetary ruler had sent word about the trespassers to Star Base. In response, Supreme Commander Varian Saar had directed the *Galactic Wind* to investigate the mystery.

Galen's team had been deposited in the ocean

so they could approach unseen in an underwater craft. They landed in a location where their heat monitors hadn't exposed human presence. After submerging the craft to conceal it, he cautioned his team once more to "be alert and quiet. They could have surveillance units or guards between us and them. We want to get close enough to study them. With luck, we can capture the entire group, be they our targets or just bold *poachis*. Keep all weapons on stun mode; I want them alive." He had ordered Renah to stay in the rear for her protection.

The men slipped forward with skill and silence, Galen in the lead. They used trees and vegetation for concealment and stealth, along with scenery-blending green bodysuits and headgear. They made certain they didn't startle any animals or birds, whose noises could give away their presence. They arrived at a small clearing and halted to study it.

"We can't go around it," Galen whispered. "The jungle is too thick on both sides. This is a perfect guard and attack point."

"Why don't I go first?" Renah suggested. "If anyone's there, I will draw him out of hiding. He would not suspect a lone woman of being a threat. If there is only one enemy, I can overpower him. If there are more and I can't fight them, you can rescue me. It's the least risky measure."

Galen knew she was correct, but he hated to endanger her in the slightest. Yet he told himself he couldn't make his decision based on personal motives. She was a highly trained and skilled officer, and her idea was cunning. "Do it, but be careful," he instructed.

Renah removed her headgear and put it aside. She fluffed her short blond hair, then discarded her weapons' belt.

"What are you doing?" Galen queried her last action, his gaze wide.

"If I go in armed, I'll be suspicious. You tested me yourself, Chief Saar, so remember I'm qualified with hand-to-hand combat."

"You're right, but don't take any chances," he cautioned again. "Stay alert, men, so we'll be ready to move in a blink."

Renah mentally prepared herself to confront possible peril, because the enthralled Earthlings present didn't know she was on their side.

Eleven

Renah walked toward the clearing she must conquer, along with her fears. If she were slain, perhaps it would be justice for all she had done to these people of Maffei. If not, she must find clever ways to assist them without exposing herself to them or to her side. At least she could give them a fighting chance to defend themselves and their world. Without her aid, they could not survive.

She pretended to be on a casual stroll. If anyone intercepted her, she would claim she was there to check on animals and birds under Salazar's protection. In case sensors or weapons were implanted in the ground, she chose her steps with care. Her heartbeat was swift, but her expression concealed her fear. Her apprehension mounted as she neared the center of the hazard. Her senses were on full alert but they detected nothing to alarm her. She thought it odd that the invaders wouldn't post guards and would be so lax with security; it wasn't like her side to make such reckless errors. How could they not realize they would be sighted and challenged, since camouflage domes were not in place? She had been told that a secluded island on Balfae would be used as a base, yet it was obvious they were not attempting to hide. If there was a change, what, she mused, could it be and why?

Renah arrived at the end of the densely enclosed area. She halted, studied her surroundings, and waited. Nothing happened. She turned and signaled that she was safe and perceived no perils, but still she was tense and suspicious. She focused full attention to the path and jungle beyond her to be ready to sound a warning if she heard or saw anything. She didn't, until noises behind her caused her to whirl to check out the problem. Galen reached her side just as she turned. He did, too; both saw the other team members staggering, falling to the ground, and writhing in anguish. They had spread out in the opening for defense strategy and wandered into cunning traps.

As Galen started to go help them, Renah seized his arm. "No! It's the mushrooms they've stepped on! See how they're spewing forth spores. Don your *breather* fast before the wind brings them to us."

Galen obeyed, snatching one from the rear of his utility belt. He passed Renah's to her so she could do the same. "Is it safe now?" he asked.

Her voice clear through the filtering mask, she replied, "Yes, with these as protection. We must summon help. Soon the spores will release a toxin into their blood. *Carraficin* will neutralize it. We have it in sick bay. Be careful, my love, because those spores create hallucinations before they immobilize; your men may not recognize us and attack. We have to work fast. One of them fired his weapon by involuntary reflex. If it was heard, we'll have visitors soon."

"We have them now," Galen warned as he heard runners approaching. "I'll signal for help before they—"

"No! They could transport into that clearing while we're too busy to warn them about the mushrooms. Without treatment, they will bring certain death within hours. We have to protect our team until we can transport out. The spores died quickly after the chambers burst, except those in their bodies."

There was no time to discuss the matter as eight men came into view and headed straight for them. Renah and Galen managed to stun five before the group reached their position and jumped them. The men appeared unarmed and didn't return their fire, which was strange but fortunate. Two men attacked Galen and one leapt at Renah, costing both their weapons during the ensuing battle. The transmitter in Galen's hand also was knocked from his grasp.

Renah avoided the burly man's charge that sent her gun flying into nearby bushes, but she delivered a blow to his stomach as he passed her. She noticed his expression of anger and astonishment. A cold sneer twisted his mouth and chilled his glazed eyes. He edged closer as he studied her for strengths and weaknesses, and she did the same to him. He pulled a laser knife from his pocket, pressed a power button, and waved it before her line of vision to scare her, then came nearer and struck at her; but Renah ducked and tripped him, allowing her time to withdraw her own flashing blade. She knew his chemically controlled mind would give her the advantage if she stayed alert. Smiling to disarm him, she suddenly sliced out and wounded his forearm. Blood seeped from a searing injury. The man tried to use his greater size and strength to throw her off balance but only succeeded in obtaining another cut for his thwarted effort. No pain registered in his expression and reaction—and probably not in his enthralled mind—so she knew he would fight her to the death.

Galen was a blur of movements as he battled the other two assailants, his body nimble and strong, his instincts sharp. He used rapid and potent blows from fists and booted feet in defense and for attack. When one was knocked backward to the ground, he quickly focused all attention on the other. He broke a nose, bruised a laranyx, and pounded kidneys. As the Earthling collapsed to the ground, his revived companion charged. The two men struck the ground hard, and rolled upon it struggling to get the upper hand. Galen managed to render him senseless with a blow to his temple just as the other *nefariant* banded his chest from behind. Galen slammed his elbow into the man's stomach several times, seized his wrist, and whirled as he twisted it to flip him to the ground. With two rapid and forceful blows to the liver area, the Star Fleet officer's last opponent was disabled.

Almost at the same time, Renah tripped her man, gained a moment to retrieve her lost weapon, and stunned him with it. Her eyes sought Galen and took in his victories. She returned his broad smile of relief and pride.

Winded from his exertions but envigorated by their successes, he grinned as he said, "We make a good team, woman."

"Yes, we do," she agreed. Renah was suffused with new energy. It was exciting to be his partner in all areas. How she wished—

"Stand guard while I call for help and explain our situation."

Renah ordered the two conscious men to gather their fallen friends. After they were in a group, she held her weapon on them in warning while Galen retrieved his transmittor and carried out his task. While they awaited assistance, he kept watch for new trouble.

Soon, a medical team in protective masks and an additional unit of Security joined them. The injured team was taken to the ship for treatment and the larger unit—armed and wary—headed for the encampment which surely was aware of their impending peril and the Maffeians' presence. To provide additional power and support if needed, the *Galactic Wind* was repositioned and readied. Two members were left to guard the captives as Galen's unit advanced toward their target area, a suspiciously quiet one.

When they reached the location, everyone was shocked to discover not a single man was alive and all supplies and weapons were destroyed!

Galen strolled around the grim setting and wondered how fifty men could end their lives rather than be taken prisoner. He ordered a search of the camp but no clues were found. Two bodies were transported to the starship for examination; the others were disintegrated with a special laser. After their tasks were completed, they returned to the attack site to gather their prisoners.

There, Galen and the others were greeted by another shock.

"I'm sorry, Chief Saar; we couldn't stop them," one of the guards related. "We didn't realize what was coming. They huddled together, pressed buttons on their belts, and disintegrated themselves right in front of us."

Galen stared at the empty spot as he concluded they had been preprogrammed like robots to self-destruct. "Not a one was taken alive! Why? What are they hiding? How could he have such evil control over them?"

"I don't know, sir, but a suicide pact is crazy."

"There's nothing else to be done here except destroy that mushroom field. Make sure you blast every one out of existence. I don't want death to come to Balfaeians or any of the animals or birds."

Back aboard the *Galactic Wind* in Security Control, Galen and Renah made a report to his father.

Renah explained her knowledge of the lethal fungi alleging she had seen them on one of the near barren planets the *Rover* had visited years ago. "My parents and the other scientists aboard assumed, if other lifeforms existed there earlier, perhaps those deadly spores had exterminated them. After two crew members fell victim to them, our medical staff learned how to neutralize their effect. Everyone aboard was shown the ship's tape of our two losses so we wouldn't wander into the same peril. This time I recognized what was happening and knew what to do." From the Dhobis' computer files she had viewed during lessons, those words were accurate, and might really be the location from where the plants had come.

"That explains why no guards were posted," Galen surmised. "It's common practice to avoid bunching up in the open, so they reasoned some of our team would burst those mushrooms and the spores would get us all. They must have known to stay on the center path for safety. We're lucky Renah didn't get injured or killed when she was on the trail as our decoy."

"Even if I had noticed mushrooms growing there," she added, "I wouldn't have realized they were the same toxic type encountered long before. I don't recall which planet it was because the *Rover* visited so many. At least we learned today to be on alert for cunning tricks, and our team is recovering in sick bay."

Varian was cognizant of how close he had come to losing his son, Renah, and their team to the shadowy threat looming over their world. He would be grateful always to her for saving their lives. "You and your unit have earned more commendations, Galen. We don't know what those *fiendals* were plotting, but you and your forces prevented it."

Renah worried if she received a third commendation, news of her presence at the incident would reach the wrong ears. Since the mushrooms were not native to Maffei, the medical staff aboard the

Galactic Wind shouldn't have known how to treat the team in time to save their lives . . . "Sir, may I make a suggestion?" she requested.

"Yes, Renah, what is it?" Varian asked.

"I think it might be wise to postpone public news of our victory and awarding commendations to us. Those involved can be notified officially of a future announcement so they'll know their work is appreciated. If it appears to our *villite* that we're defeating his forces too many times and boasting of those victories to garner our people's loyalty and support, he could become more dangerous by determining to prove we're helpless against him. So far, he's made strikes on Darkar, Caguas, Zandia, and Balfae before we could sight or halt him. If we keep revealing his attacks, the inhabitants of other planets may doubt we can protect them and might panic. If his men didn't have time to report their imminent defeat this time, our exposing and flaunting it will enlighten him to our knowledge and strategies. It could provoke him to bolder moves. I believe he intended for us to locate that base and destroy it, or it would have been camouflaged and protected."

"Why would he want us to attack?" Varian questioned.

Renah explained her theory. "To make us believe we had found and destroyed his base when that isn't his real one; so we wouldn't think to search for the real one. Does that sound logical?"

"That would explain why those thralls were ordered to take their lives, to prevent dropping clues."

Galen concurred with his father's words and with Renah's speculation. "That means he has a base somewhere else, one concealed and guarded."

"Is there another island on Balfae that isn't inhabited by its people?" Renah asked. "He might believe that's the last place we would think to look."

Varian listened closely to her words, then smiled at both. "You have yourself a woman of superior skills, intelligence, and courage, Galen. I'm proud of you, Renah, and we would be honored to have you in our family if that is your choice."

"It will be if I can convince her, Father, and I'm trying my best," Galen admitted.

"Thank you, sir" was all Renah could say under the circumstances.

"Now, back to the matter at hand. Galen, before you leave orbit, get Commander Vaux to order a scan of the entire surface to check out Renah's idea. If she's right, I'll send another ship to join you for the assault; we don't want to risk them escaping from Balfae. If she's not, I'll order scans of the other planets; that beast and his men are hiding somewhere, close enough to keep spying and attacking us."

"We'll do our best, and I'll keep you informed of our progress."

"One final order: keep our actions a secret for now; I think Renah has a valid point. There's no need to provoke trouble by humiliating him before his followers. There's little more dangerous or unpredictable than someone who's been shamed or defied or rejected."

I wonder, Renah mused, *if you know how true those words are.*

Upon the Sangers return home five days later, Jana sat with Andrea and discussed her daughter's shocking behavior.

Jana played the message on the communications device before Andrea said in a soothing tone, "We both know how love and passion can take control of every thought and emotion and action."

"But Amaya was always so level-headed and obedient. I never suspected she would do anything like this. I could hardly believe it when Varian finally told me. How could she behave so rashly?"

Andrea's green eyes softened with sympathy, as did her voice. "You mean, how could she fall in love with an alien and remain in his world?"

Jana took a deep breath. "I understand your point; we did the same things long ago. But this is different."

Andrea pushed a wisp of auburn hair from her face before she clasped Jana's hand in hers. "How?" she asked her longtime friend.

Jana's eyes met the other woman's. "I have this terrible feeling that something is wrong. You remember, I mentioned my fears before you left for Earth. I also told Varian I didn't think it was a good idea for her to go. I was right."

"Are you afraid she's only caught up in adventure? Do you doubt they could fall in love so quickly?"

"If there's one thing I do know, it's that love has no timetable. I'm sure she does love your cousin; and I'm sure Jason loves her, from all you've told me about him being a good and honest man. He even sounds like the perfect choice for Amaya. What troubles me is this sudden reckless and impulsive streak. She's never been one to cast duty and rank aside for personal desires."

"We all have our weak moments, dear friend; we've surely had ours."

Tears glimmered in Jana's eyes. "I'm afraid for her, Andrea, really afraid, and I can't explain why. I just sense something bad is going to happen to her."

"Do you have a mental bond with her like Galen does?"

"No, I don't think so. I suppose it's maternal instinct."

"Do you blame me and Nigel for leaving her behind? Are you angry with us?"

"No, of course not. Please, don't blame yourself, either. If Amaya was determined to stay there, she would find a way no matter how long or hard you searched for her. Nigel did the right thing by departing, and he's needed here. Varian has been shouldering heavy responsibilities alone. I can only hope and pray Amaya remains safe until we can retrieve her."

"Her, or her and Jason?"

"Jason, too, if he'll agree. As her message said, she knows she can stay no longer than a year without taking dangerous risks. At least she understands she cannot become an Earthling forever. I trust her to honor her word to return home next time, if no harm befalls her."

Andrea smiled encouragement. "She'll be safe with Jason; I'm certain of it. You should have seen it, Jana; she swept him off his feet that first day. I know they'll be good for each other. I watched her during our outings and she did fine on Earth. Amaya has a quick and clever wit. She's skilled and trained, so she can take care of herself."

"I hope so, Andrea; God above, I hope and pray so."

To distract Jana, Andrea coaxed, "Tell me what's been going on here. I only caught a little of the bad news from the men before they left for Star Base. I also want to hear about Galen's new romance."

The following day on Earth, Amaya strolled with Jason on a near empty beach. She was glad so few people were present so they could have privacy to hold hands and steal kisses. She savored warm sun on her back and the tickling of sand on her bare feet, particularly between her toes. She enjoyed the sounds of crashing waves, the shrill cries of numerous gulls, and the noises and sights of other sea birds. She liked the smell of the ocean air and the feel of its breezes wafting over her skin and toying with her hair. Galveston Island was beautiful and romantic to her, and life with Jason was sweet and exciting ecstacy.

Jason drew Amaya into his embrace. "These past ten days have been some of the best in my life, woman. Have I told you how much I love you and how happy I am you're here with me?"

"Many times, but tell me again and again, for I feel the same way."

Jason chuckled as he hugged her and kissed her cheek. "You're a wonder, Amaya Saar; I could never tire of being with you. I feel like the luckiest man alive. I'm glad you came into my life and I hope you never leave it. Somehow, woman, I'm going to persuade you to retire from that secret job and marry me."

"Let's not talk about such problems today," she entreated as she caressed his cheek, then nestled against him. She was relieved when he didn't press the subject. So far, she had managed to conceal any ignorance about his planet. He himself made that possible by helping her with every task. And whenever they weren't together, she watched television or listened to the radio to gather facts. She knew she was learning more each day and lessening any risk of exposure. If Jason said or asked something she did not understand, she distracted him with hugs and kisses or diverted his attention to another subject. If he was suspicious about her, it didn't show in any manner.

Jason was curious about the woman he loved and desired. He still hadn't learned much more about her life. He knew about her use of feminine wiles and sly tricks to sidetrack him on occasion. He didn't understand why she was like she was, but he knew she was anything but stupid and slow. The way she sucked up information and absorbed it like a sponge, he assumed she hadn't spent much time in the outside world, had lived some strange and secluded lifestyle. None of his veiled queries brought him answers. He hoped that when she got to know him completely and trusted him fully, she would reveal everything about herself to him. Until she did, he had to be patient and calm and trusting.

They watched the sunset as it made vivid colors on the horizon. Both knew their bond was strong and special. Both planned ways to have their remaining dream come true: a future together.

"Are you ready to go inside and make us some dinner?" Jason asked.

"I'm hungry, but not for food," she quipped with a seductive smile.

"Neither am I. Come along, woman, we have things to do."

They entered Jason's beach house and he locked the sliding door. He grasped her hand and led her to the bedroom. "Want to take a shower together? I'll wash your back and you can wash mine?"

Amaya nodded, a glow of desire and pleasure brightening her smile. She stripped off her shorts, T-shirt, panties, and bra he removed his clothes. She trailed him into the bathroom and waited while he adjusted the water temperature and flow.

"After you, madam," he said as he made a comical bow and swept one hand toward the large enclosure.

Amaya entered the shower and moved aside for him to join her. She liked the feel of the cool tiles on the soles of her warm feet and the sensuous splashing of water over her bare flesh. But her gaze was held captive by Jason's handsome face, which aroused every emotion within her and whetted her appetite for the splendid feast in store for her. He seemed to delve into her very soul and awaken each longing nestled there.

Jason noticed how Amaya's gaze caressed him long before her hands did so. She touched and moved him as no woman ever had and he yearned to make her his, now and countless times in the future. No flame of passion could burn higher than his did for her. No love could be stronger or deeper. No match could be more perfect and special. His hands rested on the gentle curve between her small waist and shapely hips. "You're the most beautiful and enticing woman I've ever seen, Amaya. I love just looking at you." His arms slipped around her body and he almost crushed it against his. He closed his eyes and allowed his senses to absorb her heady fragrance. He knew so little about her, yet he was certain she loved him as much as he loved her. Somehow he knew she was trustworthy and loyal, despite her need and vow to keep secrets from others, including him. Being a private investigator, he comprehended classified work. No doubt she could get into trouble if she revealed confidential information, and a lover was not an exception to the strict rules she must obey. He respected her position and tried to honor her promise of silence to her government and superior.

Jason's thoughts scattered as he felt Amaya's firm mounds press against his broad chest. He felt her fingers trail over his shoulders, and down his arms. She squirmed and laughed as his teeth and tongue played on her ears, throat, and collarbones.

They shared light, relaxing, and deliberate caresses, as their eager hands roved skin that was wet and slick and inviting. Their fingers wandered through and over dripping hair, often pushing soaked strands from their exploratory paths.

Amaya adored his nape-length hair, thick and wavy, dark as a night without a moon. She liked the air of mystery his hooded brows gave to his sapphire eyes, with their shade as blue and evocative as the ocean covering Zamarra's surface.

Jason sent his mouth along her cheekbone to join with hers. He savored her taste and the way her tongue titillated him with sexy swirls. Her wet skin felt even silkier than usual. His hands cupped her breasts and kneaded them to greater firmness before teasing their points into taut peaks. His mouth deserted hers to press kisses and lavish attention at them. He was delighted when she moaned in pleasure, quivered, and arched her back to give him full access to her soft flesh.

Amaya was engulfed in a white-hot heat. Every spot he touched was sensitive, susceptible. As his tongue fluttered over her peaks, the core of her womanhood ached to have him within it. Her wits were dazed by him, spinning with happiness and satisfaction, entreating him to continue as anticipation and suspense mounted. When Jason lifted his head, the four-inch span between their heights allowed her to gaze with ease into his glowing eyes that seemed to sparkle like a cerulean sky filled with tiny stars. At a *yema's* pace, her line of vision traveled his face once more. For now, he was her world.

Jason soaped a cloth and lathered her torso with slow and provocative motions. He guided it over her neck as she turned her head this way and that to let him reach every inch. He took it over her shoulders and back before journeying down each arm. He used it to play an erotic game with her fingers, then headed it to a new destination. He made sudsy circles around her breasts. He knelt to wash her long legs and lifted each foot in turn to tend them, again playing between her toes as she squirmed. "I have to get all of this sand out or we'll have a gritty bed," he chuckled.

He placed her under the water's flow to remove the bubbles from her alluring figure. Again he coated the cloth with soap and fondled her buttocks as he washed them. He nudged her thighs apart and sensually washed and rinsed the sensitive flesh there.

Amaya took the cloth from his grasp to rinse and then soap it. She slowly bathed his neck and back. Kneeling, she did the same with his legs and feet, then worked her way up his enticing torso, smiling in satisfaction as his manhood responded to her erotic ministrations. She dropped the cloth to the tiled floor and took him in her slippery grasp to arouse him to even greater need for her. Jason leaned against the wall and moaned in pleasure, willing and content to let her have her way with him. She adjusted the water's flow to remove the bubbles from him, top to bottom.

Jason reached for her and clutched her to him, his mouth sealing with hers. They wiggled and writhed as they used their naked bodies to stimulate each other and heighten their own desires. Beads of water trickled down their faces and bodies. Their caresses were no longer soft and coaxing; they were urgent and deliberate. Their breathing was shallow and swift. They could endure no more foreplay; they had to unite their bodies now.

Jason turned off the water, grabbed a towel, and dried them in a rush. He lifted Amaya and carried her to the bed. He yanked the covers aside and sank to the mattress with her. For a few minutes, they kissed and caressed before he donned a condom and thrust into her. Their bodies seemed to melt into one being. He was imprisoned by her encircling legs with ankles locked behind him. Still, that snug grip did not deter his movements or her responses.

Amaya matched his pattern and pace, eager to feed her ravenous hunger. She squirmed beneath him to create thrilling sensations for both of them. She knew he was holding back for her sake, but it wouldn't be necessary much longer as she seemed to zoom like a rocket through a joyful heaven. She felt as torrid as the sun, as if she would burst into flames and disintegrate if she didn't find a way to cool down fast. Her fingers buried themselves in his damp hair and held his mouth to hers as she seemed to attack it feverishly. Within her, it was as if a spring was winding itself tighter and tighter. Then, it suddenly reached its limit and sprang toward freedom. It uncoiled with powerful force and delight. She moaned and whispered, *"Ki, ki, ki,"* Maffeian for: Yes, yes, yes.

Jason meshed their mouths and made his strokes with swiftness and resolve. He felt spasms begin as his potent climax spilled forth into the protective shield of lambskin. His cheek pressed against hers as he breathed rapidly, continuing to thrust until they were sated. He propped his elbows on either side of her head, careful not to entrap and pull her long hair. He looked at her rosy cheeks and pleasure-glazed eyes. He had been honest earlier; she was the most ravishing woman he knew. "That was wonderful," he said. "I can't explain or understand how it gets better every time. You're something else, woman. Heavens, you drive me wild. Lordy, I love you." He wondered what she'd murmured during her climax. She didn't seem to speak Spanish so it hadn't been *"Si"*. Could it have been another language?

"I love you," she echoed. She knew she had made that language slip but prayed he hadn't noticed.

They cuddled and rested for a while, then Jason asked if she was ready to cook their evening meal together. He suggested they boil shrimp he had purchased that morning and have a salad and wine.

That suited her, since she knew how to do those things by now. She nodded before she rolled atop his naked body, gazed into his eyes, and smiled. "You are a superior specimen. Your prowess is great."

Jason chuckled as his arms banded her torso. "We do make good music together. I hope this sexy song lasts forever."

Amaya guessed his meaning and agreed. "We will sing it each day."

Jason chuckled again. "Planning to work me overtime, eh?"

"A superior officer always does his duty; I am yours."

"Frankly, I can't think of a better job or rank to have."

"The assignment also pleases me."

"Then, make it a permanent one."

"When the time is right."

Jason sent her a beaming smile. "At least I'm making progress."

"What do you mean?"

"You didn't say no or maybe this time. I think that was a qualified yes."

Amaya pretended to think as she awaited understanding of his last sentence. After she perceived its meaning, she smiled and nodded.

"Perfect, so let's go fix supper before I put pressure on you."

"Grab a quilt out of the hall closet and we'll have a picnic on the beach," Jason said, the following day.

Amaya opened the doors. *Quilt*, her mind reasoned. *A bed coverlet*. She noticed a large and colorful piece as he joined her. "Is this it?" she asked, pointing to an extra spread.

"That's for the guest room when the other one's dirty. This," he said as he removed the quilt and decided she didn't know what one was. "I fixed us a nice tropical concoction and some sandwiches."

"What is a 'concoction'?"

"A bunch of different fruit juices; it's delicious, one of my specialties." He reminded her he had to "run up" to Houston tomorrow to check on the office and would be back by dark. "Will you be all right here alone for the day, and stay inside with the doors locked?" he asked.

Amaya recalled the sixty-mile distance he had mentioned en route. "That is a long way to run. Why not use your vehicle?"

Jason chuckled. "That's just a saying; of course I'll take the car. Sometimes I think English isn't your first language; foreigners often have trouble with our slang. Am I right?"

"Yes," she admitted, to explain and excuse her errors.

"What language do you speak at home?"

"I cannot tell you. To do so would reveal my origins."

"Back to that classified obstacle again. All right, woman, have it your way. But ask me anything you don't understand."

"Thank you. I will. I just do not want to appear . . . stupid."

Jason stroked her cheek, then tugged on a long curl. "You could never look stupid, Amaya Saar. It's smarter to ask even silly-sounding questions than to remain ignorant on a matter." He led her toward the kitchen. "As soon as it gets warmer,

I'll teach you to jet ski and deep-sea dive, if you're interested."

"I enjoy learning everything you teach me."

"You still want to do that helicopter tour of the island on Saturday?"

"Yes, I like flying."

"I remember; you were an ace with that plane in Houston." .

You will be surprised by how well I can fly when we reach my world.

As they walked toward the site he had chosen between grassy dunes and white-crested water, he asked again, "Will you be all right alone tomorrow?"

"Yes, I will. But why must you go?"

Jason set down the basket to spread the quilt, flipping it several times until it unfolded and lay flat on ecru sand. "Earl and David are doing fine without me, but that new surveillance equipment still has bugs in it."

Amaya stared at him. "You have insects in your equipment?"

"That means problems. The boys don't know as much about high-tech gear as I do. I'll fix it and hurry home." *I wish I could send your fingerprints and picture through the pipeline to see what shows up, but that might get us both into trouble if my queries wave a red flag in the wrong person's face. One thing I do know—you and the Sangers didn't fly under your own names because there's no record of your arrival or their departure from Houston. As for your clothes, not a one contains a label and you don't carry any identifica-*

tion. Whomever you all work for, they don't take any chances.

Jason's mind raced as Amaya took in the setting. He knew she couldn't be a spy because she was unfamiliar with guns and didn't know how to drive. Yet she had been eager to learn how to use his weapons, and had become an expert shot after a few rounds. He'd suggested he teach her how to drive soon and she seemed eager to comply. She didn't appear to know about video and regular cameras, so any type of surveillance job was improbable, but she enjoyed looking at the pictures and watching the tapes he had made as souvenirs. He had taken her grocery shopping, and got the impression it was a new experience for her. The same was true when he took her shopping for clothes, since she hadn't come prepared for a long stay. She certainly had never ridden on a trolley or in a carriage or been to dog races, events they had enjoyed last week. Nor had she done laundry, their joint mission yesterday. It was as if all appliances and everyday chores were strangers to her.

He was baffled by her, and his curiosity was sparked continuously because there were so many common things she didn't know, even though she explained she had never been required to do those tasks and others always handled them. Yet she was seemingly unspoiled, not lazy at all. She learned everything quickly, and didn't mind doing or helping with any type of work. She must have led a very sheltered and pampered life, he reasoned, which could explain why her parents and boss were worried about her venturing into the outside world, and why the Sangers were so protective of her. As Jason's gaze drifted over her, he felt sneaky investigating her behind her back, but he wanted to learn anything that could help him keep her forever. He also knew, if she vanished from him as she had from the Sangers, he would have no idea where to find her; that reality troubled him and lessened his guilt.

Amaya gazed over the dark-blue surface and noticed occasional white-tipped waves, boats, ships, and an oil rig. The sky was as remarkably sapphire today as the ocean, and clouds were as white as the waves' crests. It was "low tide," so the beach seemed endless. Since it was a workday for most Earthlings and not "the height of the tourist season," only a few people were strolling or sitting or fishing. In the distance, she saw piers and rock jetties, stretching across the sand and ending beyond the surf. Waves lapped and foamed at parts of old wharfs with birds resting on them. A protective wall journeyed for miles as a guardian against hurricane or vicious storm. It was a lovely and tranquil setting, she concluded as she gathered a few seashells that caught her eye before she rejoined Jason on the quilt.

"I can tell you love this area and the ocean as much as I do. It's the best place I've found to escape the city. I've needed a vacation, and this is the best one I've had, thanks to you."

Amaya smiled and took the sandwich and drink Jason handed to her. As they ate and sipped, she reflected on the past ten days together. They had done and seen many things. In particular, she sa-

vored the Lone Star Flight, Railroad, and Texas
Seaport museums where she learned about past
modes of transportation. He took her to Seaside
Safari where she had viewed and touched exotic
and domestic species. She also liked the Strand
district, another historic peek into the past and a
bustling place with countless stores for shopping.
He had given her a tour of the island in and on
many kinds of vehicles, including a ride on a mo-
torbike where she snuggled against his back. They
had viewed the Bishop's Palace, gone to a movie,
and fished in the ocean. They had eaten many
kinds of foods and sampled many liquids. Best of
all, they had made passionate love at least once
every day.

Amaya knew Jason was mystified by her lack of
skill and knowledge in certain areas, but he appeared to believe and accept her replies and differences, though they were odd ones to him. He
was always patient and helpful with lessons, and
fortunately she was a good student in all areas.
She tried to stay alert to pick up information she
needed in order to have a safe and happy existence
on this planet. With Earth's crime rate so high, she
was glad she knew how to use Jason's weapons, as
she dared not use hers before witnesses. So far,
she hadn't needed to take advantage of the devices
always worn on her person.

As she glanced at her wrist, Jason asked her
what the time was. Amaya could not read the watch
he had given to her, but she did not panic at his
request. "Time does not matter when we are together," she extricated herself with a sexy smile.

"Good," he concurred as he drew her down beside him for a kiss.

After Jason left for Houston on Friday morning, Amaya stood at the sliding doors and gazed at the ocean. She knew the Sangers had reached home by now and her parents were aware of her decision to stay on Earth. She tried to imagine their reactions. Even if her father didn't understand her motive, surely her mother would; and both would want her to be safe and happy. She assumed Galen would be amused and surprised. She could hardly wait for her twin and her lover to meet; she was certain they would like each other, and Galen could teach Jason many things about their world. Jason would have no trouble fitting into a new life there, as he loved challenges and adventures. A glorious future was ahead for them if he would return home with her. Everyone would like and accept him as her mate, except, Commander Mohr.

Amaya frowned. By now, Mohr knew she had not returned and must be angry. If he discovered the reason, jealousy would consume and provoke him. Perhaps he would have her punished and demoted; surely his feelings would work against Jason's acceptance. But she couldn't worry about those grim possibilities for a year and spoil her visit. When the time came, she would decide how to handle any repercussions, or her father would, as the Supreme Commander of Star Fleet and the Elite Squad. Hopefully, no crucial assignment would arise where she was needed.

*I'm sorry, Mother, Father, but I had to do this. I have
to know if Jason Carlisle is my future. I had to give us
this chance to seek the truth.*

Amaya gazed around at the setting where she had
known such joy. A spacious living area with many
sofas and chairs drifted leftward into a breakfast
room with a side door. The kitchen adjoined the
eating section, and a laundry was at the far end.
On the street side, there was a small guest room
and bath. To her right was the master "suite" and
large bath with an oversize shower and Jacuzzi garden tub. Double sliding doors were positioned in
the eating and living areas and in Jason's bedroom,
all with splendid and unobstructed ocean views.
She favored the colors—creams, mauves, aquas,
blues—that Jason or someone had chosen for fabrics
and carpets and decorations and the comfortable
furnishings. She liked the exposed ceiling beams
and fans in almost every room. She glanced outside.
Steps from the ground halted near the dining area
door where a wraparound deck began and traveled
to a screened porch beside the master bedroom.
The wood house was elevated by sturdy stilts, which
allowed for parking and storage facilities underneath.

She didn't know how long they would remain
on the island, but she was in no hurry to leave.

A week later, Amaya was sitting on a sofa and
looking at pictures in a magazine as Jason prepared mild margaritas in the kitchen. She lowered
the book, sighed dreamily, and reminisced. A heli-

copter tour of the island last Saturday had been exciting, so had the dinner-dance cruise aboard a large paddlewheeler that night. Jason had enjoyed teaching her how to dance and pointing out sites from the upper deck. On Sunday, a visit to Moody Gardens with a tropical rain forest re-created inside a ten-story glass pyramid was fun and educational. So was the 3D IMAX Theater with animals that seemed to leap off the screen at them. Dinner afterward in the Garden Restaurant was delicious and delightful as they watched the "Dancing Waters" fountain show. That entire day in a mock paradise was a romantic and exotic adventure she would never forget. The rest of the week they had walked, biked, fished, rested, loved, and Jason had given her driving lessons. Friday afternoon they had grocery-shopped, done their laundry, and cleaned the house. Before they grilled hamburgers on the deck, they planned to enjoy a drink and relax.

Jason entered the room and set down their glasses. He tossed Amaya a *TV Guide* and asked her to see what time the baseball game came on this evening. When she appeared to panic, he asked, "What's wrong? I thought you enjoyed that game I took you to in Houston."

"I did, but . . ." *How can I get out of this without lying or being rude?*

"But what, love? Would you rather watch something else?"

"No." She passed the guide to him. "You look," she suggested.

"Something's wrong, Amaya; tell me," he coaxed.

She took a deep breath and said, "I can't read or write English."

Her tone and expression said she was serious. But, Jason mused, could a woman this smart be illiterate? No, that was impossible. Yet she always asked him to order at restaurants and there were other clues that led to a possible disability. "What do you mean? Do you have dyslexia?"

"I cannot read or write English," she clarified.

"How is that possible? You speak it well and you've done fine here except for a few times that I've noticed."

"I learned by practicing with my mother and the Sangers, and by listening to television and other devices. But slang and unusual sayings give me problems."

That explained to him why Andrea and Nigel were apprehensive about letting Amaya out of their sight. But, he reasoned, what was wrong with her explaining the language mystery. "What language do you speak at home?"

"It must remain a secret for now. That limitation is one reason my parents did not want me to come to America; they worried about me being able to take care of myself and about honoring my vow of silence. I did not tell you because I do not want you to think I am ignorant and unworthy of you."

Jason cuddled her in his embrace and kissed her forehead. "I would never think such things about you, my love, because they aren't true," he said. "Look how well you've done so far. You haven't gotten into any trouble and I'll make certain you never do. Trust me to protect you. Don't worry, I'll teach you to read and write English, or find some-one qualified who can."

Amaya nestled her cheek against his strong shoulder. "How will I explain my problem to a teacher? All information about me is classified."

"We'll figure out something," he assured her. "We must, because you can't find your way around or read warning signs if you don't take lessons. While I'm in Houston next week, I'll pick up some literature to see what steps we should take."

She lifted her head and asked, "Are you disap-pointed with me?"

Jason's tender gaze met her troubled one. "No, and I'm glad you finally told me. Don't worry, we'll solve this matter together."

"I feel I can solve all problems with you," she said, and kissed him.

Five days later, Amaya went for a stroll on the beach. Jason had been gone since Monday morn-ing because his presence was required as a witness during a trial for a case he had investigated. Before leaving, he had taught her how to use the tele-phone for emergencies and to call him. He was scheduled to return the next day. They had de-cided it was best for her to stay at the beach house rather than go to Houston with him, in case any-one was searching for her. To safeguard their lo-cation, he was to make certain he wasn't followed to that city.

Yet Amaya was too distracted to realize she was being watched from a distance through binoculars, was being observed by a dangerous stranger.

Twelve

A week later on Rigel in the Maffei Galaxy, Jana and Renah were talking in the Saars' private chambers in a tall *transascreenic* tower. The *Galactic Wind* had returned to Star Base to deliver Earthlings whom they had taken prisoner on several planets. The inquiries and tests were completed, but no leads were gleaned about their *villite*'s identity or motive; neither had a mysterious alien vessel nor *nefariant* base been found. Yet the Saars were relieved that no one had sighted Varian's duplicate at any of the trouble spots, and no one was suspicious about Galen's casual questions about his father. All infected victims the other team had uncovered were now being treated at the base Med Complex. Meetings had been held by the Supreme Council and by the Alliance Assembly of *avatars;* nobody had new suggestions on how to find and defeat their threat. There was nothing they could do except leave the matter in Varian Saar's hands and hope he and his forces could resolve it. Still, every leader and their ruler were worried about where and how the evil *fiendal* would attack next. They knew many people were aware of the troubles and were spreading the news to others; they wanted protection and swift victory.

"How is the medical research progressing, Doctor Saar?" Renah asked.

"Not good. New cases have been diagnosed and we've sent med teams to get them and bring them here. Most of the other patients have died. Their families and friends are worried about catching the virus. We've tried to assure them it isn't possible without direct blood contact with an infected person. But some don't believe us; they're being treated for traumatic depression. Despite precautions, Renah, word has leaked out about it, and I fear a panic may result. Varian and I believe we should address the grave matter publicly to educate people on how to avoid infection and to assuage their fears; the Council and Assembly disagree. They think the bad news will cause chaos and a loss of faith in them. They also suspect some citizens may try to flee to other galaxies for safety. If the virus is allowed to spread beyond our boundaries, it will turn our allies against us. Varian and I agree with them to a certain point, but saving lives must be our prime goal."

Renah knew how hard Jana and Varian were working on the problems confronting them. Yet, from what she could ascertain, their motives were good ones: love for their people and world. If the Saars had wicked or greedy feelings like those that were alleged to have compelled this vengeful plot, she could not perceive them. Nor had she learned anything about the past existence of such evil traits. But if the Saars were honorable people, now and long ago, how could . . . Renah discarded those troubling thoughts to concur with Jana. "We have no choice except to obey the commands of our rulers."

"I know, but I think they're wrong. There are times when one must take dangerous steps to achieve good for others. If everyone put himself first, the world would be a terrible place. There would be no love or unity. Those who care only for themselves and their desires are cold and miserable people, and often they are a peril to others who are not the same. They seem to live to hate and destroy."

Renah wanted the guilt-inspiring subject to change. "What would you suggest to our ruler and leaders?"

"Initiate a mandatory testing of every citizen and guest to locate all victims and carriers so we can contain the rogue until a cure is found," Jana answered firmly. "It's the only way no more people will get infected by accident or malicious intention, and anyone needing rapid treatment would be found and helped before it's too late. The results will also let us know how widespread the virus is."

"At least now you know how it got here and how it spreads."

"Thanks to my husband and son's theories. I should of had that mode of transmission investigated sooner. I knew lovemaking was a conduit, but I never imagined terrestrial prostitutes would act as syringes and purposely inject their poison into others."

"Have those alien pleasure-givers we and the other teams captured provided any clues?"

"None; they have mind blocks, too, and we can't penetrate them."

"That proves the *villite* is responsible, just as Galen suspected."

"Yes, but it doesn't help solve the problem that devil created. How could anyone do such a horrible thing to innocents? Not only did he use female carriers but he loosed infected male rapists on us. Every time one of our people has sex, willingly or by force, with those carriers, they've been murdered. Eventually, the carriers will take ill and die, but the virus doesn't affect them for months to years from what we can gather from our tests. If our chemistries totally matched those of Earthlings, we'd have more time to solve this grim riddle. But it mutates fast, and quickly becomes lethal. *Avatars* are making demands we can't meet. The populace is beginning to do the same. How can we tell our people we're powerless to help them?"

"Galen thinks that may be part of the *villite*'s plot: to incite dissension and rebellion to endanger the Alliance. If the planets lose faith and withdraw, they will be more vulnerable to attacks and possible conquest."

"That's too horrible to think about, Renah, but my son could be right. That blackheart is surely after more than simple wealth, but I can't imagine how he would hope to conquer an entire galaxy."

"As long as the Alliance stands united, he can't. But if it doesn't, he's proven he can come and go and attack at will, and we can't stop him. We don't even know how many followers or what weapons he has." Which was also true for her, as so many changes had occurred after she left them. The original plan of punishment and exposure no longer existed, and a larger and deadlier one was in effect. If only she could speak with her family to learn more of those alterations, but that was impossible since she could send messages but receive none unless it was deemed mandatory and safe in their judgment. The few that had been sneaked to her during the last four years only revealed new tactics without explaining their motives, grim actions to which she was opposed. Didn't they realize how they were endangering her life if she were discovered and captured? Why didn't they extricate her? She refocused her attention on Jana's words.

"Having the Fleet and planetary patrols on full alert didn't prevent our enemy from almost sabotaging Zamarra's environmental system. If the explosive hadn't been noticed by technicians and disarmed by experts, most Zamarraians would have perished without fresh air before they could have been rescued because an evacuation of that size would require many vessels and trips."

Renah was still dismayed at that near tragic event and was glad it had been thwarted. She listened as Jana talked about Sebok's father, the ex-*avatar* of that underwater world.

"Supreme Councilman Suran is worried they might try to shatter the protective domes and drown everyone when the ocean pours inside them. The message our unit confiscated from those captured implied they intended to ransom safety for an enormous payment, but we doubt a cargo of *katoogas* was the real motive. The teams Varian sent there haven't been able to determine how those Earthlings got into an undersea complex with portals that are heavily guarded. And they had no means of escape waiting nearby, as if they never intended to leave alive."

"It appears to be an impossible feat, Doctor Saar, yet they succeeded in gaining entry and planting explosives. One day later, Zamarra would have been destroyed. We do know they had perfect fake identities to get them aboard sea shuttles and inside the largest city, and we also know two guards are missing and presumed dead. We should be thankful those *nefariants* were defeated and captured before they wreaked havoc."

"Captured only to kill themselves before questioning. If only we could neutralize his hold on their minds . . ."

Renah gazed at Jana and noticed many points of resemblance to her lover. She realized Galen could not be the wonderful man he was if he had been reared by evil parents. "The compounds from Ryker Triloni and those in the Trilabs computer system have safeguards to prevent them from being analyzed and reproduced by others," Renah continued her speculations. "If you know how he accomplished that self-destruct marker, maybe that knowledge will tell you how to deal with the *villite's* formula tags."

Jana wasn't surprised by her query, as that scientific fact was common knowledge. "We tried that; it didn't work on his unknown chemicals. Whomever he is, Renah, he's a genius."

"Why do you think he's using Earthlings as his forces?" Renah wondered.

"Perhaps because they look like us—I mean, Maffeians. They can intermingle without notice if they have fake credentials. Either he abducted and enslaved the worst criminals on Earth, or his drugs force them to do pernicious deeds for him."

"Galen believes he will eventually reveal his motive, Doctor Saar."

"Please, Renah, call me Jana, unless you object."

"Thank you. When we're alone, I will. In public, I must show you the respect your rank and status deserve."

The older woman smiled. "That's a nice compliment and compromise. Now, let's have some *zim*."

Later, as they sipped the steaming beverage, Renah asked, "Since the virus carriers have been traced and arrested, the disease can be controlled now until you find a cure. Isn't that correct?" *Please say yes.*

"Only after we have all of them and their victims in our care; at this point, we don't. The med team has gone after new cases we discovered, so I hope further infection can be prevented. We're trying to create a vaccine that seeks out, attacks, and destroys the enemy, but nothing we've attempted in the lab has worked so far. It's as if the rogue virus sets up a force shield to protect it while it's mu-

tating into a more lethal form. We need a weapon—
a transmembrane conductor—that can pierce its
barrier so we can reach it and inhibit its alteration
until we can destroy him."

"Sort of a biochemical *simboyd* that can drill a
hole in the cell wall and shoot in its own type of
gracene gas like we did at Caguas with that enemy
ship?" Renah asked.

"In theory, yes, but everything we've tried along
that line has been too toxic and destructive to use
on our patients."

"Perhaps what's causing the mutation process
holds the key to a cure. Differences in our immune
systems, our air, food, and water?

"We're working on some of those theories now."
Jana was impressed by Renah's aptitude. "You're
a very smart woman; you could be a superior scientist."

"Thank you, Jana, but I'm happy in Security
and Weapons for now."

"And being with my son?" she hinted with a
bright smile.

Renah felt a flush warm her cheeks at the unexpected remark. "Yes, Galen is very special and
important to me."

"As you are to him and to us."

"Thank you again, Jana; you're very kind. I appreciate how you and Commander Saar have befriended me."

"You make it easy for people to like and accept
you, Renah."

"That she does, Mother," Galen concurred as
he and his father entered the sitting chamber.

"Did you two miss us or have you been too busy talking to realize we were gone?" he jested.

Later, as Galen and Renah cuddled in another chamber of the tower, she asked, "Are your parents angry about Amaya's behavior? She wasn't mentioned all evening."

He stroked her bare arm. "They're worried about her being alone so far away, especially with the *villite* raiding there; and what she did certainly shocked them."

"Did it also astonish you?"

"Yes, and no," he replied. "It surprised me that she would forget her duty and rank for personal reasons and risk getting into trouble. But, loving you as I do, I understand why she did it. If she hadn't stayed, she couldn't get to know Jason better to learn if he's the man for her. Since my mother is an Earthling and I'm partly one, I understand even more."

"You don't hate them for being involved in the threat to Maffei?"

"How can I blame them when they have no control over their actions? I do wish he wasn't using that race; it could reflect badly on Mother and others. If things worsen, it might cause resentment toward all Earthlings living here. Long ago, the ones on the Anais Colony were given a choice of remaining with us or returning home. Those who elected to leave were treated so they wouldn't remember their visit with us. Those who stayed were helped to adjust to their new lives. We know from our investigations that none of them are in on this plot."

"What do you mean by 'treated'?" Renah asked.

"It's a process that eliminates certain parts of recent memory, sort of like erasing sections of a robot's program."

"That seems similar to the *villite's* mind block?" After he nodded, she asked, "So, why can't our scientists use their knowledge to penetrate his?"

"It isn't the same treatment. Ours removes memory of recent events; his enslaves the mind to do his bidding, which is obey his order and keep silent at any cost, even if that price is their lives."

"Will recall ever occur in any of the returnees?" Renah asked.

"Never, it isn't possible, because those memory cells are gone."

"Cells . . . Your mother and I discussed many types of body cells. She said the *villite's* forms a protective shield around itself after it enters certain cells, then prevents assault on it. I wonder . . ."

"You wonder what?"

"If his mind block works along that same line. Instead of destroying or removing memory cells as they did with the Anais Earthlings, what if he knows a way to insert his orders, then creates a protective shield around them? He could add something that transmits a warning when questioned that causes a biochemical signal to be given, one that orders death." Renah knew that wasn't how the mind-control drug functioned, but it could give Jana a starting point if Galen relayed those speculations to her. She could not come right out and tell him how to break it or her family's identities would be exposed, and no doubt hers, too. She laughed. "I guess that sounds wild. I'm sure your mother and her staff have considered all possibilities."

"What else did you and Mother discuss while we were gone?"

"Many things."

"Such as?"

"The attacks we've had and medical research."

"You get along fine with her and Father, don't you?"

Renah realized his mind was traveling the wrong way. "Yes, I like and respect and admire both of them. You have good parents, Galen."

"They want to be substitute parents for you, if you don't object."

"How and why should I, my love?" she felt safe replying.

"Excellent, that makes you one of the family. After this threat is terminated, I want that part to be bigger and more important. I love you."

"I love you, too," she murmured and kissed him to stop him from talking about a future together, as they could have none.

Galen nibbled at her lips, relishing their flavor. His hands stroked her nude body to tantalize and pleasure her and himself. His lips kissed a sensuous path down her throat, lingering at her breasts until she squirmed with delight. Soon, his mouth and hands voyaged lower, bringing her desire to a feverish pitch.

Renah's head thrashed on the pillow as his tongue and fingers inflamed her with their bold and stirring actions. She felt that inner coil winding tightly again and quivered in anticipation. Soon, golden splendor engulfed her and sent her careening through glorious space like a rocket spinning out of control. As his new course brought him upward, she shifted to explore his magnificent frame. Her hands and mouth traveled his body to give him the same enticements and thrills. Within moments, she had him tensing, relaxing, and moaning over and over in a mingling of suspense and rapture.

Blissful sensations snatched away Galen's breath. He felt aflame, as if he were going to erupt like a *cario* and spew molten liquid into a sultry paradise surrounding him. He grasped her arms and guided her to a position beneath him. He thrust within her and carried them to the threshhold of ecstasy, lingered there a few minutes, then swept them through its portal.

As they lay in a state of contented afterglow, Galen held her close and possessively. "I love you with all my heart and soul, Renah Dhobi. I don't know how I would exist if I ever lost you." *That must be what you were feeling, too, my sister, when you stayed behind with Jason Carlisle. How lucky we are that we both found true and powerful loves at almost the same time. We'll be even luckier if we can hold on to them forever.*

Far away on Galveston Island, Amaya and Jason strolled on the beach at sunset. She noticed how distracted he seemed today and asked if something was troubling him.

"I just hate to leave you alone again," he alleged, but that wasn't what bothered him. He had a feeling they were being watched, yet he hadn't been able to sight anyone or anything suspicious to justify his qualms. He told himself he must be mistaken. The only person he had noticed more than once was a woman who was staying in a rental unit down the beach, and she appeared to pay little attention to them. He had been on alert since his return last Thursday and observed nothing out of the ordinary.

"I did fine last week," Renah assured him.

"I know, but I want to spend every day and night with you. I'll be back late on Friday but then I have another appointment on Monday."

"I promised to stay for a year before I return home."

Jason gave her hand a gentle squeeze of affection. "True, but a year will pass too fast to suit me. I don't want to lose a minute of it."

"You have not become tired of me?" she jested to calm his worries.

"Never in a zillion years. Are you bored with me?"

"Never in a zillion years," she echoed and laughed in joy.

The following day, as Amaya sat on the beach, she was tempted to fetch the quilt from Jason's house but was too relaxed to do so. After she finished a snack, the paper kept blowing away, causing her to retrieve it. Not ready to go inside or willing to litter, her gaze scanned the area and, seeing no one nearby, she used her wrist device to disintegrate it. As she daydreamed about her lover and absently toyed with an empty cola can, she nicked a finger on the rim left sharp by its pull tab. She examined the bleeding cut and recalled Nigel's warning about lethal alien germs. Again, she did a visual check of her surroundings before she used another function of the device to sterilize and seal the small wound with its *latron* beam. She decided to get Jason to teach her "first-aid" so she would be prepared for any future accidents, as she didn't know how to read medicine labels to select which one to apply.

Amaya pondered if she should reveal everything to Jason so he could help her stay out of jeopardy, and could understand and trust her fully. That confession would prove how much she loved and trusted him, what it had cost her to remain in his world. If the truth turned him against her, she could stay with Andrea's parents until departure time. Perhaps it was best for both of them to discover how that shocking news affected him before their relationship went much further. Besides, she reasoned, it wasn't fair to deceive him longer than necessary. Yet she needed more days of sharing, more days of peace and passion before she risked losing him. She decided she didn't want to think about such perils and problems any more today. She propped her hands behind her and leaned backward with closed eyes to allow the sun's rays to warm her face.

An hour later, Amaya watched their temporary neighbor stroll toward her. The woman had spoken to her in passing last week during Jason's absence and another time at a shop in town. Amaya didn't want to be rude, but she didn't want to begin a friendship with anyone who might cause intrusions on her time with Jason.

"Good afternoon. A beautiful day, isn't it?" the woman greeted her.

"Yes, but a storm is coming tonight." Or so the television reported.

"Nothing could be as bad as that big hurricane. Over six thousand people died. They have a film about it at Pier 21 near the Strand. You should go see it while you're here; it's awesome and scary."

"Did you witness that storm?" Amaya asked.

The woman laughed. "Heavens, no, I'm only forty-two."

In case she had offended the woman, Amaya said, "I did not know when the storm struck."

"In 1900." Francis Haver could tell the young woman was brushing her off and didn't want company. There was no point in lingering. "I hate to rush, but I have to finish my exercise and shop," she excused herself. "Perhaps I'll see you again before I leave next week."

"Perhaps," Amaya echoed with a polite smile. She watched her neighbor speed walk a short distance farther up the beach, turn, and head homeward at a brisk pace. They exchanged smiles and waves. Amaya was glad the woman was in a hurry, but didn't want a change of mind about joining her. She stood, stretched, and walked the few steps to the house. After locking the door, she went to watch television and to fantasize about Jason until it was dinnertime.

Midevening, Amaya was standing on the deck and enjoying brisk gusts and refreshing air. The moon had vanished behind clouds that said the storm was approaching, which it did very soon. A feeling of suspense and excitement consumed her as winds became forceful, thunder rumbled, waves grew loud and fierce, and lightning danced in exquisite patterns. Amaya didn't want to go inside; she wanted to experience and observe the alien storm. She wanted to witness its power and beauty, its magic and allure. No house within view had lights on. No one was on the beach. No boat was in sight. It was dark, and she was alone.

Amaya pressed the button on her wrist device and energized the personal body shield so she could remain where she was without risking injury. As winds blew, rain poured down, thunder roared, and lightning flashed, she was safe and serene in a transparent dome. She could remain there for hours until she breathed all entrapped air in the shield. She saw brilliant slashes dart across the sky or shoot into the ocean like beams from a laser. She wished she could stand in the open so the wind could play in her hair and tug at her silky nightgown. She would delight in getting drenched by the rain, but not zapped by powerful lightning;

those dazzling bolts could strike her and stun or kill her if she wasn't protected. Even if someone strolled by, she mused, the shield wasn't visible, and it was night, so she wasn't risking exposure.

Or so she assumed in grave error.

Four days later, Amaya awakened from a lengthy slumber. She felt limp and tired. Her wits were dazed, her mouth was dry, her body chilled. She couldn't move. She soon learned why she was plagued by those weird sensations. She was naked beneath a thin sheet in a cool room and she was secured to a table by straps fastened around her wrists and ankles! As her mind cleared, she knew this was not a bad dream. She had been drugged and captured! She heard voices nearby and, through a slitted gaze, saw two people in blue garments, head coverings, and masks. She didn't know who they were or where she was. She didn't know what language they spoke, as her intergalactic aural units translated any one they intercepted. She remained quiet and motionless as she judged the grim situation.

When Jason returned from Houston, he wouldn't know what had happened to her. He might think she had escaped him rather than have the "serious talk" he had mentioned before leaving. He might assume she had changed her mind about revealing everything to him and fled in panic. Even if he suspected a crime, he wouldn't know how or where to search for her.

Who were these people and what did they want

with her? Was she still on Earth, in a starship, or on another planet? She couldn't guess because she didn't know how long she had been kept drugged. But from the way she felt, it had been a long time. All she knew was that she had been napping on the sofa when someone seized her from behind and held an odd-smelling cloth over her mouth and nose. There hadn't been time to rouse herself and resist, as whatever was on that cloth worked fast to render her unconscious. Yet, she remembered, many hands were involved. One had imprisoned her left arm, one banded her throat to hold her head still, one gripped her right arm, and one used the dazing drug. At least two people, she reasoned, but perhaps more.

If she could get free of the bindings and use— Amaya panicked: the device on her wrist was gone! *Kahala* save her, she was powerless! She was too far from home to send a mental message to her twin. No one was coming for her for almost a year. Only Jason knew she was missing, and there was no way he could reach her or help her. She should have told—

"Ah, so my priceless treasure is awake at last. Greetings, Amaya Saar, I'm Doctor Karnes. We're going to have an interesting time together. You can't imagine how delighted I am to be the one to find you."

Amaya stared at the man whose face was almost concealed. All she could see were brown eyes and pale skin between his blue mask and hair covering. He looked to be about her height and appeared to have a slim build. If she could get free, surely she could best him and escape.

"Come now, don't be shy or stubborn. I know you understand and speak English. Do you prefer to call me Douglas or Doug instead of Doctor Karnes? Will that put you more at ease?"

"English." that means I'm still on Earth and in America!

"Don't frighten her, my love," a female voice cautioned.

Amaya's head jerked in the other direction. She knew those eyes and that voice. They belonged to the woman she had met on the beach. Her gaze widened in disbelief.

"That's right, Amaya, it's me: Frances Haver, psychic extraordinaire. That first time we met each other, you dropped a seashell you had been clutching. I picked it up, and have never received more potent and astonishing vibes in my life. I watched you for days until I was certain I was right about you. Then I called Doug and told him the news, but he didn't believe such a wild tale, even though he knows I'm no fake. I finally convinced him to come observe you. Thanks for convincing him for me."

Douglas ordered in an excited tone, "You're going to tell me how that gadget we took off your wrist works and how you created that force shield. I can become rich and powerful and famous with those inventions. I'll have the world kneeling at my feet. As for you, my lovely specimen, I want to know everything about you and your world: its technology, how and when you arrived from it, if you're alone or there are others like you on Earth. Why you came. *Everything.*"

Amaya didn't respond.

"Soon you'll talk, and you'll tell me everything I want to know."

"Cooperate, Amaya, it's in your best interests," Frances coaxed. "Doug isn't a cruel man, unless he's sorely provoked."

The research scientist disconnected a feeding tube. "We've already begun our tests on you so we know you aren't from Earth," he revealed. "The materials of many of your clothes aren't known on our planet. You don't have fingerprints like ours. Your blood cells, tissue samples, EKG, EEG, nails, hair, teeth, and DNA, to name a few I've noticed, are different. You have no tonsils, adenoids, and appendix, but no scars from their removal. Your spleen is not like ours. CAT scans and X-rays reveal some type of computer chips in your ears and brain; we want to know what they're for because we could hurt or kill you removing them for testing. I'm certain you don't want us to dissect you for answers, right?" Douglas asked when she looked alarmed. "We're being careful not to infect you or injure you; I don't want to lose my valuable prize. Of course, if an autopsy is necessary, that will be a last resort."

"What are you going to do with me?" Amaya asked.

"As soon as I complete my preliminary study of the samples and X-rays I've already taken, I'll test your reflexes; IQ; hearing, senses of sight and smell; bone marrow; endocrine, autonomic, and central nervous systems; your immune and respiratory systems; and your metabolism. I plan to do an in-vitro fertilization of the egg I collected from you to see how our species fuse and match, using my sperm, of course. I'll do a dye test of the kidneys, brain, and heart to study their functions and any dissimilarities. We have a lot of work in store for us and it will take a lot of time. It's best if we become friends and help each other. While I have to analyze my data, you think hard and decide if you're going to cooperate. One way or another, Amaya, I will get my answers. If you do as I say, after we're finished, I'll release you. If not . . ." Douglas smiled and shrugged. "We'll cross that bridge when we come to it."

"I want my clothes."

"You won't be needing them for a while. Just relax and think for now. Come along, Frances; we have work to do."

Amaya watched the smug couple leave the large and sterile chamber. Within moments, the brilliant overhead lights dimmed to a soft glow. The room's chill lessened. What was supposed to be soothing music was heard. She noticed a ceiling corner camera for spying on her. Her mouth was still dry and she hadn't been offered anything to drink. She felt bandages on the inner surface of her elbows and sore spots elsewhere. She knew she had been stripped, examined, tested, and invaded during a drugged state by Dr. Douglas Karnes and possibly his staff. She was at this evil man's mercy. She was only a laboratory specimen to him, a path to wealth and fame and power. The same was true of Frances

Haver; Amaya was aware the psychic had been touching her during the conversation and seeking mental rapport. Since she was trained to defend her mind against such tricks and skills, she had thwarted that domination.

Amaya knew she was in big trouble. She had been rash and careless and exposed herself to a terrible *villite*. She couldn't prevent him from doing as he pleased with her for now, but she would tell him nothing about herself and her world. He could torture her if he desired, but she would hold silent. He could inject her with his truth serum and drugs, but her *Rendelar* process would foil his attempts to extract information. She was trapped and she had to come up with an escape plan.

Thirteen

Jana stared at her husband in astonishment. "They did *what*?"

Varian exhaled in anger and frustration. "Seven of those enthralled Earthlings breached security at Star Base and tried to assassinate the *Kadim*, Council members, and Assembly of *avatars* during a meeting. Nigel and I arrived just in time to prevent their attack."

"Is everyone all right? Were Draco or any of the others injured?"

"No, moonbeam, but it was close. If Nigel and I had gotten there a few minutes later, there's no guessing the damage they could have wreaked. When we found two guards dead, we knew something was wrong and sounded the alarm. We stopped them at the conference-chamber doors."

"Did you take any prisoners to question?"

"None. The moment we appeared and fired stun beams on them, they took their lives, just as the others have done."

"How did they get on Star Base and to that off-limits level?"

"They had fake identities that were so well made even I might not have questioned and halted them.

They had electrocards and the password codes; I changed both after the incident. Nobody has possession of them now except our leaders, me, and Nigel. Security cannot be breached again without information supplied by one of those eighteen people. If it does occur, we know where to search for a leak. Whoever is behind this threat seems to know everything about our world, our defenses, and safeguards. His forces bypass us with ease."

"That doesn't sound good, my love." Jana's voice carried her alarm.

"I know. I hate to consider a spy or traitor, but it's pointing in that direction. How else could he know exactly where, when, and how to strike? Even if we defeat them at the last minute they've still gotten too close. He knew exactly what was needed and supplied it to his men. Now, I have to discover who he is or who's helping him."

"Do you have any ideas on how to proceed?"

"Not yet. I did check the travel schedules of everyone in power, but none of them were suspicious. I don't think Draco, Suran, Brec, or any of the *avatars* are involved."

"Who else knew such things before your changes today?"

"Me, Nigel, and Security chiefs. This time, I didn't supply chiefs with our new safeguards. If any of them needs entrance to that area for an acceptable reason, one of us will have to admit him and stay with him. Those electrocards and verbal codes haven't been changed in years, but there are no past rulers still living who could have given his to our *villite.*"

"Wouldn't that mean one of those men must be involved?"

"Unless there's another way he could have gotten—or is getting—facts, and I can't imagine what that could be. Our leaders have been through the *Rendelar* process so they can't be forced to reveal facts, even with drugs. I know our enemy has some powerful and unknown formulas, but nothing can neutralize or weaken or penetrate *Rendelar.*"

"That's what our lab studies have confirmed. Of course, we've only used blood and tissue samples from surviving prisoners who carry his chemicals in their bodies; we can't analyze and duplicate his formula to test it on a *Rendelared* volunteer."

"And speaking of duplicates," Varian interjected, "at least mine vanished after his Darkar visit. I'm relieved Galen found no further evidence of him."

"Are you sorry you sent him after Amaya and that medical research? Did you need him here more than on those two missions?"

"No, both are needed. That also takes him and Renah out of danger for a while. And they deserve a little rest after all the hazardous assignments they've handled lately."

"Do you think Galen can locate her?"

"If anyone can find Amaya, it's our son," Varian said with conviction. "I ordered him to give her no choice about returning home."

Jana sighed, her concern apparent. "I hope force isn't necessary."

"So do I. I doubt it will be once he explains the

troubles here. She'll probably be upset she gave in
to personal desires when she was needed."

"I agree, but Nigel said he decided not to tell
them anything until they were en route home. If
he had exposed our troubles, I know she would be
here now. To make their mental link work, Galen
must get within a certain range of her. Earth is a
big place to search if they've left Texas or America."

"I hope she wasn't that foolish or dazed by love.
I don't like her being there without help nearby
and so ill-equipped to protect herself. By remaining on Earth without more preparation and precautions, she took a big risk of exposure. But as
long as her head is clear, she can respond tele-
pathically. He'll find her, moonbeam, so don't
worry."

"What if she wants to bring Jason Carlisle back
with her?"

"I gave Galen permission to use his best judg-
ment in that matter. It's possible Andrea's cousin
will not want to move to another galaxy. You know
most Earthlings think aliens are monsters, enemies. He may not be able to deal with the truth
about her."

"I hope all goes well; I don't want to see Amaya
hurt. What did Commander Mohr say when you
told him you sent for her?"

"I haven't related that information to him or to
any others. We want to keep this mission a secret.
We don't want our *villite* to interfere with our attempts to copy Earth's research data on their virus.
Their studies might be of no help with our mu-

tated strain, but it's worth a try. After Amaya is home, we'll handle any reprimand needed."

"Will she be in deep trouble?" Again, Jana's maternal concern was strong.

"I don't know; I haven't decided how to deal with her defiance. As a father and mate, I understand her feelings and actions. As an officer and her superior, I can not allow those emotions to intrude on my judgment. If she weren't a Star Fleet officer and Elite Squad member, there would be no problem to resolve, but she disobeyed orders and is absent without leave."

Jana loved her daughter but knew she could not interfere. She prayed Amaya was safe and the repercussions of her decision would not be grave.

Two days later, more bad news arrived: Supreme Councilman Breccia Sard's son died on one of their planets after contracting the new virus.

A shocked Jana halted her laboratory work to listen to her husband.

"He was on duty on Therraccus, actually on leave. He met and spent off-time with one of those female carriers; no doubt he was her assigned target. We traced her and have her in custody, but we don't know how many more of those lethal weapons our *villite* has roaming the Alliance. She could be the only one we missed locating, or he could have loosed more of them on us; we'll know soon because new cases will appear. We released her image on public transmission and asked anyone who's been in contact with her to notify the local authorities, and they'll send word to me. We said she was carrying a contagious germ which required anyone who had been near or with her to come in for decontamination and injection. That announcement should compel any other victims to come forward for treatment. As for Brec's son, by the time he returned to duty, it was too late; he died quickly from a lung infection. His body is on the way to this complex for autopsy."

"How is Brec taking the tragic news?" Jana asked in empathy.

"As we would if it were Galen or Amaya. If we don't kill this rogue virus soon, any one of us could be struck down by it."

"If only we could find a cure," Jana murmured in despair.

Varian drew her into his embrace and said, "You will, moonbeam. Perhaps the information Galen will bring home will help you and the others."

"I hope so, but I have enormous doubts it will be of any value to us. Earth doctors and scientists have searched for a cure to their strain for years without success, and ours moves swifter than theirs does. It would be wonderful, a miracle, if we could find vaccines for both strains. Presently, we're studying differences between us and terrestrials to see if we can discern why the virus mutates in Maffeian systems. The answer could be a key to unlock the door to the virus's powers. The only victims who have survived infection are the ones we're keeping in germ-free isolation, but to live in sterile seclusion forever is no answer." She sighed in frustration. "Poor Brec."

"Losing his son couldn't have come at a worse time for him or us. He and the other Council members are trying to convince the Androasian Empire and Pyropean Federation not to place us in a state of galactic isolation and quarantine. If they seal off their borders with armed patrols, we couldn't pursue any possible suspects across them or ask them to intercept and return them. Since they're so alarmed by this incurable virus, they could resort to blasting any vessel into oblivion that encroaches on their territory. Innocent people could perish and suspects would be lost to interrogation. So far, their ears are closed to negotiations."

"How did they learn of our problem?" Jana asked.

"Untraceable messages were sent to *Effecta* Agular and Supreme Ruler Leumi yesterday. Probably from our *villite* to cause more trouble. If only we could learn how that *fiendal* comes and goes at will, and how and where he obtains his inside information. Now, I have to leave, moonbeam; we both have plenty of work to do. I'll see you tonight. Be careful."

Jana stood in her husband's comforting embrace for a few minutes and shared several tender kisses and gentle caresses. "I love you, Varian. You be careful, too. This *villite* is after anyone in power, so you're bound to be a prime target. So are our rulers and their families. And Nigel and Andrea."

"I've assigned Alliance Force guards to all of

them. I don't want any loved one kidnapped to be ransomed for information."

Frances Haver peered through a slot into the barren and locked room where Amaya Saar sat in a corner in a hunched position to conceal as much of her nakedness as possible. "Are you hungry and thirsty yet?" the psychic asked. "Do you want your clothes? All you have to do is answer our questions and you'll receive them."

Amaya ignored the woman and kept her chin resting on her raised knees and her eyes closed. She despised the two people who were holding her captive and the things they were doing to her to extract information, facts she refused to disclose. They had threatened and attempted to intimidate her in countless ways. They had performed numerous medical tests on her, none of which she had been able to resist after being rendered unconscious by disabling gas sent into the cell she inhabited like an animal. Now they were angry and frustrated. They had denied her food and liquid for two days. They refused to let her have clothes, a bed, a chair, a bath, or anything that would lessen her discomfort. The only things in the room except her body were a metal container for waste products and a camera mounted high in one corner for observing her.

"Come now, Amaya, let's be friends, or at least allies. Stop this silly silence and defiance; they aren't accomplishing anything except torment for you. Talk to me."

Amaya remained motionless and silent as she cursed the woman. Her bare flesh was chilled but she would not request she be moved to more comfortable quarters. She was hungry and thirsty but she could not obtain nourishment at such a price. They would get nothing from her except what they took by force. If necessary, she would die to retain her honor and remaining secrets. This trap was a result of her own doings, so she must accept the consequences. Yet she hated to think of how her family, Jason, and her friends would suffer because of her careless and self-indulgent actions. She would perish alone and they would never know what happened to her. She gave mute apologies to each of them for the torment they would endure.

"We've tried not to frighten or harm you, but Doug is getting impatient with you," Frances asserted. "You know how gentle he's been with every test and examination. He wants to know how to work that device we took off your wrist. We saw the things it did when you used it on the beach and on the deck during that storm. We know that metal doesn't exist on Earth, and those symbols are unknown to us and our data banks. If you care about your safety and release, give us information about you and your people."

Amaya was bombarded with questions that were being repeated numerous times.

"Are you alone? How did you get on Earth? Why were you sent? Are you a scientist? A test subject for survival and mating? How long have you been on Earth? When and how were you planning to leave? How do you block my mind probes even when you're unconscious? How does your space travel work? What kind of weapons and technologies does your race possess? What about medicines? Why is it so terrible to share such helpful facts with us? We've kept *you* a secret from our government and scientists; I know you don't want us to turn you over to them. They would not be as gentle as Doug and I have been. Cooperate, Amaya, or matters will worsen for you and others."

What "others" did the woman mean? Amaya wondered in alarm. The only person they could know about was Jason Carlisle. What if, she fretted, they abducted her lover and brought him there to use as a weapon against her? What if they tortured him to extract answers from her? Could she remain silent and watch him suffer? Could she allow them to kill him? What would he think, say, and feel after discovering her secret identity in such a vile manner?

"Suit yourself," Frances answered Amaya's silence, "but you'll be sorry you didn't cooperate."

If or when I get free, you'll wish you could have read my mind and saved your miserable and greedy lives! I must escape, after I destroy all of their records about me. I have to locate Jason and protect him from harm. But can I dupe you two with faked friendship and assistance? I must try something daring or they'll never allow me out of this prison. But what?

"Have you told Franklin about her?" Frances asked.

Douglas looked up from the microscope. "No,

and I hope I can keep her a secret for at least a while longer. Since I'm in charge of this research facility, no one dares to question me about anything, and I don't allow anyone in this section. Graham doesn't come here often, so I hope to keep her hidden from him and everybody else. That shouldn't be a problem since I usually make my reports to him by phone. He would take control of her and our work if he discovered her existence. The old coot's seventy now and he's desperate for a fountain-of-youth drug. Despite the bastard's billions, he can't buy a life extension or replace damaged body parts. He would view this beautiful alien as a source of power, wealth, and healing. He'd probably want me to give him her perfect organs, or demand she be dissected for crucial answers to life's mysteries. But Franklin Graham isn't going to be the one to profit from Amaya Saar. *We* found her; we own her; she's going to make us rich and famous and I won't need his backing for my private research. This secret facility is his, but contrary to his beliefs, I don't belong to him; and neither does my research and grand prize."

"He's powerful and dangerous, Doug," Frances refuted. "He's chewed up men and spit them out for lesser offenses than you're committing. If he learns you're deceiving him on his property and under his support, there will be hell and damnation to pay. He'll destroy us. You'll be ejected from here, and he'll have Amaya and all of your files."

"Not if we're careful, and not if we're finished with her soon."

"But she won't cooperate. I've tried everything on her."

Douglas sent the psychic a devilish grin. "Not everything, my sweet lover. I have an idea. Listen," he ordered.

After he explained his ploy, Frances laughed in joy and agreed with him. "You're the cleverest man alive, and the sexiest. That's why we get along so well: our desires and goals are matched." She unbuttoned his lab coat and peeled it off his shoulders, then she unfastened his belt and lowered his zipper. He lifted his hips from the large stool for her to wriggle the trousers to his ankles. She knelt and feverishly nursed his manhood into a hard and slick tool, then propped her feet on the stool's highest rungs and clasped his biceps to ride the wild stallion within her.

Douglas pressed her forehead to his shoulder and held it there with a hand on her nape. His traveling gaze halted on Amaya's naked body on the nearby monitor and he fantasized about rapturous sex with the ravishing alien while he had her strapped to a gurney. For a while, Dr. Douglas Karnes forgot the woman atop him was a genuine psychic who was picking up disturbing and infuriating perceptions.

A still-vexed Frances went to see Amaya, whom she knew had been given food and drink by her guileful lover. She had been tempted not to carry out his devious ploy, as it had compelled her to leave the facility for almost a week, leave Douglas alone with his lustful cravings. Yet she knew from their intimate greeting earlier that nothing sexual had happened between the two during her long absence. If it had, she fumed . . .

Amaya heard the slot being opened but didn't look in that direction. She assumed it was the scientist returning. At last he was giving her nourishment three times a day, keeping her cell at a comfortable temperature, and had ceased his medical tests. During his many recent visits, he asked questions and chuckled when she refused to speak with him. But he wouldn't give her garments or covers, which he said she could use as "weapons to take her life."

"I have a surprise for you today, Amaya. We have guests: the McKays."

Amaya recognized Frances Haver's voice and caught those shocking words. Her head jerked upward and her gaze darted to the opening where the woman's smirking face was visible. A shudder of fear swept over her.

"They're friends of yours, right? And you don't want to see them harmed because of your foolish pride and stubbornness? I couldn't locate your terrestrial lover, so I figured his relatives would fill our needs. When I went to see them in Houston, I told them you had an accident and we needed to reach Jason Carlisle or your family. Jason isn't to be found anywhere and they didn't know how to contact your family. Imagine that. They said you had come visiting in April with their daughter and her family, but they didn't know how to reach them either because they're in the Secret Service. Tell me, Amaya, are the Sangers visiting your world while you visit ours? Is contact and alliances with E.T.'s something else our government is keeping secret from us? Does Jason know you're an alien? Where was he going when he left home?"

Amaya stood, ignored her nudity, and approached the sealed door. Her angry gaze glared into Frances's cocky one. "The McKays know nothing about me; they cannot help you; release them. They are old and ill. I do not know the whereabouts of Jason Carlisle, and he is ignorant about me. You have done terrible and cruel things to me; I demand our release."

"Well, I'll be damned, it's about time you responded to me! All I needed was the right stimulus, and I have it. If you cooperate, the McKays won't be harmed. If you refuse, I can't imagine what Doug will do to them. Or to Jason after he's located. From the way you two were so lovey-dovey, I suspect you care a great deal for him, unless he's just a specimen to you. I suppose you can't love him too much or he would know the truth about you. Still, you might not want to see your pet project harmed. I can't help you protect him and the others if you rashly provoke Doug."

Amaya ignored the woman's questions and remarks about her feelings for Jason. "If they are harmed, you will be slain," she replied. "You do not comprehend the great power you challenge. You and your people are primitives compared to my race. Soon they will come and you will perish for this crime. To save yourself, you must free me and the McKays."

"They can't find you here, and neither can our government, so don't bluff me. Without that gadget on your wrist, you're helpless. You don't have any supernatural or superior powers in mind and body or you would have used them on us by now. You don't scare me or Doug."

"A homing device will guide them to me, and you will be punished." Amaya saw a reaction of surprise and alarm, as she'd hoped to extract with her lie. If they could be panicked into moving elsewhere, it might provide her with a chance—no matter how slim—to escape. Even if only *she* got away, she could find Jason, and together they could rescue Andrea's mother and father, her best friend's grandparents. She was responsible for their peril, so she must help them avoid injury and death. If anything happened to Avi's family, she would never forgive herself; nor would the Sangers and her own parents forgive her.

"Where is this alleged homing device? You couldn't have activated one because there was no time and there's been no occasion since your capture. You're lying."

"The homing device automatically begins its signal if I do not prevent it by pressing a certain button at a certain time each day."

"It's inside that wrist gismo, isn't it?"

"Yes, but you cannot disarm it. Any attempt to destroy or disassemble the unit will result in a large explosion; as a safeguard, it self-destructs."

"Is it too late to turn off the signal if I let you hold the device?"

"No; they will think it is a malfunction when the signal ceases."

"This is only a clever trick to get your hands on that weapon, isn't it? I don't trust you, Amaya, and I don't believe you. And I'm not a fool! If a rescue team comes here and threatens us, we'll kill you and the McKays before they reach the inner lab. We'll know the instant exterior security is breached, so they'll never reach you in time to save your life."

"They can penetrate your primitive security system with ease. Bring me the device and I will disarm it to save the McKays' lives. I will not activate my weapon or the force shield; you have my word of honor." Amaya faked an expression and tone of honesty.

"So, it does contain a weapon! A laser beam of some kind."

"That is correct."

"How are the beam and shield activated?"

"I cannot tell you; I am sworn to secrecy by my leader."

"Even if your life is at stake?"

"Yes, and I will obey."

"Even if the lives of friends or allies are at risk?"

"Yes. I do not wish to have them harmed, but I cannot expose such power and secrets to any Earthling, for any reason." She awaited the woman's next move as their gazes met and battled.

"Put this on and have a visit with the McKays. We'll see if their lives truly mean nothing to you. Get dressed and I'll return for you soon."

Amaya picked up the bodysuit Frances had stuffed through the large slot and dropped to the floor. The communications slit was closed and locked. When she heard the hissing of gas being pumped into the room at the ceiling, she donned the outfit in a rush before she lost consciousness and was bound to be taken elsewhere to speak with Jason's aunt and uncle.

Amaya awakened with Grace and Martin standing on either side of the gurney to which she was secured by straps at her ankles and wrists. The elderly couple was leaning over and their faces revealed expressions of concern. She wriggled to glance around the laboratory to find no one else present. Yet the red light on the ceiling camera indicated they were being monitored, no doubt by the despicable pair, Frances Haver and Douglas Karnes.

Grace stroked her hair. "Are you all right, dear? You look so pale and weak. They told us you're very ill and needed us because they couldn't locate Jason. Do you know where he is so we can phone him?"

Amaya shook her head as she deliberated what to tell them and how.

"We've tried to reach him for days at his office, home, and the beach house; but he must be out on a case. As soon as he returns, he'll get our messages and join us here. Tell us how to contact your family or Andrea."

"I cannot."

Martin eyed her as he asked, "Because of your confidential job or because you really don't know where they are?"

"Their location and work are a secret I am sworn to protect."

"But you're very ill, Amaya; you need your family," Grace reasoned in a gentle tone. "I'm sure they would want to know and to come to you. What's wrong with you, dear? Why are these straps necessary?"

Amaya began her revelations in a careful manner to prevent shock to the elderly couple. She knew she must enlighten them to their jeopardy. "The woman who brought you here and the man who spoke with you lied. I am not ill. I'm their captive. They drugged and abducted me from Jason's home after he left for Houston. They want to use you to force me to betray everything about myself and our Secret Service work. If they could find Jason, he would be captured and used against me. I am sorry I endangered you, but I cannot tell them anything."

Martin gaped at her, then turned to stare at the sealed door for a moment. "What are you talking about, Amaya? We weren't kidnapped. You must be confused; it's probably the medication or your illness. Frances Haver is a famous woman, a renowned psychic; she wouldn't do anything illegal; in fact, she's helped police all over the country solve many crimes. We met the physician who's treating you, Douglas Karnes; he has excellent credentials. None of us is in any danger. They just need facts about your medical history so they can help you get well. You've been unconscious on and off, so they needed written permission to treat you; that's why they were trying to contact your family, or Andrea, or Jason. People are lawsuit crazy these days and they didn't want to take any risks."

Amaya had been shaking her head in disagreement as Martin spoke. "She tricked you into coming here to use you as weapons against me," she announced after he finished. "I am not sick, and I'm bound so I can't resist them or escape. They are evil people, sir, and we are all in danger. See that camera?" She nodded toward it with a raised head and the couple obeyed. "They're watching us and listening to us now. They've kept me locked in a bare room with no clothes for many days, without food and drink. They have done cruel things to me. They threatened to harm you both—and Jason, too—if I do not tell them my secrets. If I am forced to talk, the Sangers' lives will be in peril," she added in deceit to compel them to grasp the seriousness of the situation. "They want to know all about our planet's workings and technology. They said such facts will make them rich, famous, and powerful. They want the names and locations of my leaders and our other workers. Does this place look like a hospital to you? Do I look ill? Do I look as if I'm being treated kindly, being treated as a patient? They are evil enemies and we are in danger. You are prisoners now. If you do not believe me, try to leave this place or ask to use the telephone."

Martin McKay somehow knew she was telling the truth. "Those sorry, good-for-nothing . . . They won't get away with this! The police and Jason will find us and arrest them. Don't you tell them anything, Amaya, and don't worry about us. They wouldn't dare hurt me and Grace."

"They might, sir." She glanced from an angry Martin to a worried Grace. "I'm sorry, but I cannot tell them what they want to know."

The older man patted her arm. "We don't want you to be a traitor and reveal government secrets, do we, Grace?"

"No, Amaya, you mustn't allow terrorists to get our nation's secrets."

"I'll get you out of these harnesses," Martin said, and began to unfasten one of her wrist bindings. "How dare they treat a lady like this! I'll—"

"I can't allow you to do that, Mr. McKay," Douglas said as he arrived in a hurry and halted the man's actions by shoving away his arthritic fingers.

"Get your hands off her and me!" Martin warned. "This is an out—"

"Step back, you old coot, or I'll hurt you," Doug threatened.

"You and who else?" Martin scoffed as he glared at the man in blue.

"Me," Francis injected as she pointed a pistol at the elderly couple.

Grace shrieked when she noticed the weapon and Martin skirted the gurney and wrapped an arm around his frightened wife. "It's all right, dear; I won't let them hurt you." He glared at the psychic. "Why are you doing this, Miss Haver?" he asked.

As Douglas resecured the loose fastening,

Frances told the McKays there wouldn't be any trouble if Amaya answered their questions.

"You're both crazy. You can't get away with this. Surely you don't expect her to betray her country to traitors like you two?" Martin turned an alarmed gaze on Amaya. "Don't you tell them anything, Amaya, no matter *what* they do to us."

"She doesn't work for our government; she's an alien from another planet, from another galaxy. She will tell us what we want to know about her and her race. Our world needs the knowledge she possesses in that stubborn head of hers. We'll get it out of her one way or another; you'll see."

"An alien from outer space?" Martin scoffed. "You two are insane."

"You stupid old man, she *is* an alien!" Douglas shouted. "I have proof. I've done all kinds of tests on her body. We were witness to strange things she can do. Tell them who and what you are, Amaya."

The Maffeian woman refused to comply. "My work and identity are secrets."

Douglas seized Amaya's chin. "We'll see how brave and silent you are in a day or two. Frances, lock our new guests in room six. No food, water, medication, or lights. Soon they'll beg her to co-operate with us. As for you, Amaya Saar, let's see if my drugs will loosen your memory or electric shock will spark your tongue to oblige me."

Frances looked at Douglas. "It's been two days and we haven't broken her will yet," he fretted. "What are we going to try next?"

Douglas glanced at the alien female on the monitor. "Drugs and pain don't seem to work. She's well trained to resist them. Most people would have cracked by now. I have to admit she's unique."

"Are you going to get rougher with her, or torture the McKays like you threatened? I know you held off on them to avoid risking their lives. Either she isn't scared or she'll hold silent at all costs."

"It looks as if I'll have no choice if she doesn't talk by tomorrow. I want to extract everything we need from her then get the hell out of Graham's facility. I don't want to risk him or that Carlisle paying us a visit. Since you couldn't locate him, he's probably out searching for her. At least we didn't make any slips he can trace. You did steal the tape out of his answering machine so he won't get the McKays' messages about her?"

"Yes, right out of his bedroom. His home security is most lacking."

"You didn't really phone his office and beach house, did you?"

"I'm not stupid, Doug; I faked those calls in front of them. If we decide to abduct Jason Carlisle, it has to come as a surprise. Frankly, I think it's dangerous to drag him into this situation unless it becomes necessary. A man in his line of work and with his connections is trouble."

"I agree; that's why I didn't send you back out after him. Now, let's look ahead. Are you ready to continue with my next test?"

Frances didn't want Douglas to fertilize Amaya's

confiscated eggs with his sperm. "I don't like this crazy experiment, you mating with an alien."

"It's for science. I have to know if our chemistries are compatible. Why are you angry? I'm not going to bed with her."

"What are you going to do if the procedure works?"

"Study the results, maybe grow a test tube baby to—"

"You can't be serious! That's going too far. Absolutely not, Doug."

"Okay, I'll think about it a while longer," he lied. *Tomorrow, I'll find a lengthy errand for you to run while I do this test. I must know if interspecie mating is possible, and a baby should make Amaya more cooperative.*

Fourteen

Amaya's eyes flew open and her body stiffened in alert when she heard the voice inside her head. She could hardly believe what was about to happen. It was Galen sending her a telepathic message! Her twin was coming to rescue her! If she wasn't dreaming or hallucinating . . .

Amaya called herself to full alert because the mental signal was faint and she was surprised it had awakened her. Thank *Kahala* she wasn't drugged beyond receiving it. She concentrated on responding.

Galen, I can hear you, but your range is weak. I'm in terrible danger. I've been captured. I don't know where I am. Please find me and help me.

Amaya! Are you injured? Are enemies with you?

No, but I'm a prisoner and they took my wrist unit.

Keep contacting me so I can locate you.

I'm in a secret complex, but I don't know where it is. I don't know how many people are here. I've seen two, a male and a female. They said there was exterior security and they're armed with alien weapons, guns.

Your signal is getting stronger, so I'm nearing

your location. In Earth miles, you are far from the city you visited. I'm orbiting you now. I see a large structure, *many trees, an enclosure fence, and vehicles. I have your readouts on my monitor. Stay calm. I will be there soon.*

Be careful; these people are evil and perilous. There are monitors for watching me, other chambers, and the corridors.

Inside the structure, four other bodies are registering on my sensors; two are very close to you and two are a short distance away. All are asleep.

Those nearby are Andrea's parents. The enemies captured them to force me to reveal my secrets. They know who and what I am, but I have told them nothing. A psychic discovered me and betrayed me to her doctor lover. They used me as a lab specimen. It's been terrible. I had little hope left.

There are other bodies registering outside the structure: two are at the enclosure fence, out of intrusion range; one is near the structure. I can see him now on my monitor. Where is the Earthling male you love?

They abducted me when he was not home so he does not know what has happened to me or where I am. I'm sure he's searching for me.

Describe him to me. Amaya complied. *Relax, my sister, you will be safe soon. I have many things to tell you.*

How are Mother and Father? Are they angry with me?

Only worried about your safety.

Is that why they sent you after me?

That and other reasons. I will explain when you are with me. I must think of other things now. I will see you in a few preons.

Amaya was relieved she had been allowed to keep on the bodysuit, though she wished they had provided her with shoes and undergarments. She watched the door and waited to be freed. Time seemed to crawl by like a *yema*. She was eager to see her brother, eager to release the McKays, eager to locate Jason and explain everything. She knew she must return home because it was not safe for her on Earth. She prayed Jason loved her enough to accept the truth and to move to her world.

The lights went on, the door was opened, and Galen's tall frame seemingly filled the space from jamb to jamb. Though he was wearing headgear, she recognized him easily. Amaya squealed with delight, ran forward, and flung herself into his outstretched arms. "It's so wonderful to see you. I've missed you. I love you. I've never been this afraid in my life."

Galen stroked her hair with one hand and hugged her with the other. "I love you, too, Amaya, and you nearly scared me witless when you wouldn't respond to my callings. We kept increasing the range of our probe until you heard me. I've missed you, and I have a surprise for you. We found this man lurking outside and seeking entrance."

Amaya's misty gaze perceived Jason standing in the hallway. His expression and stance were odd, almost accusatory. "How did you find me, Jason?" she asked.

"I tracked you here and I met up with your friend outside."

Amaya grasped the way he said "friend" and surmised the reason for his cool mood. "Galen, I want to introduce you to Jason Carlisle, the man I love, the man who enticed me to stay behind and get into this mischief. Jason, this is Galen Saar, my twin brother. You couldn't notice the resemblance with his visor on."

"Your brother?" Jason echoed as the stranger removed his helmet.

Galen smiled and grasped Jason's wrist in a Maffeian handshake. "It is an honor and pleasure to meet the man who stole my sister's heart. We will get acquainted later after this matter is handled. Amaya, we must hurry; we cannot remain here much longer. Does he know about us?"

"Not yet. Jason, will you wait inside this chamber for me while I speak with Galen? There are private things I must tell you before we leave."

Jason complied as he worried this was the moment he had dreaded: someone had come to take her from him. He had been near crazed by fear since her disappearance. He had followed clues to this location, only to learn she didn't require his help. He needed a hug and kiss himself! He needed words in private. He didn't want to lose her; he had to convince her to stay and marry him.

Galen spoke privately with his sister in the hallway before leaving with his team to carry out their tasks.

Amaya joined her lover and gazed into his sapphire eyes. She smiled, then embraced him. "I'm happy you came to rescue me. I love you and I feared you were lost to me forever. All hope was almost gone."

Jason clasped her face between his hands and looked into her glowing eyes. "I've been out of my mind with worry. Did they hurt you?"

"I'm fine. You can tell me later how you found me. Time is short and there's much for me to reveal. I must return home; I'm not safe on your planet. I love you and want to become your mate, but that isn't possible here. When you asked me to stay behind, you didn't know how hard that decision was for me. I'm not from Earth, Jason; I live in another galaxy; I am an alien being from another world," she stressed for clarity.

Jason didn't laugh because her expression and tone told him she believed what she was saying! He stared at the woman he loved as if she had lost her senses. He wondered what the kidnappers had done to her to create such delusions. Before he could try to clear her wits, she jumped ahead with her implausible story.

Jason hoped her brother returned soon because she needed urgent medical treatment to rid her of these hallucinations. If she was only trying to escape from him, she could fabricate a more convincing tale. He assumed she'd been abducted because of her confidential work, perhaps in an attempt to obtain classified material. There was no telling what kinds of drugs and torments had been used on her. In her troubled state of mind, he shouldn't tease or pressure her. "Just relax, my love; it's over now," he soothed when she concluded telling him everything that had led up to her abduction by the psychic and Douglas Karnes. "Don't think about such things."

Amaya perceived that he doubted her words and sanity. "My captors discovered what I am when I was careless at the beach, and they've been treating me as a lab specimen. When they couldn't find you to use as a weapon to extract my race's secrets, they abducted the McKays. Galen is rescuing them now and they'll be returned home. Andrea hasn't told them about her new life; her parents were led to believe the Sangers work for the Secret Service to conceal the truth. Your world would panic if it knew of our existence and visits. Some forces would try anything to capture and misuse us and our knowledge." She realized she was being sketchy but explanation time was limited.

"You have to calm down, Amaya; you're confused and scared. This kidnapping has you mixed up. You'll be fine as soon as you're out of here and you get some rest. You aren't an alien, my love."

"Yes, Jason, I am. But I haven't altered my lifeform; this is how I truly look. Our races are almost alike in appearance. I am not a monster as your movies portray extraterrestrials, but I am an alien to you. As you can see from me and Galen, intermating is possible and safe. Other Earthlings live in our world, but no government on your planet knows of us, and it must remain that way until Earth advances to our level of technology and the many problems of this planet are resolved. I'm not crazy or suffering from delusions or trauma. You must believe me because I have to return home to Maffei tonight."

"Is this a wild scheme to get away from me and to prevent me from searching for you later?" Jason asked accusingly. "You want me to think you've gone nuts or you require deprogramming, so you're being hauled off to a secret government institution for treatment? If that Secret Service claim is phony, why not use it on me, too? Why this absurd charade?"

"I love you, Jason, and you deserve to hear the truth. I—"

"Truth, Amaya? You want me to believe you're an alien from outer space? Believe Andrea is married to one and lives in another galaxy? Believe Avi and Thaine are half alien? Believe you're about to hop a spaceship and leave Earth forever?"

"I swear those are facts. I know I sound insane and my story sounds incredible. I swear I love you and everything I've said is true."

He had to call her bluff. "What proof do you have to offer me? I can't believe this wild story without evidence."

"Wait a moment while I summon Galen to bring my wrist unit and I'll give you proof."

He watched her close her eyes in intense concentration. He avoided a cynical tone when he asked, "I suppose you're using telepathy?"

"Yes, Galen and I can communicate this way because we're twins."

Soon, Galen arrived and handed Amaya the item Jason had assumed was a watch or data bank, and gave her other objects to use. How, Jason mused, had her brother known what she wanted unless—

Galen looked at Jason. "Believe her because she speaks the truth about us," he said. "We are Maffeians from another galaxy, but we're no threat to you or Earth. My sister loves you and trusts you; that's why she's revealing our secret. Now, you must hurry, Amaya," he added to her, and left.

Amaya explained how the device worked as she strapped it on her wrist and related how she had exposed herself to Frances and Douglas by using it several times while they were spying on her. She noticed that Jason remained silent and alert, and dubious. "I need your knife," she said to him.

After passing it to her, he watched Amaya cut her finger, then use a beam to seal the cut to perfection. "That's a neat trick; demonstrate on me," he asked.

Jason was stunned when she did so, and gaped at his finger in surprise. Still, that didn't make it an alien instrument, only a secret and clever one. He observed as Amaya placed objects on the floor and disintegrated them without a trace. Again, he reasoned, it could be some highly advanced government weapon or she was a gifted magician.

"This is my force shield; try to touch me."

Jason's probing hands came into contact with an invisible dome-shaped barrier covering her. No amount of pressure or pounding could shatter or penetrate it. An eerie sensation filled him.

Amaya spoke into a small unit. "Lieutenant Amaya Saar requesting private communication with Lieutenant Thaine Sanger."

Moments later, a reply came from the Earthling's cousin. "Thaine here, Amaya. How are you? What do you require? Over."

"I'm fine now, but your cousin is with me and needs a word or two to convince him I'm from another world. Over."

"Jason is with you? Over."

"I'm here, Thaine. Where are you?"

"Over," Amaya added for her astounded lover.

Thaine chuckled as he responded. "On a ship orbiting your location and waiting for the landing party to return for departure. Over."

"Departure to where? Over," Jason finished that time in recall.

"Tell him the truth, Thaine, but quickly. Over."

"The planet Rigel in the Maffei Galaxy, our home. That's where we live and work. Amaya, too. We're Star Fleet officers. Over."

"That's crazy; it isn't possible. Over."

"Believe it, Jason, because it's true. Come and see for yourself. Over."

"Thaine, use the sensors to tell Jason what you see down here. Over."

As his cousin described the sights and movements in and around the complex, Jason stared at the communicator, then looked at Amaya.

"That's fine, Thaine. Thanks. We'll join you soon. Over and out."

"Don't be worried or refuse to trust her, Jason. If you decide to go with us, you'll be safe and happy; I promise. Over and out."

Amaya met Jason's bewildered gaze. "He's right. Will you come with me to my world and become my husband? I love you and need you, but I can't live here. Another exposure could be worse."

"You're asking me to move to another galaxy and marry you?"

"Yes. I know that's a big decision and this is a stunning revelation, but I lack the time to explain it further or to give more proof. We must depart soon or risk exposure. If you need more time to search your feelings for me, I'll return next year with the Sangers for your answer. If you don't love me or want me, tell me and I will not return. To come with me, you must give up all you know and possess here. There is no time to sell your belongings, and your money has no value in my world."

Jason studied her expression. Even if he didn't believe her, should he play along and accompany her to see what he discovered? "You're serious and sane, aren't you?"

"Yes. I was going to tell you everything, but I was captured. I feared you would not love and want a female from another world and race. I had to give you time to get to know me as a person. I am an officer in Star Fleet and a member of a secret squad of military specialists. Much like you, I investigate and solve crimes. I'm a *Spacer* pilot. Those are crafts similar to your space shuttles but swifter and superior; that's why your airplanes and Space Center Houston intrigued me. I work in Security at Star Base on our capital planet when I'm not on special assignment or a secret mission. My brother is the Security and Weapons Chief on our lead starship. My mother, an Earthling like you, is a research scientist. My father is head of Star Fleet, the Alliance Force, and our special units. He's a rich and powerful man; his grandfather was our past ruler. There's so much to tell you about me, my world, and my people; but time is fleeing. Will you come with me?"

"This is mind-staggering, Amaya. I knew you were different and a huge mystery surrounded you, but I didn't expect *this*. Another galaxy? Aliens?"

"I know it's hard to believe. You'll have many adventures and challenges to face. I, my family, and the Sangers will help you learn to adjust. Life together in the Maffei Alliance will be wonder—"

The door opened and Galen poked his head inside the room, cutting off her sentence. He looked at his sister and sent the telepathic message: *It's time to finish and depart. Does he believe you? Is he coming with us?*

I don't know. Amaya fused her entreating gaze to Jason's keen one. "I must help them destroy this place and all records exposing me, then leave. Do you want me to return next year for your answer?"

"No, I want to come with you now. Is that all right?" he asked Galen.

"It's permissible. Father said I could decide after meeting you. You're welcome to join us. If you change your mind later, you can return next year with the Sangers."

"Thanks. Do I have time to write a paper giving all I own to Aunt Grace and Uncle Martin in case I don't return? I'll say I'm joining the Secret Service with Amaya and the Sangers; I don't want to fake my death and grieve them."

Amaya hugged him. "Yes, if you hurry. Where are the McKays?"

Jason noticed the monitoring system. "I'll tape a message using their video equipment. What did you tell them about all of this?"

"For now, they believe we're a Secret Service rescue team. Later, they won't remember tonight; Amaya will explain my meaning. Let's go. The Med staff and security team are ready to carry out their tasks."

Two hours later, Frances Haver and Douglas Karnes had no memory of the last few months; they were lying a short distance from the structure and with "evidence" to make it appear they had sabotaged the undisclosed research facility. The guards at the front gate were "asleep" and would report they didn't see or hear anything. Every test and file concerning Amaya Saar was destroyed. Her belongings were returned. Jason's car was disintegrated without a trace so it wouldn't be found near the inexplicable crime scene. The McKays were safe at home; any recall of the shocking events of the past few days was erased from their minds. On their kitchen table was a videotaped message leaving everything Jason Carlisle owned to them; it included an assertion he was now working with the Sangers and his new wife in a classified rank and couldn't be reached.

He had collected personal keepsakes from his villa that he wanted to take with him. A cassette tape with the McKays' frantic message about Amaya which was on an answering machine in his home office was destroyed, as Frances had missed finding it in the locked downstairs room.

Jason was developing a growing sense of belief in the "impossible." Aboard the enormous *Galactic Wind* and with Amaya at his side, they had all left orbit to voyage "homeward."

As soon as Galen enlightened Amaya about the many troubles in their world, he planned to introduce her and Jason to Renah. Then, all four could get acquainted during the return trip. Until the twins completed their discussion, Thaine Sanger was keeping his second cousin occupied with undeniable proof of everything Amaya had told Jason earlier.

As for Renah, she paced her quarters and worried over the last order from her family which had been passed to her shortly before this trek.

"I shouldn't have stayed on Earth, Galen; I should have been home helping to battle this threat. I was selfish to indulge my own desires when my world is being attacked."

"You did what you had to do, Amaya, what anyone in your position would have done, including me and our parents," Galen assured his sister. "How many times during our lives does true love come along? Once, if we're lucky. If we sacrifice that glorious opportunity, even for duty, we might never find it again. You had to stay to test your feelings, and Jason's. It's not as if you could have seen him tomorrow or next week or next month;

you would have been galaxies apart. I understand you had no choice, so do Mother and Father. Of course they were upset and worried, but they aren't angry. They only want to see you safe and happy, as do I. Besides, you didn't know we were in peril; Commander Sanger withheld that news. Father knows you would have returned had you known. And even if you *had* returned on schedule, there was nothing you could have done that we haven't thought of. This *villite* is too clever to be thwarted quickly. Besides, we had to go to Earth for that data."

"Thank you, Galen, for trying to make this easier on me. That virus is terrible; I heard about it many times during my stay. I hope Mother and her staff can conquer it soon. I don't know if it will help her any, but the scientist who captured me found my spleen and lymph nodes more highly evolved than the Earthlings'; and they're major parts of our immune system, which the virus assaults."

"I don't know if she's considered and studied that; we'll pass along the information to her when we reach home. She's staying on Rigel with Father so she'll be near the Star Base Med Complex. All of our best scientists and doctors are gathered there to research and treat the victims. Father is working from there, too. They have living chambers in the Pandor Tower nearby. I'm anxious to return and work against our enemy. At least that replica of Father hasn't made another appearance, or hadn't before we departed. We'll both be assigned to tracking and arresting the virus. I can't think of a worse period in our lifetime. If only we could extract clues from the Earthlings we capture, we could make sense of this mystery."

"Our *villite* appears to have planned every angle. I agree with you and Father that it is strange for him to possess such knowledge without having inside help. But I can't imagine any of our leaders betraying us. We've known all of them for most of our lives, and I trust them. It would be a terrible blow to Father and to our world if one of them is a traitor."

Amaya's eyes suddenly held a question, "Do you think Father would assign Jason as my teammate?" she asked Galen.

"He might, because Jason is unknown in our world and that could be an advantage for us. We'll teach him what he doesn't know and get him prepared during our return voyage. Now, tell me everything about Jason and your adventures on Mother's old planet."

Amaya's body warmed, her cheeks glowed, and her emotions soared as she responded in detail. She witnessed the anger in her brother as she related her capture and treatment by Dr. Karnes and Frances Haver. Yet Galen wasn't a cruel man, so he hadn't ordered their deaths as punishment. He listened with great interest as she told him many things about Earth and its inhabitants. She finished with, "I love Jason with every part of me, Galen; I can hardly wait for you to discover and enjoy such feelings."

"I already have, my radiant sister; that's why I understand and accept your decision to remain with him, even at the risk of your life and career."

Amaya studied his sparkling face. "Who is she? How did you meet? When? Where? Does she love you?"

Galen chuckled. "You can fire questions as fast as a laser weapon. *Kahala,* it's good to have you back with me. Do you recall the beautiful woman with short *platinien* hair who was at my side during your rescue?" Amaya nodded. "She's Lieutenant Renah Dhobi, a member of my Security and Weapons team. She transported into my life the day you left for Earth, and captivated me the moment we met. After this threat is over, she's going to become my mate."

"Has she agreed? Or is my brother still pursuing her?"

"She loves and desires me as much as I do her."

"So, you handsome ex-*reacher,* tell me everything about this perfect woman."

After Galen finished his revelations, Amaya smiled at him and jested, "I can see you have a case of love sickness as bad as mine. Perhaps we can share a mating ceremony later, give Mother and Father two new family members on the same day. I assume they will be delighted to see us take this big step. We could have a large party and invite all of our friends. I'm sure the Sangers would enjoy sharing such a moment with us."

"That sounds excellent to me, but we should check with Renah and Jason first. I doubt the Sangers will be surprised to see him with us."

"I hope everyone likes him."

"Everyone will except Commander Mohr, right?"

"At least it will make him stop chasing me. Honestly, Galen, I tried every way I could to discourage him."

"If he were Jason Carlisle, you wouldn't want him to cease."

"If he were Jason or even like Jason, we'd be mated already. Now, why don't we join Renah and Jason so we can all get acquainted?"

"That pleases me. Any time away from her and I get lonely."

"It is strange how powerfully love has affected us. Let's go find our future mates."

Amaya entered the guest quarters which had been assigned to Jason. His second cousin was with him. Both men stood as she approached and sat down with them. Her gaze drifted over the man she loved and who had given up so much for a life with her. "Has Thaine been overwhelming you with information about us and our world?" she asked.

Jason grinned and nodded. "I've seen and learned a lot and there's still plenty to absorb. This is about as much of a shock to my system as Earth was to yours. Now I see why you said you believed in aliens and space travel, and I surely won't argue their realities. A man couldn't ask for more proof than I've been given. But it's exciting and stimulating, not scary at all. I guess I'm not as smart and perceptive as I thought or I would have picked up some clues over the years when my cousins came to visit. You, too, woman."

Thaine chuckled. "We were always careful not

to drop any clues or make any slips; at least, ones we couldn't cover fast."

"Don't forget, our mothers are Earthlings and we're part Earthling," Amaya added. "But Thaine and Avi were better prepared for visits than I was. After I decided to go with them, there wasn't enough time to train me fully. I feared you would think I was stupid for not knowing common things and tasks. Your language and sayings and customs made me crazy at times."

Jason grasped her hand and held it. "I would never think of you as being ignorant, but I did think it was odd there was so much you didn't know. I assumed you'd led a pampered and sheltered life, and were from another country where things were different. When I first came aboard, it was like being in a foreign country; I couldn't grasp a word being said. Now I can understand anything anybody says to me because I have those little implants in my ears and head. Those are clever and valuable devices."

"That's what Karnes thought when they were exposed by his tests."

Amaya didn't want to think about her terrible experience, so she asked, "What have you two been doing during my meeting with Galen?"

"Thaine gave me a tour of this ship; it's huge, mind-boggling, like a town in itself. I was allowed to visit the bridge and take in the awesome, breathtaking view. Now I know how the astronauts feel when they watch Earth from space or the moon. Thaine introduced me to many nice people, including Commander Vaux. I'm astounded by the advances of your world, and I'm still in shock about my cousin being married to a man from another planet. The most amazing part is how this already seems natural to me."

"I told you I come from a peaceful and healthy galaxy, but that's no longer true," Amaya turned to Thaine. "Did you explain matters to him?"

"There's little I haven't told him, Amaya, but it will take time for all of it to settle in," the man replied. "My cousin is adapting quickly. He'll have no problems in our world. Now, why don't I leave you two alone to talk?"

Amaya stood and hugged him. "Thank you for everything, Thaine; you're a good friend. We'll meet in the Stardust Room for dinner. Galen is bringing Renah."

"Now that he and Sebok are giving up their freedom, I suppose I should search for a mate," Thaine confessed. "Since all of you had such good luck, maybe I will, too."

"You will," Amaya assured him, "because you're a wonderful and handsome man."

"Despite all you've learned about our troubles, are you still sure you made the right decision to come along?" Amaya asked, as soon as they were alone.

Jason realized how worried she was about her family and everything that was occurring in Maffei. "Yep. I'll help in every way if I can."

Amaya was relieved by his response. "Before we discuss other matters, tell me how you found me."

"When I found you and your things gone, I admit I panicked. Then, I realized you wouldn't have left before talking to me or leaving me a message on one of my answering machines. At first, I figured your people had come and taken you away. I could tell the place had been searched, so that confused me, made me suspicious. Since I believed you were in the Secret Service and those people usually have enemies, I was afraid one of them had abducted you, come after you for information. I knew you hadn't returned to Aunt Grace's because I spoke with her, before she and Uncle Martin vanished. I checked with neighbors at the beach, and the lady across the street saw you leave with the woman from the rental unit. Actually, she told me she saw you helped to a car by that woman and a male friend because you appeared too sick and weak to walk. That sounded odd."

Jason leaned closer to Amaya and crossed his legs. "The hospitals and clinics on the island and in Galveston had no record of you being brought in for treatment; that made me suspect you'd been drugged. I remembered feeling as if we were being watched several times and recalled bumping into Frances Haver on more than one occasion. I recognized her from TV, newspapers, and magazines because she's famous for helping police and private investigators solve crimes. I should have trusted my gut instinct and been more careful, but I couldn't sight anything suspicious, so I assumed I was wrong, paranoid."

Jason rested a hand on her thigh, needing to touch her as if to prove to himself they were together and she was safe. "I went home to get some things I needed for a full-scale investigation and heard Aunt Grace's message on the answering machine in my downstairs office; that's my business line. When I went to my bedroom to check my home line answering machine to see if there was more information or an update on it, the tape was missing. I knew somebody had been in the villa and stolen it. As with most criminals, Amaya, she made an error by assuming I had only one phone machine; that second tape gave me clues to follow. By searching their homes and checking other sources, I traced Frances to Douglas Karnes and him to Franklin Graham. I snooped into records and files and located his ownership of that secret facility outside of Houston, and played a hunch. I spotted Frances's car there. I was nosing around looking for a way inside when Galen appeared. He seemed to know who I was and said he was there to rescue you, said I could join him. Now, explain to me what happened to you."

Amaya revealed her frightening episode once more, and received an even stronger reaction than she had from Galen.

"I should have killed them for what they did to you."

Amaya held his hand in hers. "Amnesia was sufficient punishment. My people do not believe in killing unless it is necessary. Besides, my love, it was partly my fault for exposing myself to her."

"Nothing gave them the right to treat you like an animal. If they had harmed you, I *would* have killed them."

"They wanted my secrets too much to hurt or destroy me. I'm sorry the McKays were captured and frightened, and it's good they won't remember what happened. If they hadn't taken my wrist device, I could have stunned them and escaped. It was foolish to use it on Earth."

"You and Thaine showed me what it does; it's an amazing weapon."

"You'll have one, too," *if Father allows you to become my teammate.* "Only contact with the owner's fingerprints will make it function. That's why Karnes couldn't make it work. He never thought of placing my finger to the buttons to obtain clearance. If he had, that would have been awful. Usually I'm not careless or impulsive, Jason, but I wasn't thinking clearly."

"At least you're safe and we're together."

"We'll never be parted again." *If I can get you on the Elite Squad with me and if I'm not placed in confinement for a defiance of orders.*

"What if your parents don't like me and accept me?"

"How could they not do so when Galen and I do, and you are the cousin of my mother's best friend since childhood. There is no way they would dislike or reject you."

Jason pulled her into his arms. "I love you, Amaya Saar. I'll never be sorry for making this decision, no matter what happens in your world. I know you can't live in mine, so we'll find a way to make it work in yours."

"If I had searched the entire Universe, I could not have found a better man; we are perfectly matched, and we'll be happy together."

"I have no doubt that's true."

Their lips met in a heady kiss that led to another and another. As their hands caressed and stroked, heat seemed to radiate from their bodies like fiery suns that enflamed themselves and each other.

"Amaya, Amaya, I love you so much," he murmured in her ear, and felt her quiver with delight and suspense.

Amaya could hardly pull away to say, "We have to leave, my love, and join the others. I wish we could stay here alone, but Galen wants us to meet his new love. Later, I will sneak a visit with you."

"Sneak?" he teased with a sexy grin.

Amaya lifted her hand and ruffled his sable hair. "Yes, do not forget we are aboard a starship and I am an officer. I must be careful with my behavior. I am already on reprimand for being absent without permission. I shall have to—how do you Earthling's put it—'face the music' after my return. I might be lowered in rank, put on extra duty, or lose a month's pay for my actions. No matter, it was worth it. It *is* worth it," she corrected.

"Leaving everything I know and just about everything I owned behind is worth it to be with you. In the years to come, we'll look back on this episode and view these as small sacrifices for a beautiful future."

"I'm certain we will. Shall we freshen up and join the others?"

"After one more kiss and hug."

Days later on Rigel, a terrible explosion took place in the enormous research complex. All data and samples were destroyed. All patients were slain. All bodies awaiting autopsies and burial procedures were lost. Many staff members were killed or injured. Security was heightened and an investigation was begun. No attackers were captured alive; not even their bodies were recovered after self-disintegration following a successful assault.

Jana Greyson Saar was one of those injured. She was taken to the medical center for examination and treatment where her lacerations were sealed with *latron* beams, and excess fluid and blood were drained from those sites. Unconscious from a forceful blow to her head, Varian sat beside her *sleeper*, held her hand, and prayed for her recovery. Andrea and Nigel waited in worried silence nearby and prayed.

Varian looked at his best friend. "He's gone too far with his evil and cruelties. I'm going to kill the *villite* when I catch him, Nigel, with my bare hands."

"I'll help you do the good deed myself. We've got to find a way to expose him and stop him. Stars above, why is he doing this? Who is he?"

"*Gehenna* be damned, I have no idea! It makes no sense. He orders random attacks on our planets. He infects us with an incurable virus. He develops and uses a duplicate of me to get his weapons and supplies. He has cloaking ability we can't penetrate. He gets his men past our security. He fakes credentials to match real ones. He uses enthralled Earthlings, then disposes of them as if they're useless debris. He kills or orders killings without a care. He even slays the sick so we can't find clues in their bodies to rescue ourselves from his madness. His mind-control formula is more powerful than our *moondust;* resulting comas are as deadly as those induced by our *stardust.* What does he want from us? When is he going to reveal himself and his motive?"

The ex-Science and First Officer of the starship *Wanderlust* said, "I've searched my brain and our records, Varian, but I can't find the name or names of anyone alive who could have such a grievance against us. I can't imagine who possesses the powers he has at his command. In all of our years and travels, we've never come across anything like this. I've entered everything we know into the computer and even it can't come up with possible suspects or solutions."

"I don't know where or how to search for him, Nigel. I feel helpless and useless."

"Nobody could do more than you're doing, Varian."

"If I were doing better, Jana wouldn't be lying here fighting for her life. I'm to blame for this; I should have ordered tighter security. I should have posted guards around her."

"That wouldn't have stopped them; they were dressed in Security uniforms and had Security clearance codes and electrocards. If you and I had been standing guard, we would have been duped into letting them pass. He's almost making it so we suspect everyone of being an enemy."

"One thing I have noticed, Nigel: he doesn't breach any new security or safeguards. That makes me think he has access only to old codes and information. I was in the process of altering every one of them when I received the news about Jana. As soon as she wakes up and I make certain she's all right, I'll finish that job."

"You stepped up the search for his base, so maybe it will be spotted."

"When it is, I'm going there myself to destroy it and challenge him."

"Nigel, Varian," Andrea whispered. "Perhaps you shouldn't be talking like this in Jana's room. It's amazing what a person hears even when unconscious. She needs quiet and rest. If you two want to speak outside or go work against our enemy, I'll summon you the moment she awakens."

"Andrea's right," Varian conceded. "If Jana can hear us, we shouldn't be saying anything to distress her."

"I know you're worried about her, but I'm sure she'll be fine," Andrea assured him. "Jana is strong and brave; she'll recover. She must."

"The doctor said her brain is bruised by the fall," Nigel reminded. "As soon as the area heals, she should be fine. He's removed the fluid and the swelling has decreased. He said sleep is the best thing for her right now."

"But you also heard what he said about possible complications."

"Possible, Varian, not absolute. Stay optimistic."

"I'm trying, Nigel, but it's damned hard seeing her like this. If anything happens to Jana because I didn't protect her . . ." He took a deep breath because he couldn't finish that horrifying statement. He wished Galen and Amaya were here with him and their mother. He knew their daughter would never forgive herself if Jana was lost during her absence. Somehow, some way, he had to defeat their ominous threat.

What none of them mentioned was the doctor's alarming word about awaiting the results of one other test, for DISD: Distructive Immune System Disorder. Jana had been cut by broken debris and splattered with blood. In her laboratory were tubes, petri dishes, and glass slides with infected blood and tissue samples which had been shattered and flung about during the attack. It remained to be seen if those deadly foes had come into contact with her open wounds. If so, they all knew, there was no hope for her survival. At this very minute, the rogue virus could be invading her system and destroying her defenses.

Varian's quivering hand stroked her damp brow and his gaze roamed her exquisite features. She was the most beautiful and desirable woman he knew. She was kind, gentle, loving, smart, and courageous. He remembered the many times he had almost lost her long ago to several enemies, but generous fate had saved her for him. Would it do so again? If a life was demanded this time, make it his, he prayed, not hers. *Come back to me, moonbeam, to walk in starlight at my side and to enjoy love's splendor. What is my life without you?*

Fifteen

As the *Galactic Wind* traveled at starlight speed toward the capital planet of Rigel in the Maffei Galaxy, Galen and Amaya Saar were unaware of the new events in progress there. To prevent worrying them when they were so far from home, Varian did not send word about their mother's attack four days before. Yet an anxious Amaya paced Jason's quarters on the enormous vessel, as if sensing something was terribly wrong. "I'm sorry I'm so tense tonight," she said when he tried to calm her. "I won't be able to settle down until I check out the trouble at home for myself. There must be something I can do—we can do—to help expose and defeat this *villite*."

"Maybe there is, after we study the matter together. Since I'm an outsider, maybe I can spot a clue those close to the situation have missed."

"I hope so, Jason; it sounds as if we'll require any assistance we can find." She sat down with him on the *seata* and snuggled against him. "You've done splendidly with your weapons' training and you've learned so much about our planets. You've made many friends. I can't see any problem with your adjustment and acceptance. You've been an excellent student."

"There's just so much to learn; three galaxies are involved, not just one planet. It's a big task, woman."

"I can imagine it's awesome for you, as it was for your cousin and my mother when they first came to Maffei. I can assure you they'll be helpful and understanding of your position."

"I'm eager to meet your parents and to see my relatives again. Despite all the trouble your world is having, at least you have treaties with the other two largest and closest galaxies. I can't even imagine wars between such powerful and sizable factions."

"As I told you and you viewed on those history tapes, we weren't always allies. The year before I was born, we were almost at war with both. Thank *Kahala* those old leaders and their provokers are gone. I hate to envision today's events if either Prince Taemin Tabriz or Prince Ryker Triloni were alive and challenging us, especially Prince Ryker. I've told you about him."

"Are Galen and your father certain nobody from those other galaxies are involved in this threat?" he asked.

"As positive as they can be. Besides, neither possesses the scientific and technological advances being used against us. And neither ruler would evoke intergalactic war by attacking us; we're more powerful than they are, and we have twenty-six-year-old treaties they don't want broken."

"Can you be certain no one in either world has

followers, friends, or relatives who would seek revenge for the Tabrizes or Trilonis?"

"They wouldn't have waited this long to exact vengeance. It certainly wouldn't be justice, not after what those two men did to provoke war and attempt conquest. We're fortunate Prince Ryker died in an accident because his grandfather would have attacked us for revenge. As to Prince Taemin, his own father banished him and his people agreed he could never return home. In exile and isolation, he has no power or followers; at least not on the scale required to be our *villite*. He may even be dead by now."

"It must have been hard on Jurad to have been betrayed by his own son. Taemin was lucky he wasn't put to death as a traitor."

"By Pyropean law, a royal can't be slain even for a crime, only exiled. Most of our *nefariants* are held captive on a penal colony. A force shield around the prison planetoid makes escape impossible. There are separate colonies for males and females. They're allowed to roam and survive as they will; being cut off from everything they know and everyone they love is their punishment. We have no parole system as Earth does. Once you are placed there, it's for life. And our interrogation process is flawless. A *nefariant* doesn't get a trial; it isn't necessary. If he's guilty, the *Kadim* sentences him; our ruler's word is law."

"Too bad Earth doesn't have a similar process; it would save taxpayers a lot of money on trials and appeals, and no innocent person could be harmed."

"Then, people like you wouldn't have jobs."

"If crime was brought under control, that wouldn't matter."

"If Earth's problems were handled differently, things would be better for everyone there. In my world, only government forces are permitted to have weapons; we have virtual reality units for diversion, to take minds to other places for pleasure; we have no poverty. Some people are richer than others, but no one goes hungry, homeless, sick, or jobless. Robots, androids and machines do many of our chores. We have few natural disasters and, those we do have, are quickly controlled. Most of our inhabitants are happy and obedient to our laws. We have population control, which is necessary to provide enough space, food, and work for our people."

"How many children will we be allowed to have?"

"Three, but most people elect to have only one or two. Birth control is the man's responsibility: error-free *liex* injections every three months. That's what I gave you the other day since you came unprepared."

Jason and Amaya shared passionate memories by seductive gazes.

"When do we get to start working on a child?"

"After we're united by law. First we'll need time to decide what jobs we want to do, where we want to live, and get settled."

"Do you want to continue working in Star Fleet?"

"Only until this threat is defeated. I'm ready to retire and become a mate and mother," Amaya confided. "I'm eager to have our first child. Are you looking forward to having another one?"

"Yes. I still miss my son and I'm sure I always will, but he's gone."

"I love you, Jason Carlisle, and we will make a happy family."

"I have no doubts, Amaya Saar. I love you, woman."

"Show me how much you love me and need me," she coaxed.

"It will be my pleasure," he murmured in a sexy tone.

"It will be *our* pleasure," she corrected with a laugh.

Hand in hand they entered the adjoining chamber, then undressed. They lay on the *sleeper* and embraced as they kissed, taking and giving pleasure until their desires were so aroused they could wait no longer to join their eager bodies. A condom was unnecessary this time, and the flesh-to-flesh contact was sheer bliss. Together they climbed upward toward passion's pinnacle, where they lingered and savored the glorious landscape before they continued their trek toward rapture and contentment.

In the golden afterglow of their blissful adventure, Jason and Amaya snuggled, sharing kisses and light caresses.

Amaya sighed in tranquility. "I'm so happy you're here with me."

"I can't think of any other place I'd rather be. You're a fascinating and totally satisfying woman. I knew you were the one for me the moment I saw you at Aunt Grace's house. The more I came to know you, the more I wanted and needed you. I'm glad I snared you."

"I feel the same way. We're so fortunate, my love."

After a short rest in his embrace, Amaya said she had to leave.

"Want to take a shower together first?" Jason asked.

"If it's anything like the other one we shared, I'd never get out of here tonight," she jested, then kissed him. "I'll see you in the morning."

In Galen's quarters, he and Renah had just made love.

As Galen caressed her sated body, he murmured, "Soon, we'll be too busy and will lack the privacy to indulge ourselves in this fiery manner."

His words brought reality crashing down on Renah. She couldn't help but reply, "Please don't speak of such things tonight."

Galen shifted so their gazes could meet. "What's wrong, my love? You seem so scared and worried lately; that isn't like you."

Renah cuddled up to his comforting body. "I've never felt those things so potently before. I'm afraid everything good will be destroyed and evil will take its place." *Evil I rashly assisted.* "I'm afraid you'll be stolen from me." *I know you will be stolen from me, and I'm to blame.*

Galen kissed her forehead. "You'll never lose me, Renah, never."

Yes, heart of mine, very soon. Kahala, *how you will*

hate me and our days together. "Hold me, Galen; I need you more tonight than ever. Love me again, for soon we could be parted by death." *Or by my wickedness.*

"I won't let anything happen to either of us or to our love."

As his mouth covered hers, Renah raged against the predicament she was in; she yearned for release from it and the freedom to have the man beside her whom she loved. Before leaving for Earth, she had been given a vial of active virus and ordered to infect Galen with it! Although she would be required to cease the passionate affair with him to do so, that wasn't her motive for traitorous disobedience. She would fail in that horrifying mission because she could not slay her forbidden love. Her side now plotted to torment their unreachable enemies through the wanton destruction of their families, and demanded her help with the Saars. She could not harm Galen, would not harm Galen. Yet she dared not expose herself and the truth to him. Until she could escape to Seri or trick her side into retrieving her, she must pretend to obey her parents' orders while secretly aiding her lover and pray that neither side wised up to her deceptions. She dreaded the return to Rigel next week when her family would discover her defiance.

Three days later, Galen, Renah, Amaya, and Jason sat in the guest quarters assigned to the Earthling male because it was the largest and quietest place to visit and converse on their last evening

together. They had finished a delicious meal and
were now sipping wine.

"We'll reach Star Base tomorrow," Galen remarked. "I'm anxious to see Mother. From the way
Father looked and sounded, she was in bad condition for a while. She could have been killed in
that assault on the research complex last week.
When I get my hands on the *villite* who's responsible, I'm going to make him regret that action
and everything else he's done to our people."

"I'm relieved she's healed and back at work,"
Renah said.

"So am I, Renah," Amaya answered. "How could
anyone be so cruel and evil as to murder sick people
and destroy the complex seeking a cure for their
disease? We have to stop that heartless beast."

"Obviously he doesn't want your mother and her
staff to find a cure."

"I agree, Jason," Galen said, "but he won't stop
us from pursuing him no matter what he does to
intimidate and hinder us. Father said they had es-
tablished a new laboratory complex and are treating new cases of the virus. That means all victims
and carriers haven't been located and contained."

"Or he's infected more while we were gone,"
Renah pointed out. "Galen and I were sure we
and other teams had them all gathered and receiving treatment. Why doesn't he stop this vicious-
ness?" *Please, Father, Mother, don't continue along this
perilous and wicked course; it is wrong and cruel.*

"We can't allow it to become an epidemic,"
Amaya said. "We have to track down its origin

and destroy any containers or carriers he has left."

"It's not that easy," Galen told her. "We can't find his base or his ship."

Amaya mused on all the facts she'd learned. "Have you tried reprogramming the anticloaking device? Perhaps he's using a different frequency for his shield beam. Since he appears to be so clever and to have possession of our secrets, perhaps he knows the one our penetrating device uses."

Galen looked at his twin as he deliberated her words. "You might have something there, my cunning sister; we'll try it after our return." He smiled and said, "It's good to have you back, Amaya."

"Thank you, Galen. Father said they received the data we transmitted to the new research complex. I pray it helps Mother and her team solve this lethal mystery. At least they can compare Earth's strain to ours, and they can search for biological differences in our immune systems which might explain why and how our rogue mutates and works so fast. Father said Mother is suffering occasional delusions from that head injury, but the doctor expects them to cease upon total recovery. At least she wasn't infected by contaminated blood samples during the assault."

Renah had to struggle to conceal her anger at what had happened to Jana. Had she known about the heinous attack she would have certainly tried to stop it. She hoped her parents would not try again, but Jana was one of their primary targets. She was relieved Varian had stepped up all security.

Security, her troubled mind echoed. While in Security Control with Galen during the communication with his father, she had overhead Varian give his son the new security codes for Star Base. She would report them to her parents after arrival or they would think her a traitor and might create havoc to discover her motive; that news should appease and dupe them for a while, and there was no risk to the Maffeians because security had been increased at the base. Also, she must report Amaya's suggestion about the enemy ship's cloaking device frequency, as her parents were aboard that vessel and she could not allow them to be found and destroyed. *As soon as you can find a way to escape Maffei, you must leave, Renah. If your parents punish and banish you, so be it, but you must stop helping them slay those you've come to love and respect and other innocents.*

When Amaya arrived at the Saars' temporary home on Rigel, she and Jana shared a long and joyful embrace. Both were relieved to see the other safe and well.

Jana held her daughter at arm's length and roved her with a misty gaze. "It's wonderful to have you here. I've been so worried about you."

"It's wonderful to see you, Mother, and I've been worried about you, too. Are you all right? Father told us about the attack. I love you and I should have been here to protect you. I'm sorry I disobeyed, but I had to stay behind."

Jana didn't want to spoil their reunion with upsetting talk, so she ignored grave matters for now. "I understand, Amaya; I would have done the same thing if it had been your father involved. And I'm fine now, so stop fretting." She glanced past her daughter to the handsome stranger. "Why don't you introduce me to the man who caused you to behave in such an unusual fashion?"

With an arm around Jana's waist, Amaya half turned to grasp her lover's hand and pull him closer. "Mother, this is Jason Carlisle, Andrea's cousin and the man who stole my heart. Most unexpectedly," she added. She squeezed his hand as she continued, "Jason, my mother, Doctor Jana Greyson Saar, the best mother a person could have."

"Welcome to our world, Jason. Andrea has told me many good things about you. I'm pleased you came with Amaya. If there is anything I can do to assist with your adjustment, you've only to ask."

Jason noticed his love's resemblance to the beautiful and gracious woman who looked more like a sister than a parent. Jana had those same multicolored eyes and exquisite features, but her hair was golden blond compared to Amaya's ash-blond shade. "Thank you, Doctor Saar. It's an honor and a pleasure to meet you. I hope you and Supreme Commander Saar won't be upset with Amaya for what I coaxed her to do. I love her and want to marry her when the time is right for all of us."

Jana was elated by their guest's manners and character. He was a tall, handsome, and virile male like her beloved mate, with strong features and a splendid physique. "According to my best friend, we couldn't be more fortunate with our daughter's choice. I'm sure Andrea's right. I have one small request: please call us Jana and Varian. We— Here's my husband now," she said, smiling and slipping from her daughter's grasp to join him. "They're here, Varian: our children and their loves are finally back with us. I was hoping you'd be home soon to share in our happy reunion."

"Good to have you and Renah home safe, Galen," Varian greeted warmly. "This must be Jason standing with my errant daughter," he teased Amaya, and hugged her. "I'm also glad to have you home, Lieutenant Saar, so I can relax again."

Amaya hugged him once more and kissed his cheek. "I missed you, Father, and I love you dearly. I brought someone very special back with me." She turned to her love. "Jason, this is my father."

Varian clasped the visitor's wrist in greeting, and Jason responded as he'd been taught during the return voyage. The two males scrutinized each other during their introductions, and both were pleased by their perceptions.

"Amaya speaks highly of you, sir; I'm honored to meet you."

"Your being here speaks highly of her opinion of you, Jason. Welcome to our chambers and family. I'm sure you'll enjoy your many challenges here. If there's anything you want or need, don't hesitate to ask me or Jana. After you're settled in, I can arrange enlightenment in any needed areas."

"Thank you, sir; you and your wife are kind and generous. A woman as unique as Amaya could only come from a special family, so it will be a privilege to become part of it in the near future, with your permission."

"Granted, Jason. Since you know Amaya well by now, you must realize she always finds a path to get her way," Varian jested.

Jason nodded and smiled.

As the others chatted and shared news, Renah observed their genial rapport and genuine love and respect. She liked these people and didn't want to see them harmed. How she wished she could become a member of the Saar family, but that wasn't possible. They were so different from what she had been told since birth. She couldn't imagine them doing the evil deeds which had been related to her countless times. Once more she wondered if they had changed, or if her parents were mistaken and misguided. The couple standing near her would never plot the vengeful acts. They would never entice or force their children to assist in inciting such chaos. If only she knew the whole truth of what happened before her birth . . . She knew some of the facts from historical tapes and security files, but other portions were so secret that they weren't recorded anywhere except in the minds of those involved, those who had survived bitter treachery.

"Come, Renah, you and Jason sit on either side of me," Jana invited their two guests. "Galen and Amaya can discuss serious topics while we have fun."

"Please don't tell my love and future mate all of my flaws and weaknesses, Mother," Galen begged.

"Mine, neither," Amaya concurred with her chuckling brother as she smiled at a grinning Jason.

"Don't worry, you two, only words of truth will escape these lips."

"Considering the mischief my friends and I got into, even truth can be damaging to my shiny image," Galen comically scoffed.

"I'm sure Renah knows you well enough by now, my dear brother, to realize in which areas you've changed for the better," Amaya jested.

"I assure you, she makes me behave myself," Galen murmured.

"Galen is a wonderful person, Renah," Amaya said in all seriousness. "We all love him and would not trade him for another son or brother."

Galen made a humorous bow from the waist. "I thank you and my love thanks you. Please, Mother, prove to her she made a good choice in me."

"That decision needs no proving," Renah responded in boldness. *I only wish I could stand by it forever, for we are perfectly matched in all but one area. I love you, Galen Saar, as much as you will soon despise me. I only hope I can do one final good deed for you before my contact approaches me and risks my exposure: perhaps that vial of active virus will assist your mother's research if I can sneak it to her somehow.*

As Jana and her son continued their playful banter and Varian chuckled in enjoyment, Amaya and Jason furtively observed the distracted Renah, as they had done on the ship on several occasions when her moods seemed odd.

* * *

The following afternoon while Varian was giving Jason a tour of Star Base and introducing him to friends, Amaya spent time with her mother in Jana's new laboratory, one heavily guarded on the exterior and interior.

"Does your head injury still trouble you, Mother?"

"No, it seems fine and my tests yesterday were normal. And, no, I'm not still seeing things—people—who aren't there; I know your father told you and Galen about those hallucinations; I wish he hadn't worried you two."

"Perhaps you returned to work too soon and worked too hard."

"It happened twice, Amaya, both times when I wasn't here. Once, I was taking a relaxing stroll with Andrea and the other, I was dining with your father. I thought I saw someone I knew long ago, but I was mistaken."

Amaya sensed some uncertainty. "Are you positive?"

"When I took a second look, it was evident I was wrong. There's no way I could have been right," Jana added. "I'm fine now, Amaya. There have been no further incidents of delusion, so don't worry about me."

Amaya could imagine how those episodes had shocked and alarmed Jana, so she dropped the distressing topic. "As you wish, Mother."

Jana laughed and said, "If I had a *katooga* for every time your father used to say that to me, I would be rich."

"You are, Mother," Amaya replied with merry

laughter. "You were wealthy on Earth, too. I wish I could have visited your own home and the space firm. I saw and learned so much there; your old world is fascinating."

"And primitive and dangerous. You could have been harmed, Amaya."

"I know, but I wasn't. If Galen hadn't rescued me that night, Jason would have."

Jana noticed the glow in her daughter's eyes and on her cheeks after she mentioned Jason's name. "I can see why you chose him and love him."

"I do, Mother, with all my heart and being. He's wonderful; he's perfect. Do you know he helped us destroy that evil medical complex? Does any of that data we gathered help you?"

"It's looking hopeful for the first time since this havoc began. One of my teams is investigating the differences you mentioned about our spleens and lymph nodes this very moment. Your defiance and capture might not be bad after all; perhaps generous fate kept you there and exposed you to them for this worthwhile purpose, and Jason is the reward for your sufferings."

The women exchanged smiles before Jana continued. "I'll explain how the virus functions. The victims who mated with infected Earthlings were attacked by the rogue; then, it quickly mutated inside their bodies; and the strain was spread to others. It affects us differently than it does Earthlings or part-Earthlings. Those two groups have damaged immune systems or some disability, but it works slower in them for some reason. Most of them produce some antibodies in the blood and urine, but we do not. Yet, even with them, the antibodies are not strong enough to kill either strain. Only two of the women we located who had infected lovers reveal no antibodies or virus in them following one or more sexual contacts; we're trying to discover how and why that natural immunity occurs. The gene charts they copied are priceless because they reveal any dissimilarities, and all sites for possible attack in their species. We're trying to reconstruct the progress we had made before the lab, our specimens, and patients were destroyed; fortunately—and our *villite* doesn't know it, I hope—there was a copy of our tests and studies in another research section, all except that last day's work. We're attempting to engineer genes and cells that will reprogram or sneak past the body's immune defenses. Until now, everything we've tried was considered an invasion and challenged; only that clever rogue slips past them, and we can't figure out how he manages that feat."

"It sounds as if your creations need a force shield for protection until they're in position to attack the enemy; then a means to lower the shield for a moment to fire its weapons and reenergize before it's assaulted."

"That sums it up perfectly, Amaya; you inherited some of my skills in science and research. Perhaps this field will interest you after your retirement from Star Fleet. I assume you don't want to trek around the galaxy and leave Jason behind for long and lonely spans. And we do want grandchildren."

"You're right, Mother, and I hope you and Father have them soon. I would adore living on Altair and working with you in your research complex there. Perhaps Father can help Jason find a position he will enjoy."

"I'm certain that can be arranged; your father seems pleased with your choice, as am I. It will be wonderful having you two live near us. Altair is a large and fertile planetoid, so we'll all have privacy, and we'll be there to help with the children when you and Jason need time alone. I'll discuss the idea with him later; I'm sure he'll agree. Right now, his mind and energies are occupied by our perils. Our enemy strikes anywhere and everywhere without warning. Since the death of Brec's son, families of our leader are under guard because they appear to be his current targets. As he told you, Amaya, we've been cut off by Pyropea and Androas because of the virus threat; they've told us they don't have any cases in either galaxy and they don't want to risk its spread to them. Your father, Nigel, and the Council have a conference set with them next week. Our *villite* made certain they turned against us."

"Perhaps with good cause, Mother. If he has his base on one of their planetoids close to our boundary, he's prevented us from crossing them to investigate or to pursue any suspicious craft. I told Father my speculation and he's asked both rulers to have their patrols check out any possible locations. That beast has to be close enough to us to spy and attack, yet our forces can't find their base in our world. It seems logical and clever."

"Yes, Amaya, it does; and you were smart to think of that. I'm sure your father is delighted to have you back at work for us."

"Thank you, Mother, but I feel as helpless and ignorant as he does. That *villite* seems to know our every move and secret. Earlier, you said you'd made a marvelous discovery during this trouble. What is it?"

"Oh, yes, I almost forgot to tell you. It will be valuable to Star Fleet Security. While working on our foe's mind-block formula, we couldn't analyze or neutralize his, but we discovered a new truth serum that will bypass the *Rendelar* process. We've already tagged the chemical with Ryker's technology so it can't be reproduced by enemies, and we've made a vaccine for our side to upgrade our defensive process. For now, we're keeping it a secret because we don't know where spies might lurk. Next week, we'll give injections to our ruler, leaders, and Security members. Until then, don't mention it to anyone. You're the only person besides your father and my staff who know of its existence. We haven't even told Galen and Renah. It's powerful, Amaya; anyone who's been *Rendelared* but hasn't had the vaccine can be successfully interrogated with our formula."

"That's wonderful news, Mother, especially if clues point to one of our leaders or a Security team member whom we need to question but whose secrets are protected by *Rendelar*. You're a genius."

"Please don't use that word," Jana entreated in an uncharacteristic, harsh tone. "It was always Ryker's description of me. I'm sorry, Amaya, I didn't mean to sound foolish. It's just that those days long ago were difficult and frightening for me. I wish it wasn't a known fact I was his mate after my arrival in Maffei, but it was necessary to release that news to obtain my inheritance and peace. It took me a long time to lessen that memory. People think we married because we were both scientists and needed mates, but you know the truth. Sometimes I feel guilty about not sharing those facts with your brother, but it would accomplish nothing useful. You and I have always been close. As a woman, you understood I needed to talk to excise torment. Besides Andrea and Nigel and the Supreme Council, no one else alive knows what really happened between me and Ryker or how he truly died. Even with *Effecta* Maal gone, the terrible truth could cause problems with the Androasians. Despite his evil and coldness, Ryker Triloni was loved and respected by his people. Thank heavens, there's no way anybody can learn of those horrible events."

"I believe it's best to leave them in the past where they're safe. You and Father aren't to blame for what happened; you two handled matters in the best way. There is a safeguard we should take: Jason should have the *Rendelar* and new vaccine processes when he joins our family. Just being around us, he'll glean information we don't want enemies to learn."

"You're right; I hadn't thought of that. At least our world's secrets are safe with Renah since she's in Security and has access to them, and to us after she and Galen mate. We'll upgrade her *Rendelar*, too."

Selecting words with care, Amaya started to ask Jana what she thought about Renah Dhobi, but was halted when her communicator signaled an urgent message. She lifted it from her belt and responded, "Lieutenant Amaya Saar here. Over."

"Lieutenant Saar, your father requests your immediate presence in his chamber at Star Base," a man's voice related. "Over."

Amaya almost panicked by the summons. "What's wrong? Is this an emergency? Over."

"We've had an attack here, but no one is injured and damage is minimal. Report to him as soon as possible. Over."

"I'll be there soon. I'm in Med Complex now. End transmission. Sorry, Mother; we'll finish our talk later," Amaya said.

"After you meet with Varian, let me know what's happened."

"I will, but don't worry; he said everything and everyone are fine."

Amaya and Jason sat before Varian's desk and listened as the Supreme Commander gave orders concerning discovery of who had betrayed the new security code for the base. No one was injured and damage was minor, but the enthralled Earthlings had reached a level only use of the altered code made possible. The foes had as before, self-destructed before capture could occur. A packet of explosives survived the assault to indicate their evil intentions.

"What you two will be doing is classified and doesn't go beyond this office." Varian looked at his daughter. "I enlisted Jason in the Elite Squad to be your teammate. He underwent the *Rendelar* process earlier as protection; he fully understands the situation and that he's been made immune to truth serum by a traitor or our enemy. I want you to visit our leaders—all are present on Rigel at this time—under the pretense of introducing them to Jason. Also find cunning ways to make contact with any Security chiefs currently on Star Base. Study them for clues, but don't risk exposure of your mission. If anyone appears suspicious, contact me immediately. Otherwise, report to me after you finish. Speed is important, but don't rush to the point of being careless." He turned to Jason. "Follow Amaya's lead," he told him. "Make this appear as friendly visits, nothing more. I'm aware of what kind of work you did on Earth, so you're highly qualified and skilled to handle this task."

"Thank you, sir, and I won't let you down."

"Neither will I, Father," Amaya assured. "We'll be careful and alert."

"I have other teams checking out your theories about our *villite's* cloaking device and base. Commander Mohr has been notified you're on special assignment, and that you were on a secret mission during your extension on Earth, so there will be no reprimand for your absence without leave approval. He was told your assignments came from *Kadim* Procyon and were revealed to no one except me; therefore, Mohr cannot question or resist either action."

"Who is Commander Mohr?" Jason asked.

"My superior when I'm in Security here between assignments," Amaya explained. "But Father has the highest rank and authority next to the *Kadim* and Council." *I'll explain other things about Mohr to you later, my love.* "Is that all, sir?"

"Yes. Perhaps you can casually join one or more of the *avatars* for dinner and carry out some investigating tonight. I don't like suspecting those men of treachery, so I want this distasteful matter settled quickly."

Amaya knew Varian was troubled by this necessary course of action against longtime friends and prestigious leaders. "We'll begin immediately, Father, and keep you advised of our progress. Before a week passes, we'll have all of them absolved," she said with confidence. "Then Jason and I will work on how he's truly obtaining his information. What are Galen and Renah doing today?"

"They're investigating our breach in security. They're studying the surveillance monitor tape and entrance computer file to see if they can come up with clues about those fake credentials and uniforms. Those men didn't even attempt to use the old access code, which would have sounded an alarm; they only used the new one, and few people know it—those I'm having you and Jason check out for me. They're also examining the bag of explosives left behind and trying to learn how those Earthlings landed on Rigel. Using printouts of their pictures from the monitor tape, maybe they can locate somebody who saw them and retrace their path to us. Renah's a very special woman and a highly skilled officer, Amaya, a perfect choice for your brother. Considering her excellent qualifications and record, I intended to assign her to the Elite Squad, but Galen and I think she's serving our current needs better where she is. So far, their personal relationship hasn't interfered with their duties, and they make a good team."

"You like and respect her very much, don't you, Father?"

"Yes, I do; and she's done exceedingly well since her family's tragic death. She and Galen are fortunate they found each other. If this trouble had been known before she arrived on the *Galactic Wind,* she might have been assigned elsewhere and they might not have met."

How true and convenient and timely . . . "You said she requested the *Galactic Wind,* if I remember correctly."

"Yes, she wanted to work under Vaux and on our lead starship. In her place, I would have made the same request; and she was qualified."

"Galen told us her history; she's a fascinating woman." *One I'm surprised none of us ever met or heard about before her transfer . . .*

"That she is, just like my wife and my daughter."

"Thank you, Father. We'll leave now and get busy on our mission."

"Be careful, Amaya, Jason; this enemy is cunning and dangerous."

"We'll guard each other, sir," Jason assured. "I appreciate your confidence in me and I'm grateful for this chance to work with Amaya and to help you."

"It's good to have you here with us, Jason. Keep her safe for us."

"I'll do my best, sir; you have my word of honor."

While Galen was studying the monitor tape again and printing out pictures of the intruders, Renah opened the bag of explosives and placed them on the counter for examination. Noticing a tiny pocket that was almost concealed from view and casual hand contact, she sneaked the slender vial from her utility belt pouch and slipped it into the cavity only a minute before Galen finished his task and joined her. As Renah spread out the items for their scrutiny, she asked, "Did I get everything?"

Galen reached into the bag and made a discovery. "What's this?"

Renah glanced toward the satchel.

"There's a little compartment with something inside. I can feel it, but my fingers are too large to recover it. See if you can free it."

Renah wiggled her fingers into the slit and retrieved the hidden vial. She held up the tubette. "What do you suppose it is? There's only a small amount, too small to be useful as a liquid explosive."

Galen took it from her hand and shook the container. "Looks like water or medicine. I'll break the seal and take a smell."

Renah stayed his hand. "What if it's something hazardous to inhale or touch?" she asked. "If it's harmless, why would *nefariants* have it? What would they carry in such a small vial that could be deadly in that amount?"

Galen's eyes enlarged, then suddenly narrowed. "Do you suppose it could be that lethal virus? Do you think they planned to inject somebody here?"

Renah pretended to ponder his speculation. "An injection would be certain death, so that's possible. Perhaps one of them had an infusion device on him before he self-disintegrated. We should have the contents analyzed."

Galen's expression brightened. "We'll take it to Mother; she'll know how to handle it safely." His tender gaze settled on Renah's face. "Wouldn't it be wonderful and due justice, my love, if this mistake of theirs led Mother to a cure?"

"Yes, it would. I'm so happy you found the vial in the pouch. As tiny as it is, we could have missed it. If this is the virus, an active sample will prove a treasure to the med staff. There's no telling what secrets this vial can reveal to her."

"Let's trek, woman; a scientific discovery may be awaiting us. We'll work on our other tasks later; this is more important."

"We must be careful no one learns about this find. We don't want to provoke the *villite* into making another strike at the new laboratory."

"You're right, as usual. We'll tell only Mother."

The following day, Amaya and Jason sat in Varian's office to give their shocking report. She glanced at her lover for encouragement before she spoke. "There was a social gathering of the assembly of *avatars* last night, and Jason and I were invited to attend. The Supreme Council members were present, too. We had a chance to study each of them during the evening."

"Your mother and I were invited, but we had to decline," Varian clarified. "She was working on a new discovery, hopefully one of great importance."

"I know; she told us when we stopped by to visit her. You might think we're crazy, Father, but we believe we've located your spy and traitor. To make certain, we'll need your cooperation to set a trap."

Varian leaned forward and stared at his daughter. "Who is it?"

Sixteen

When his daughter hesitated and looked worried, Varian asked again, "Who is it, Amaya? What evidence do you have?"

"No proof, Father, just suspicions; and you aren't going to like them."

"I've never known you to be wrong before."

"I wish—and hope—I am this time, but I doubt it; and Jason agrees. Since our *villite* knows our actions and secrets, he must have a traitor or a clever spy among us. It has to be someone with access to security codes and procedures and prior knowledge of our plans, someone who would have a means to send out undetectable reports. It's Renah Dhobi, Father."

Varian gaped at Amaya, then Jason, then Amaya again. *"What?"*

"We believe it's Renah. We've studied the files and dates, and it all makes sense. Officer Fein was killed in an alleged accident just after her old ship was decommissioned because too many 'accidents' rendered it too expensive to repair. Those incidents landed Renah on the *Galactic Wind* just before the first episode occurred on Darkar with your replica, that followed her visit there with my brother. I think she must have learned the shield lowering and complex entry codes that day and passed them to her leader who used them and your duplicate to raid Trilabs."

Amaya spoke slowly and clearly. "She ensnared Galen from the start, for the purpose of eliciting information during . . . private moments. Perhaps the *villite* gave her a formula with which to enchant Galen, as Shara Triloni did to my grandfather long ago and wreaked havoc in our world and family. Renah has contact with you—Supreme Commander of our forces—Mother—one of our chief researchers, especially on the virus project. Those connections provide her with the means to sneak information from both of you, or from Galen after his visits with the two of you. She has access to undetectable communications from Security Control aboard the ship, so she can pass along our secrets without us knowing. She suddenly appeared in Maffei four years ago after the *Space Rover* mysteriously was lost; that left us no way to challenge her identity claims, except by DNA tests, which she must assume we would never attempt since she's become almost part of our family. Because of the high position she's obtained in Star Fleet and on the *Galactic Wind* and with Galen, she's been involved with the events on Caguas, Zandia, Balfae, Mailiorca, Zamarra, and Rigel: privy to our thoughts and actions before, during, and after those assaults. An attack occurs at Star Base as soon as she returns and learns about the new code."

So far, Varian could not argue her points.

"Renah leaves for Earth to supposedly help seek

clues about our virus, and the research complex is destroyed so no comparisons are possible. When she's sent to help defeat the *nefariants* on Balfae, they kill themselves before our forces can reach them, as if they knew our team was approaching. And remember she knew about the toxic fungi which doesn't exist in our galaxy. I know she's appeared to help our side on numerous occasions, but we believe those were tricks to conceal her true identity and role. Also, she had no choice but to participate or risk exposure. And what better ways to win our trust and to earn an accepted place among us? Think about what she's done, where she's been, and what she's had access to since she entered our lives and world. Jason and I have watched her carefully since meeting her on the voyage home; there is something about her that makes us uneasy."

Amaya placed her arm around his shoulder. "With two simple and quick tests, we can make certain. Blood and tissue samples will reveal her race, be it Maffeian or not; and will prove if she is the Dhobis' child, as their medical histories are on file. Interrogation with Mother's new truth serum will compel her to answer any and all of our questions; *Rendelar* will not protect her from its power."

"Do you realize what you're asking of me, Amaya? If she is innocent, Renah will hate us; she will reject Galen. My son, your brother, will never forgive us for suspecting and interrogating her. Renah, our spy . . ."

"If I did not believe this with all my heart and

mind and the survival of our world was not at stake, Father, I would hold silent until I gathered hard evidence. There is no time left to do so; victory demands swift and desperate actions. You asked me and Jason to search for the truth and we think we've found it, but speed is crucial. If Renah learns we suspect her, she could panic and vanish. Only you and the *Kadim* have the authority to issue the order needed to judge her. I realize this is hard for you to believe and accept, as you have known Renah longer than we have. Perhaps she found herself in a trap from which she could not escape after being given this wicked assignment. Perhaps she didn't know the extent of their plot. Perhaps she truly loves Galen and has tried to help us without her leader's awareness, or ours. We will not learn her motives or his until she is questioned. I know you can't make a swift decision, so think about it. Can I bring you anything to drink?" After her father shook his head, Amaya went to the *servo* to obtain refreshing liquids for herself and Jason.

Varian almost leapt from his chair and stalked to the *transascreen* to stare outside as he deliberated the stunning news and pondered how to handle it. If Amaya was right, this plot went into motion years ago. But how could sweet and gentle and intelligent Renah be a part of such monstrous evil? He hated to imagine the repercussions if he agreed to interrogation and she was innocent; or worse, if she were guilty. That reality would crush Galen, and it would torment Jana. Yet Amaya and Jason were right: the survival of their world and people

were at stake. He couldn't forget how Renah had
behaved oddly on certain occasions, such as avoiding public commendations and wanting vital ideas
to appear as Galen's or remain a secret. She had
entered their lives just before chaos broke loose,
and she was in the midst of most episodes. She
possessed all of the information the *villite* needed
for his strikes against them, and she had the perfect means and opportunities to pass along new
facts. As incredible as it seemed, it all made sense.
Though his choice was hard, Supreme Commander Varian Saar made the only one possible.

Kahala *help you, Renah Dhobi—or whoever you are—if
you have used and betrayed my son's love and aided our
enemy in this vicious threat.*

Varian turned and looked at his daughter and
her future mate. They were holding hands and
patiently awaiting his difficult decision. He knew,
as Amaya's father and superior, she would obey
his order. He took a deep breath and slowly exhaled. "I'm proud of you two; you did a superior
and swift job. Bring Renah to your mother's laboratory as quickly and quietly as possible, and if
you can, without Galen's knowledge. They're staying at Pandar Tower and might be together this
moment. If so, trick her away from him. I'll meet
you at the lab so we can carry out this matter before the day ends."

"I'm sorry I had to be the one to deliver such
bad news, Father."

"I know, Amaya. But if you're right, only you
could have guessed it. Renah has gotten too close

to us for us to suspect her of such treachery. I pray it isn't true, but somehow I fear it is."

An unsuspecting Renah headed for Jana's laboratory with Amaya and Jason. "Galen will wonder where I am when he finishes his shower," Renah worried. "Perhaps I should have left him a message with yours."

"That would spoil the big surprise we're planning for him," Amaya said with a light laugh. "Mother and Father are waiting for us. After we finish, we'll summon him immediately. This won't take long. Do you miss him already? I know I miss Jason every *preon* he isn't with me."

Renah sat beside Amaya in the bubblelike tube taking them toward the research complex. "He's such an important part of my life; I can't imagine one without him in it."

Renah glanced at the scenery they passed but didn't really notice it. Her mind was in a turmoil because she had made a difficult decision. Tomorrow she must confess the truth to Galen and take her punishment, as she could no longer play her deceitful and wicked role. As soon as they were aboard the *Galactic Wind,* she would send that shocking news to her parents and give them time to escape with their lives. Then she would expose herself to Galen so he could halt this madness she had helped create. *One last night with you, my love.* "Yes, it would be agony; but sometimes we suffer terrible losses from events beyond our control."

Amaya perceived the anguish in Renah's voice,

but she had a duty to perform. "You mean, like the tragic accident that took away your parents?"

"Life can be short and cruel at the moment one least expects defeat."

Amaya gave the girl's hand a gentle squeeze to disarm her. "Don't worry, Renah; you have a wonderful life ahead with Galen. He loves you more than anyone, including his family; that's how true love should be."

Renah gazed into Amaya's eyes, ones whose color matched Galen's. The resemblance between the twins was strong and compelling. "Does he?"

Amaya responded with undoubtable honesty. "Yes, Renah, I swear. He's never loved and will never love anyone as he loves you." She noticed how her words caused the other woman's eyes to mist in odd sadness, and she could not deny the truth and sincerity of Renah's reply.

"I have never loved and will never love anyone as I love him. I will do whatever I must to make certain he is never harmed."

The automated transportation vehicle halted and the clear side panel opened for them to depart. Jason stepped from the seat behind them, then assisted the two women. They passed through tight security at the entrance and on the second level. They approached Jana's laboratory and pressed the call button. The door swished open and they went inside; Amaya kept talking to distract Renah. Just as it was closing, Renah, Amaya, and Jason were seized by strangers. Others held Jana and Varian captive nearby. A man came forward and placed an infusion device against

Renah's bare arm. A soft hissing sound was heard as a drug was injected into her flesh.

Before Renah could resist or argue, she was completely dazed. The last thing she remembered was the man stepping to Amaya to do the same, or so she thought as blackness claimed her mind and weakness her body.

The android caught Renah before she collapsed to the floor; he placed her on an examination table as ordered.

"Prepare her for questioning and do your other tests while I return these units and erase their memory banks," Varian said. "After we're finished and she awakens, she won't have any recall of this being a trick. If she's innocent, we'll say we were attacked by enemies, resisted after she was unconscious, and the enemy self-destructed as usual. If she's innocent, no one will know the truth of what happened here except the four of us. For Galen's sake, that's necessary. I'll return soon."

Jana, Amaya, and Jason gathered around the table.

Jana looked at her daughter. "Are you sure, Amaya?" she asked.

"Yes, Mother, I am."

"Then we have no choice. I'll get started on the tests. Turn on the tape machine so everything will be recorded for Galen to watch later."

Amaya obeyed, and Jana rolled a medical apparatus to the table. She lifted Renah's arm and inserted it into a circular band. She set the controls to draw blood and to take a tissue sample. The automated instrument began its painless tasks after sterilizing the areas involved. When a buzzer sounded, Jana removed the tube and microscopic slide, walked to another unit, and inserted them in separate slots. She programmed it to analyze her entries and to compare the date with the Dhobis' records, then waited for the results in silence and dread.

Amaya and Jason stood nearby without talking. Neither could decide if they should pray for positive or negative answers. Renah's innocence would be wonderful, but guilt would supply them with the means to unmask and defeat their enemy. Jason slipped his arm around Amaya's waist and drew her close; she rested her head against his chest and quivered in suspense.

Jana's gaze roamed the serene face of the unconscious girl as their past visits and talks filled her mind. She thought of the anguish her son would endure after Renah was exposed to him, and her heart went out to him as if he already knew the harsh truth. She feared her son would never be the same after this devastating episode. She recalled how she had felt when she believed for a time that Varian had betrayed her; those events long ago almost had ripped out her soul, and they had caused great sufferings and her near death at the hands of his half brother. Only Ryker's demise and Varian's love had freed her from that dark and perilous trap which a vengeful woman had dug for her. She and Varian had confronted and thwarted evil, hatred, greed, and revenge; they had escaped lethal enemies and their deadly snares several times. Could Renah have a justifiable motive, as Varian had had years ago?

As the medical analyzer indicated completion of its studies, Amaya replied, "We'll know the truth very soon. Check the blood and tissue readouts."

Jana did so with visible reluctance. She stared at the results on the screen, then glanced at her daughter in confusion and sadness.

"What is it, Mother? Are we wrong?"

Varian returned as their daughter asked that question and joined his wife at the testing unit, as did Amaya and Jason. "What is it, moonbeam? Have we made a terrible mistake or discovered a much needed fact?"

Jana's astonished gaze locked on Varian's entreating one. "She isn't the Dhobis' child; it's medically impossible. She's part Maffeian and . . ."

"What else?" her anxious husband coaxed.

"Part Pyropean," Jana murmured just above a whisper.

"Pyropean?" Amaya and Varian echoed together.

"Are you certain?" Varian asked in surprise.

"Positive, my love; there is no error."

Amaya reasoned, "Why would the Pyropean Federation attack us? We have a treaty with them. Auken Leumi is a good man and wise ruler. He wouldn't dare challenge us."

Jana said, "Perhaps he isn't part of the plot and threat, Amaya."

"Your mother's right. Give her the truth serum, moonbeam, and let's hear who's responsible and why."

She glanced toward the monitor and spoke as if her son were there to hear her words. "I'm sorry,

Galen, but our world is in grave jeopardy and we must do this deed."

"He'll understand, moonbeam; we can't let our people suffer and die, even to spare our son from grief. Continue."

Jana infused the new serum into Renah's vein. "She's ready."

Varian leaned over the prone female. "What is your name?" he asked.

In a soft voice, she responded, "Renah Tabriz."

Varian and Jana gaped at each other across the table.

Jason and Amaya exchanged quizzical looks.

"Who are your parents, Renah?" Supreme Commander Saar asked.

"Prince Taemin Tabriz and Canissia Garthon Tabriz."

Varian and Jana stared at each other in disbelief and shock.

"That's impossible, Renah: Canissia Garthon is dead; she was killed in an accident long ago. How could you be her daughter?"

"She is alive. She was rescued before the ship exploded."

"How? By whom?"

"By Yakir, *Raz* of Seri, a galaxy beyond Androas. His scientists were testing a long-range teleporter beam to use during emergencies for rescues when it was impossible for their ships to reach an endangered vessel in time to save its crew and cargo. They reasoned that if the process failed, she would be dead anyway, so they were not risking her life.

It succeeded and she took refuge with Yakir in the Serian Empire. They became close friends."

Cass alive and plotting revenge for all these years . . . "How did Taemin join up with her and become your father?"

"Mother begged Yakir to search for him in exile and to reunite them. Yakir complied. They became mates, and I was born to them."

Varian looked at Jana, who was pale and shaken by this news. It was as if two enemies had arisen from the dead to torment them again. Both had tried to slay them in the past and both had failed. Now they had returned. "Why were you sent to Maffei?" he began his questioning. "What happened to the *Space Rover?*"

"I came here to help obtain justice and retribution for crimes against my parents. The *Space Rover* was destroyed after its files were stolen for my training and to establish and protect my stolen identity. I was told her crew was taken to a planet in Seri to live in captive freedom by Yakir's command."

"Do you mean, training to become Renah Dhobi?"

"Yes."

"Was there a real Renah Dhobi aboard?"

"No, but that was never reported to the Maffeians.

"Is Renah your real name?"

"Yes. In Serian it means Seed of Beauty. Yakir named me."

"Why are you helping your parents in this vicious plot against us?"

"I love them. I do not want them slain. I was

taught from birth to hate the Saars, their friends, and the Maffeians. I was trained to help them acquire justice and retribution for crimes committed against them."

"What crimes?"

"For the destruction of my grandfather, Councilman Segall Garthon. For bringing about my father's exile. For using and betraying and trying to murder my mother. For their many sufferings and losses as results of greed and treachery on the part of the Saars and their friends."

Varian and Jana listened to the many lies Renah had been told, then gazed at each other in shock. They needed more facts.

"How did we destroy your grandfather?"

"He was coerced into leaving the Council to save my mother's life when Varian Saar threatened it. Grandfather died in shame and sadness."

"Explain this in more detail, Renah."

"The Saars, *Kadim* Trygue, and their friends wanted control of Maffei. Grandfather resisted and battled their desire to take over this galaxy; he stood in their path to victory. To get rid of him, they used my mother to force him to remain silent and to withdraw from the Council. They put Breccia Sard in his place and Varian took command of Alliance forces in Sard's place. Draco Procyon took *Kadim* Trygue's place as ruler after Varian's grandfather died. Suran took Draco's place on the Council. They are all friends and traitors who now rule Maffei. Sard helped Varian many times, so they punished him by slaying his son when he could not be reached. Suran's planet of Zamarra was attacked when *he* could not be reached. Draco is being proven an unworthy and helpless ruler since he cannot be reached. Other Maffeians are being punished to hurt those who aided my parents' enemies and who allowed them to remain in power."

In her drugged state, Renah was compelled to respond in honesty. "My mother tried to gather evidence to expose Maffei's threat and to vindicate Grandfather; Varian pursued her and attempted to silence her with death by exploding her escape vessel. He also wanted her dead for other reasons. She was to marry him before he went to Earth and found Jana Greyson. Jana was not a temptation to him until many Maffeian males craved her; then he wanted to keep the alien for himself. He could not because of their laws, not until he was able to change them. He pretended to auction her to Draco, and his friend agreed to hold her for him until he could lay legal claim to her. Jana knew of Varian's lust and greed and evil. She asked Mother to help her escape, and Mother did so. But Varian had found a sly way to get her freed because he would not take a slave as a mate. *Kadim* Trygue pretended she saved his life and earned her freedom. Mother knew Jana was free, but she wanted Varian to suffer loss and humiliation such as she had endured when he discarded her before everyone."

Amaya glanced at Jason who was listening intently to the tale.

Renah continued. "Mother took Jana to Ryker Triloni's planetoid because she knew Varian and his friends could not land there without Ryker's permission, not even by the *Kadim's* order, as Ryker was the only man above his law and reach, and they dared not challenge or offend Ryker. Jana mated with Ryker for protection and spite toward Varian, and Ryker accepted her because he needed an heir and knew Varian was obsessed with her. Mother believes Ryker was murdered so Varian and Jana could mate and could get control of Trilabs. Mother suspects Jana was freed so she could get close to Ryker for those purposes. She said Jana's price for assistance was abolishment of the *charl* laws and practice. Jana was to get them Trilabs and mate with Varian in exchange for her freedom and that of all other *charls*, most of whom were from Earth. Mother realized Jana had tricked her into helping her get rid of Ryker, get control of Trilabs, and take Varian from her. Varian also wanted to get rid of Mother because he realized she knew those evil secrets and would expose them. Varian told Mother he was only using Jana to get what he wanted and needed for himself and his people, but when he bonded to Jana, Mother knew he had lied. She showed me tapes of the bonding plans between Varian and herself, so I knew she spoke the truth."

Varian and Jana realized which faked announcements she meant.

"Renah, how did we get your father exiled?"

"Varian and his side wanted and needed a truce with Jurad and Pyropea, but Father stood in their way because he didn't trust them and had too much influence over his father and people. They made Prince Taemin appear to be a *villite* and traitor who was out to kill his father, take over Pyropea, and provoke war with Maffei and perhaps Androas. My parents were friends for years before the real trouble began. He told me of their wicked plans to destroy him and have him banished, since a prince cannot be slain or imprisoned. Their 'evidence' was so cunning and strong that Father lost everything he loved. He tried to warn his friend Ryker about their treachery, but Ryker did not believe anyone would dare to challenge him or attempt to slay him. He was wrong."

"What do you mean?"

"They needed to get rid of Ryker and get control of Trilabs, and they needed a truce with *Effecta* Maal and Androas. As with my grandfather, father, and their people, Maal Triloni and the Androasians were too influenced by his grandson and heir, and they were nearing intergalactic war with Maffei. Ryker wanted war and conquest as punishments for his mother's humiliation and betrayal by the first Galen Saar, my Galen's grandfather. My parents told me how he seduced, promised to wed, and discarded Ryker's mother for the first Amaya—*Kadim* Trygue's daughter. Galen charged that Shara had tricked and drugged him while en route to become Jurad Tabriz's mate. But Shara had her revenge; she killed Galen and Amaya. My parents say that all Saar men use and betray women to get their wishes, as Varian did with my mother. She said rumor proved the son of Varian was the same, but that is not true of Galen. My parents said Varian and his friends helped Maal's rival assume control of Androas. By the time Varian and his allies finished their evil work, they said, they controlled Maffei; had truces with Androsia and Pyropea; had gotten rid of Ryker, Maal, my grandfather, and my parents. Now, Varian's friends and allies are in total control of the Tri-Galaxy, with Varian as the head of all military forces and has them convinced he's perfect and all powerful."

"What are their goals, Renah?"

"Those are many: exposure of past crimes and the real *villites*, justice dispensed to their enemies, vindication of themselves and Grandfather, retribution for their sufferings and losses, and the return of their good names and properties and former status in their worlds."

"Do they believe such violence and crimes will obtain those goals?"

"Only part of them, but that is acceptable to them."

"What is the thrust of their plot?"

"In the beginning, it was to expose and punish the Saars, their friends, and Maffeians who allowed their sufferings to occur; to destroy the intergalactic truces and isolate Maffei; to obtain retribution through theft, and to vindicate themselves of past crimes. It changed after I was in place."

"Changed? How? Why? When?"

"Why, I do not know. When, after I was carrying out my duty to them and had entrapped myself. They did not tell me about the lethal virus. They did not tell me about attacks on the planets. They did not tell me innocents would suffer and die. They did not tell me revenge was their major goal."

"Why do they use Earthlings as thralls?"

"To hurt Jana Saar, and to turn Maffeians against her and Varian. Also, *Raz* Yakir would not allow his people to invade another galaxy. He gave them a ship, supplies, weapons, but no forces. They voyaged to earth and collected evil men to enslave and use. I did not know about the females or the virus carriers until a contact alerted me not long ago. I did not know the Earthlings would die."

Varian continued his interrogation of Renah.

"How does the mind block work?"

"I do not know; it is a creation of the Serians, an advanced race."

"Is there a cure for either strain of the virus?"

"No. Not unless Doctor Saar and her staff find one."

"How does their cloaking device work?"

"On a different frequency."

"We tried another one, so how can that be true?"

"I told them to change it after Amaya Saar suspected the truth."

"Why did you tell them?"

"So my parents would not be attacked and killed."

"Are they on the ship now?"

"Yes."

"Where are they orbiting and striking next?"

"I do not know."

"Where is their secret base located?"

"I do not know."

"Was Fein murdered so you could get aboard the *Galactic Wind*?"

"Yes, but it was supposed to be only a crippling accident."

"What were the attack plans for Caguas, Zandia, Mailiorca, Zamarra?"

"I was told Caguas and Zandia were for obtaining supplies and money to finance and fuel our forces; I did not know they were to be destroyed. Mailiorcan *majee* were to be endangered but also not destroyed. I did not know about Zamarra's threat until it occurred. I did not know about the toxic fungi beds until Galen's team wandered into them."

"Was it your mother Jana saw after her head injury?"

"I believe it was. *Raz* Yakir knows how to shapeshift."

"Is that how someone impersonated me on Darkar?"

"Yes, my father."

"Why did Taemin go there?"

"I was told to obtain needed chemicals and weapons, to copy Ryker Triloni's formulas for reproduction, and to insert a computer virus in that system to render it useless to the Maffeians. The last two objectives were impossible because of safeguards and failsafes."

"How did your parents get our secret codes and procedures?"

"My mother learned them from her father long ago when he was a member of the Supreme Council before he was destroyed by Varian Saar and his friends. I reported the ones for Darkar and the changes after my return from Earth because I knew they could not breach upgraded security and it would trick them into believing I was not a traitor to them."

Varian asked her to explain her last words.

"I have been secretly giving Galen Saar and his side assistance. I was going to confess everything to him tomorrow so he could halt the plot."

"Why would you confess to Galen?"

"Because I love him and cannot let him and his family be harmed. They are good people; perhaps they have changed over the years. Galen's love and acceptance have changed *me*."

"Why haven't you told Galen the truth?"

"At first I believed my parents' teachings and hated the Saars and their friends who had wronged them. I came to love and desire Galen, and to like and respect his family. I have made other friends and learned many things about Maffei, things which caused me to doubt my parents' words and motives or to suspect they were mistaken. If I confessed, I feared Galen would hate and destroy me and my parents. I wanted to cease my evil and to escape before he discovered my betrayal, but I had no way to leave Maffei. And I knew if I vanished, I couldn't continue to aid Galen and protect him. If I abandoned my role, I feared they would do terrible things out of anger. I realized matters were worsening and only I could halt this madness by confessing all to him. I betrayed my parents to aid his cause, but I knew it would not matter to him after he learned the truth about me."

"Will your parents punish you for your betrayal?"

"I do not know, because they are consumed by hatred for the Saars and their friends."

"What is your deepest desire in this tragic situation?"

"To make it all only a bad dream so I can keep Galen Saar and the existence I have found here, so I can become a part of his family, so this evil will cease to exist, so innocents will suffer and die no more. I wish my parents could forgive and forget and survive."

"How can you accomplish those goals, Renah?"

"I cannot; it is impossible. To halt this evil plot, I must lose Galen's love and respect and those of his family. I am doomed. It is too late. I have committed too many crimes."

"Won't your good deeds and assistance matter to the Saars?"

"No, for I have misused and betrayed them, and many have died."

"Would you ally with the Saars against your parents?"

"I cannot help kill my mother and father."

"But they are wrong and dangerous; they have misused you."

"Yes, but they are my parents and I love them."

"Why did you decide to make a confession tomorrow?"

"Because I feared more changes in the original goals. I feared more families of leaders would be slain. I feared more virus would be introduced and spread, and more planets attacked. I feared they would make another attempt on Galen and his mother."

"What attempt did they make on Galen?"

"They ordered me to infect him with the virus while en route to Earth."

The Saars and Jason exchanged horrified looks. Jana paled in fear.

"But you didn't do it, did you?" Varian asked in dread.

"I could not. I love him. I sneaked the vial to him for his mother to use to find a cure. I feared they would try to infect him in another way."

"Who came up with the idea of the virus? Why?"

"Mother, but Father agreed with her. I don't know why."

"When did you learn about the virus? How did it make you feel?"

"After it was spreading. I was angry with them. I was forced to admit they would never give up their goals unless exposed and chased from Maffei. I was going to contact them tomorrow with the news I was confessing to give them time to escape before I did so. *Raz* Yakir offered them refuge if they wanted to return to Seri after exacting their revenge."

"How do you contact them?"

"From Security Control on the *Galactic Wind;* I have a secret code and frequency to use, and transmission on a security device is undetectable. Other times, they sent messengers to me while I was on Rigel."

"Did you tell them Amaya Saar was on Earth?"

"Not until we were leaving for Earth and I knew they could not beat us there to capture and harm her, which they would have attempted earlier if I had disclosed her location. I could not, though we were strangers then."

"You don't know when or where or how they'll strike next?"

"No."

"Why did you accept and carry out this mission, Renah?"

"I believed my parents' words and thought I was right to help them. I was trained from birth for my role and never questioned or defied them."

"Varian, either I need to give her another infusion or she'll awaken soon," Jana said. "Do you have more questions for her?"

"None that I can think of at the moment. Amaya?"

"None, Father; I think you covered everything."

"Why don't you summon Galen and view the tape with him?" Jana suggested. "Then you two can decide on a course of action. We must move ahead quickly before they discover her exposure. I would like to awaken Renah and tell her the truth about her parents and the past; she deserves that much for all she's endured and the help she's given us."

"I agree. But I think Galen should hear the truth, too. Sedate her while he watches the tape. Afterward, you can speak with her in the conference room, and Galen can witness it through the observation screen. I think he should hear both sides before he and Renah speak privately."

"I hate to imagine how this terrible news will affect our son."

Varian held Jana in his arms for a minute as he murmured, "So do I, moonbeam, but Renah is guilty, no matter her motives."

"What will happen to her?"

"Only the *Kadim* can judge her and decree punishment."

"But Draco doesn't know her and love her as we do," Jana pleaded. "She was caught in a trap her parents created with lies and held there by love for them."

"I know, but Draco is our ruler and she is guilty of many crimes."

"She's changed since knowing Galen and us. She's contrite and she helped us. Will she lose her life or be condemned to a penal colony?"

Varian grimaced. "I don't know, moonbeam, but both are strong possibilities. We'll have an answer from Draco before nightfall."

Seventeen

Renah opened her eyes and lifted her head from the back of a long *seata*. She was in a large chamber that held a long table with many chairs in the center, several relaxation areas in its corners, and wall units with viewing equipment at both ends. An enormous *transascreen* allowed her to see outside to numerous gleaming towers of various sizes and shapes and a purplish-blue sky. Wispy pale-yellow and pinkish clouds and a passenger shuttle crossed her line of vision.

"How do you feel?"

Renah turned and looked at Jana. "Fine," she replied, and shook her head in confusion. Where are we? What happened? Was anyone harmed?" she asked, fear racing through her body and mind.

Jana was aware of the observers concealed behind a wall unit: Varian, Amaya, Jason, and a sullen Galen. She had spoken with her son for a few minutes after he had watched the interrogation tape. He was stunned to discover his love's identity and role in their world's peril. He could hardly believe she was capable of such treachery and duplicity. He felt as if she had made a fool of him; he was hurt, confused, embittered, and angered.

"We're in a conference chamber near my laboratory. The complex is secure and everyone is safe." *Except you.* "Galen will be with you soon. First, we must talk."

Renah focused a quizzical gaze on Jana. "About what?"

"The truth. Your parents. What really happened in the past. And what you have done to our world and to my son." Jana saw Renah pale and shudder; she watched the girl's silvery gray gaze widen and her lips part.

"You know who I am, don't you?"

"Yes, Renah Tabriz; I know everything. Everything," Jana stressed.

Jana's use of her real name confirmed her fears. "How? When?"

Jana explained how she had administered a new truth serum to the girl and she had revealed everything.

"Does . . . Galen know?" a stunned Renah asked.

"Yes, but only after the questioning session; he never suspected you." The expression of anguish in Renah's eyes and on her ashen face moved Jana deeply. "I asked to speak with you before he does and before . . ."

"Before I receive my dire punishment," Renah finished for her. "I think it is best for Galen if we do not meet and talk. Any further interrogation should be handled by Supreme Commander Saar. I'm sure Galen has been injured enough without having to be in my presence again. I only wish I could have been the one to expose myself to him."

"He knows you planned to take that course of action tomorrow."

"Is he all right?"

"I'm certain you can imagine how he feels at this moment."

"Yes, he's hating and cursing me and wishing me dead. He's right."

"You truly love my son, don't you?"

Tears welled in Renah's eyes. "Yes, but that does not matter after what I have done and because of who I am. I deserve his hatred and any punishment deemed necessary for my wicked deeds."

Amaya grasped her brother's hand and squeezed it as Galen clenched his teeth, narrowed his gaze, and stared straight ahead. She heard her twin's telepathic cry: *Damn her, Amaya, damn her. I would have died for her, given her anything, loved her forever. Sebok warned me, but I did not listen because she had cast her magical spell over me.*

Amaya closed her eyes and responded in kind: *Sometimes loving, forgiving, and understanding are harder than dying to protect a loved one. Perhaps you will learn that difficult lesson from Mother's words to her.*

"I'm going to tell you the truth about what happened long ago, because your parents lied to you and misused you and your love for them," Jana said. "This story is long and painful; so allow me to finish before you ask questions, make comments, or debate my words. You will learn things even Galen does not know in their fullest because Varian and I tried to bury the past for our sakes and for the good of our people."

"Why are you telling me such secrets?"

"Because you deserve to hear them for trying to help us and because of what you have come to mean to us and our son. If intergalactic peace had not been at stake, these secrets would not exist to be misused by enemies."

"How can you trust me with them after all I have done?"

"Because you will be unable to repeat them to anyone," Jana replied, and Renah understood her meaning: her memory would be erased before punishment. "You know from history tapes about the *charl* practice the Maffeians used after an alien virus rendered most of their females sterile. For their race to survive and recover, they took slave-mates from the Milky Way Galaxy. Twenty-six years ago, I was abducted from Earth by Varian to become one of them. En route to Maffei, we were trained and prepared to become inhabitants and mates here. During that time, Varian and I fell in love, but it was against regulations for him to select a member of his female cargo for himself. As you know, women were auctioned to the highest bidder during stops at each planet, sold to men who were qualified to obtain a mate. On Lynrac, I met two elite visitors from another galaxy: Supreme Ruler Jurad Tabriz and his son and heir, Prince Taemin. Jurad wanted to purchase me to become Taemin's wife; he actually *demanded* me in retribution for Varian's father allegedly stealing Princess Shara Triloni from him long ago. From our past nine stops, Varian knew word had spread about his affection and desire for me, so he surmised Jurad wanted vengeance on the Saarian bloodline and to compel Maffei to humble itself to appease him. To protect my life and happiness, Varian refused, and the law said a buyer must be Maffeian."

Renah's smoky gaze widened in astonishment.

"You also know that the first Galen was Shara's escort across Maffei; that marriage was to forge a treaty between the Pyropean Federation and the Androasian Empire. During the voyage, Shara craved Galen and seduced him by means of potent drugs. After Galen came to himself, he rejected Shara and exposed her deceit. Shara refused to bond to Jurad, inciting hatred and treachery charges from the Pyropeans and Androasians. When *Kadim* Trygue and our Council refused to punish Galen and he mated with Amaya Trygue, matters worsened. Ryker was born from Shara's seductive deception; he was reared to hate the Saars, the *Kadim,* and Maffeians who protected and admired Galen. Ryker grew to be a scientific genius, and purchased Darkar for his home and complex; he was too powerful and dangerous for Maffeians to challenge or reject. Ryker lived for the day he could exact revenge on those he hated. Ryker Triloni was handsome and virile, rich and powerful, and cunningly deceptive. He was truly a rare and superior wizard in science and technology. In public, he could be utterly charming, when it suited his purposes. In private and on the sly, he persuaded *Effecta* Maal, his grandfather, to attack and conquer Maffei. Maal waited only for Ryker's signal to proceed."

Jana did not hesitate before adding, "Much the same was true of your father; Taemin yearned to conquer Maffei and Androas and rule the Tri-Galaxy. He tried to influence Jurad in that direction, but Jurad was too smart to challenge us, especially with Trilabs in our sector and Ryker allegedly our ally. Taemin and Ryker were . . . friends of a sort, but mostly they used each other, and would have slain each other without a second thought if the need arose. Your mother had relationships with both men; they all exploited each other for procuring their separate and sometimes intermingled goals and needs."

Jana was relieved Renah didn't interrupt her story. She walked to the *transascreen* and gazed outside. She felt it wasn't beneficial or necessary to disclose the fact her auction was an illegal farce between her lover and their current *Kadim.* "Sometimes, as you've learned, Renah, love demands great sacrifices from us. Varian could not bid on me at my auction because he feared Ryker or Taemin or another enemy would strike at me to hurt or to manipulate him. He also had a lengthy mission ahead out of Maffei and feared I would be imperiled during his absence if he laid claim to me and left me behind. He was compelled to pretend he felt only desire for me, but not enough to take me as his *charl;* to prove to his enemies he didn't love me, he carried out my sale. Draco knew the truth and purchased me with the hope and belief Varian would change his mind after those threats ended. For me to react convincingly to Varian's behavior, Draco did not tell me of his future plan to help reunite us. I felt betrayed by Varian, even though he had always warned me we could not become mates. I was as hurt, confused, embittered, and angered as my son is today. Since I believed Draco was my permanent owner, I tried my best to adapt and to become a good mate, because there was no other choice. I did not want to provoke Draco into selling me to another man who might not be as kindly as he."

Pick your words carefully, Jana. "Varian realized it was a mistake to lose me. He came to Karnak and confessed his feelings to Draco; a resale was legal when a relationship did not work out as hoped, and Draco and I had not consummated our union. Varian purchased me and left me on Eire with his grandfather, the *Kadim*. I managed to foil an assassination attempt, and I was given my freedom; Varian insisted on completing several vital missions before he told me I was free to choose to marry him or to leave him. He realized—after what he had done—he would have to earn my trust, and forgiveness. He knew he needed time to prove we were perfectly matched; and his motives for betraying me had been sincere, and of grave importance to my survival and to peace for his world. I loved him, and true and powerful love comes along rarely." *Hear me well, Galen.* "I would have believed him and accepted him if we had been given that recovery time, but two enemies stole it from us: Ryker and your mother."

Jana turned, leaned against the clear surface, and looked at Renah. "Before I came to Maffei, your mother had craved Varian Saar for years. She wanted him because of who and what he was, the perfect choice for her mate; and because she believed he would one day become the *Kadim*. It is true they were lovers on occasion, but Varian always told her he did not love her and they had no future together. After my arrival, Canissia despised me because Varian and Taemin desired me and later, Ryker. Her hatred and jealousy was evident to everyone. She dreamed of the day she could destroy me."

Jana talked as she fetched throat-soothing water from a *servo*. "Ryker supplied her with potent drugs which allowed her to extract secrets from her father, planetary *avatars,* and regional *zartiffs,* and sometimes security forces. Canissia sold or gave those secrets to Taemin and to Ryker. Before Varian could tell me the truth, Canissia kidnapped me and gifted me to Ryker, hoping he would torture and kill me. Whether he did or not, she knew Varian would not take me back after Ryker . . . possessed me. To trick me, she made false tapes from conversations between her and Varian, talks which said he was going to give me to Ryker as a peace token or to another man to get rid of me, and she claimed he was going to marry her. To hurt and provoke Varian, Ryker forced me to become his legal mate, though we never had a physical union. Ryker claimed he forced the *Kadim* to free me, as he wanted a mate not a *charl*. Varian suspected the truth but could not prove it or provoke Ryker into denying Maffei its chemical and military needs or into war with Androas, of which he was heir. Imprisoned on Darkar, there was no way for me to seek the truth or disclose my peril."

Jana returned to the *seata* and sat sideways to face

Renah. "Ryker challenged Varian to a death duel
for my possession, ownership of Darkar and Trilabs,
and the Saar estate and name. Ryker never believed
Galen wanted him and had tried to obtain him or
that Varian wanted peace and a brotherly relationship. Shara and Maal had poisoned his mind for
years. Varian was forced to meet with Ryker to prevent my death. Nothing Varian said or did reached
Ryker's evil and twisted mind and frozen heart. To
save himself, me, and Maffei, Varian had to take
Ryker's life. There was a crucial secret only Ryker's
family, your mother, and Varian knew."

Varian tensed as he wondered which secret Jana
was about to reveal. He hadn't told her what to
say, but she was doing an excellent job so far.

"Ryker and Varian were like twins. From the
time he was born, Shara and Maal concealed that
amazing fact with falsely colored irises, hair, skin,
and other alterations. It was auspicious Ryker continued that ruse until his death. After my rescue,
Varian and I used it to arrange what appeared an
unquestionable accident on Caguas so Maal would
not be provoked into retaliation. We visited Maal
and Jurad as Ryker and Jana Triloni to initiate
peace treaties. We used a cyborg of Varian to make
public peace between the half brothers so Varian
would not fall under suspicion later. We also made
Ryker appear a changed and better man before his
death. But your mother suspected it wasn't Ryker
with me. She and Taemin kidnapped us to gain
Trilabs and to kill us. We escaped and exposed
Taemin's plot, which included a plan to slay his
father and become ruler of Pyropea. Jurad knew

we were telling the truth because Taemin was caught in the process of his evil treachery; that's why Taemin was exiled, not because of what Varian and I told Jurad. Surely you realize Jurad would not take our word over his son's without proof he himself witnessed and could not deny."

Jana added another relevant topic of interest to Renah. "Your grandfather, Supreme Council member Segall Garthon, was asked to step down because he was guilty of treacheries. Besides the facts Canissia stole from him, he confessed he had related secrets to his daughter, never imagining she was exposing them. He was weakened in heart, mind, and spirit by his child's deceit. As a traitor, Canissia's capture and punishment were ordered by *Kadim* Trygue. She tried to escape, after kidnapping me and Andrea Sanger to torture and slay us for revenge. She knew the penal colony codes and took us there. Those men are barbaric savages. But Varian, Nigel, and their crew aboard the *Wanderlust* reached us in time to rescue us. We tracked Canissia toward one of our boundaries. She refused to surrender. Her ship was disabled; still she refused to yield. It was about to explode and end her life, but she would not permit a rescue and capture. We watched helplessly as the vessel exploded and assumed she was dead."

Jana's mind quickly searched for any points she had missed. "The announcements your mother showed to you were fakes to protect my life while I was on Darkar and to draw Canissia into the open to be snared. I swear to you, Renah, Varian never loved or misled your mother about his feelings or intentions toward her: I did not steal him from her because she never possessed him. As with you and Galen, I could not help falling in love with him, though I believed it was forbidden and futile. We made every attempt possible to save your mother's life that day, despite all she had done to us. We did not lie about your father's crimes. We did not betray or destroy your grandfather; he did that himself by his blind trust and love for his daughter and by her treachery. Yet his image was left intact and unstained by the men in power because they knew he had been misused. We did not murder Ryker to obtain Trilabs. Following Ryker's death, we found his private journals and tapes which revealed many crimes, including murders your mother had committed for him and her own purposes, but we could not use them as evidence because they revealed too many secrets about his work, Maffei, and other vital matters.''

Jana rushed onward. "Your mother hates Varian for rejecting her and for discovering the truth and trying to capture her. She hates Draco for helping Varian obtain me as his mate. She hates Breccia for helping Varian expose your grandfather and her, so she killed his son. She hates Suran for his part in the downfall of her and your grandfather, so she tried to destroy Zamarra and his people. Those men are not in power because they are Varian's friends and aided some sinister plot of his. They were next in line as ruler and leaders long before I came to Maffei and these troubles began. They are good and honest leaders: that is why the people love, respect, and obey them.''

Jana completed her revelations. "Canissia hates me most of all because Taemin, Varian, and Ryker wanted *me* for various reasons, not *her.* If she could not have her first choice, she would settle for her second or third; but all three rejected her for a mate. She always believed I thwarted her dreams and plans when, as a *charl,* I was helpless to control my own destiny. It is true I offered to exchange my help for abolishment of that law and freedom for all *charls,* but the Council knew and agreed it was time to eliminate that practice. It maddened and enraged her to watch me succeed when all she was and had were being destroyed; she could not admit she was to blame for her misery and losses. She was spoiled, arrogant, cruel, and vindictive. She had everything any woman could desire—beauty, wealth, power, elite status, freedom—but they were never enough for her. She wanted no rival in any area. She also wanted to be a ruler, and tried to acquire that goal through one of the heirs to Maffei, Androas, or Pyropea."

Jana noticed how alert Renah was. "What they have now is isolation in a foreign galaxy, dependence on Yakir's generosity, no elite status, no wealth, no power, captivity of sorts, bitterness, hatred, and a denounced prince and exiled female for mates. They hold us to blame for that bleak situation. Canissia and Taemin would be content to see Varian, me, our children, and the Council dead; and to gain possession of Trilabs to rule and exploit this galaxy from Darkar. With possession of that complex and planetoid, we would be at their mercy. But they can wreak death and destruc-

tion on us and our world with their attacks and
that virus, but they cannot conquer us, and they
will be defeated. Don't you see, Renah; they cannot
be vindicated because they were guilty. They can
never return to their worlds where they are *villites*.
You must face and accept the real motives behind
their assault: revenge, greed, and a lust for power.
You must confront and admit the bitter reality that
their hearts and minds are consumed by evil. I am
certain they will never surrender even to survive,
just as I am convinced only death can release them
from their self-induced torments and from making
another vile attempt on us in the future."

Jana moved closer and placed a comforting hand
on Renah's, clasped tightly in her lap. "I know from
past episodes how persuasive and devious Canissia
and Taemin can be. You're not totally responsible
for who you are. Reared to hate and destroy us, you
had no chance of a normal life; no choice but to
aid your parent's scheme. I realize you were tricked,
abused, and blinded." *I hope my son does, too. Forgiveness will be hard for him, but I pray not impossible.*
A match between Galen and Renah was perhaps
fated, Jana reasoned, just as hers had been with
Varian. Renah had proven there was a lot of good
in her, and she was worthy of joining their family,
but that decision must be Galen's alone. Jana could
not guess if his love was strong enough to overcome
this obstacle. She prayed Galen would not do ir-
reparable damage to their relationship before he
mastered his pain and soothed his injured pride.

"If your parents truly loved you, they would not
have asked you to become a part of their plot,"

Jana said. "They put your life in peril and deceived you. I could not do that to a child of mine. As wicked as they are, I cannot understand why Canissia and Taemin would behave so cruelly to their own blood. If you truly love Galen and were willing to sacrifice your life and freedom to protect him and all he holds dear, help us, Renah, to end this madness and grief. If you refuse, your suffering and losses—and Galen's—will be for naught. If you agree, I will entreat *Kadim* Procyon to exonerate you and spare your life. I will beg Draco not to condemn you to the penal colony or to death; I will suggest total memory deletion, reeducation and training, and a new identity and existence elsewhere: tasks I will oversee myself. You have my word of honor." With Galen observing and most likely unsure of his feelings, Jana could not give the girl words of hope for a future with her son. "Do you have any questions or remarks before I end this meeting and summon Varian and Galen?"

Renah grasped Jana's hand. "Do not force Galen to see me," she pleaded. "Surely I have broken his heart, humiliated him, and damaged his spirit. I could not bear to view the hostility and coldness in his eyes."

"I understand, Renah, but that is not within my power. Galen is your superior officer and he was closely involved with your . . . misdeeds."

Renah fought back tears. "I wish I had never been a part of such wickedness, or I had jettisoned my involvement sooner. I wish I had escaped and spared him this misery, but I cannot alter the past. I want to thank you, Jana, for explaining matters to me and for being so kind when I do not deserve it."

"You earned that right by trying to assist us, Renah. I know your parents, so I understand how they duped you with lies and preyed on your love and loyalty to them. You are a good person; you have changed and bettered yourself since coming to Maffei. You could never return to your old feelings and way of life. I have deep affection and admiration for you, and gratitude for your help. I will do everything I can to extricate you from this predicament. Do not lose hope or embitter yourself. Your hardest task will be self-forgiveness."

Restrained tears broke free and slipped down her cheeks. "No, Jana, that will be losing Galen's love and respect and trust, and a life with him. I place my fate in yours and Commander Saar's hands. I concede to defeat."

Jana pulled Renah into her arms to comfort the tormented girl who appeared so young and vulnerable, so plagued by guilt. So filled with anguish and contrition. She had experienced those same emotions and reactions, and her heart ached with empathy and her mind raged in anger at the Tabrizes. After the girl's tears and tremblings were brought under control, Jana said, "Relax here while I go speak with Varian. He will join you soon for your answer."

"Answer?" the silvery eyed female echoed in confusion.

"To the question, will you help us defeat your parents. It will not be a quick or simple decision, so give it grave consideration. I shall see you again after your talk with Varian." Jana stood and departed.

Renah stared at the closed door; she knew it was sealed against her escape, just as her black fate was. She walked to the *transascreen,* leaned her forehead against it, and closed her bleary eyes. "I'm sorry, Galen, for how I have wronged you and your people. I know you will never believe me or forgive me, but I love you with all my heart and soul. If I could return to the past, I would not make these same terrible mistakes. What I would give to make this only a bad dream."

In the observation chamber, Galen stood near the secret viewer panel with his palms flattened against it. He stared at the woman out of his reach and her knowledge. His heart throbbed in a vise of agony. His mind raged at cruel fate for dealing him this stunning defeat. His spirits were low and trampled. He felt almost numb with grief, yet sensations of anger and resentment attacked him for brief moments. His gaze was bright with unshed tears. Never had he felt more helpless, assailed, and weak. "Why, Renah, why?" his voice hoarsened by emotion murmured. "How could you do this to us, to my family, to my people?" Inside, he knew, but it was too late to matter. Surely his mother realized Renah's crimes were punishable by death; she was a spy, an enemy. Citizens were dead or injured; planets had been attacked and almost destroyed; Darkar and Trilabs had been breached. She had stolen and passed along their security secrets and procedures. The son of Supreme Council member Breccia Sard had died from their lethal virus. The undersea world of Supreme Council member Suran had been threatened. Attempts had been made on the lives of the *Kadim*, Council, Assembly of *Avatars*, and their loved ones. Attacks had occurred at Star Base and at the medical and research complexes. Fein had been murdered. His own mother had almost lost her life. How could the woman he loved and thought he knew commit such evil?

Yet, as the troubled man watched and listened, doubts surfaced and pulled at him like strong and persistent currents. His mother, whom her side had tried to kill, had not turned against Renah! In the powerful grip of truth serum, Renah had made startling revelations about her feelings and actions. *It wasn't all lies and tricks,* his heart argued in her favor; *she loves you and helped you. But she's an enemy,* his keen mind retorted. *She's done terrible things.*

"Galen, are you all right?" Amaya asked from behind him. Varian had left the chamber earlier to join Jana. Jason also had left to give the twins privacy to speak and for her to offer much needed comfort.

Galen turned to face his sister. "I don't know, Amaya. Until a few hours ago, I had a bright future with a wonderful woman. Now, my life couldn't seem bleaker or darker; she's a stranger to me."

"Give it time, Galen; give yourself time before you speak with her. At this moment, it's hard and painful for both of you. Let shock, anger, bitterness, and disappointment fade. She does love you, my brother."

"How can you be so generous to her when

you're the one who suspected and exposed her? You know what she's done to us."

"Yes, but we all know why, Galen, and that should matter to you."

"What difference do my feelings make, Amaya? Her life's doomed, so she's lost to me forever."

"Not if Mother persuades the *Kadim* to spare her life. With a fresh identity and no past memory, perhaps you could pursue and win her again."

"She wouldn't be the same person I met and fell in love with after she's . . . reprogrammed like an android! My Renah doesn't even exist! She was just playing a role with me."

"Was she, Galen? I don't think so; neither does Mother. If you truly love her, don't end this relationship. I realize you're hurting and humiliated, but so is Renah. Consider what she's been through since she left home and came here. Imagine her childhood with evil parents like that other family? She was caught in a black hole, Galen, and she did her best to cope and help after she got to know us and realized her actions were wrong. *Kahala*, Galen, it was her *parents*, who trained and gave her orders! She loved them and trusted them, just as we love and trust our parents. If we were told those same lies, we would have joined their cause to seek justice." She lowered her gaze. "Are you angry with me for being the one to expose her?"

"No, Amaya. In fact, I'm happy we finally found a way to strike at those beasts. I'm going to capture those two and kill them."

"No, Galen, do not place their blood upon your

hands. Despite what they've done, they're Renah's parents; one day, that will matter to you."

"Look what they've done to us and what they've taken from me: the only woman I've loved and wanted, my future mate. I have to get out of here before I erupt. Let Father decide her fate; I cannot." Galen fled the chamber in anguish.

Amaya looked through the impenetrable panel at the defeated Renah. She understood Galen's frustration and fury, as she had never before felt this impotent. Her brother was right about one thing: Renah was lost to him, whether or not she complied with their plea for further assistance. Amaya took a deep breath and went to join her mother in the laboratory.

Varian entered the conference chamber where Renah was being held. He approached her, stared at her for a moment, then sat down. He knew she must be frightened and worried, as it had been hours since Jana had left her alone there. He noticed she didn't speak or move, only stared at the floor in shame and torment, and surely in dread of her unknown fate.

"Renah, once we begin our pursuit of your parents, can the Serians use that long-range transporter beam to rescue them from their ship?" he asked.

Without looking at him, she responded, "No, sir. Shortly after the experiment with Mother, the device and its creator were destroyed in an explo-

sion. All notes were lost so another one could not
be made."

"What frequency are they using for their cloaking shield?"

"I do not know, but it was changed recently from
their old one."

"Do you have any idea how, when, and where
they will strike next?"

"No, sir. When I am given information on tactics, it is afterward. I can send out messages, but
I receive them only by contact at their timing by
keeping them alerted to my schedule and location."

"You can't reach your contact?"

"No, sir. He just appears when they think it's
safe to approach me."

"Could you summon him during an emergency?"

"Yes, but that would terminate all contact once
he and I are exposed."

Varian realized she was cooperating so far, but
would she continue to do so, he wondered, after his
next question? "Could you lure your parents to Luz,
a planetoid just inside the Pyropean boundary, by
saying you've stolen a *Spacer* with cloaking ability
and escaped and you need rescuing?"

"I'm certain they would come after me since
they trust me now."

"Would you do that for us?"

Renah lifted her eyes and looked at Varian. "Yes,
sir."

"What would you demand in return for your
assistance?"

"You mean, in return for betraying my parents, inciting their hatred, and causing their deaths," she said sadly. "I demand nothing. I will do it to save Galen and everything he loves."

Varian breathed a sigh of relief. "As soon as we finish our strategy talk, I'll take you to a unit where you can send your first message to them."

"How can you trust me? How do you know I won't trick you and escape?"

"Because Galen will be leading the capture team and you would not endanger his life. And because I do trust you, Renah, just as Jana and Amaya do. The reason for my delay was due to a meeting with the *Kadim*. Draco viewed your tapes and has agreed to follow Jana's suggestion." Varian hoped she didn't notice his use of "tapes" instead of tape; he'd also shown Draco the one of the conversation between Jana and Renah, as there was nothing on it that their friend and ruler didn't already know. "You will not be slain and you will not be sent to a penal colony: that is our reward to you."

Renah admitted a memory loss wouldn't be so terrible under the grim circumstances of forgetting her black deeds, dead parents, and lost love. "That's compassionate and generous, sir, in light of my guilt. Thank you."

"Thank *you*, Renah, for helping us to save many lives and worlds."

"There is one request I want to make, sir."

In a gentle tone, Varian asked, "What is it?"

"Could you keep me and Galen separated during this final mission? I don't want to face him and I'm certain he would prefer not to see me."

"Granted, if possible. Let's make our plans, then you can rest before our departure."

After they finished and Varian left her while he made final preparations, Renah sat on the *seata* and wept in despair, shame, guilt, and apprehension. She knew she soon would lose her parents, Galen, her friends, and her life in Maffei. *Forgive me, Mother, Father, but I must stop this madness and there is only one way to do so. Forgive me, Galen, for what I have done to you and your world. I pray my parents will believe me and come, so this can be over.*

Yet Renah feared they might be suspicious and refuse to appear, feared they might reach the rendezvous sight first with a larger force of *nefariants* and set an inescapable trap for them. She also feared Galen and his family and Jason would be slain. Once her treachery was exposed, there would be nothing she could say or do to save their lives. *"Kahala* protect those I've come to love, for they do not deserve to die. If lives must be sacrificed, make it mine and my parents'."

Eighteen

As the cloaked *Galactic Wind* journeyed toward the planetoid of Luz and they awaited their roles in the crucial mission ahead, Amaya and Jason talked together in his assigned quarters on deck one. "How is it possible for all of your planets to have livable environments and for travel between them to be accomplished with such ease?" he asked. "I know your starships are fast, but still the intervals are great, aren't they?"

Amaya surmised he was trying to distract her and was grateful. "There isn't as much distance between our solar daystar and our planets as the outer lying ones of the Milky Way Galaxy which are cold and hostile to human and animal existence," she explained. "Our pattern of bodies is almost like a giant staircase with globes sitting on its thirteen steps; each planet is only a short range—farther left and outward from the sun than the world before it. Since all orbit at similar rates, they stay positioned in a manner which keeps them close enough for fast interplanetary treks, particularly at starlight speed. Our ozones are strong and have not been damaged or depleted as Earth's has been, so we can live closer to our sun without hazards. Only one of our worlds is aligned with another and almost shadowed by it: Kudora; it moves on the same schedule and in a path behind Therraccus; therefore, it is always in a sort of twilight and is covered by ice and snow. Its people and animals, as with Earth's polar regions, have adapted to those demands. Without direct sun rays for warmth and light, Kudorans live in domed cities and are pale-skinned." *Like Commander Mohr, who—thank the stars—has not seen me or given me any problems since my return. No doubt he has heard about our love and conceded to defeat; I hope so.* "We'll reach the Pyropean boundary soon and sneak across it to Luz. By tomorrow, we'll be heading home in victory."

"What if we're sighted?"

"It's nearly deserted and barren except for a race of mutant *greebs* and odd creatures. It's also in a parsec without planets nearby so it's visited rarely, and our scanners report nothing suspicious in that sector."

"What if they're there—Pyropeans or *villites*—but cloaked like us?"

"We have an anticloaking device which would detect either. Pyropea does not possess the detection-resistant technology our *villite* is using, a gift from those Serians. Besides, with our accurate guess of the Tabrizes' cloaking frequency, we know their location and we'll reach Luz before them. We've reset ours so they can't track us. After our cloaked ship is in orbit, Renah will land in a *Spacer.* As soon as we transport down and our precautions are taken, she'll send them her coordinates."

Jason hated to think of his love and her family being in jeopardy, as it was unknown how many men were aboard the en route enemy vessel. He also worried about the Tabrizes having a superior weapon. "Won't their sophisticated monitors and scanners pick us up?" he asked.

"No, not with our personal force shields in place after we conceal ourselves. You have your wrist device on and know how to use it. Once the Tabrizes land and join Renah, we'll surround them and capture them. Only my father, brother, you, and I will be with her. Renah says they'll come alone to speak privately with her. While we're on the planetoid's surface, the *Galactic Wind* will disable their ship and capture their men. Soon, the Tabrizes will be defeated and peace will reign once more, and we can begin our future together."

"That sounds wonderful; I'm more than ready to take that big step."

"Me, too." Following several kisses, Amaya cuddled close to him on the cozy *seata*. With time short and without total privacy, they could not allow themselves to become aroused. "It's strange—perhaps fated—how this threat will end on Luz, where my parents crashed years ago when Taemin and Canissia tried to kill them. As Father told us, Luz can be a dangerous place and the Tabrizes, unpredictable," Amaya reminded him, "so we have to be on full alert. I think he chose Luz because of its historical meaning to them, and because it makes it easier for us to terminate this peril in secrecy."

"Has Renah been told her fate?"

"Father revealed it after we left Rigel. Since only we five will come into contact with the Tabrizes, no one aboard will discover her true identity and what's she's done. The *Kadim* and Supreme Council are the only other people who know about her misguided role, and it will forever stay in the dark."

"You agree with their decision to allow her to remain as Renah Dhobi?"

"With the help she's given us, and the woman she's become, she deserves exoneration. Her talents and intelligence make her an asset to Star Fleet. I believe we can trust her."

"Does Galen concur? How has that stunning news affected him?"

"He's kept to himself while analyzing his feelings. I hope he forgives her. To reject her would be a great loss and bring further tragedy because they are so perfectly matched and are so deeply in love, even if Galen doubts that truth at this agonizing moment. I spoke with Renah earlier; she has no illusions about a future with Galen. She thinks that he can never forgive or love her again. That's heart-crushing to her, but she will not force herself on him. May *Kahala* be kind to them as they seek a course around this gigantic obstacle, alone or together."

Varian sat in Commander Vaux's borrowed quarters with his somber son. "I know you haven't seen Renah yet, and that's been wise for both of you considering your torn emotions," he said to Galen. "I realize how hard this situation is on you, but you have to come to grips with it and make a decision about her. What she did was wrong, but I can understand her actions. *Kahala* knows, I did similar things to your mother long ago out of a sense of duty and, at times, desperation and blindness. I tricked her, misused her, and deceived her for reasons I truly believed were right and necessary. It's much the same with Renah and you. I'm not taking her side and I'm not telling you to take her back; those are serious decisions only you can make. If you can't forgive her and put this matter behind you, it's wrong to resume your relationship and to mate. Without love and trust, there is no chance of happiness."

Galen listened with his heart and mind, but didn't respond.

"There are some points you should consider," Varian went on to elaborate. "Renah saved you and your team from those toxic mushrooms on Balfae, and she risked exposure to tell you their cure. Her simboyd idea at Caguas prevented many deaths and much damage when she could have held silent. She helped destroy Zandia's threat when she could have found way to feign a mistake or she could have enticed you not to send her on that mission. She didn't imperil Amaya's life by telling the Tabrizes she was on Earth alone. She kept most of our strategies and knowledge a secret from her parents. She didn't use opportunities to assassinate us, destroy this ship, or plant explosives at Star Base. She didn't infect you with that virus and she slipped us clues about it, along with that vial. She didn't give them our security codes and procedures for Base; Canissia already knew them from the past. At great risk to herself, she remained with us to provide assistance and to protect you. She believed her parents' charges against us and didn't know to what extent they would go for revenge. In all honesty, she's supplying us with a path to victory. Those actions will cost her, Galen. Can you imagine betraying me and your mother and being responsible for our deaths for any reason? Before you cut Renah from your life, be certain you can live without her."

Later that afternoon, Varian received an astounding message from his wife. He summoned Galen, Amaya, and Jason to reveal it to them.

Varian, Amaya, and Jason went to Renah's quarters on deck two. The tormented female was not confined to them but was remaining in seclusion during the awesome voyage to confront and betray those she loved and had sided against. Only security team members and Elite Squad units were aboard, as there were men amongst them who could operate every section and function of the starship. The regular crew and its superior officer had been given leave on Rigel until their ship's return. Varian Saar, past commander of the *Wanderlust,* was in charge of this furtive mission and carefully selected staff. Their clandestine actions would be explained later by saying they were ordered by the *Kadim* to check out a slip by a captive and were ordered to conceal their movements to avoid being discovered and thwarted by the *villite* who seemed to have a cunning way of breaching their security measures. It would be reported that this commander and crew penetrated the enemy vessel's cloaking shield, pursued the *nefariants*, and battled them to victory. Only the *Kadim*, the Council, the Saars, Jason, and Renah knew the rest of the story. If the Tabrizes survived the impending attack, the insidious couple would not be allowed to expose their daughter; nor would the enlightened Maffeians.

Renah stepped back to permit the visitors to enter her quarters. When she noticed that Galen was not with them, a contradictory mingling of sadness and relief filled her. She had removed the sunny shade on her short hair and returned it to her original color, and she observed how Varian halted a moment and stared at her fiery mane and silvery-gray eyes. "I hope this doesn't displease you, sir," she said to Varian, "but I wanted to face my parents for the last time as myself."

"Renah, that's what I've come to reveal; I have stunning news for you: I've just learned Canissia Garthon is not your mother and Taemin Tabriz is not your father."

She gaped at him in confusion. "What are you talking about? I don't understand."

"Jana was going to alter Canissia's old medical record so you couldn't ever be traced to her and exposed, but the data Jana retrieved reveals you can't be Canissia's daughter." Varian watched Renah's gaze widen in astonishment. "As a result of a minor accident and treatment on Lynrac long ago, Taemin's blood factors are on file; they do not match yours, so he cannot be your father. Jana ran your DNA pattern and factors through the comparison system, but she could not find a match, so she can't venture a guess as to who your real parents are. Since it isn't the Tabrizes, that explains how they could misuse you so vilely. I can't say I'm sorry about this unexpected development. In fact, I'm delighted you aren't their child."

Amaya and Jason witnessed Renah's bewilderment and shock. They, too, could hardly believe this turn in events. The same was true of Galen who was pacing and thinking things over in his quarters.

"They aren't my bloodline parents? Is Doctor Saar positive?"

"Yes. You were reared, trained, and misguided by strangers."

"Who are my parents, sir? How did the Tabrizes get hold of me?"

"We don't know, Renah, and we probably will never know unless they tell us on Luz. It is a fact you are part Maffeian and part Pyropean."

The redhead deliberated this information but its reality changed nothing for her. "I never imagined they were lying to me about anything, everything. I wonder if *Raz* Yakir knows who I am. If so, will he tell me?"

"As soon as we're finished here, we'll contact

him and ask, right after the Serians receive a warning not to interfere in our fates again. I doubt—"

A signal for permission to enter cut off the remainder of Varian's sentence.

Galen looked at his father, then his sister and Jason; he quickly glanced at Renah before returning his somber gaze to Varian. "Father, we're almost there, so time is brief. May I speak with Renah in private?"

Varian studied his son's expression. "Renah, is that permissible with you?" he asked. "Time is short and perils are many."

Renah knew she could be slain during the impending mission; she should allow Galen to relate his feelings now, to unburden himself. She nodded, then waited for the others to leave them alone.

Galen took a deep breath as his gaze scanned her flattering changes. The color of her fiery hair enhanced her beauty and appeal; it heightened the allure of her smoky eyes and tawny hue of her complexion. She looked vibrant and even more feminine, sultry and irresistible. The red tresses which framed her exquisite face suited her even more than the sunny strands she had used as a disguise. Despite her strength and courage, there was a fragile and vulnerable air about her. "I'm grateful for your help, Renah. What you're doing is difficult, but it will save many lives and prevent much destruction. You're very brave and generous to assist us. I've stayed away until now to give us both time to deal with our emotions, but that's proving to be harder than I imagined it would be. All of the time that I believed we were a personal and professional team, you were working against me and my people. You shattered my faith and belief in you, and my confidence in myself and my instincts."

Renah looked at the injured and suffering man who remained at a distance, as if he could not bear to come nearer and risk more wounds. Yet she read no great hatred and scorn in him, and was relieved. "I know, Galen, but I hope I can earn your trust again, and your forgiveness. What I did to you and your people was wrong, but I cannot undo those evil deeds. All I can do is apologize and try to right them and repair the damage. The only thing I can say in my defense is that I was blinded and deceived by people I thought were my parents and who convinced me to aid their cause. As soon as I saw the truth, I tried to lessen the evil until I could halt it without getting my parents slain. I was trapped between opposing forces whom I loved. I was confused, afraid, and tormented; I didn't know what I should do or whom to trust and help. In my predicament, I made many terrible mistakes and I'm sorry."

Her words—and those he recalled from the taped sessions—seared his troubled mind and tugged at his aching heart. Then and now, she looked sincere and honest. To be fair, she had been as tricked and betrayed as he was. While his gaze drifted over her, he murmured, "It's as if the woman I knew and loved never existed, as if Renah Dhobi was a glorious dream or an illusion; Renah Tabriz is a stranger, an enemy I should despise and reject and battle."

Tears misted her eyes, but she kept them from flowing down her cheeks. "I'm not your enemy, Galen; I hope I am your ally and your friend."

"After what I've witnessed, that will take awhile to believe and accept. I thought we had an honest relationship, that we were perfectly matched, that our bond was unbreakable. I'd never loved a woman as I loved you. You were my heart, my soul, my future."

Each time Galen used the past tense, it knifed Renah to the core. She had *expected* to lose him, yet hearing the results of her duplicity staggered and agonized her. She was too impeded by warring emotions to plead or reason. She just waited for him to continue unburdening himself on her dejected shoulders.

"Sometimes I think it would be easier for me if you were totally guilty; then I could hate you and put this episode behind me one day. I feel like a Tri-Galaxy at war: part of me understands and wants everything to return to the way it was between us; part of me does not grasp what you did and warns me to reject and avoid you forever; and part of me knows neither of those two are possible. Right now, I'm miserable with you and miserable without you. I need a soothing truce with you and with myself; but I don't know what to do to obtain the best treaty for us. I have only one remaining question: Do you truly love me?"

Renah stared at him, as that was not the query she had expected. "Why are you asking me that today?"

He had heard her vow love for him amidst the

power of truth serum, but he needed to hear it come from her conscious thoughts. "Was my conquest only a necessary part of your assignment?"

"No. It was at first, but it changed quickly and easily, as soon as I got to know you. I had believed what my . . . Canissia told me about the Saar men being insensitive users and discarders of women and I had heard the rumors about you being a *reacher* so I thought you deserved any pain and humiliation you received from me during my mission. Very soon I realized both stories were false and you were a special man. You stole my heart and changed me forever. I'm sorry I hurt you, and I swear I will never do so again by intention."

"Do you love me, truly love me?" he persisted.

"I will always love you and I'll never repeat such evil misdeeds. Can you ever forgive me? Can we be friends again one day?"

"Is that all you want from me now: to be friends and allies?"

"No, but that is all I can ask since I have so wronged you. If you can love me and accept me again, that must come from you. It is selfish and unfair for me to pressure or coax you into taking me back."

"This has been hard on me, Renah. I love you, but I don't know if we can overcome this obstacle. Before we can attempt to repair this damage, I must make certain I have truly forgiven you, that I can put this darkness behind me and can trust you. If I can't do those things, there is no chance for us."

She took a few tentative steps forward, but halted

when he did not do the same. "Is there anything I can say or do to make this easier for you, no matter what your decision will be?"

"No, Renah, this is something I must handle myself. I need more time to examine my feelings and to adjust to what's happened."

Renah yearned to run into his embrace and be surrounded by it. She longed to kiss him. Yet she knew she must not entice him. "I understand," she said simply.

Galen's gaze was fastened to hers. He craved to hug and kiss her. He hungered for this episode to fade since it could not vanish. He had to be assured of his feelings for her and hers for him, feelings which must be strong enough to carry them beyond this trying point, feelings strong enough to establish a new and better bond. They loved each other and all lies were removed from between them. Surely they could weather this solar storm—

Galen's wrist communicator signaled an impending message; he lifted his arm and responded into it, "Chief Saar, over."

"We have to prepare for our mission, Galen," Varian said. "We're nearing orbit. Over."

"We'll join you in bay one shortly. Over. Out." He looked at Renah. "We must leave now. We'll talk again afterward."

Renah awaited her alleged parents' arrival. She was aware of the four people concealed nearby and protected from enemy sensors by individual force shields and deflector beams. She gazed at her surroundings. She was in a large clearing which was encircled by rough and difficult-to-travel terrain of arduous hills, craggy peaks, steep slopes, rocky ravines, and various-size boulders in giant piles. Tall and precipitous bluffs of several mountain ranges jutted from the hard ground, their rugged pinnacles and crevices filled with snow and ice. Afternoon sun dazzled off the ivory blanket as if it were splattered with brilliant gems.

Prickly plants and sticker trees were barren of vegetation during Luz's winter season. Any formations visible were brown and black and occasional blue. Nowhere within view was the ochre sand and russet dirt of other seasons. The aquamarine sky displayed a mingling of clouds and gases in scarlet, flame, chartreuse, and violet. On the far horizons, the largest and highest mountains were marbled silhouettes before the colorful background. With the ground frozen, *keelers*—deadly and vicious vipers—were burrowed deep in hibernation and presented no threat. Wind gusted in odd whooshing and whining sounds; often its force shook branches free of powdery snow or breezes swept over boulders and scattered fresh flakes on them across the terrain. It was a near desolate, harsh, and isolated place.

Renah's clear helmet, thermal jumpsuit, and gloves insulated her body against the climate's icy assaults. A small unit strapped to her back provided fresh air inside her headgear. Yet a strange chill and tension suffused her. She wished her parents would hurry so she could complete this formidable task. Her motive for rushing was not to avoid the elements; it was because she yearned to have this menacing matter behind her and to earn a chance to forge a new bond with Galen. She wanted to bury her dark past today and to seek a radiant future tomorrow. Were both goals, she mused in suspense, possible? Even if she succeeded with the first, the second—

Renah discarded wishful thoughts as she saw a small shuttle with Serian symbols appear, approach, and circle her location. She removed her vizard and looked upward. The craft hovered for a few minutes, as, no doubt, the rendezvous setting was checked for hidden perils. Only a one-seater *Spacer* was visible, as the other team members had transported to the surface and taken cover after concealing their tracks. The shuttle landed, an aperture opened, and a walkway was extended to the ground. The Tabrizes appeared in the orifice and their gazes scanned the area for hazards. Renah waved to them, but did not leave her position as she needed to lure them away from their craft. She watched her "parents" walk toward her. She feigned a smile as her "mother" and "father" studied her in bewilderment. Despite her sixty-two years, the cinnamon-haired Canissia was still beautiful, slim, supple, and smooth-skinned, she exuded a sensual and arrogant aura. Taemin, eleven years younger, was virile and handsome. A regal bearing from his days as a Pyropean prince lingered in his carriage and movements. He, too, projected a seductive and vain air. Their personalities and characters were similar, making them a perfect match as allies and mates.

Canissia snuggled inside a fake fur cloak, her voice harsh as she questioned Renah. "Why did you disobey and leave Maffei and summon us here? We have important work to do. Your message said you had to see us immediately. What happened? Why didn't you put your news in a coded report? Sneaking off like this could imperil our plans and jeopardize your role in them. This trip was reckless and unnecessary. How will you explain it to them?"

She watched wind whip through Taemin's long and silky hair, and through Canissia's long and curly fiery tresses. She noticed she received no loving embraces, cheerful smiles, or warming words to indicate they were glad to see her after lengthy separation. This seemed more like a business meeting with an acquaintance to them than a family union with a daughter. Only their plot mattered to them. "I was in danger of exposure so I had to flee," Renah tried to explain. "Surely you did not wish me to stay and take such a risk."

"It was better to leave if our plan was threatened," Taemin replied gruffly. "Are you sure there was no way you could have repaired whatever damage you created?"

Again Renah realized that only the safety of the plot mattered to them, not any risk to her survival. "No, sir, and it was not of my doing. Supreme Commander Saar ordered a full investigation into the breaks in security and a thorough check into anyone in a position to be a traitor. Since the attack on the medical complex which injured his mate, he is seeking clues as one obsessed by revenge. It did not help to protect matters when you revealed yourself to Doctor Saar," Renah added to Canissia. "That was reckless and detrimental to your goals."

"Jana and Varian believe I am long dead, so it was no risk to us."

"If that is true, why is he searching for any indication you survived?"

"He suspects I'm alive and behind this threat?" Renah noticed her astonishment and vexation. "He does not believe his mate is seeing things. You gave him a vital clue to his enemy."

"You should not have taunted that alien witch," Taemin scolded. "Jana is too intelligent to be duped by shapeshifting; she's a scientist."

"I do as I please, and that pleased me deeply. Soon, she and Varian will be dead and my trick will not matter. Did you give Galen the infusion?" Canissia asked Renah.

"No, it was too risky. He could have contaminated the entire crew, including me, during our long voyage. Secondly, there was no logical way to explain how he contracted the virus during flight, so I would have fallen under suspicion. Also, I would have been compelled to cease my physical relationship with him to avoid infection, which definitely would have exposed me. I discarded the vial to prevent being caught with it in my possession. Now, I have many questions which need answering."

Canissia glared at the quizzical girl. "What questions?"

"Why did you change the original plan and do such horrible things? What manner of twisted jus-

tice is this? Why use a lethal virus that has no cure
and attacks randomly?"

"An alien virus brought Jana Greyson to Maffei
to invade and ruin my life," Canissia scoffed, "so
an alien virus—a mutated strain from her old
world—is the perfect choice for striking at my
nemesis—a scientist who cannot repel it and a crisis
which will incite hatred toward her and all Earthling females who stole Maffeian women's places.
Varian chose her over me, discarded me before everyone as if I were debris! As if that wasn't enough
torment, he tried to exterminate me, and he destroyed my father, your grandfather! I lost everything because of them and their friends; so will
they. I will let them taste humiliation and pain before they taste death. They destroyed my life and
my family. I'll destroy theirs."

"And you agreed to such horror?" Renah asked
Taemin.

"Yes. The Pyropeans banished me and made a
truce with Maffei. What we are doing will break it
and provoke war; both sides will be punished. My
people will beg for my forgiveness and return to
save them, once Trilabs is in our grasp. The Pyropean throne is mine by birthright! Varian, Jana,
and their friends stole it from me. They humiliated me. They had me sent into exile; I was forced
to live as poor and savage as a *greeb*. That anguish
slowly killed my father, your grandfather. Canissia
found me and rescued me; I owe her my loyalty and
help."

"But entire planets are being threatened by dev-
astation. Sick and dying people were killed during

the med complex attack. Crimes and violence ran
rampant until *nefariants* were captured. Men have
been murdered. Women and children have been
injured. Families have been torn apart. Earthling
forces have been ordered to self-destruct. And I
was placed in the center of such enormous cruelties and perils. Why?"

"We are battling enemies, Renah." Canissia
fumed. "We thought you understood and agreed
to help. Why this sudden doubt and defiance?"

"I agreed to help obtain justice, retribution, and
vindication. None of those things are possible with
the actions you are taking. Too many innocents are
being injured and killed. Your plot has soured and
become toxic to all of us. It is past time to terminate
it and return to Seri. You have wounded them
deeply and painfully, so they have been punished
for wrongs against you. What more do you desire?"

"We cannot stop until our enemies are dead,"
Taemin replied.

"But all of Maffei is not the enemy," Renah refuted. "Upon whom and where can you justify
more strikes? Tell Yakir to release the *Rover* crew."

"He can't; they're dead," Canissia snapped in
impatience and anger.

Renah shuddered. "You told him to slay them?"

"Of course not, foolish girl; Yakir would never
do so. We got rid of them because we could not
allow them opportunities to soften Serian hearts
during our absence. If they'd been freed, they
could have exposed us."

"This vicious war with Maffei has gone too far;
it must halt now."

"What have they said and done to turn you against us?" Canissia demanded. "Have you allowed the Saars to work their devious magic on you? Have you become a slave to Galen Saar? Has he blinded and enchanted you? We're your parents, Renah; you owe us loyalty, respect, and obedience."

Renah knew the team nearby could hear the conversation via a hidden transmitter. She had tried her best to extract information from Canissia and Taemin before any attempted capture. She realized more queries about future plans would be suspicious, so she withheld them. Before she gave the team a signal to join her, she asked, "Are you *really* my mother and father?"

Taemin exchanged odd looks with Canissia. "What do you mean?"

Renah explained alleged circumstances that led to this query. "I was forced, like everyone else, to take blood and tissue tests to prove I am not a carrier or victim of the virus you unleashed upon them. I feared the results would expose my true identity. I was going to alter your old medical records to prevent a match with mine, but that wasn't necessary. You know why. Who am I?" She faced them squarely upon conclusion. "Why did you rear me as your child and weapon? Am I just as expendable as your enthralled Earthlings?"

"What lies and foolishness do you speak?" Taemin shouted.

"Tell me the truth," Renah persisted as she stared at them. "I saw my test results; I saw Canissia's medical records; I saw Prince Taemin's. You are not my parents."

"You have lived as our child since you were born," Taemin asserted. "Is that not enough to make you ours?"

"Who are my real parents?" she held firm in her questioning.

"We do not know," Taemin asserted. "We found you abandoned and claimed you as our own because your colorings matched ours. We could not have loved and wanted you more if you had been from a union between us."

Renah wondered why Canissia was allowing Taemin to respond each time. "If you had loved me as your own, you would not have imperiled my life with your hunger for revenge. Do you forget I have earned a place of trust in Star Fleet Security and in the Saars' circle; I have access to secret records and I have read them; they do not match the tales you told to me. You were not betrayed and used long ago; you did evil things and were exposed and punished. I was not reared as your daughter; I was programmed as a robot to become your tool of vengeance."

"Have you exposed us to the Maffeians and Saars?" Canissia sneered.

"I wanted to speak with you first to learn who and what I am."

"That means you're going to reveal the truth to them?" Canissia asked.

"How can I return to Maffei after what I have done? Though I am not your child and I was deceived, I am guilty of many dark deeds against them. They would not forgive me. I am doomed."

"You must come with us, Renah, to be safe," Taemin said.

"No, I will not be deceived and used by you again."

"We cannot allow you to go free and jeopardize our plans."

Renah stared at Canissia. "Are you going to kill me to silence me?"

Canissia pushed wind-blown strands of copper hair from her face. "I hope you will not make it necessary. If you behave, you can serve our purposes elsewhere. Once Trilabs is in our grasp, you will be rewarded and can travel where you desire. If you like, we will give Galen Saar to you as a slave to do your every bidding. As for the other Saars, they will be enjoyed by us, then annihilated. If you become our enemy, Renah, your fate will be the same." She turned to her husband. "Do you agree, Taemin?"

The ex-prince sent her a salacious grin and nodded.

"How can you be so cruel? If you accepted, loved, and reared me as your true child, how could you take my life?"

"Because you have turned against us and could destroy us. Hear me, Renah: nothing and no one will prevent us from obtaining our desires."

"I'm glad you're not my parents and I'm nothing like you, because you're both evil. I'm leaving to return to the *Raz* and live with the Serians," she contended, as that ruler's rank was the verbal signal to spring their trap. Now, as ordered by Galen, she was to put a safe distance between them.

As Renah whirled and headed toward the *Spacer,* Taemin shouted, "Halt! You must come with us and obey, or perish here on Luz."

"I don't think so," Varian argued after he lowered his force shield and stepped from hiding, followed by Amaya, Galen, and Jason: all were armed and ready to attack. "Surrender or prepare to die."

"Varian!" Canissia shrieked, then glared at Renah. "You little traitor! If you were my child, you would never do this to me! I should have known you were not strong enough to withstand Saarian magic and cunning."

"You should not have deceived me and sent me there," Renah replied. "Did you think I would not discover the truth and try to right my wrongs? Have you forgotten I was also reared and trained by kind and gentle Serians, not just by your hateful influence? I cannot allow evil to continue."

"This is Galen's fault, isn't it?" an enraged Canissia shouted as she and Taemin steadily backed away from the encroachers.

As the group joined Renah, she saw her alleged mother lift a hand to use a *lazette* strapped to the woman's palm. Renah knew of Canissia's penchant for that manner of surprise attack and guessed the woman's intention. She reacted with haste by leaping in front of the man she loved and shouting a warning to the others to get down. They rapidly dropped to their knees to dodge incoming fire. After taking the blast meant for Galen, her body was jolted backward against his chest.

Galen almost lost his balance from the force of the unexpected blow. He caught Renah in his arms and lowered them both to the wintry ground, his weapon drawn and pointing at their targets. He was ready and willing to defend her with all his might and prowess and, if necessary, with his life. He kept his gaze locked on the action and tried to stay alert as he prayed for her survival.

Before Canissia could get off another shot or Taemin could draw his weapon, Amaya and Jason fired their guns and disarmed the two *villites*. Amaya's skill and precision caused Canissia's hand to jerk backward from an impact which disabled her *lazette* and numbed her hand. Jason's accurate aim sliced through Taemin's holster and caused it to drop to the ground; a rapid second shot rendered its weapon useless.

The assailed couple took instant action; they turned and ran toward their craft to escape, the icy ground no threat to their cleated boots.

"We need them alive and uninjured," Varian reminded his team.

They pursued the couple with a headstart on them, their special footgear and agile limbs also traversing the frozen terrain with ease. They fired warning blasts which zinged through the frosty air and struck the white surface around their foes. Canissia and Taemin were determined to reach safety, so they ignored the shots which scattered loose snow and melted holes in the ice. When Amaya and Jason focused their aims on the craft and disabled it, the couple changed directions and fled into a jumble of concealing rocks.

Varian received a vibrating signal that should mean the enemy vessel was in their control.

"There's nowhere to run or hide!" he shouted. "You're trapped! Your ship has been captured! Your shuttle is disabled. Surrender!"

"Never, you *gichata!*" Canissia yelled. "Come after us if you dare!" She and Taemin worked their way deeper into the arduous terrain.

"As you wish, but you'll be sorry!" Varian warned the couple.

With the situation now being handled by the others, Galen felt safe to examine Renah. He sighed in relief when he detected a heartbeat and shallow breathing. He realized Canissia's weapon had been set on stun, not kill, whether by oversight or intention. For a staggering few minutes, Galen had feared Renah was dead, her life given to save his, sacrificed in undeniable love. As he held her close and thanked *Kahala* for sparing her, he heard loud noises and gazed in that direction to see a group of large, apish primates leaping from behind or atop boulders. Scraggly and tangled manes grazed their hulking shoulders. Snoutish noses sniffed the air and sent forth snorts which formed brief clouds in the frosty air. Beady black eyes darted about to study the trespassers. Huge lumps and sharp bony ridges etched their alien features. Wiry whiskers stuck out from their faces. Big ears did the same on the sides of massive heads. Any flesh visible beneath their shaggy, hairy coverings was a pale yellow. What must be their leader pummeled his broad chest with balled fists and made menacing sounds. His lips sent forth unintelligible words. On a rugged hill, the startled couple was surrounded. Mutant after mutant scrambled forward one at a time to poke at the two captives, then returned to the circle of chattering companions. Canissia and Taemin, standing back to back, slapped and kicked and shouted at their taunting attackers to scare them; but those tactics failed.

Varian, Amaya, and Jason halted their pursuit while still in the clearing. Their weapons had been set on stun in the hopes of capturing their enemies for interrogation. Under the power of the new truth serum, they had hoped to learn if there was a cure for the virus, if there were other carriers or vials which needed to be located, where to find and how to disenthrall the Earthlings, and if other threats were in progress.

"We can't go in there to rescue them; there are too many *greebs* to battle," Varian said. "We'd be at a strong disadvantage. We'd entrap ourselves, and leave Galen and Renah in jeopardy. Much as I want them, we can't take that risk."

"Should we summon help, Father?" Amaya asked, knowing that could reveal their knowledge of Renah's identity to others aboard.

Varian saw the leader bound onto a boulder, pucker his mouth, and make blowing sounds. He realized it was a signal to others when he heard responses from the rocky ranges. He knew from past experience that communication was impossible and they were unwelcome intruders on the creatures' territory. He recalled how strong and aggressive the hairy primates were from the time they had attacked him and Jana years ago. If captured, they would be torn to pieces and devoured for food—something the Tabrizes also realized.

"Look!" Jason shouted. "It's too late. They . . . self-disintegrated."

Varian saw surprise register in the wild brutes after the couple glowed for a few moments and vanished, but the loss was quickly forgotten by their simple minds. He assumed they would be stalked next, and the odds were too great to battle; not even their skills could disable so many creatures before they were reached by countless others. Somehow, he could not order his ship to fire on these beings whose behavior was normal for their evolutionary level; with their own targets dead, it was unnecessary to injure or slay these primates.

Amaya assumed her father was deliberating his next course of action, but time was short. "Father, we must call for help or leave quickly," she advised. "Those creatures are after us. They're everywhere; we're outnumbered."

As rocks and sticks were thrown toward them, Varian said, "Let's get Galen and Renah and transport so we won't have to kill the creatures. We'll recover the _Spacer_ by remote control and we'll blast the shuttle into oblivion from the ship. Move out; they look angry, but they're advancing with caution!"

The three hurried back to Galen and Renah.

"How is she son?" Varian asked in a rush.

"Alive, but I don't know her condition. She hasn't awakened yet. What happened? Where are the Tabrizes?"

"Gone. Dead. We have to get out of here fast; the _greebs_ are agitated." Varian called the ship and ordered their hasty retrieval.

Suddenly, a loud explosion was heard and a brilliant light was seen in the darkening sky far above and slightly left of their location.

"What was that?" Jason asked Varian.

"I don't know. I hope our ship isn't under attack. We'll know soon."

Nineteen

While Galen carried Renah to sick bay, Varian and the others went to the bridge to check out the commotion just before they left the planetoid's surface. "What happened?" he asked the Elite Squad officer in charge.

"After we received your signal that you had your targets under control and it was time to demand the enemy vessel's surrender, we did so," he explained, "but they refused to yield. I kept trying to warn you of a problem, but you had your transmitter off to verbal communication and didn't respond to my vibrator clue. We kept your position shielded against them in case they were sent an assault order from your targets below. A few minutes before you requested transportation, they closed their channel to our reception. For some reason, they destroyed their ship as we were recovering your team."

Varian explained in a rush. "Either the Tabrizes sent their mind-controlled men an order to blow up the ship or they had a remote device they used to initiate a self-destruct sequence before they killed themselves," he theorized. "I suppose to prevent us from obtaining their records or to endanger us." Varian told the weapon's operator to obliterate the shuttle on Luz. He said to do the same to the *Spacer* as there was no time to recover it. "As soon as he finishes eliminating all clues to us," she said to the navigator, "get us out of here fast before a Pyropean patrol comes to investigate that mysterious explosion. Take us straight to Base."

After all signs of their encroachment were removed, the cloaked *Galactic Wind* hit starlight speed and left that sector. As they trekked toward the intergalactic boundary, the officers met to discuss the episode.

"Who were they, sir?" One asked. "Why are they attacking Maffei?"

Varian had decided what and how much he would tell them, with the *Kadim*'s permission and knowledge. He watched the four men react with astonishment as he gave the names of Canissia Garthon and Taemin Tabriz. He then related the background of the nefarious pair and how they had been plotting revenge in a faraway galaxy. "They captured and enthralled Earthlings because the galaxy which befriended them refused to challenge us," he explained, "but they did gift those *fiendals* with a ship and supplies. Everything else they stole. We didn't have time to get much information before those mutants attacked."

Another officer explained they had picked up the *greebs'* presence but couldn't get a warning out. "I was worried when I saw the large number of readings, but you didn't request a rescue so I held off."

Varian had ordered all visual and audible sensors

to be kept off, saying it was to prevent detection in case their enemies had superior technology for scanning; in reality, it was to prevent Renah's exposure. The moment the Tabrizes fled, he alerted his ship to attack the other one and to monitor the ground action by searching for heat images from enemy lifeforms.

"I'm glad you obeyed," Varian concurred, "because we weren't sure if those *villites* had only one vessel. I dreaded to think they had another ship on a different cloaking frequency that could be waiting for the first one to draw us out of hiding."

"Your strategy worked, sir; and that clue Doctor Saar obtained from one of those prisoners before he died was accurate."

"It was clever to use Lieutenant Dhobi as bait," the third officer remarked. "Who would suspect a beautiful female of being tricky and dangerous? Her message on their frequency cunningly lured them into our trap."

"And I had Jason Carlisle standing by to assist her with duping them. Being an Earthling and a stranger, I surmised he could fool them into believing he and a disguised Renah wanted to join their forces. Even if the *villites* didn't trust them, they had to come check out who had their code and how they got it. Since our ship and my team weren't picked up by their scanners, they assumed Renah was alone until they were out of their shuttle and questioning her. I doubt they even suspected a snare since Pyropea and Androas have us quarantined. I only wish we could have gotten more facts."

"At least our threat is over; that was our main goal," the fourth man asserted, and the others nodded their agreement.

"After that *villite* used a replica of me to get inside Trilabs," Varian continued his explanation, "I had to come and see for myself if our clue was real and this trap worked; and we had to keep our plan a secret since we didn't know how our enemy was breaching our security measures. I suspect Canissia had information she stole from her father years ago; we hadn't changed codes or procedures since Segall left the Council and died. We had truces and were at peace so there appeared no need to do so."

"I know our people will be happy this peril is over," another officer said. "We can have things back to normal within a few weeks at most."

"Unless we have trouble about their leaders," his colleague hinted.

Varian was ready to handle that with his team. "Since Prince Taemin was involved, this matter will be classified top security to prevent any repercussions from Pyropeans who remained friends of his or those who still grieve over Jurad's death. I don't think it will serve any good purpose to expose their identifies. Publicly, we'll report we pursued and destroyed the *villite* leader and his ship: an alien from another galaxy, which is true."

"That sounds wise, sir. With Taemin's crimes in the distant past, his people might only see a strike against their royal bloodline. We shouldn't accuse him openly. And bringing Canissia's new deeds to light would darken her father's image. Supreme

Councilman Segall served us well long ago; he doesn't deserve that. To expose their identities could do more harm than good."

The other team members nodded in agreement.

"Our scientists still have to find a cure for that virus, but it's time to put this dark plot behind us and repair their damage," Varian said. "The entire team will receive commendations for their roles in this mission, but expose its details to no one. I know the *Kadim* will want to thank each of you personally after our return to Rigel. I'll express my gratitude here and now; thank you, men, for a fine job."

The group talked for a while longer before Varian said, "Since everyone's had a busy day, we'll file our reports tomorrow. Alert me if anything shows up on our sensors before we reach our territory. Dismissed."

Amaya and Jason went to sick bay to check on Renah and to give her brother the results of their meeting. They found her anesthetized while recovering in a life-support/medical unit which healed her injury and monitored her condition until all bodily functions returned to normal. They spoke in a private corner with a relieved Galen before heading for Jason's quarters to relax and share their passions.

Later in the alcove where Renah was resting after removal from the unit, Galen sat beside her as he told her the fates of the Tabrizes and their ship. He related what the public would be told about the trouble and the gaps in the attack team's knowledge. He perceived her sadness over her confrontation with the reality of her alleged parents; in a tragic turn of events, she had lost her false and real parents in the same day. It was as if Renah Tabriz had been wiped from existence. He knew she must feel confused and alone as she faced dealing with her shadowed past and creating a new life for herself. "Your true identity will remain a secret," he told her. "You must put the past behind you; from here on, you will live as Renah Dhobi in everyone's mind. Because of what you have done for us, you won't be slain or penalized or have your memory erased. You can't be a part of Security for a long time, if ever again, but you can remain in Star Fleet if you so choose. To safeguard your secret, you'll have to request a transfer or people will wonder why a heroine of our great mission had to step down. Saying you want to be away from the line of perils for a time would sound logical to everyone." He grasped her hand and held it. "I'm sure it won't take long for you to prove yourself to the *Kadim* and Council and to be reinstated if that's your goal. They will insist on questioning with the new truth serum; that's understandable given the circumstances." He saw her nod in agreement and acceptance.

Galen stroked her hair. "You have a chance for a fresh beginning, and you deserve it; let the past go, Renah, and be happy. The fact you were reared by the Tabrizes doesn't matter to me or to my family because you're nothing like them. We accept you as the woman you are now. You overcame and survived their evil."

As her smoky eyes misted, he caressed her cheek to comfort her. "You shouldn't have risked your life that way; you could have been killed if her weapon hadn't been set on stun. You're lucky it was, and so are we."

"I had to do it, Galen, because I love you with all my heart and it was my fault you and the others were in jeopardy. I shouldn't have been such a coward and permitted the danger to continue as long as it did. But at least by remaining quiet, I was in a position to get information from the Tabrizes to pass along to you. I feared if I was removed from my role, things would be worse for your side."

Galen didn't interrupt when she halted to take a breath. He sensed she wasn't finished and needed to lighten her heavy burden.

"I was also selfish in not wanting to lose you so soon," Renah admitted. "I should have trusted more in you and in our love. I kept hoping and praying my par— the Tabrizes would stop their evil and leave. When I realized I was deluding myself and it was increasing, I had to side against them. That was a tormenting decision for me. You know the rest. I swear you can trust me; I would never betray or trick you again." She lowered her gaze for a moment. "I hope you can learn to forgive me one day and allow me a chance to earn your respect and affection again."

Galen gave her hand a light squeeze and smiled. "You don't need to try, because you have them already. I love you; I never stopped loving you even when I was consumed by ill feelings, emotions I've conquered. I want you, Renah. I need you to be part of my life, my future. I know it was difficult and painful being torn between me and your parents, and being compelled to go against all you had been taught since birth. You made great sacrifices to end the threat against us, and I'll always be grateful to you, always be proud of you."

Renah's heart raced in suspense. "Does that mean we can be friends again?" she asked, in case she had misunderstood his words.

"More than friends, Renah, if you're willing; I want you to become my mate after our return to Rigel and our reports are filed. You fulfilled your end of the bargain and the Council will honor theirs. We're at peace again, thanks to you, and you're free to make your own choices within limits. My family and I love you and want you to join us."

She trembled in anticipation and prayed she wasn't still unconscious and this was only a taunting dream. "Are you saying you want me to . . ."

Galen finished for her, "I want you to become Renah Saar as soon as it's possible. We're perfectly matched, woman; we were destined and fated for each other. What is your answer?"

Tears of joy brimmed her eyes. "Yes, a million yeses, my love."

"Excellent, because I wasn't going to accept no or even a maybe," he jested with a chuckle and a roguish grin.

Renah sat up and hugged him. "Fate is being very generous to me."

"To us, my love," he corrected, then sealed their

lips in a heady and bonding kiss which revealed the depth of their feelings to each other.

"Despite everything that's happened since your arrival, you aren't sorry you came to Maffei with me, are you?" Amaya asked.

Jason pulled her closer to him. "Never; we've had some exciting adventures and I've learned a lot about your world. Besides, we were fated to wed the moment we met. No, the moment we were born."

Amaya cuddled in his embrace as potent emotions engulfed her. "I believe that with all my being, and I love you with all my heart."

Jason trailed his fingers up and down her bare arm. "So, you'll become Amaya Carlisle soon?" Without halting his motion, he amended, "Wait, let me do this right. Will you do me the honor of marrying me, Amaya Saar, and making me the happiest and luckiest man on Earth? Make that, the entire Universe."

Amaya shifted her position so her gaze could meet his. "Yes, and I've decided to resign immediately from Star Fleet to start creating a family with you." She couldn't replace his lost son but another child would lessen his tragic loss.

Jason's blue eyes blazed with desire and his body flamed with it. "That more than suits me. Your mother's suggestion about us living on Altair and you working with her and me with your father also appeals to me. I'm glad he agreed. I like and respect your family, and it looks as if we'll all be happy now, if Renah said yes to Galen."

"I have no doubt she did. They love each other as much as we do. Galen and I had good examples in our parents." She decided the time was right to explain her world's marrying ceremony to Jason, and gave her intention. "It is a little different from Earth's: we stand before a *mintu* and announce our decision to become mates; we sign a document making it legal and, *pralu*, we're a pair forever. We have no divorce; once a public commitment is made, it's binding for life. Only the *Kadim* or a criminal offense can dissolve a union."

"We won't ever need your ruler's assistance in that area. If you tried to escape me, I would chase you from one end of the Universe to the other. If I couldn't change your mind, I'd hold you captive until you did," he jested.

"If you hadn't agreed to come home with me, I'd be the captor today. Surely you couldn't expect me to allow a prize like you to elude me." Amaya laughed. "After I'm wearing your bonding bracelet, everyone will know I am yours. We'll select one while we're on Rigel."

"Ah, yes, the Maffeian substitution for the wedding band in my culture. I noticed your mother wears both. Would you like to do the same?"

"Since I'm part Earthling, that would please me. Father can tell us who made Mother's. Now, there is something I want to ask you: If Galen and Renah are willing, we can have a simultaneous signing. We can invite our friends as witnesses and have a celebration, a wedding reception by Earth's description. Is that all right with you?"

"Sounds like fun, just so we honeymoon alone," he teased.

"I know the perfect place for us: an island on Eire. It's secluded, romantic, and has all the amenities we'll require."

"The only thing I'll require is you at my side, Amaya. You're the food, water, and air for my soul. I love you, woman."

"I love you, Jason. We're going to be so happy together."

Amaya's eyes were fixed on Jason's handsome face, one whose expression revealed love and desire. Just a glance from him called to life every inch of her being. Without trying, he whet her appetite for a feast only he could provide. His sapphire gaze seemed to possess the power to delve into her very soul to claim it. His need for her reached into her core and ignited her senses into flaming desire. She longed for him to make love to her again, as recent events had prevented sufficient unions to sate her hunger, a hunger that seemed perpetual. "Do you know how much I enjoy just gazing at you? Just touching you? Just seeing your smile or hearing your voice? Just being with you?"

"I hope as much I enjoy those same pleasures." His arms encircled her and pulled her against his chest, her supple curves a delight to roam. He closed his eyes and inhaled her titillating fragrance. He nibbled at her earlobe and trickled kisses down her throat. Her flesh was soft and smooth. His fingers wandered into her long hair and enticed locks to curl around them as he savored this special moment. He had won her heart and her hand in marriage. He had responded to her allure the instant they met; now his dreams were realities—she was his.

Amaya's hands rounded his head and toyed with his black hair. She let them slide down his neck and across his broad shoulders. She teased her fingertips up and down his spine, then traversed his torso front and back. His frame was so sleek and hard, yet as sensuously pliant and silky as *magee* spinnings. He was splendid, magnificent. He was the ideal choice with whom to spend her life, day and night.

Jason gently cupped a breast and kneaded it to firmness with a taut peak, then massaged the other into pointed readiness. His teeth played with the rosy brown bud before doing the same to its partner. As his palm continued to stimulate the pinnacles, his lips journeyed up her chest and over her chin. His mouth fastened to hers with kisses which were deep, slow, and pervasive at first, then fast, greedy, and light. His tongue coaxed hers to dance with his.

Amaya sighed dreamily as Jason's lips made another journey down her throat and up her breasts. He was like solar flames searing over her, burning away anything preventing pleasure. Every part of her was sensitive, susceptible, responsive. Her wits seemed to spin. She experienced sensations too numerous and wondrous to count.

Jason was thrilled by the way Amaya took and

gave during lovemaking. She wasn't shy, modest, or restrained with him. His heart pounded with pride and adoration, spreading fiery blood throughout his body. His hard maleness pressed against her and it craved to be within her. His breathing was fast and shallow, as was hers. She clung to him and released moans of rising passion. She appeared as aroused as he was. Her head tossed and her body writhed as she surrendered her all to him. He moved deeper and faster within her and she matched his rhythm and pace.

Their joined bodies moved blissfully as their restraints were cast aside. They kissed and caressed until victory was obtained. They drank every drop of nectar from passion's cup, then nestled together in sated fatigue.

"I love you, Amaya Saar, more than I thought possible to do so."

She kissed his shoulder. "I love you, Jason Carlisle."

"I could have searched forever on Earth and never found a woman to compare with you."

She rested a leg across his and cuddled closer. "I could have searched forever in my galaxy and never found a man to compare with you."

Whether it be in starlight or sunshine, they knew they would always feel this powerful way and would share glorious splendor with each other.

Days later on Rigel in the Pandar Tower, the Saar family and their two impending members dined together. Reports had been filed, and precautions had been taken to safeguard certain secrets. The news was accepted by a grateful populace who praised their forces and ruler, and held victory celebrations throughout the Maffei Alliance. The mission team was enjoying shore leave. Commendations had been awarded. Jana was given the colorful details of the episode on Luz, then was asked about her progress against the Destructive Immune System Disorder.

"We haven't found a cure for DISD but we have several hopeful paths to follow," she replied, "We've been using the gene map and studying how genetic mistakes are corrected in the DNA strands in cell nuclei. If we can master that process, it might help us engineer a cell that can resist the virus. We know uncorrected mutations in those strands cause diseases. We're attempting to locate or make a protein tag that will signal the body to attack the alien enemy and to produce healing antibodies."

Jana set aside a cup of *zim*. "There are a few exciting developments. We found two people who were infected by carriers who've managed to fight off the invader. Three others have tested positive, yet they show no signs of immune system destruction or illness. If we can discover why and how their white corpuscles aren't being affected, we might extract clues from them to guide us toward a vaccine. From what we've learned so far, their cells seem to have a sturdy barrier which the invader can't penetrate. What we don't know is what makes theirs stronger. The same mystery exists on Earth with their AIDS, and with certain African women. While I was studying the data we copied from American scientists, I discovered that intriguing fact and checked it out with our cases. Needless to say, we were stunned we had overlooked that possibility because known victims had succumbed and died so rapidly after infection. The medical and research teams are concentrating on that fact for now. As with the Earthlings, we don't know yet if it will prove to be useful."

Jana continued. "For those already infected, we need something to act as a key to open a portal in invaded cells so we can strike at the enemy. Scientists on Earth have been working to defeat their virus for years; hopefully one civilization will come up with a cure the other can use. We have been able to halt the spread of the virus; we've had no new cases lately and all patients are being treated at Med Complex where we can protect them from lethal illnesses while awaiting a vaccine. No more carriers have surfaced, so we think we have it contained for now. We won't stop seeking a cure until this mystery is solved."

After Jana finished, Varian told her the other good news. "Our neighboring galaxies were notified our military and medical threats are over, so normal relations and travel have been reestablished today. *Avatar* Kwan reports the *magee* of Mailiorca are procreating nicely. *Avatar* Faeroe says the mines on Caguas are back to normal. Kael sent word the rain forests of Zandia are being replanted. Zamarra's fresh air system is at peak level, and Balfae's island sanctuary has recovered from invasion. All damage has been repaired on Base and at the medical and research complexes."

"What about the Serians, Father?" Amaya asked.

"*Raz* Yakir and his people were warned not to repeat their prior mistake and to stay out of Maffei's affairs. Yakir claims he didn't know the extent of the Tabrizes' hatred and threat; he assumed they were seeking justice from past enemies who had wronged them, not attacking our entire galaxy and in such insidious manners. Yakir said he preferred not to have any future contact with Maffei and would forget the Tabrizes' existence. We agreed, so Renah's past life with them will remain a secret."

Varian smiled at Renah. "I'm sorry we couldn't get any information about your real parents. Yakir swears he doesn't know who they are. He said that when Canissia returned with Taemin, they had you with them and claimed you were his and she accepted you as her daughter. I hope you realize your true identity does not matter to us, Renah. You have proven yourself worthy to be a Maffeian citizen and a member of the Saar family."

"Thank you, sir; thank you, everyone, for accepting me."

"Plans are almost finalized for the dual bonding ceremony next week," Jana announced happily. "That will give our friends throughout Maffei time to reach Altair to witness it and join in on our celebration. Everyone we've invited is coming. It will be wonderful to see them again. It's been years since I've visited with some of my friends from Earth and Varian's old ship."

"If Avi and Sebok had their way, they would

make it a triple bonding,'' Amaya injected. ''They're holding theirs on Rigel next month. Even Thaine is actively searching for a mate; he doesn't want to be left out of the fun with his best friend and cousin snatched up by me and Renah.''

''Andrea and Nigel are ecstatic that one child is taking a mate and the other is seriously looking for one,'' Jana said. ''This way, all of your children can grow up together as friends, just as the rest of you did.''

''Just as you did with Andrea, Mother, and Father did with Nigel. It amazes me how fate entwined all of our lives. Who could have imagined I would meet and fall in love with Andrea's, Avi's, and Thaine's alien cousin?''

The others laughed, then chatted for hours about their futures.

In a private chamber later, Renah rested against Galen's chest. ''I'm so happy I can hardly believe I'm this fortunate,'' she murmured. ''At times, I fear this is only a beautiful dream and I'll eventually be awakened to ugly reality.''

Galen cupped her face and lifted her head to lock their gazes. ''It's not a dream or an illusion, Renah. We're real and we're together, now and for the rest of our days. You're the best thing that could have happened to me. Except for our children, what else could I hope for to make me complete? We're enough alike to be ideal equals but different enough to hold each other's interest forever.''

"I'm so glad you gave me a second chance to—"

Galen's fingers pressed against her lips to silence her words. "The dark past is over, Renah; the only thing that concerns us now is a bright future. A union between us was meant to be or one wouldn't have worked out for us. Everybody makes mistakes, my love, including me and my family; but we can't dwell on them or let them be destructive. We're all stronger and better people because of the problems and perils we've faced and surmounted. The episodes we've endured brought us closer together. Besides, we've shared many exciting adventures and challenges which bonded us tighter."

Renah's loving gaze roamed his expression, and she knew every word he spoke was true. Just being with him enthralled her. A fierce and gnawing hunger chewed at her, not only because it had been so long since they had shared passions, but also because of her joy at being given another chance for a splendid future with him and for having redeemed herself. Her hands clasped his face and drew his head downward to kiss his lips.

Galen's arms banded her waist and held her with possessiveness. He carried her to the *sleeper* and removed their boots and garments. After adoring her with his eyes, he hugged her as they sank to the inviting surface. Her gaze and mood—as well as his—exposed their mutual needs, their search for a stronger bond, their willingness to challenge anything and anyone to be together.

As their naked bodies pressed close, the contact staggered their senses. Their mouths melded and they explored their sweet surrender. Enslaved by each other and sheer bliss, they sought paradise together. It was as if a magical and powerful spell had been woven around them, one which bound them for all time with its silky but strong strands. They took and gave and shared every skill and sensation they knew. Their hips undulated on the bed in a matched pattern and at the same pace. They knew they would never be parted again; they knew destiny had pushed them together. Their love was deep and their passion was overwhelming.

When they could withstand the entreatments of their bodies no longer, they moved to starlight speed and trekked the wild and wondrous reaches of splendor as one body, one spirit, one glorious culmination.

"You are my heart, Renah, and I will cherish you for all time."

"You are my heart, too, and I will cherish you forever."

Amidst contented kisses and tender caresses, he asked, "Will you take a leave with me after our bonding so we can spend our first months on Altair creating our new life and home?"

"Yes, I have decided to work with your mother and Amaya, if that is agreeable with you. I don't want to return to Star Fleet duty, much as I enjoyed it. I only want to be your mate and to have our children and to work on Altair in science and research."

Galen silently thanked his mother for her timely suggestion and offer, one meant to keep her family close and safe. "You're matchless, Renah."

"No, because you are my match, my perfect match."

"Truer words could not be found in the Universe. I love you."

"More beautiful words could not be found anywhere, and I love you."

Days later on the planetoid of Altair which orbited Rigel, Varian and Jana stood on the highest balcony of their palatial tri-level abode. They were happy to be home, to have peace, and to await the day their twins would begin unions as special as theirs.

Varian rested his cheek against Jana's temple as she stood with her back leaning against his chest, his sable hair a dark contrast to her honey tresses. His arms were around her body, and hers overlapped his. In tranquil silence, they savored their contact and the view of lush gardens beneath a star-studded indigo sky with a full moon and silvery clouds. A soft breeze wafted over them. Heady smells of various flowers and bushes drifted upward. Birds and animals imported from Rigel, some visible in the brilliant moonlight, sent forth entertaining sounds. The android servants were in rest modes following the completions of their chores, so they would not be disturbed. The research complex and staff chambers were located on the other side of the planetoid to give the Saars privacy; it was reachable with ease and speed in air-rovers which skimmed the surface. Anything that wasn't grown or made on Altair could be purchased on Rigel, a fast shuttle ride away. Their enormous home and the complex were protected by individual force shields and cybornetic guards, so both were safe and secure.

As she relaxed in her husband's gentle embrace, Jana reflected on her stimulating and satisfying life with Varian and in the Maffei Galaxy, a life which began long ago as a captive *charl* and amidst perils and enemies. So much had changed over the years, except for their love and passion which were strong and eternal, predestined. She thought about Amaya and Galen and their loves and where the two couples would build their homes and about the grandchildren she and Varian could be enjoying next year. Until those dwellings were completed, the couples would live with them on the lower levels, as the top one held their private chambers. With the twins and their soon-to-be mates arriving the next day and their guests coming soon, this was a special night to be spent alone in several ways . . .

"I never thought to see the day when a son of ours married a female reared by Canissia and Taemin, or our daughter is united to an Earthling like you," Varian said softly. "Isn't it strange how fate works sometimes?"

Jana turned and looked into Varian's blue eyes. "Yes, my love, it is."

He studied her playful grin. "What's the significance of that look, moonbeam?"

"I mistakenly believed we were preparing for a period alone before our twins gave us grandchildren to help rear. Now I discover my virile husband forgot his *liex* injection during this lengthy and distracting crisis, just as he did long ago. On Earth, we call it déjà vu."

"What do you mean?"

"When my lab was sabotaged, so were our records, our schedules. I missed the reminder of your injection, so I guess I'm partly to blame."

"To blame for what, Moonbeam?"

"Your keen wits are off-duty or dulled by me, Supreme Commander Saar, because you're missing my clues," Jana teased. "I'll be clearer; we're about to enter the realm of parenthood again. I'm pregnant. My test today revealed it's only one child this time. It's a good thing Maffeians have long and healthy life spans so we'll be around long enough to see this baby grown."

Varian stared at her. "A baby? You aren't teasing, you're pregnant?"

"Absolutely, Rogue Saar."

He chuckled. "You haven't called me that name in years."

"Because you haven't been one in years. Who else but a rakish space pirate would seduce and enthrall me and get me in this condition?"

"Ever since the night we met on Earth in Andrea's garden, my life has been a constant series of adventures with you, my alien temptress."

"You mean, a series of perils and passions. You promised me many surprises and excitement, and you've certainly kept your word. How ever will I reward you for this new challenge and treasure?"

"For a start, by assigning your staff to work on the virus cure so you won't expose yourself to any medical risks."

"Yes, my love. I will analyze data only. What else?"

As they stood beneath romantic starlight, Varian jested, "*Kahala* help us and guide us in the exciting and unpredictable years ahead." He gazed into her glowing eyes and caressed her abdomen. "I wonder what's in store for this fated child . . ."

"I hope a life as happy and satisfying as mine has been with you. Will you join me inside and feed this ravenous hunger I have for you?"

"I've never been one to shirk my duty."

"No, you haven't, so get busy obeying my commands."

"What's your first order, moonbeam?"

"I'll tell you inside," she murmured in a seductive tone, grasped his hand, and led him to their *sleeper.*

Varian touched several buttons which cast the room in a soft glow, sent forth lovely strains of music, and emitted an exotic fragrance. They undressed each other with leisure and enticement, then embraced. Their lips met in a heady and stirring kiss. There was always an instant spark between them, one which ignited swiftly and flamed brightly without coaxing.

He leaned away to look at her. "You're as beautiful and alluring now as on the night we met. I love you, Jana Greyson Saar, with all my heart."

"You're as handsome and virile as on the night we met, my love. I can't imagine my life without you in it. I love you with every breath I take."

"You never cease to amaze and please me, moonbeam."

"And I hope I never do, Rogue Saar."

He smiled, and his blue eyes sparkled. "Somehow I know you never will." He sank to the soft surface of the *sleeper* with her in his arms.

Together, the handsome Maffeian and beautiful Earthling sought the rapture of a union which spanned two galaxies, was as powerful and large as the Cosmos, and burned brighter and hotter than the stars which filled it.

Two hearts joined by fate. Aliens no more;
Light conquered Darkness; fiery passions soar.
On wings of magic, those lovers wished to ride;
How lucky they conquered a Universe so wide.
Starlight and Splendor, though wondrous they
be;
What destiny awaits child number three . . .

Author's Note:

If you enjoyed this futuristic romance, I hope you'll look for and read sagas I and II in the Moondust Series published by Pinnacle Books: *Moondust and Madness,* where it all started between Jana and Varian; *Stardust and Shadows,* the continuation of their romance and adventures; *Starlight and Splendor,* the romances and adventures of their twins.

If you want to know what happens to child number three, saga #4 will be released in the fall of 1995 as *Moonbeams and Magic,* also by Pinnacle Books.

If you would like to receive a Janelle Taylor Newsletter, book list, and bookmark, send a Self-Addressed Stamped Envelope (long size best) to:

Janelle Taylor Newsletter
P.O. Box 211646
Martinez, Georgia 30917–1646